# Bruckner's Symphonies

Few works in the nineteenth-century repertoire have aroused such extremes of hostility and admiration, or have generated so many scholarly problems, as Anton Bruckner's symphonies. Julian Horton seeks new ways of understanding the symphonies and the problems they have accrued by treating them as the focus for a variety of interdisciplinary debates and methodological controversies. He isolates problematic areas in the works' analysis and reception, and approaches them from a range of analytical, historical, philosophical, literary-critical and psychoanalytical viewpoints. The symphonies are thus explored in the context of a number of crucial and sometimes provocative themes such as the political circumstances of the works' production, Bruckner and post-war musical analysis, issues of musical influence, the problem of editions, Bruckner and psychobiography, and Bruckner's controversial relationship to the Nazis.

JULIAN HORTON is Lecturer in Music at University College Dublin. He has contributed an essay to *The Cambridge Companion to Bruckner* (forthcoming) and has also published articles and reviews on Brucknerian topics in *Music and Letters* and *Music Analysis*.

# Bruckner's Symphonies

## Analysis, Reception and Cultural Politics

Julian Horton

CAMBRIDGE
UNIVERSITY PRESS

CAMBRIDGE UNIVERSITY PRESS
Cambridge, New York, Melbourne, Madrid, Cape Town, Singapore, São Paulo

Cambridge University Press
The Edinburgh Building, Cambridge, CB2 2RU, UK

Published in the United States of America by Cambridge University Press, New York

www.cambridge.org
Information on this title: www.cambridge.org/9780521823548

First published 2004
Third printing 2006

Printed in the United Kingdom at the University Press, Cambridge

*A catalogue record for this book is available from the British Library*

*Library of Congress Cataloguing in Publication data*

ISBN-13  978-0-521-82354-8  hardback
ISBN-10  0-521-82354-4  hardback

A. R. Horton
*in memoriam*

# Contents

# Preface

Although work on this book has, in the most immediate sense, spanned a little over four years, some of its aims and ideas have had a much longer gestation period. The initial impulse stems from the sense of dislocation that accompanied my first encounter with the critical orthodoxies surrounding Bruckner's symphonies, especially in the older English-language literature, marked above all by a feeling that entrenched views emphasised concepts or criticisms that bore little relation to my own experience of the music. In many ways, the studies comprising this book collectively represent an effort to close this gap: to establish grounds for understanding Bruckner that do justice to an unmediated sense of music-historical and analytical significance that I have never quite managed to reconcile with prevailing debates.

This, however, is not to propose yet another round of Brucknerian revisionism. As I shall argue, the perpetuation of the revisionist impulse has in some respects been one of the most debilitating aspects of the musicological reception of Bruckner. Nevertheless, it is hard to deny that the symphonies are still attended by an array of clichés, which hardly contribute beneficially to our understanding of the composer or his work. Whilst many of these preconceptions have lost musicological credence today, their hold on public perception has endured. Two strands of criticism have proved especially durable, and it is hoped that what follows accelerates their demise. On the one hand, the old accusations of formlessness, naïve atavism or the simplistic imitation of Wagner have persisted with remarkable tenacity, despite the longstanding irrelevance of their formative cultural-political context. On the other hand, the defence against these criticisms has often involved a kind of special pleading, imbuing the music with a type of constitutive otherness or detachment from the Austro-German mainstream that is in its own way just as damaging. Much work has recently been done to unravel or dispose of these mythologies in specific instances; yet there remains the need for a study that advances, so to speak, on a broad front, tackling issues and their attendant methodological dilemmas as part of an expansively defined critical problem. This book is an attempt to supply such a study.

Undertaking this project has necessarily entailed the adoption of what might be described, in the most modest sense, as an inter-disciplinary approach. The motivation for this is not so much a purposeful postmodernity, *pace* the views of Jean-François Lyotard and many others after him, but rather a kind of musicological pragmatism, born of the conviction that critical difficulties are best addressed as part of a general nexus of analytical, textual, philosophical, historical and social matters. There is scarcely an issue in Bruckner scholarship that does not, by its very nature, straddle some kind of disciplinary boundary. If we try to constrain such issues within the areas on which they appear initially to be centred, we ultimately defer consideration of the critical problems that they pose. Editorial questions, to pick perhaps the most contentious Brucknerian topic, are certainly also analytical questions; they similarly engender problems of reception history, cultural politics and philosophical orientation that cannot be detached without disabling the critical process. Rather than retreat into disciplinary or methodological specificity as a way of dealing with the fact that multiple versions and editions of a Bruckner symphony exist, it seems more constructive to allow the context of disciplinary interactions to guide our critical and interpretative responses.

Inevitably, this technique has required engagement with a wide range of texts and areas of scholarship, and this in turn has entailed seeking advice from a diversity of sources, not all of them musicological. In terms of the provision of materials, I am greatly indebted to the Music Collection of the Austrian National Library, for making vital manuscript sources and texts available. Similar acknowledgements are due to the British Library and Cambridge University Library, both of whom supplied many key resources, and to the Medical Library of University College Dublin, for providing important psychoanalytical texts.

At the same time, it seems appropriate at this stage to make one significant apology. As I write, *The Cambridge Companion to Bruckner* is in press. Leaving aside my own contribution to this volume, it contains a wealth of important new scholarship, to which, for reasons related to the chronology of preparing the present study, I have not alluded. In the light of this publication, the arguments I have proposed will undoubtedly require modification. I apologise to the authors represented therein if any of my work neglects their contributions or else glosses, without acknowledgement, ideas they have put forward.

A great many people also deserve profound thanks for their help, contributions and encouragement. I am profusely grateful to all at Cambridge University Press involved in the book's preparation, production and marketing. Particular thanks must go to Paul Watt for his assured handling of design and the process of production, to Michael Downes for his patient and careful copyediting, and to Vicki Cooper for overseeing the project in its latter stages. An immense debt of gratitude is also owed to Penny Souster, without whom this book, like so many others, would not have been born or come to fruition. I wish her every happiness in her retirement.

The early stages of research and planning occurred during my tenure of a Junior Research Fellowship at Trinity College, Cambridge, and I would therefore like to offer sincere thanks to the Master and Fellows of that institution. My colleagues at University College Dublin likewise deserve considerable praise for their continuing support. Harry White's encouragement and many constructive suggestions are greatly valued, now as always. Wolfgang Marx and Patricia O'Connor offered much apposite criticism of the text and help in translating aspects of the German-language literature. Helen Smith deserves particular gratitude for her unending patience with my technological shortcomings, and for more instances of practical assistance than I can reasonably enumerate. Máire Buffet, Therese Smith, Adrian Scahill and Thomas McCarthy have all graciously accommodated the demands of preparing a study of this magnitude in the midst of three busy academic years.

Elsewhere, many individuals have given invaluable assistance. Lorraine Byrne read early drafts of parts of the book, and made considered and generous remarks. Jill Varley appraised aspects of my German translations, and offered helpful corrections. Rachel Wingfield and Lorenz Welker proffered essential advice on psychoanalytical matters, specifically in connection with the nature and diagnosis of Obsessive-Compulsive Disorder, and thereby gave professional guidance in a field in which I am a complete amateur. Fruitful conversations with Nick Marston on the subject of sonata deformation have vitally informed the analysis of that topic, and I am grateful to him for allowing me to include terminology he has suggested, particularly the concept of reformation. One reader, of whose identity I remain unaware, offered very positive criticism at a key stage of preparation. Your comments are greatly appreciated, whoever you may be.

I must reserve special acknowledgements for two people. The first is John Deathridge, whose careful reading of the text was vital in bringing it to completion, and for whose wisdom and support in this project, as in many others before it, I am deeply grateful. The second is Paul Wingfield, who furnished penetrating and detailed critiques of many features of the book's content and style, and who has provided more selfless advice and help over the years than I can ever hope to repay.

Finally, profuse thanks are due to my family, and especially to Janet, for encouraging and sustaining my Brucknerian preoccupations and the endless amounts of work they seem to generate.

J. H.
Dublin
May 2004

# 1 Introduction: the critical problem

Stephen Johnson concluded a recent article about Bruckner and the cultural politics of Nazi Germany with the following exhortation:

> What is certain is that as regards performance and textual fidelity, and maybe much else, Bruckner's music stands in urgent need of reassessment . . . Let's hope that this time it can be done with something like impartiality.[1]

In making such an appeal, Johnson by no means expresses a novel attitude amongst Brucknerians. Protestations of misunderstanding, calls for reappraisal and concerns about the dense problems generated by the music form possibly the most consistent feature of the composer's reception. Perhaps to a greater extent than the music of any of his contemporaries, Bruckner's music has come to be defined by its attendant problems.

The issues comprising 'the Bruckner problem' in the broadest sense have been both geographically specific and geographically indifferent. On the one hand, Germanic and anglophone reception histories have followed markedly different paths. The appropriation of Bruckner during his lifetime by the more extreme elements of Viennese Wagnerism, and subsequent right-wing annexations culminating in the Nazification of his music, quickly established the symphonies in the Germanic canon at the cost of a lasting affiliation with fascism. In Britain, by contrast, Bruckner was, until fairly recently, widely regarded as a defective continental curiosity, and despite an increasingly secure place in the repertoire, his defence as a 'canonical' composer is often still necessary. In America, he has received more systematic support than in Britain, thanks to the founding of the American Bruckner Society and its Journal *Chord and Discord*, although the secure position of the music in the American concert repertoire is also recent. Whereas Austro-German musicology has long sought theoretical, historical and philosophical strategies for dissecting Bruckner's music, post-war Anglo-American musical analysts have all but ignored it. On the other hand, problems and preconceptions have persisted that are not circumscribed by national trends. Editorial involvement with Bruckner's works has become increasingly international. Many of the infamous textual difficulties generated by Bruckner's revisions and editorial collaborations have recently received fresh attention from European,

---

[1] 'Bruckner: Guilty or Not Guilty?', *Independent* (10 January 1996), p. 7.

American and Australian scholars. Similarly, the critical tendency to conflate music and biography has not been geographically restricted, but is apparent in the work of writers as diverse as Donald Francis Tovey, Robert Simpson, Constantin Floros and Carl Dahlhaus.

The single factor uniting these trends is consistently their revisionist motivation. During and shortly after the composer's lifetime, this arose from the desire to defend him against the ridicule of Hanslick and the Brahmsian faction, and usually involved belittling the Brahmsian concern for classical formal archetypes in the face of Bruckner's bold modernism, which, as one reviewer put it, 'is precisely greatness and sublimity in symphonic artworks'.[2] Later in the twentieth century, reappraisal in Germany was restyled as a rearguard action against cultural decline, as for example in Karl Grunsky's nationalistic characterisation of the 'struggle against Bruckner' as a symptom of anti-German artistic decadence.[3] Such protestations took on a more forceful, institutional conviction during the Second World War. In an ironic inversion of the earlier emphasis on Bruckner's progressive credentials, the Nazis perceived anti-Brucknerian feeling as another facet of degenerate, Judaeo-Bolshevik modernism.[4] After the war, supporters in Britain bemoaned the mistaken alignment of Bruckner and Wagner, while Austro-German musicologists countered pre-war characterisations of the symphonies as the epitome of absolute music with programmatic readings.[5] In the last decade, the revisionist inclination has been taken up by American musicologists, who have stressed the need to remove the layers of prejudice that Bruckner's music has accrued.[6] Johnson's 'urgent need of reassessment' has a long, diverse and sometimes politically controversial lineage.

[2] Anonymous review of 21 December 1892 in *Das Vaterland*, quoted in Franz Grasberger, 'Das Bruckner-Bild der Zeitung "Das Vaterland" in den Jahren 1870–1900', in Rudolf Elvers and Ernst Vogel, eds., *Festschrift Hans Schneider zum 60. Geburtstag* (Munich, 1981), p. 126. See also Benjamin Korstvedt, *Bruckner: Symphony no. 8* (Cambridge, 2000), p. 6.

[3] See for example Grunsky's *Kampf um deutsche Musik!* (Stuttgart, 1933).

[4] The *locus classicus* of Nazi Bruckner reception is Goebbels' 1937 Regensburg address, published in Helmut Heiber, ed., *Goebbels Reden* (Düsseldorf, 1971), pp. 281–6. On this matter, see Matthias Hansen, 'Die faschistische Bruckner-rezeption und ihre Quellen', *Beiträge zur Musikwissenschaft* 28 (1986), pp. 53–61; Benjamin Korstvedt, 'Anton Bruckner in the Third Reich and After: An Essay on Ideology and Bruckner Reception', *Musical Quarterly* 80 (1996), 132–60; Bryan Gilliam, 'The Annexation of Anton Bruckner: Nazi Revisionism and the Politics of Appropriation', in Paul Hawkshaw and Timothy L. Jackson, eds., *Bruckner Studies* (Cambridge, 1997), pp. 72–90; Leon Botstein, 'Music and Ideology: Thoughts on Bruckner', *Musical Quarterly* 80 (1996), pp. 1–11.

[5] See for example Constantin Floros, *Bruckner und Brahms: Studien zur musikalischen Exegetik* (Wiesbaden, 1980).

[6] See Paul Hawkshaw and Timothy L. Jackson, Preface to *Bruckner Studies*, p. xi.

Many of the claims made in the spirit of reappraisal are contradictory to the point of aporia. Bruckner has been praised as a Wagnerian and for having nothing to do with Wagner; as a composer of absolute music and of programmatic symphonies; as a dangerous modernist and a venerable reactionary; as an unworldly mystic and a ruthless pragmatist; as an apolitical innocent and as provider of the soundtrack to German military expansionism. And although some of these readings respond decisively to manifest extremism – few today would seek to defend, for example, the Nazi appropriation of Bruckner – the near-continuous state of reassessment has in many ways become as much of a problem as the matters it has sought to address. Partly, this is the product of a prevalent scholarly specificity. Attempts to resolve individual matters of reception, philology, analysis and interpretation have been consistently preferred over studies addressing 'the Bruckner problem' in the broadest critical sense. As a result, the consequences for other fields of enquiry of conclusions reached in one area of research are infrequently examined in detail. This is especially true of the vexed question of the editions. Decisions regarding the content of an edition have profound consequences for the conduct of an analysis, but research often stops short of investigating this relationship.

More fundamentally, the persistence of revisionism may be attributed as much to the absence of a critical overview as to the presence of intractable scholarly problems.[7] And here we broach the central motivation of this book: to investigate 'the Bruckner problem' in the broadest sense in a comparative, rather than a disciplinarily specific, fashion. This responds to the basic conviction that a path through the musicological difficulties generated by Bruckner's music, and more precisely by the symphonies, can be cleared by treating them as points of interdisciplinary convergence, rather than simply as isolated problems demanding isolated solutions. Such an approach, it is hoped, could be instrumental in breaking the repeating cycle of reappraisal that in many ways comprises the enduring common ground of Bruckner scholarship. The greater part of this study will be given over to a series of case studies that prosecute this aim by exploring the consequences of allowing problematic issues to intersect, or to be refracted through a succession of diverse methodological debates and applications. The technique is purposefully pluralistic and critical: it seeks to test the self-containment of fields of enquiry, not to consolidate methodological specificity. By way of introduction, this chapter offers brief surveys of four key fields of debate that will be examined in more detail at a later stage – issues of reception history,

[7] For a recent response to this matter, see Albrecht Riethmüller, ed., *Bruckner-Probleme* (Stuttgart, 2000). This corporate volume, although it seeks to provide a cross-section of problematic issues, does not do so comparatively, but by addressing problems successively through individual contributions.

editorial policy, biography and analysis – with the twofold purpose of obviating revisionist tendencies and establishing guidelines for more detailed consideration.

## Trends in reception history

Germanic and Anglo-American Bruckner reception over the past hundred years has been defined to a large extent by differing responses to the question of Bruckner's canonical membership. In Germany and Austria, the symphonies entered the repertoire relatively rapidly, and critical discussion consequently focused on a body of work, the canonical status of which was comparatively firm. In Britain and America, there has been a much more gradual progression from widespread hostility to canonical acceptance via protracted critical debate.

Before the Second World War, British opinions of the symphonies were almost unanimously negative. In an emphatic rejection of Bruckner's own hopes for his works in England, the first performance of the Seventh Symphony in London in 1887 met with little sympathy. Charles Barry voiced criticisms that were to become standard objections:

> Reasons for [the symphony's failure] may be found in extreme length – a fault substantially aggravated by lack of proportionate interest –, in an exaggerated and spasmodic manner only allowable when the composer follows the changing and contrasted sentiments of a poetic text, and in an extraordinary mixture of scholasticism with the freedom of the Wagnerian school.[8]

Forty-two years later, the situation was scarcely different. A review of a performance of the Fourth Symphony on 6 November 1929 ascribed the work's critical reception to a paucity of material, concluding that

> [Bruckner's] command over form, which is not allowed to abdicate, but which is the servant of his ideas, does not suffice to compensate for [the material's] diffuseness. One feels that the musical material of the symphony is not really strong enough to support so vast a structure.[9]

The first London performance of the Eighth Symphony, given by the London Symphony Orchestra under Klemperer on 20 November 1929, provoked a similar response. *The Times*'s critic noted the work's 'peculiar difficulties . . .

---

[8] Charles Barry, 'Richter Concerts', *Musical Times* 28 (1 June 1887), p. 342, quoted in Crawford Howie, *Anton Bruckner: A Documentary Biography*, vol. II: *Trial, Tribulation and Triumph in Vienna* (Lampeter, 2002), p. 543.

[9] *The Times* (6 November 1929), p. 12. All reviews before the mid-1960s were anonymous, being ascribed simply to 'a correspondent'.

great length and the curious disjointedness of its structure', whilst the *Daily Telegraph* judged it inaccessible to anyone not from Upper Austria:

> If you are not an upper Austrian . . . you are content to accept its often rather ponderous rhetoric as belonging to those spacious Teutonic days when every first-class composer not only demanded a big orchestra, but was generally oblivious to the possibilities of a small one.[10]

Performances of the Sixth and Seventh Symphonies in 1936 elicited tentatively receptive comments, mingled with the old complaints of tedium and formlessness. A reviewer for the *Musical Times* found the outer movements of the Sixth 'burdensome' and the inner movements flawed, but attractive enough 'to raise the name of Bruckner in this country'.[11] The same journal received the Seventh in an identical manner: Bruckner 'conceives fine characters' but is unable to 'unify their action', as a result of which the work 'raised [Bruckner's] stock' without securing his reputation.[12] Immediately after the war, journalistic resolve stiffened again. *The Times*'s correspondent observed on 21 May 1948 that British and American audiences had no time for Bruckner in particular, and for what he described as 'the Austrian Nationalists' in general, including also Mahler and Schoenberg in this category. He therefore likened Bruckner to Stanford, as a composer-organist whose fame did not extend beyond his national boundaries. Inevitably, material deficiencies were cited as the chief obstacle, particularly Bruckner's 'appalling lengths' and 'redundancies'.[13]

A succession of articles that appeared in the 1950s and 1960s attempted a critical accommodation. In the late 1950s, Deryck Cooke and Robert Simpson conducted a war of words in the *Musical Times* against predominantly hostile preconceptions. Dyneley Hussey's faint praise proved especially provocative:

> Tiresome though he may be, one cannot but end up liking the old bore and admiring the patent nobility of his aspirations. His most tiresome habit is his way of pulling up dead at frequent intervals, and then starting the argument all over again, usually with repetitions of what has already been said. One has the impression . . . that we are traversing a town with innumerable traffic lights, all of which turn red as we approach them.[14]

Cooke responded with forceful accusations of musical ignorance: '[Hussey's] review only demonstrates that where there is no understanding of a

---

[10] *Daily Telegraph* (6 November 1929), p. 8.
[11] 'Bruckner's Sixth Symphony', *Musical Times* 77 (1936), p. 454.
[12] Ibid., p. 1032.   [13] *The Times* (21 May 1948), p. 7.
[14] 'The Musician's Gramophone', *Musical Times* 98 (1957), p. 140.

work . . . there can be no real evaluation'.[15] Consistently, reappraisal involved dissociating Bruckner from the mainstream symphonic models against which he had previously been measured. A *Times* article of 1960 entitled 'Antipathy to Bruckner Still Felt' asserted that the symphonies 'are not argumentative after Beethoven, Brahms and Wagner', and should properly be understood as combined products of the organ loft, Catholicism and Bruckner's rural childhood, whilst a similar article of 1964 described the music as 'monolithic, concerned exclusively with God and religion'.[16] William Mann consolidated this view in 1967, regarding the symphonies as assertions of faith, rather than as following the 'struggle–victory' archetypes of the Beethovenian symphony.[17] Uncritical acceptance of the music is finally evident in Joan Chisell's 1969 review of a performance of the Fourth Symphony under Horenstein.[18]

This progression is reflected in the British musicological literature. Tovey's essays on the Fourth and Sixth Symphonies and Gerald Abraham's scattered comments in *A Hundred Years of Music*, published in 1935 and 1938 respectively, betray varying degrees of contempt. Both employed comparison with Brahms as their point of orientation. Abraham used Brahms as a benchmark of competence against which Bruckner compared unfavourably:

> Bruckner's long-drawn ideas generally lack both the fertility of good themes and the beauty of genuine melodies: take, for instance, the opening subjects of the Second, Seventh and Eighth Symphonies.[19]

Tovey similarly invoked the Brahmsian comparison as a context for Bruckner's manifest technical inadequacy. His analyses vacillate between an acceptance of the quality of individual passages, and patronising description of formal deficiencies:

> [Bruckner's] defects are obvious on a first hearing, not as obscurities that may become clear with further knowledge, but as things that must be lived down as soon as possible . . . Listen to [his art] humbly; not with the humility with which you would hope to learn music from Bach, Beethoven or Brahms, but with the humility you would feel if you overheard a simple old soul talking to a child about sacred things.[20]

---

[15] Letter to the editor in ibid., p. 266.     [16] *The Times* (18 November 1960), p. 18.
[17] 'Bruckner's Structures in Perspective', *The Times* (21 July 1967), p. 6.
[18] *The Times* (22 March 1969), p. 19.
[19] See Gerald Abraham, *A Hundred Years of Music* (London, 1938), p. 199.
[20] Donald Francis Tovey, *Essays in Musical Analysis*, vol. II: *Symphonies (II), Variations and Orchestral Polyphony* (London, 1935), p. 72.

For Tovey, Bruckner's problematic angle of relation to the mainstream could be reduced to a dichotomy of form and content: an uneasy conflation of Wagnerian style and a conception of form 'as understood by a village organist'.[21] Julius Harrison was even more abrupt, dismissing Bruckner in two sentences: he was a 'pedantic' and 'self-conscious' Wagnerian, whose symphonies 'are in no wise worthy to rank with those of the great masters'.[22]

The trend towards accepting Bruckner by arguing for his distinct status crystallised with Robert Simpson's *The Essence of Bruckner*, still the most extensive English-language study. Again, the symphonies are considered essentially anti-Beethovenian, concerned not with the dynamic overcoming of struggle or the heroic assertion of the subject, but with the 'patient search for pacification', the gradual removal of obstacles to the calm expression of the material's essence.[23] When Bruckner fails to achieve this, it is for Simpson because he has not recognised the incompatibility of this ambition with the conventions of symphonic form. He cites the Third and Fourth Symphonies as the most problematic works in this respect, detecting an open conflict, in the first movement of the Third and the Finale of the Fourth, between the implications of the material and the conventions of sonata form. The subtext is once more that Bruckner places an emphasis on spiritual revelation that separates his music from the essentially secular orientation of the symphonic mainstream. The teleological processes of the Beethovenian symphony could thus only impede Bruckner's works, because they rely on a concept of maintained structural ambiguity that was anathema to the eternal verities of Bruckner's faith. This idea was reiterated by Wilfred Mellers, who perceived Bruckner to have transformed the symphony into a 'confession of faith', and by Deryck Cooke, for whom 'Bruckner . . . abjured the terse dynamic continuity of Beethoven, and the broad fluid continuity of Wagner, in order to express something . . . elemental and metaphysical'.[24]

Over the last fifteen years anglophone scholars, particularly in America, have embraced new approaches to Bruckner. William Carragan, John Philips, Paul Hawkshaw and Benjamin Korstvedt have attacked anew the dense philological problems; Korstvedt, Bryan Gilliam, Margaret Notley and Stephen McClatchie have provided novel perspectives on many aspects

[21] Ibid., p. 121.
[22] See 'The Orchestra and Orchestral Music', in D. L. Bacharach, ed., *The Musical Companion* (London, 1934), pp. 127–284, this quotation p. 237.
[23] See *The Essence of Bruckner* (London, 1962), p. 232.
[24] Wilfred Mellers, *Man and His Music* (London, 1962), pp. 685–6; Deryck Cooke, 'Anton Bruckner', in *The New Grove Late Romantic Masters* (London, 1985), pp. 1–73, this quotation p. 49.

of reception history; Timothy Jackson, William Benjamin, Edward Laufer and Derrick Puffett have brought fresh analytical strategies to bear on the music. In general, Bruckner's position in the repertoire has been consolidated and, late in the day, he has gained admittance to what Korstvedt describes as 'the American musicological canon'.[25] Nevertheless, the conception of Bruckner as an anti-dynamic composer has persisted. Benjamin Korstvedt recently affirmed Simpson's conviction that the Brucknerian coda embodies pacification rather than overcoming:

> [T]he conclusive cadential preparation [of a Bruckner symphony] does not present itself as the final paroxysm of a long symphonic struggle, but rather as a self-possessed expression of splendour . . . the final tonic major is not wrested from the darkness with Beethovenian might, but granted to us with awesome ease.[26]

Korstvedt concurs with Derek Scott in understanding the source of such gestures to be 'lux sancta, the holy light of salvation for the believer', rather than the enlightened humanism of Beethoven.[27] Timothy Jackson similarly considers the symphonies as religious narratives in which the heroic subject is always ultimately redeemed by faith.[28] Even today, a haze of otherness clings to Bruckner: he has, to an extent, been granted canonical space only by distancing his music from the symphonic tradition he sought to inhabit.

All this stands in stark contrast to the trajectory of Germanic scholarship. Before the war, writers in the post-Hegelian tradition made extravagant claims for Bruckner's music-historical significance. August Halm, Ernst Bloch and Ernst Kurth all saw in Bruckner the synthesis of a dialectical music-historical process that defined western music since the Enlightenment. For Halm, Bruckner initiated a musical culture that synthesised the antithetical tendencies of fugue and sonata, embodied in the music of Bach and Beethoven respectively.[29] Hence, whereas in Halm's view fugal counterpoint subordinated form to thematic material and the sonata principle subordinated material to the demands of the form, in Bruckner's symphonies the 'culture of theme' discovered in Bach re-emerges in a symphonic context:

[25] See *Bruckner: Symphony no. 8*, p. 2.      [26] Ibid., p. 49.
[27] See Derek Scott, 'Bruckner and the Dialectics of Darkness and Light', *Bruckner Journal* 2 (1998), p. 12.
[28] See Paul Hawkshaw and Timothy L. Jackson, 'Bruckner, Anton', in *The New Grove Dictionary of Music and Musicians*, 2nd edn, ed. Stanley Sadie (London, 2001), vol. IV, pp. 475–6.
[29] See August Halm, *Von zwei Kulturen der Musik*, 3rd edn (Stuttgart, 1947), and also *Die Symphonie Anton Bruckners*, 2nd edn (Munich, 1923).

Bruckner is the first absolute musician of great style and complete mastery since Bach, the creator of dramatic music – which is the enemy and conqueror of music drama. If the fugue wanted to be fertilised by the spirit of the new music, it had to create contrast in the manner of treating the theme while leaving its thematic unity intact.[30]

Halm intends this synthesis in a broader sense than the simple importing of fugal techniques into the sonata design, a device of which Beethoven also made considerable use. Rather, Bruckner's engagement with Wagner's chromatic style elevates his melodic material above the concisely motivic themes of Beethoven and into a realm where the subordination of melody is no longer a prerequisite for the construction of sonata forms: 'Bruckner . . . finds [in Wagner's harmony] a new purpose, a new content for melody. Not a service to form, to something superordinate, but something which it could create in itself.'[31] Halm's ideas were taken up by Bloch, who construed Bruckner as realising the symphonic potential of Wagner's style without the baggage of dramatic, programmatic or overtly poetic allusion.[32] Halm and Bloch effectively up-end Wagner's aesthetics of music drama: rather than conceiving of the symphony as a stage en route to music drama, they consider music drama as 'the not-yet emancipated symphony', to use Carl Dahlhaus's phrase.[33]

The construction of such historical schemes found its most substantial expression in the work of Ernst Kurth.[34] Halm's formula of 'Bach, Beethoven and Bruckner' became 'Bach, Wagner and Bruckner' in Kurth's work. His underlying contention was that the motivating force in musical history is the resolution of voice-leading tension, understood not simply as an acoustical phenomenon, but as the build-up and discharge of melodic 'energies' that, in a Schopenhauerian turn of thought, amount to manifestations of a creative 'will'. In Bach's music, and generally in the contrapuntal style of the high Baroque, melody is perceived by Kurth as dominating harmony and form. After the hiatus of classicism, which suppressed music's essential linearity beneath a pervasive homophony, Wagner's mature chromatic style introduced a type of harmony motivated by chromatic alteration, and therefore reinstated voice leading as a governing principle. In Kurth's view, Bruckner's achievement lay in his application of Wagner's 'intensive alteration technique' to the creation of symphonic forms, made possible by devising a

---

[30] *Von zwei Kulturen der Musik*, p. 17, quoted in Carl Dahlhaus, *The Idea of Absolute Music*, trans. Roger Lustig (Chicago, 1989), p. 125.

[31] *Die Symphonie Anton Bruckners*, pp. 218–19.

[32] Ernst Bloch, *Vom Geist der Utopie* (Berlin, 1923).

[33] *The Idea of Absolute Music*, p. 123.       [34] See *Bruckner*, 2 vols. (Berlin, 1925).

type of material process that organised symphonic structures around the accumulation and discharge of melodic tensions. Unlike the classical sonata principle, in which motivic processes articulate a tonal scheme, Bruckner's sonata forms are driven by melodic intensifications, of which tonality and harmony are structural effects. Consequently, Kurth conceived of Bruckner's forms as compounds of 'symphonic waves' (*symphonische Wellen*).[35] In a revision of Halm's model, Bach's 'culture of theme' and Wagner's 'culture of harmony' became a 'culture of form' in Bruckner's symphonies.

These historical narratives were given a disturbing slant by the Bruckner reception of the Nazi period, with commentators turning the Hegelian method to overtly political ends: the ethnocentricity implicit in the views of Kurth and Halm became explicit in National Socialist cultural politics. Bruckner's music was considered in the highest sense purely German; consequently it stood as a bulwark against the degenerate, cosmopolitan forces of musical modernism, which in practice were considered synonymous with an imagined Judaeo-Bolshevik conspiracy. At a time when British reception still largely viewed Bruckner as marginal and incompetent, German reception was marked by a crescendo of hysterical lionisation that secured him as an institutionalised artistic symbol of the regime. As a consequence, post-war Germanic scholarship has understandably sought less controversial directions. As editor of the complete edition, Leopold Nowak set about a reappraisal of the aims and methods of the *Gesamtausgabe*, which had become infused with the politics of the Third Reich.[36] The trend in pre-war discourse towards establishing Bruckner as the quintessential composer of absolute music gave way to attempts to read the symphonies as consciously programmatic, for example in the work of Constantin Floros, while Bruckner's historical context and Austro-German reception has been traced in some detail by Floros, Manfred Wagner and Christa Brüstle, amongst others.[37]

---

[35] The concept of the symphonic wave is elaborated in *Bruckner*, vol. I, pp. 279–319. See also *Ernst Kurth: Selected Writings*, trans. and ed. Lee Rothfarb (Cambridge, 1991), pp. 151–87.

[36] On this matter see Hansen, 'Die faschistische Bruckner-Rezeption'; Morten Solvik, 'The International Bruckner Society and the NSDAP: A Case Study of Robert Haas and the Critical Edition', *Musical Quarterly* 83 (1998), pp. 362–82; Benjamin Korstvedt, '"Return to the Pure Sources": The Ideology and Text-Critical Legacy of the First Bruckner *Gesamtausgabe*', in *Bruckner Studies*, pp. 91–121.

[37] See Constantin Floros, *Bruckner und Brahms*, and 'Historische Phasen der Bruckner-Rezeption', in Othmar Wessely, ed., *Bruckner-Symposium Bericht. Bruckner Rezeption* (Linz, 1983), pp. 93–102; Manfred Wagner, 'Bruckner in Wien', in *Anton Bruckner in Wien: Eine kritische Studie zu seiner Persönlichkeit* (Graz, 1980), pp. 9–74; Christa Brüstle, *Anton Bruckner und die Nachwelt: zur Rezeptionsgeschichte der Komponisten in der ersten Hälfte des 20. Jahrhunderts* (Stuttgart, 1998).

The revisionism of post-war Germanic reception has fulfilled an entirely different function to that of post-war Anglo-American reception. German-language commentators did not struggle with the question of Bruckner's canonical membership, which the Nazi misappropriations did not endanger, but tried to escape the grand historical narratives and overtly ideological self-justifications of pre-war scholars in favour of a more cautious, positivistic approach. Both strands of reception, however, exhibit a common ambition to divest Bruckner of a problematic status that earlier scholarship was perceived to have exacerbated.

## The problem of the editions

The problem of a self-perpetuating revisionism is nowhere more keenly observed than in the question of the editions. The composer's multiple revisions, for which there is still no consensus explanation, have combined with philological difficulties of alarming complexity to create a situation that a century of research has failed satisfactorily to resolve.

In 1969 Deryck Cooke published a series of articles under the collective title 'The Bruckner Problem Simplified', the purpose of which was to provide a conclusive solution to these matters.[38] Cooke asserted that the burgeoning variety of scores – amounting to the first publications, the critical editions of Haas, Orel, Oeser, and later Nowak, and the (at the time) unpublished first versions of the Third, Fourth and Eighth Symphonies – could be reduced to a reasonable total by observing some simple guidelines. To begin with, the editions published during and shortly after Bruckner's lifetime should be rejected *en masse*. As far as Cooke was concerned, their editors 'collaborated in misrepresenting Bruckner's intentions', and they are therefore 'not versions by Bruckner'.[39] Secondly, the discrepancies between the editions of Haas, Orel and Oeser and those of Nowak are for the most part insignificant. The First, Fifth, Sixth, Seventh and Ninth Symphonies vary so little that, for Cooke, the two versions are in each case 'one and the same Bruckner score in two slightly different editions'.[40] Thirdly, we should reject the first versions of the Third and Fourth Symphonies as of no more than scholarly interest, since they are not 'alternative performing versions, but scores which Bruckner discarded on the way to his first definitive versions'. Cooke applied the same rationale to the first version of the Eighth, whilst admitting that this 'was actually Bruckner's first definitive score of the work'.[41]

---

[38] Deryck Cooke, 'The Bruckner Problem Simplified', *Musical Times* 110 (1969), pp. 20–2, 142–4, 362–5, 479–82, 828, reprinted in *Vindications: Essays on Romantic Music* (Cambridge, 1982), pp. 43–71. All quotations from *Vindications*.

[39] Ibid., p. 47.     [40] Ibid.     [41] Ibid.

This leaves the Second Symphony, the remaining two versions of the Third Symphony, the Fourth Symphony and the 1890 revision of the Eighth. Again, Cooke cut tersely through textual discrepancies. He selected Haas's edition of the Second Symphony, rejecting Nowak's edition of the 1877 revision on the grounds that Bruckner's collaboration with Johann Herbeck in preparing this score amounted to an early example of the kind of interventions that rendered the first editions irrelevant. Cooke preferred Oeser's edition of the 1877 version of the Third Symphony for the same reason: the 1889 version on which Nowak based his publication was developed in collaboration with Franz Schalk (Nowak eventually published his score of the 1877 version in 1981). Haas's score of the Fourth Symphony was also Cooke's first choice, because Haas's primary source was a copy of the 1880 version made by Bruckner in 1890, that is to say after the 1886 revision on which Nowak based his edition, a chronology which for Cooke rendered the 1886 score redundant. Finally, he favoured Haas's edition of the Eighth Symphony. The restorations of passages from the 1887 version of the Adagio and Finale made by Haas are accepted on the grounds that their omission was motivated by collaboration, and because their absence impaired the work's formal balance. Although he admitted that Nowak had 'musicological rectitude on his side', Cooke felt that Haas could take the moral high ground, since 'Schalk's interference in the revision must itself be considered unethical'. The textually accurate Nowak score is therefore 'a piece of musicological pedantry which makes no structural sense at all'.[42]

In the thirty-four years since its publication, Cooke's tidy reduction has progressively fallen apart.[43] Notwithstanding considerable advances, most notable of which are the foundations for determining the scope and quantity of versions for a given work laid down by Manfred Wagner and others, the current state of scholarship emphasises a dramatically expanded range of legitimate sources and editions.[44] There have been four main areas of contention. First, more recent publications have rendered Cooke's synopsis inadequate. The *Gesamtausgabe* under Nowak and others has subsequently published the first versions of the Third, Fourth and Eighth Symphonies, along with rejected further versions of the slow movement of the Third Symphony and the Finale of the Fourth. Moreover, in the case of the Second Symphony, Cooke's judgements were erroneous because neither Haas nor

---

[42] Ibid., p. 68.

[43] For a recent consideration of Cooke's essay, see Dermot Gault, 'For Later Times', *Musical Times* 137, pp. 12–19 and Korstvedt, '"Return to the Pure Sources"', p. 92.

[44] See for example Manfred Wagner, *Der Wandel des Konzepts: Zu den verschiedenen Fassungen von Bruckners Dritter, Vierter und Achter Sinfonie* (Vienna, 1980).

Nowak based his edition purely on Bruckner's first completed version, a problem that is addressed in a new publication edited by William Carragan.

Second, recent reassessments of the collaborations between Bruckner and his editors suggest that Cooke's blanket dismissal of the first editions was somewhat simplistic. This issue has been taken up by Benjamin Korstvedt, who contends that the relationship between Bruckner, the Schalk brothers, Max von Oberleithner and others was more complex than has been supposed. In many cases, Bruckner was to an extent complicit with the editors' decisions, and consented to leave the final stages of preparation in their hands. With reference to the Eighth Symphony, Korstvedt observes that:

> The textual situation . . . is messy and cannot support simple, black-and-white answers; so, while the 1892 edition may not be 'pure Bruckner' – whatever that might be – to all appearances Bruckner authorised it, and for that reason it needs to be taken seriously. If we simply dismiss the 1892 edition in the name of honouring Bruckner's 'real intentions', we paradoxically do something that contradicts the composer's own actions.[45]

This view may be justified on other grounds. Many of the changes in the first editions, particularly concerning the notation of dynamics, tempo markings and expression, reflected contemporary notational and performance conventions. And although Bruckner himself adhered in manuscript to older conventions, there is evidence to suggest that he would have expected the details added in the first editions to be realised in performance. Korstvedt concludes that the editors simply made explicit what was already implicit in Bruckner's scores. The first publications are thus in a sense historically 'authentic', because they notate aspects of contemporary performance practice that later Urtext editions removed. If Korstvedt is right, the textual situation takes on an unprecedented complexity. At least for the Second, Third, Fourth, Seventh and Eighth Symphonies, all of which were published during Bruckner's lifetime and involved varying levels of collaboration or intervention, any concept of a single authoritative text must be abandoned, and we become committed to an irreducible pluralism.

Third, the legitimisation sought for the *Gesamtausgabe* in the terms of Bruckner's will, and in other remarks of the composer regarding the validity of his unedited manuscripts 'for later times', both of which Cooke tacitly accepted, has also come under critical scrutiny. Again, Korstvedt has

---

[45] *Bruckner: Symphony no. 8*, p. 91. Suspicion over the Haas editions is not recent: see for example Emil Armbruster, *Erstdruckfassung oder 'Originalfassung'? Ein Beitrag zur Brucknerfrage am fünfzigsten Todestag des Meister* (Leipzig, 1946) and Wilhelm Oerley, 'Von Bruckners eigener Hand. Revision der Revision', *Der Turm* 2 (1946), pp. 138–42.

been instrumental in this respect. He notes that the will, which bequeathed manuscripts of the symphonies, the three great masses, the *Te Deum*, Psalm 150 and the cantata *Helgoland* to the Imperial Library and entrusted their publication to the firm of Josef Eberle, makes no direct suggestion that these scores should be the sole sources for subsequent editions. Neither does it make any claims that posterity would validate Bruckner's original versions, the inference in fact being drawn from a letter to Felix Weingartner of January 1891 concerning the Eighth Symphony. In Korstvedt's view, these two pieces of evidence have been hijacked as justification for a particular philological strategy, which Cooke's article unquestioningly upholds.

Fourth, Cooke's general preference for Haas has been challenged on political grounds. For some commentators, seminally Emil Armbruster and more recently Matthias Hansen, Morten Solvik and Benjamin Korstvedt, the links between the first *Gesamtausgabe* and Nazism renders Haas's scores ideologically dubious.[46] The National Socialist Party was intimately involved with the funding of the project, and populated its motivations with Nazi ideology. To an extent, Haas's critical methods reflected contemporary politics: he was not simply concerned with reproducing the autograph sources, but also with saving Bruckner posthumously from what were considered to be the pernicious interventions of Jewish elements. Haas's philological method was therefore compromised; he frequently sacrificed textual accuracy in favour of spurious ideological justifications. More generally, the motivations behind the *Gesamtausgabe* carry potentially disturbing ideological connotations, being caught up with notions of textual purity and the resurrection of an *echt Deutsch* cultural icon that racial and political forces had allegedly tried to tarnish. Although Cooke noted that Haas was replaced for political rather than professional reasons, he did not recognise the extent to which politics affected editorial method. His support for Haas therefore runs the risk of defending texts that are potentially tainted with fascism.

There are other gaps in Cooke's arguments. His dismissal of the first versions of the Third and Fourth Symphonies on the grounds that they were not performing versions is untenable. The fact that these scores were not performed before they were revised does not render them illegitimate: the absence of a performance is not evidence that Bruckner considered them to be preparatory drafts. In the case of the first version of the Third Symphony, the lack of performance was due to repeated rejection by the Vienna Philharmonic, rather than the composer's desire to withhold material that had not reached its definitive form. The first version of the Fourth

---

[46] Armbruster, *Erstdruckfassung oder 'Originalfassung'?*; Korstvedt, "'Return to the Pure Sources'"; Solvik, 'The International Bruckner Society and the NSDAP'.

Symphony was in fact played in part by the Vienna Philharmonic at a test
rehearsal in 1875, and was rejected as a result. The notion of progress towards
a definitive form that should be taken as a benchmark of authenticity is
deeply problematic. Aspects of Cooke's defence of Haas's score of the Eighth
Symphony are also suspect. Haas's edition does not simply conflate two
versions, as Cooke suggested. The section Haas added in bars 609 to 617
of the Finale does not come from the 1887 version: although its harmonic
framework derives from a passage in that score, the melodic material was
largely an invention of Haas himself. Lastly, Cooke's view that Nowak's edition of the Finale 'makes no structural sense' is a serious overstatement.
The cuts simply abbreviate some sections of the form, without in any way
compromising their structural integrity. If abbreviation of the recapitulation amounted to a formal defect, other movements by Bruckner would
also have to be considered defective, for example the finales of the Sixth and
Seventh Symphonies.

At present, there is by no means general agreement about the best course of
editorial action. Some scholars, notably Paul Hawkshaw and John Philips,
have opposed Korstvedt, arguing that the meaning of Bruckner's will is
unambiguous, and that it is rash to forsake scores that are indubitably only
by Bruckner in favour of material that, at best, betrays dual authorship.[47]
Hawkshaw points out that many of the *Stichvorlagen* for the first editions
have been lost, so that, notwithstanding earlier collaborations, it is impossible to determine whether changes were introduced without Bruckner's
consent between the preparation of each engraver's copy and its publication. Worse still, in some cases, for example the F minor Mass and the
Fifth Symphony, the Schalk brothers and Max von Oberleithner clearly did
exclude Bruckner from the process of preparation. Hawkshaw concludes that
'there is no justification for performing or studying anything as authentic
Bruckner other than the versions identified by Haas and Nowak', since 'no
modern editorial policy, however all-encompassing, should defend sources
produced as a result of the composer being *deliberately removed* [italics
in original] from the circumstances of their preparation'.[48] Hawkshaw is
also cautious about the outright rejection of Haas's editions, observing that
'the horrific politics surrounding the origins of the first *Gesamtausgabe* are
neither philological nor musical grounds for throwing out the rest of his
editorial conclusions'.[49]

---

[47] Paul Hawkshaw, 'The Bruckner Problem Revisited', *Nineteenth-Century Music* 21
   (1997), pp. 96–107; John A. Philips, review of Korstvedt, *Bruckner: Symphony no. 8*,
   *Music and Letters* 82 (2001), pp. 323–8, and particularly p. 325.
[48] Ibid., p. 104.      [49] Ibid.

While such fundamental disagreements persist, the editorial situation will continue to be 'one of the most vexatious in all musicology', as Cooke described it. This complexity may not simply arise from the inability of musicologists to find an editorial common ground. The circumstances surrounding the revisions and initial publications generate enough information to justify widely differing editorial perspectives. Frequently, differences of opinion turn on the interpretation of Bruckner's inherently ambiguous remarks, or, in the case of the argument over the Haas editions, on assumptions about the influence of politics that are really themselves based on ideological as much as factual considerations. Thus, although Cooke's arguments can easily be debunked, counter-arguments laying claim to an absolute philological rectitude may be equally unstable, since an uncontentious stance with respect to textual 'authenticity' is in many cases unrealistic. Ultimately, we may have to recognise that resistance to an unchecked pluralism will often involve interpretative or analytical decisions rather than the establishment of an unequivocal textual authority, a process that unavoidably entails recourse to approaches lying outside the domain of philology.

## Biography and music

If editorial problems have resisted satisfactory reappraisal, the tendency to read biographical information as inscribed in musical style and material has proved actively detrimental: there can be few composers whose work has suffered so chronically from the equation of life and works as Bruckner. Faced with music of forbidding length, complexity and originality, commentators have resorted, both critically and apologetically, to explanations based on the peculiarities of Bruckner's personality and background. The conflation of biography and interpretation has produced conceptions of the symphonies that have endured, despite the manifest gap between constructions of Bruckner's 'simplistic' personality and the astonishing modernity of his works.

The most common connection made between music and personality has been the accusation of naivety: the claim that Bruckner was 'childish as an artist and childlike as a man'.[50] Whilst the composer's personal naivety is at least sustained by considerable anecdotal evidence,[51] the demonstration of musical naivety is frequently based simply on the identification

---

[50] 'Kindlich als Künstler und kindisch als Mensch'; see Manfred Wagner, *Bruckner: eine Monographie* (Mainz, 1983), p. 1.

[51] The standard biographical source for much of this evidence is August Göllerich and Max Auer, *Bruckner, ein Lebens- und Schaffensbild*, 4 vols. (Regensburg, 1922–37).

of 'naive' material in the symphonies, as for example in Tovey's opinion that 'the defence of Bruckner . . . would defeat itself by attempting to claim that there is nothing helpless about the slow movement of the Romantic Symphony', or that the second theme in the Finale of the Sixth Symphony is 'the most naive of all Bruckner's second subjects'.[52] This view gains complexity when it is linked to the complaint of formal incompetence. Bruckner's apparent intellectual simplicity is translated into an inadequate understanding of symphonic form, and so his music betrays a rift between the pretensions of the material and its poorly understood formal context.

These objections have been countered in a number of ways. Before and during the Second World War, right-wing exponents in Germany and Austria turned Bruckner's naivety into a virtue by regarding it as evidence of an unsullied rural purity, free from what they saw as the pernicious influences of liberal urban intellectualism. His music therefore expressed a kind of Germanic *völkisch* essence, which had been obscured in other composers' work by an unhealthy intellectual self-consciousness.[53] Elsewhere, Bruckner's naiveties have been reinterpreted as mystical rumination: his religious convictions afforded access to a realm of experience that was at odds with the pervasive post-Enlightenment humanism of the time. This is consequently the innermost meaning of his music; as Geoffrey Sharp remarked, 'his mysticism is latent on page after page of his most inspired music – in itself an irrefutable indication of the depth of his elephantine genius'.[54] More recently, the biographical evidence itself has been freshly scrutinised. There are indications that Bruckner was far from intellectually retarded. He gained an advanced education not only in music but also in physics and Latin, and was quite able to keep up with contemporary academic debates if they aroused his interest. Neither was he as socially inept or parochial as has been suggested, having spent the greater part of his life in large urban centres and risen in his career with a fair degree of shrewdness and calculation. This biographical revision forces a renewed appraisal of the music: if Bruckner's personal naivety can be disproved, then the accusation of musical naivety, being based on an equation of character and musical material, becomes untenable.

---

[52] *Essays in Musical Analysis*, vol. II, pp. 75 and 83.
[53] The Bruckner reception of the Third Reich is replete with such opinions, and usually involved invocation of the so-called *Blut und Boden* ideology. See for example Goebbels' Regensburg speech, and also Reinhold Zimmermann, 'Anton Bruckner: der große Lehrermusiker', *Der Deutsche Erzieher* (12 June 1937), p. 370. See also Bryan Gilliam, 'The Annexation of Anton Bruckner'.
[54] Geoffrey Sharp, 'Bruckner: Simpleton or Mystic', *Music Review* 3 (1942), p. 53.

If the clichés surrounding Bruckner's personality have proved hard to sustain, the image of Bruckner as an organist-composer has become entrenched in the literature. Debate about this issue in pre-war Germany, typified by the respective views of Max Auer and Alfred Lorenz, had little effect on a large body of post-war writing, which continued to style Bruckner's material and orchestration as organistic and rooted in his background in church music, often without any kind of detailed substantiation in musical analysis.[55] Generally, the composer's orchestration is taken to resemble organ registration in its apparent tendency to offset orchestral groups as distinct 'block' sonorities. This is considered to oppose Wagner's orchestration, which is more concerned with mixing sonorities, and certainly the line of French orchestration from Berlioz to Debussy, which appears to place material in the service of texture. Although Lorenz's views on this matter had political implications – the detachment of Bruckner from the organ loft, and therefore the Church, carried distinct political overtones in Nazi Germany – he nevertheless made observations that deserve attention. Lorenz pointed out that the kind of block oppositions discovered in Bruckner, which he called the 'group principle' (*Gruppenprinzip*), relate more closely to the distinction between *concertante* and *ripieno* found in the Baroque concerto grosso than to any kind of organistic texture. As he rightly observed, the group principle and its alternative, the 'mixture principle' (*Mischungsprinzip*), are both prevalent in Bruckner's orchestration, and can be found in equal measure in music from Beethoven to Wagner. For Lorenz, both techniques are engrained in a tradition of orchestration originating in the high Baroque, and have nothing to do with Bruckner's roots in church music. We need not accept the ideological overtones of this argument to recognise its implications: Bruckner's orchestration is considered organistic because of a superficial affiliation with a biographical fact, rather than through close analysis of the music and its precedents.

Numerous other connections between life and works have been made. Bruckner's recurrent nervous conditions, expressed most seriously in his nervous breakdown of 1867 and the feverish revision period of the early

---

[55] Max Auer, 'Anton Bruckner, die Orgel, und Richard Wagner', *Zeitschrift für Musik* 104 (1937), pp. 477–81; Alfred Lorenz, 'Zur Instrumentation von Bruckners Symphonien', *Zeitschrift für Musik* 103 (1936), pp. 1318–25. Other examples of Auer's view can be found in Alfred Einstein, 'Bruckner, Anton', in *The Grove Dictionary of Music and Musicians*, 3rd edn, vol. I (London, 1927), p. 482; Hans Redlich, 'Bruckner, Anton', in *The Grove Dictionary of Music and Musicians*, 5th edn, vol. II (London, 1954), p. 971; Hans-Hubert Schönzeller, *Bruckner* (London, 1970), p. 164; Denis Arnold, 'Bruckner, Anton', in *The Oxford Companion to Music* (Oxford, 1983), p. 278; Donald J. Grout, *A History of Western Music*, 5th edn (New York, 1996), p. 583.

1890s, have been employed to explain some of his compositional habits. His tendency, for example, to number bars in various phrase groupings beneath his scores – the so-called 'metrical grid' – has been considered a compositional effect of his numeromania, or compulsion to count and record quantities of objects. The use of cumulative repetitions of motives in his music has been explained in a similar way: it comprises an obsessive counting of thematic ideas arising from a deep-seated compulsive urge.[56] Bruckner's predilection for revision could also be explained psychologically, as another product of the persistent insecurity manifest in his inability to deal with the attacks of Hanslick and the liberal press and his excessive concerns over financial security. And this is to say nothing of the murkier issues of Bruckner's repressed sexuality (he never married, nor had any extended relationships with women), or his interest in corpses and the paraphernalia of death, both of which make the symphonies inviting targets for a Freudian reading.

Again, more pragmatic explanations have been sought for Bruckner's psychological peculiarities, notably by Manfred Wagner, Norbet Nagler, Peter Gülke and others.[57] Although it is true that his anxieties were exaggerated during periods of nervous ill health, for the most part Bruckner's numeromania could be taken simply as mathematical curiosity, his sexual repression as an imposition of his Catholic faith, and his frustrations over money and criticism in the press as understandable practical concerns. The relationship between these issues and the compositional process could also be circumstantial. The revisions are in some estimations too systematic to be the products of psychological disturbance. As Timothy Jackson has argued, the layers of bar numberings in the scores are not in any sense tied to his periods of nervous ill health, but represent a consistent and logical feature of the way Bruckner composed. Repetitions in his music, although prevalent, are always functional, and frequently assist processes of intensification articulating important structural downbeats. Altogether, the conflation of biography, compositional process and interpretation of the music is often based on connections that do not withstand close scrutiny.

---

[56] See for example Cooke, 'Bruckner, Anton', p. 359 and Jackson, 'Bruckner's Metrical Numbers', *Nineteenth-Century Music* 14 (1990), pp. 101–31.

[57] See *Bruckner: Eine Monographie*; see also Norbert Nagler, 'Bruckners gründerzeitliche Monumentale Symphonie: Reflexionen zur Heteronomie kompositorische Praxis' in Heinz-Klaus Metzger and Rainer Riehn, eds, *Musik-Konzepte 23/24: Anton Bruckner* (Munich 1982), pp. 86–118, Peter Gülke, *Bruckner, Brahms: zwei Studien* (Kassel 1989), and Martin Geck, *Von Beethoven bis Mahler: die Musik des deutschen Idealismus* (Stuttgart 1993).

## Bruckner and musical analysis

Johnson's revisionist admonition has especial urgency for the field of analysis. Canonical preoccupations, perhaps combined with a more general atmosphere of musicological disdain, have created a neglect amongst Anglo-American analysts that has only recently begun to be redressed. The dual influence of Schenker and Schoenberg on the analysis of the tonal repertoire has only exacerbated the disparity between the analytical reception of Bruckner and that of his significant contemporaries. There is no body of analytical literature for Bruckner akin to that developed for the music of Brahms or Wagner, both of whom have yielded to analysis along broadly Schenkerian or Schoenbergian lines.

Schenker's negative reception of Bruckner, which was part of a music-historical model that excluded any composer embracing a post-Wagnerian or post-tonal idiom, has impeded acceptance of Bruckner by analysts, despite general rejection of Schenker's historical and aesthetic thinking. Even when attempts have been made to apply Schenker more widely, Bruckner has generally been ignored. Felix Salzer's *Structural Hearing*, which analyses music from Machaut to Hindemith in an attempt to prove the widespread applicability of Schenker, examines no music by Bruckner.[58] Moreover when Schenkerians have approached Bruckner, it has required conspicuous justification. Edward Laufer purposefully styled his analysis of the Ninth Symphony as a refutation of Schenker's view:

> Surely Bruckner's compositional technique of repeatedly working in certain
> motivic ideas beneath the surface . . . and making these form the guiding
> framework on which the foreground is placed is at the heart of Schenker's
> concept of the organic nature of a great work of art.[59]

Laufer's primary concern is membership of an analytical canon: with justifying Bruckner's inclusion in the corpus of music to which Schenkerian theory is applicable. He achieves this by showing that Schenker's technique remains relevant notwithstanding the historical and aesthetic preconceptions of its creator.

Bruckner has proved similarly resistant to Schoenbergian ideas of thematic process. Analysts defining Bruckner's thematic techniques have sought explanations beyond the notions of developing variation that have been considered central to the Beethovenian tradition: Stephen Parkany has purposely returned to Kurth's ideas of thematic 'becoming' as a way of understanding the development of material in the Adagio of the Seventh

---

[58] Felix Salzer, *Structural Hearing* (New York, 1952).      [59] *Bruckner Studies*, p. 255.

Symphony;[60] Benjamin Korstvedt has resuscitated Werner Korte's concept of thematic 'mutation' in the Eighth Symphony;[61] Warren Darcy, in part following the work of James Hepokoski, has identified sonata-form 'deformations' in Bruckner relying on fulfilled or negated 'teleological processes' and static material repetitions, rather than the Schoenbergian concept of the *Grundgestalt* and its elaboration.[62] The issue of Bruckner's distance from the analytical norms of developing variation is summed up by Carl Dahlhaus:

> Musical logic, the 'developing variation' of musical ideas . . . rested on a premise considered so self-evident as to be beneath mention: that the central parameter of art-music is its 'diastematic', or pitch, structure . . . Bruckner's symphonic style, however . . . is primarily rhythmic rather than diastematic, and thus seems to stand the usual hierarchy of tonal properties on its head.[63]

For Dahlhaus, the root of Bruckner's special status is a tendency to invert the relationship of rhythm and pitch. Whereas developing variation, which Dahlhaus identifies in Schoenbergian terms as the 'musical logic' of 'the classical–romantic tradition', treats interval content as the defining factor of the symphonic theme, for Bruckner the 'ground level' of thematic identity was rhythm, with pitch and interval content being malleable around an invariant rhythmic pattern.

Analysts have also broached questions of tonal, topical, expressive and metrical strategy. Paul Dawson-Bowling, William Benjamin and Robert Pascall have all drawn attention to aspects of tonal structure in the Eighth Symphony, noting with varying degrees of caution the influence of the modal mixture engendered in the main theme of the first movement on the structure of the piece.[64] These studies however remain isolated: the striking

[60] Stephen Parkany, 'Kurth's *Bruckner* and the Adagio of the Seventh Symphony', *Nineteenth-Century Music* 11 (1988), pp. 262–81.

[61] Korstvedt in *Bruckner: Symphony no. 8*, pp. 31–2. Korstvedt draws on Werner Korte, *Bruckner und Brahms: Die spätromantische Lösung der autonomen Konzeption* (Tutzing, 1963).

[62] Warren Darcy, 'Bruckner's Sonata Deformations', in *Bruckner Studies*, pp. 256–77.

[63] Carl Dahlhaus, *Nineteenth-Century Music*, trans. J. Bradford Robinson (Berkeley, 1989), p. 272. See also Dahlhaus, 'Anton Bruckner und die Programmusik: zum Finale der Achten Symphonie', in *Anton Bruckner: Studien zu Werk und Wirkung, Walter Wiora zum 30. Dezember 1986* (Tutzing, 1988).

[64] See Paul Dawson-Bowling, 'Thematic and Tonal Unity in Bruckner's Eighth Symphony', *Music Review* 30 (1969), pp. 225–36; William Benjamin, 'Tonal Dualism in Bruckner's Eighth Symphony', in William Kinderman and Harald Krebs, eds., *The Second Practice of Nineteenth-Century Tonality* (Lincoln, 1996), pp. 237–58; Robert Pascall, 'Major Instrumental Forms: 1850–1890', in *The New Oxford History of Music 1850–1890*, vol. IX (Oxford, 1990), pp. 534–658 and especially p. 591. See also

extensions of tonality, and particularly the range of tonal relationships governing the structure of sonata form, which are widespread in Bruckner's
symphonies, await the attention of a large-scale study. Robert Hatten's analysis of topical and expressive devices and Joseph Kraus's investigations of
phrase rhythm are even more exceptional. Although Bruckner's dialogue
with the topical characteristics of the Beethovenian symphony and his
acutely hypermetrical sense of structure constitute major elements of his
symphonic style, they have evaded general analytical consideration.

As a focus for analysis, Bruckner has been a victim of the theoretical and
canonical preconceptions upon which the mainstream of analytical practice has been based. Commonly adopted notions of thematic process, and
the influential prolongational model of tonality, both evolved in response
to a common practice that was considered to culminate in the music of
Brahms. Bruckner's perceived tangential relationship to the mainstream is
thus more a matter of the shortcomings of theory than it is a measure of
Bruckner's compositional practice. In the domain of analysis, the demand
for reassessment has far-reaching implications: doing analytical justice to
Bruckner may involve nothing less than a wholesale revision of what we
consider the norms of 'the classical–romantic tradition' to be.

## Conclusions

Comparison of these areas of debate reveals one point with particular clarity:
attempts to explain problems in any one area without recourse to a deeper
interpretative or contextual engagement, or simply as the effects of problems
in other fields, are likely to fail. Thus, although the Nazi appropriation of
Bruckner affected British reception both during and after the Second World
War, antipathy cannot be explained either as a reaction to fascism, or as
a response to an inherently 'totalitarian' property of the music. In truth,
hostility to Bruckner was more pervasive in Britain before the war than it
was afterwards, the post-war period marking a pronounced upward trend
in the composer's fortunes. Moreover, the development of Bruckner reception in Britain was very similar to that of other composers whose music was
either rejected or ignored by National Socialism. Parallels can be found in
the British reception of Janáček's music, which was until fairly recently also
dismissed as marginal or incoherent.[65] The objections raised against Janáček

Julian Horton, *Towards a Theory of Nineteenth-Century Tonality* (Ph.D. diss., Cambridge, 1998), pp. 128–270.

[65] For a survey of British responses to Janáček, see Paul Wingfield, *Janáček: Glagolitic
Mass* (Cambridge, 1992), pp. 116–24.

are strikingly similar to those levelled at Bruckner: in particular, a belief in the incoherence of his music arising from its repetitive and fragmentary character. Conversely, other composers who suffered fascist appropriation, perhaps most systematically Handel, retained a secure place in the British concert repertoire and provoked no comparable accusations of incompetence.[66] The convergence of music and politics in Bruckner's case is not the source of the critical problem, but one of its facets.

The influence of textual issues can be understood in the same way. The idea, for example, that misunderstanding of Bruckner was linked to the reception of the first editions is not borne out by the literature.[67] Neither Tovey nor Abraham modified their opinions in any way after becoming familiar with the first *Gesamtausgabe*. For Abraham, the new editions simply 'de-Wagnerised' Bruckner, and therefore made his defective technique all the more apparent. Tovey rejected the *Gesamtausgabe* versions on the simplistic grounds that the first editions 'were all accepted and published by [Bruckner] as expressing his final intentions'.[68] Conversely, the Germanic literature that most forcefully asserted the formal coherence and music-historical importance of the symphonies relied entirely on the first editions. Hans Grunsky's analysis of the Ninth Symphony, which made extravagant claims for the dialectical logic of the work, was based on Ferdinand Löwe's edition, with which Bruckner had no contact at all, having died seven years before its publication. The reception of Bruckner in its critical or apologetic aspects is not tied to the resolution of philological problems. Coherence, incoherence, competence and incompetence have been detected regardless of the editions used.

Comprehension of these matters is better served by looking beyond the individual issues comprising the 'Bruckner problem' to the philosophical contexts from which they emerge. The differences between Germanic and English-language reception are the respective products of idealist and positivist, or empiricist, philosophical mindsets. Consistently, the theoretical preconceptions hindering the understanding of Bruckner in Britain and America amounted to Germanic ideas that were detached from their roots in post-Hegelian idealism. In the early twentieth century, British musical

---

[66] On the 'aryanisation' of Handel, see Erik Levi, *Music in the Third Reich* (London, 1994), pp. 77–81, and also Pamela Potter, 'The Politicization of Handel and his Oratorios in the Weimar Republic, the Third Reich and the Early Years of the German Democratic Republic', *Musical Quarterly* 85 (2001), pp. 311–41.

[67] The idea that the *Gesamtausgabe* obviated the question of Bruckner's compositional competence is commonplace: see for example Schönzeler, *Bruckner*, pp. 149–50.

[68] See Tovey, 'Retrospective and Corrigenda', in *Essays in Musical Analysis VI: Miscellaneous Notes, Glossary and Index* (London, 1935–9), p. 144.

thought relied heavily on diluted appropriations of the central European *Formenlehre* tradition, deploying its normative concepts of the classical formal patterns, whilst abandoning its overtly Hegelian motivations. Tovey's 1911 essay on sonata form drew on the formalistic aspects of A. B. Marx's theories, as perhaps filtered through their reception by Prout. It advanced a concept of the form that was not agreeable to the main characteristics of Bruckner's music as Tovey perceived them. He considered the type of compositional technique appropriate to the sonata form as antithetical to the Wagnerian thematic technique, and therefore to Bruckner's symphonic style:

> It is unlikely that really vital sonata work will ever be based on the kind of Wagnerian leitmotiv system, until the whole character of instrumental form shall have attained the state of things in which the movements are not separated at all.[69]

Such views are consistent throughout the British literature. Simpson also considered Bruckner's basic difficulty to be his attempt to make a fundamentally anti-classical style accord with classical forms, and Lionel Pike's detection of a conflict of types of symphonic logic in the Fourth Symphony invokes the same dichotomy. Appropriations of Schenker and Schoenberg have followed a similar path. Schenker's aesthetics of the masterwork conveyed an ethnocentricity that rightly proved unpalatable in post-war America; Schoenberg's theoretical writings were plundered for their analytically applicable concepts, but the barely concealed Hegelianism that underpinned them was generally ignored.[70] Yet it is precisely this rejected philosophical context that has proved instrumental in making sense of Bruckner, especially the application of dialectics as an analytical or music-historical method. Halm, Kurth and Bloch stood within a tradition of dialectical thought that Bruckner's music could also be considered to inhabit. They could therefore place it historically in a way that Anglophone scholarship, with its selective absorption of Germanic musical theory, could not.

---

[69] Donald Francis Tovey, 'Sonata Form', in *Encyclopaedia Britannica*, 11th edn (London, 1911), p. 398. Tovey's writing is replete with such assertions: 'Bruckner conceived magnificent openings and *Götterdämmerung* climaxes, but dragged along with him throughout his life an apparatus of classical sonata forms as understood by a village organist'; 'Bruckner's difficulty [in composing slow movements], is . . . his conscientious objection to write anything so trivial and un-Wagnerian as a symmetrical tune'; 'you must not expect Bruckner to make a finale "go" like a classical finale. He is in no greater hurry at the end of a symphony than at the beginning.' See *Essays in Musical Analysis*, vol. II, pp. 121, 75 and 77.

[70] On the philosophical background of Schoenberg's ideas, see Janet Schmalfeldt, 'Beethoven's *Tempest* Sonata and the Hegelian Tradition', in Christopher Reynolds, ed., *The Beethoven Forum*, vol. IV (Lincoln, 1995), pp. 37–71.

These observations elaborate in brief a methodological conviction that
will be fundamental to the ensuing case studies: we are more likely to engage
both Bruckner's symphonies and their attendant problems substantially
if they are considered both reflective of, and susceptible to, more general
philosophical and methodological contexts and debates. To this end, a variety of musicological and non-musicological authorities and ideas will be
invoked in an attempt to address questions arising from the conflation of
disciplinary concerns: Adorno's negative dialectics will be combined with
topical analysis as a means of reading the Finale of the Third Symphony as
reflective of its historical context; Louis Althusser and Jean-François Lyotard
offer ways of assessing the analytical consequences of Nazi appropriation;
conceptions of influence from Carl Dahlhaus to Harold Bloom, Mikhail
Bakhtin and Julia Kristeva will be called upon in order to explicate the
ways in which the symphonies embody the musical and extra-musical agendas of the post-Beethovenian symphony; the association of personality and
compositional habits, and the claim that the types of psychological otherness that Bruckner has been considered to exhibit emerge in his music,
will be tested through an attempt to ground such readings in both music-
analytical and psychoanalytic method. The two remaining studies depart
from this precedent, whilst retaining aspects of its critical pluralism. The
chapter on analysis shuns adherence to a single theoretical model in favour
of the analytical testing of various techniques and the canonical or historical assumptions they court. Chapter 6 unearths the analytical marginalia of
textual research in order to resuscitate analysis as a means of policing textual
plurality.

## 2 Bruckner and late nineteenth-century Vienna: analysis and historical context

Attempts to place Bruckner's symphonies in a historical context have focused especially on three areas of enquiry: the role of the symphonies in the cultural politics of late nineteenth-century Vienna; the relationship of the music to the composer's background and education; the programmatic content of the works as it was construed by Bruckner and his contemporaries. The first of these fields has been most prominent in recent research, motivated in part by renewed musicological interest in ideological and political issues.

Conceptions of the symphonies in the context of their political climate are generally based on an equation of politics, compositional influence and broad definitions of the music's character. They relate Bruckner's absorption of Wagnerian stylistic features, and the evident monumentality of the symphonies, to a complex of corresponding cultural and political factors.[1] By these terms, reading the music in a historically sensitive manner involves disentangling it from 'the crust of latter-day reception', as Benjamin Korstvedt has put it, which has obscured the political resonances of Bruckner's Wagnerian affiliations and the function of the monumental symphony as an artistic symbol of the right-wing, nationalist politics that gained ground in Vienna in the 1890s.[2] Whatever Bruckner's personal involvement with these movements, the ideological ramifications of the Brahms–Bruckner debate, as represented by the rhetoric of Hanslick on the one hand and of Göllerich, Stolzing and the Schalk brothers on the other, form the ideological basis for a historicist reading.[3] Bruckner's engagement

---

[1] Thomas Leibnitz, Matthias Hansen and Manfred Wagner have linked the reception of the symphonies to the waning of Viennese liberalism, whilst the post-Wagnerian elements of this context have been stressed by Margaret Notley and Benjamin Korstvedt. See Leibnitz, *Die Brüder Schalk und Anton Bruckner dargestellt an den Nachlaßbeständern der Musiksammlung der Österreichischen Nationalbibliothek* (Tutzing, 1988); Hansen, *Anton Bruckner* (Leipzig, 1987); Wagner, 'Bruckner in Wien: Ein Beitrag zur Apperzeption und Rezeption des oberösterreichischen Komponist in der Hauptstadt der k.k. Monarchie', in *Anton Bruckner in Wien. Ein kritische Studie zu seiner Persönlichkeit* (Graz, 1980); Margaret Notley, 'Bruckner and Viennese Wagnerism', in Timothy Jackson and Paul Hawkshaw, eds., *Bruckner Studies* (Cambridge, 1997); Benjamin Korstvedt, *Bruckner: Symphony no. 8* (Cambridge, 2000).

[2] See *Bruckner: Symphony no. 8*, p. 9.

[3] The political affiliations of Göllerich, Stolzing and the Schalk brothers cannot be considered equivalent. Stolzing and Göllerich had close links with the pan-German

with Wagner is crucial in this respect. The problem of integrating Wagner's stylistic and expressive innovations into the closed forms of the symphony, with which Bruckner was undeniably engaged, becomes the means through which ideology is manifest in musical material.

In contrast, approaches grounded in the factors conditioning Bruckner's artistic and personal development have tended to regard the music as anachronistic rather than contemporary: it does not encapsulate the nationalist politics of *fin de siècle* Vienna and their Wagnerian associations, but harks back to the Upper Austrian *Vormärz* mentality of monarchic and Catholic authoritarianism, and therefore to a pre-Enlightenment mindset.[4] This view understands both the technical features of the music and its religious significations as modernised archaism. Bruckner's unshakeable Catholicism, expressed in his works through the various topics of sacred style, is consequently quite different from the reconstructed political Catholicism of right-wing figures predominant in the Viennese political life of the late 1890s, principally Karl Lueger. The faith embodied in the symphonies is rather an unreconstructed remnant of the Austrian Baroque, or even of the Middle Ages. Other aspects of Bruckner's compositional habits could be taken to corroborate this view, for example his persistent desire to base progressive compositional techniques in established artifice. The historical basis for understanding the music should, in this sense, be located in the poietics of the symphonies, not in their immediate political context.

Programmatic interpretations assert a more concisely aesthetic type of historically informed analysis. Efforts to understand the symphonies through the brief programmes left by Bruckner, seminally Constantin Floros's analysis of the Eighth Symphony, are underpinned by the assumption that works of the nineteenth century are best comprehended via the hermeneutic strategies of the time, in which terms they become inseparable from the narrative impulse through which music was frequently rendered meaningful.[5] Floros's analysis, and Korstvedt's more recent assessment of

movement of Georg Schönerer, an affiliation the Schalks did not necessarily share. See Notley, 'Bruckner and Viennese Wagnerism' and also Wagner, 'Bruckner in Wien'.

[4] Such views are common in the English-language literature, as for example in Deryck Cooke's assertion that, in Bruckner's music, 'the stance is not Romantic, but medieval: indeed, the mentality of the Austrian Catholic peasantry, which Bruckner to a very large extent retained, was essentially a survival from the Middle Ages'. See *The New Grove Late Romantic Masters* (London, 1980), p. 50. For a consideration of Baroque elements in Bruckner's music, see Carl Dahlhaus, 'Bruckner und die Barock', *Neue Zeitschrift für Musik* 124 (1963), pp. 335–6.

[5] See Constantin Floros, *Bruckner und Brahms: Studien zur musikalischen Exegetik* (Wiesbaden, 1980), pp. 182–235, which approaches the Eighth Symphony from the point of view of the programme left by Bruckner. The programme is treated more cautiously in

the significance of the Eighth Symphony's programme, rely on the basic idea that understanding of the work is conditional on a reconstruction of the aesthetic sensibilities attending its composition and early reception. This approach carries with it an ideological agenda: especially in the German-language literature, programmatic interpretation has been a response to the Bruckner literature of the Third Reich and before, which forcefully asserted the symphonies' credentials as absolute music.

The theoretical assumptions underlying such approaches demand critical attention. Regarding the symphonies as symptoms of their political circumstances is problematic, primarily because the connection between Viennese politics and Bruckner's compositional intentions is nebulous. There is no strong evidence to suggest that Bruckner had direct involvement with the politics of the Wagnerian movement that supported him.[6] Certainly, his more overt musical Wagnerisms, most obviously the quotations from *Tristan* and *The Ring* in the first version of the Third Symphony, were hardly intended as political symbols, even if they were interpreted as such by politically interested parties. In fact, the Schalk brothers, Göllerich and others went to considerable lengths to fabricate a Wagnerian context for Bruckner that bore little relation to the real extent of Bruckner's involvement with Wagner.[7] Association of the Scherzo of the Eighth Symphony with the *deutscher Michael* character of German folklore was more politically suggestive, since it carried symbolic connotations for the pan-German movement with which Bruckner would undoubtedly have been familiar. Yet even in this regard, Bruckner's remarks were isolated, and show little awareness of an active political symbolism.[8] We are therefore led to the conclusion that cultural politics is sedimented in the music as an effect of 'the spirit of the age' in a generally Hegelian sense, and Bruckner's intentions are more or less removed from the equation. In addition, the music-analytical elements of this argument tend to remain rather generalised. At best, they emphasise isolated Wagnerian characteristics as the musical manifestation of political

Carl Dahlhaus, 'Bruckner und die Programmusik: Zum Finale der Achten Symphonie', in *Anton Bruckner: Studien zu Werk und Wirkung, Walter Wiora zum 30. Dezember 1986* (Tutzing, 1988), pp. 7–32. See also Korstvedt, *Bruckner: Symphony no. 8*, pp. 49–53.

[6] On this matter, see for example Notley, 'Bruckner and Viennese Wagnerism', pp. 69–71.

[7] Cosima Wagner's diary entry for 8 February 1875, one of her very few references to Bruckner, is instructive in this regard, standing in sharp contrast with the polemics of Bruckner's Wagnerian supporters: 'We go through the symphony of the poor Viennese organist Bruckner, who has been brushed aside by Herr Herbeck and others because he came to Bayreuth to ask R. to accept the dedication of a symphony! It is terrible what goes on in the musical world.' See *Cosima Wagner's Diaries: An Abridgement*, ed. Geoffrey Skelton (London, 1994), p. 227.

[8] See Notley, 'Bruckner and Viennese Wagnerism,' pp. 69–71.

orientation; at worst, they point to vague categories of affect, such as monumentality or monolithic textural features. It has proved hard to pin cultural
context down to precise and detailed analytical evidence.

The question of intention emerges in different forms in biographical
and programmatic approaches. There is no reason why we should privilege
Bruckner's cultural background as a basis for historical analysis; assertions
to the contrary rapidly become entangled in the intentional fallacy. Conceiving historical analysis as a hunt for the compositional manifestations of
the cultural conditions of Bruckner's psychological development relies on
the difficult assumption that this background has a preferred status over the
diverse cultural circumstances of Bruckner's compositional maturity. This
approach also fights shy of detailed analysis, favouring amorphous conceptions of Catholic mysticism, rustic simplicity, dogmatic assertions of faith
or a governing baroque mentality over clear classification of the analytical materials engendering formative cultural circumstances. Programmatic
reading is similarly difficult, not least because it seriously overestimates
the explanatory power of Bruckner's observations. The programme of the
Eighth Symphony was furnished a posteriori in a letter to Felix Weingartner
of 1891, and to say that its scope is restricted would be something of an
understatement. In fact, it is little more than a sketch, concerned only with
the coda of the first movement, the general character of the Scherzo, and
isolated moments in the Finale.[9] Whilst Floros's analysis is illuminating,
it has to overcome significant obstacles, most seriously the absence of any
remarks from Bruckner regarding the Adagio. Floros circumvents this problem by orientating his analysis of the slow movement around Josef Schalk's
more detailed programme, a piece of fiction that cannot be traced back
to Bruckner, and which was at the time widely considered to be more of

---

[9] Bruckner's programme runs as follows:

> In the first movement, the trumpet and horn passage based on the rhythm of the
> theme is the *Todesverkündigung*, which gradually grows stronger, and finally
> emerges very strongly. At the end: surrender.
>     Scherzo: Main theme, named Deutscher Michael. In the second part, the fellow
> wants to sleep, and in his dreamy state cannot find his tune; finally, he plaintively
> turns back.
>     Finale: at the time our Emperor received the visit of the Czars at Olmütz, thus,
> strings: the Cossacks; brass: military music; trumpets: fanfares, as the Majesties
> meet. In closing: all themes; (odd) [*komisch*], as in Tannhäuser in Act 2 when the
> King [*sic*] arrives from his journey, everything is already gloriously brilliant. In the
> Finale there is also the death march and then (brass) transfiguration.

Letter of 27 January 1891, in Max Auer, ed., *Anton Bruckner, Gesammelte Briefe* (Regensburg, 1924), translated in Korstvedt, *Bruckner: Symphony no. 8*, p. 51.

a hindrance than a help to Bruckner's cause.[10] Moreover, Floros can only deploy Bruckner's comments as a basis for understanding the whole work by linking aspects of the programme to specific motivic materials, and then extrapolating extra-musical meanings from motivic processes about which Bruckner said nothing. Thus, although the aesthetic context through which music was comprehended cannot be dismissed, the use of the remaining fragments of programmatic explanation as a hermeneutic starting point often requires the analyst to supply interpretations that have little basis in historical information.

Other routes into the historical meaning of Bruckner's symphonies could be suggested. Little effort has yet been made to link the works to their context via topical analysis; Floros's analysis relies principally on motivic rather than topical observations.[11] Although topics in late nineteenth-century music do not stand within a general web of extroversive semiosis in the sense often posited for musical classicism, Bruckner nevertheless deploys clear topical allusions that have extra-musical connotations. Also, the choice of historical contexts has been rather selective. Concentration on the politics of the symphonies' early reception, or on Bruckner's Upper Austrian background, has led to a neglect of the historical milieu that in fact covers most of his compositional maturity: the period of constitutional liberalism roughly between 1860 and the mid-1890s. Similarly, approaches based in a more general philosophical location of music within the post-Enlightenment development of western culture, most obviously that of Theodor Adorno, have not been applied to Bruckner. Finally, historical reading could proceed deductively rather than inductively: instead of establishing a context, which is then mapped onto the music's technical details, we might establish a

[10]  See *Bruckner und Brahms*, pp. 197–203. Schalk provided his programme for the first performance in 1892. See Leibnitz, *Die Brüder Schalk und Anton Bruckner*, pp. 170–2 and Korstvedt, *Bruckner: Symphony no. 8*, pp. 49–50. Contemporary supporters of Bruckner could be forthright about Schalk's programmatic efforts. Carl Hruby, for example, described them as 'fatuous nonsense'; see *Meine Errinerungen an Anton Bruckner* (Vienna, 1901), p. 18. Hruby accused Schalk of simply providing Bruckner's enemies with ammunition, and corroborated this view with some particularly uncompromising remarks of Bruckner himself on the subject (see ibid., p. 19). The programme for the Eighth Symphony was regarded by Hruby as the worst of Schalk's efforts: 'these chronic poetic fits were irremediable, and on the occasion of the first performance of the Master's Eighth Symphony the world was once again blessed with the arrival of a "programme", one which put all previous efforts in the shade'. Ibid., p. 19 and also Johnson, *Bruckner Remembered* (London, 1998), p. 120.

[11]  A recent exception is Robert Hatten's 'The Expressive Role of Disjunction: A Semiotic Approach to Form and Meaning in the Fourth and Fifth Symphonies', in Crawford Howie, Paul Hawkshaw and Timothy Jackson, eds., *Perspectives on Anton Bruckner* (Aldershot, 2001), pp. 145–84.

detailed analytical view of the music, which is then read for its contextual implications.

The Finale of the Third Symphony in its 1873 version provides a clear model for such an analysis.[12] The movement conveys a topical discourse that works closely with other parameters of the music, and which evokes issues permitting a grounding in key political developments in late nineteenth-century Austria. At the same time, its material processes and gestural character have obvious resonances with Adorno's conception of nineteenth-century music as concerned with the negative critique of the universality of high classicism and its social implications. The symphony represents a vital stage in Bruckner's symphonic development, as the first work to elaborate systematically the elements of his later style. The existent multiple revisions suggest that it engendered a compositional problem that Bruckner never satisfactorily resolved. As I hope to show, the source of this problem may lie not only in the work's technical aspects, but also in its embodiment of irreconcilable social and ideological forces.

## The Finale of the Third Symphony

### Analysis

The attempt to apply topical categories to nineteenth-century music encounters one fundamental obstacle: the model of topoi as a bridge between musical style and social function that plausibly operated in the eighteenth century can no longer be effectively maintained. When Leonard Ratner observed that 'from its contacts with worship, poetry, drama, entertainment, dance, ceremony, the military, the hunt, and the life of the lower classes, music in the early 18th century developed a thesaurus of *characteristic figures*' [italics in original], he identified a relationship between the development of musical material and the conventions of society that fragments in a post-Enlightenment context.[13] The novel stylistic features that developed after Beethoven at once build upon and coexist with eighteenth-century topical types and styles. Thus, whilst the social resonances of the

[12] The textual situation of the Third Symphony is perhaps more complex than that of any other work by Bruckner. It underwent two major revisions, in 1877 and 1889, in addition to which Bruckner also provided an extra version of the Adagio. For a detailed study of the early development of this work, see Thomas Röder, *Auf dem Weg zur Bruckner Symphonie: Untersuchungen zu den ersten beiden Fassungen von Anton Bruckners Dritte Symphonie* (Stuttgart, 1987).

[13] See Leonard Ratner, *Classic Music: Expression, Form and Style* (New York, 1980), p. 9 and more recently V. Kofi Agawu, *Playing with Signs: A Semiotic Interpretation of Classic Music* (Princeton, 1991).

new styles of the early nineteenth century – notably the monumental public gestures of the symphony, the domestic contexts of the Lied and the piano miniature, the affectations of bel canto and French grand opera and their pianistic transplantation into the salon and concert hall – have clear social significance, ramification within the kind of stylistic and social totality that Ratner implies is no longer possible. At best, these affiliations cohabit with a fund of reified topical references that fulfil functions within retained classical forms and genres, of which the symphony was the most prestigious example.

These considerations do not necessarily disable topical analysis of the nineteenth-century repertoire. Rather, they split the topical and affective content of music after Beethoven into two parallel categories. Novel stylistic elements actively reflect their contemporary social circumstances. Older topical affiliations are effectively redeployed: they do not arise from a direct contact with current modes of social behaviour, but take on such new meanings as their context demands. This second category is therefore in itself a binary phenomenon. It at once embodies an anchorage in tradition, and also reconstitutes traditional elements in new semiotic contexts. The result, however, is a diversity of contextual associations that cannot be held together under the general rubric of a socially grounded 'romantic style'. At the very most, this stylistic concept constitutes a synthetic aspiration, not a goal that is attained and sustained.

This reified network of topics is very much evident in Bruckner's music; indeed, his manipulation of topical discourse represents one of the prime means by which the symphonies gain both historical and social significance. Example 2.1 shows the opening of the second theme group in the Finale of the Third Symphony. This passage conflates two seemingly incongruous topics: a polka in the strings is superimposed onto a chorale in the woodwind and horns. As has been frequently noted, Bruckner himself reportedly ascribed a narrative significance to this material, noting that 'the polka represents the fun and joy of the world and the chorale represents the sadness and pain'.[14] The structural functions of these allusions – their place within the topical discourse of the movement and their relevance for a more general extroversive semiosis – have however received scant attention.

---

[14] Bruckner allegedly made these remarks to August Göllerich, whilst walking past a house from which dance music was issuing, near the Sünhaus where the body of the architect Schmidt lay. Quoted in Göllerich and Auer, *Anton Bruckner. Ein Lebens- and Schaffensbild* (Regensburg, 1922–36), vol. IV/2, p. 663. See also Ernst Decsey, *Bruckner: Versuch eines Lebens* (Berlin, 1919), p. 126; Robert Simpson, *The Essence of Bruckner* (London, 1967), pp. 75–6; Dereck Watson, *Bruckner* (Oxford, 1975), p. 84.

Example 2.1  Third Symphony (1873), Finale

Second group – combination of polka and chorale

The juxtaposition of topics indicates a broader generic allusion: the second group as a whole constitutes a chorale prelude. As Table 2.1 reveals, the group is organised around nine strains of the chorale. Strains 1 to 6 follow a consistent pattern: the first strain exposes the basic material; the rest are antiphonal responses between horns and wind developed out of this material. Strain 8 is a transposed variant of strain 1, to which is appended an extensive continuation that successively fragments the chorale material and

Table 2.1 *Third Symphony (1873), Finale*

Structure of the Second Group

| *Chorale* | | |
|---|---|---|
| 1st strain – statement (bb. 69–84) | 2nd strain (85–97) | 3rd strain (97–107) |
| *Polka – distribution of motives* | | |
| Statement | b3, b4, b5 | b4, b5 |
| *Chorale* | | |
| 4th strain (107–14) | 5th strain (115–22) | 6th strain (122–30) |
| *Polka* | | |
| b4, b5 | b3, b5 | b4, b5 |
| *Chorale* | | |
| 7th strain (130–4; interrupted by Tristan quotations) | | 8th strain – reprise (161–92) |
| *Polka* | | |
| b5 | | b3, b4, b5 |
| *Chorale* | | |
| 9th strain (193–208) | | |
| *Polka* | | |
| b3, b4, b5 removed; only texture remains | | |

metrically compresses the antiphony of winds and brass. The ninth strain concludes the group with a prolonged cadential assertion of F. Table 2.1 also shows that this structure is punctuated by a digression halfway through the seventh strain in bars 134 to 160, in which the *Hauptmotiv* of the chorale mutates into a reference to the *Liebestod* from *Tristan*, a process traced in Example 2.2. This reference is in turn liquidated in bars 144 to 146, ceding to *cantus-firmus*-like allusions to the first movement of the Second Symphony, from which the accompanying polka texture has been removed. The quotations are also referential within the symphony, invoking a similar passage in bars 463 to 477 of the first movement. The intertextual references have a disruptive structural effect: the chorale-prelude texture breaks down under their influence, leading ultimately to a caesura.

The references to chorale and polka in the second group form part of a network of topical oppositions in the 1873 version of the Finale that was variously obscured or truncated in the 1877 and 1889 revisions. Example 2.3 traces the characteristic conflations or successions of topics in the first and third groups. In the first group, the 'heroic' principal theme in the brass and winds, itself a chromatic transformation of the trumpet fanfare

Example 2.2  Third Symphony (1873), Finale

Transformation of chorale into *Liebestod* and Second Symphony quotations

Example 2.3 Third Symphony (1873), Finale

Topical discourse in exposition, first and second groups

Example 2.3 (*cont.*)

that opens the symphony, is set against turbulent quaver figurations in the strings broadly evoking a *Sturm und Drang* texture.[15] Characteristically for Bruckner, the unison third theme resembles an expanded plainchant, an

[15] I am aware that this is a contentious category, given its original appropriation from eighteenth-century theatrical and literary, rather than social or ecclesiastical, conventions. In the present context, however, its status is rather different from its classical deployment, since Bruckner does not refer directly to a contemporary literary context,

Example 2.3 (*cont.*)

bars: 257

3: Third group, distorted plainchant informs *Sturm und Drang* texture

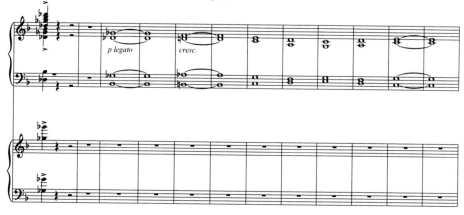

bars:   277

4: Third group: unadorned chorale/*cantus firmus* at end of exposition

association reinforced by the quasi-liturgical intonations of the brass, and distorted by the syncopated imitation of the violin figure *per arsis et thesis*

but to a reified topical construct, which is not necessarily affected by the ambiguity of its eighteenth-century origins. On this matter, see Elaine Sisman, 'Haydn's Theatre Symphonies' in *Journal of the American Musicological Society* 44 (1990), pp. 292–352; R. Larry Todd, 'Joseph Haydn and the *Sturm und Drang*: A Revaluation' in *Music Review* 40 (1980), pp. 172–96; 'Sturm und Drang', in *The New Grove Dictionary of Music and Musicians*, ed. Stanley Sadie, 2nd edn (London, 2001), vol. XXIV, pp. 631–3; James Webster, *Haydn's Farewell Symphony and the Idea of Classical Style* (Cambridge, 1991); Neil Zaslaw, 'Music and Society in the Classical Era', in Neil Zaslaw, ed., *Man and Music in Society: The Classical Era* (London, 1989), pp. 1–14.

in the bass. This material alternates in the third group with two topical digressions. The passage between bars 221 and 244 has pastoral resonances, arising from the consistent musette pedal C in the violas and the hunting calls in the horns. The progression to the climax of the group in bars 257 to 277 redeploys the plainchant material as part of a *Sturm und Drang* texture, underscored by the prevalent diminished-seventh harmony. At the close of the exposition, this texture cedes abruptly to an unadorned chorale texture in the horns.

The juxtapositions within the theme groups are complemented by broader topical oppositions between groups. Thus the chorale prelude comprising the second group opposes the essentially post-Beethovenian symphonic associations of the heroic/*Sturm und Drang* conflation in the first theme. Similarly, the conflations of topics within the first two groups contrast with the alternation of topics in the third group. These oppositions are further emphasised by the nature of the transitions between groups. Each group stands as a distinct structural unit. In the 1873 version at least, Bruckner made no effort to link groups with preparatory modulations or melodic elisions.[16] The division between first and second themes is marked with a general pause, and the D(7–9) chord that concludes the first group does not resolve as a dominant onto G, but as an altered augmented-sixth chord onto F sharp. The pianissimo dominant preparation of F at the end of the second group is interrupted abruptly by the fortissimo unison third theme in D flat. In this way, the exposition sets up a notion of discontinuity that becomes crucial to the subsequent progress of the form.

Elaborating on a remark of Ernst Decsey, we can reduce this topical discourse to a dialectic of the secular and the sacred; of the human, earthly or natural and the metaphysical or transcendental.[17] The first group is entirely concerned with secular topical associations. In the second group, the dialectic is displayed within a single theme: the polka embodies a secular dance type; the chorale a sacred style. The third group first of all opposes the sacred

[16] The disjunctions of the 1873 version were successively stripped away in the 1877 and 1889 revisions. They are partly retained in 1877 (although the various intertextual references are removed), but in 1889 a systematic effort is made to smooth over the characteristic caesuras between groups with bridging material. See for example the transition between first and second themes in the exposition. The separation of groups in this manner owes an obvious debt to Schubert, particularly the Eighth and Ninth Symphonies.

[17] Decsey saw this opposition as basic to Bruckner's style in general: 'es gilt von ähnlichen Kombinationen in der Achten und in der Ersten, ja im Grund von seinem gesamten Schaffen. Immer wieder hat der Künstler die beiden Gegensätze gebunden: Erden- und Himmelslust, Endlichkeit-Unendlichkeit, Sinnenwelt und Jenseits, Sehnen und Glauben, Natur und Gott, Leiden und Verklärung.' See Ernst Decsey, *Bruckner: Versuch eines Lebens*, p. 126.

and the pastoral, and then absorbs the plainchant material into the climactic *Sturm und Drang* section. At the end of the exposition, no attempt is made to resolve these oppositions. The chorale style is reasserted in the closing bars, but it follows the climax in bars 273 to 277 after another abrupt textural disjunction.

The development unfolds a topical narrative that brings these various elements into direct conflict. This takes place in three stages, each of which is again separated by an abrupt disjunction. The first section, bars 310 to 358, is entirely concerned with first-group material. After the caesura in bar 358, the second section also opens with a restatement of the first theme, but then moves towards a confrontation between the sacred and secular topical elements of the exposition. From bar 399, the *Hauptmotiv* of the second-group chorale is introduced over the *Sturm und Drang* quavers in the strings, together with a diminished form of the first-movement *Hauptthema* in the flutes and oboes. The effort of the chorale to assert itself against the first group is however decisively negated at the climax in bars 415 to 420. The quaver patterns remain in the strings, and the chorale material is replaced by the distorted plainchant of the third group in the trumpets and upper winds. Yet the structural security of this climax is also rapidly undermined. In bars 419 and 420, the whole orchestra takes up the plainchant figure, and this is followed abruptly by two bars of silence. Two further attempts to install a textural and structural stability are also emphatically negated. The four bars of chorale prelude in 423 to 426 are immediately interrupted by a further intervention of the third subject, and this once again leads to an abruptly imposed general pause. There is furthermore no sense of continuity or structural necessity relating the variant of the chorale prelude in bars 433 to 468 to the preceding climax; rather the chorale prelude is simply resumed after its disruption in bars 426 to 427. The sense of disjunction persists at the point of recapitulation. The chorale-prelude texture is liquidated in bars 460 to 467, and the first theme returns from bar 469 following yet another caesura, without any harmonic preparation or sense of material retransition in the classical manner. The topical combinations at the climax of the development are shown in Example 2.4.

The development is an object study in negation and structural discontinuity. The confrontation of sacred and human elements does not lead to a triumphant synthesis of the two, but to a climax in which the chorale is ousted by the 'negated' plainchant. This in turn produces a structural fragmentation that undermines the synthetic or resolutory effect of the ensuing recapitulation. The reprise of the first theme is imposed as a formal convention rather than a result of the sort of apparent structural necessity embodied in the classical recapitulation. The discontinuities that are present

Example 2.4  Third Symphony (1873), Finale

Topical confrontation in development

Example 2.4  (*cont.*)

in the exposition, and which overwhelm the synthetic efforts of the development, are consequently exacerbated rather than alleviated. In the second group, the references to *Tristan* and the Second Symphony are removed and replaced, in bars 574 to 580, by a fragmentation of the texture and a two-bar caesura. Similarly, the third group follows the second after another general pause, rather than the sudden interruption at the parallel point in the exposition, and the plainchant material in bars 581 to 618 is broken up by persistent textural disjunctions. The pastoral topics return in bars 619 to 636, but are halted by yet another general pause.

The burden of establishing a synthesis of the movement's dialectical topical tensions is transferred to the coda. A first attempt to accommodate the different topical allusions within a single texture is initiated in the passage beginning at bar 637. As Example 2.5 reveals, this section conflates three topics: the third-group plainchant is present in the clarinets, oboes and violins, whilst the violin tremolandi also allude to a *Sturm und Drang* topic; the violas return to the *Sturm und Drang* quaver patterns of the first group; the brass, basses, oboes and bassoons introduce the heroic first theme, and the trumpets take up first subject of the first movement from bar 641. As the passage progresses, however, topical elements are successively removed, until, by bar 666, only the *Sturm und Drang* texture remains in the strings over sustained octaves in the brass and woodwind. The consequence of this topical liquidation is again the intervention of a caesura.

The decisive factor in securing a synthetic conclusion to the work is the disjunct reminiscence of material from the first, second and third movements in bars 675 to 688. In a passage clearly alluding to the retrospective gesture that opens the Finale of Beethoven's Ninth Symphony, and which preempts Bruckner's later use of the same device in the Finale of the Fifth Symphony, the second theme of the first movement and openings of the Adagio and Scherzo appear successively before the final transition to the coda begins at bar 689. These allusions perform a kind of structural catharsis. Following their intervention, a variant of the *Sturm und Drang* material of bars 258 to 277 returns, culminating in the brass fanfare that prepares the coda. The position of the quotations in the structure, and the enabling function they seemed to perform in allowing the movement to reach its conclusion, suggests that the tacit source of discontinuity in the Finale has been the structural burden imposed by the earlier movements, a burden that can only be removed once it has been acknowledged through quotation. The coda then attempts an overcoming of the movement's topical oppositions by presenting the principal topics simultaneously within a single texture, a gesture that prefigures the conflation of themes at the end of the Eighth Symphony (see Example 2.6). The strings maintain the *Sturm und Drang*

Example 2.5  Third Symphony (1873), Finale

Topical combinations in third-group recapitulation

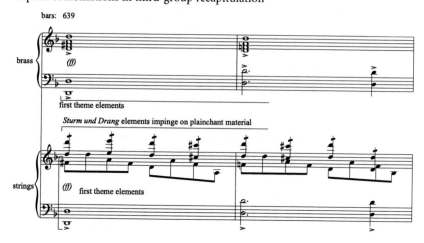

elements, the flutes and clarinets contain a version of the plainchant motive, the trombones intone the rhythm of the first theme, and the trumpets allude to the chorale-prelude associations of the second group by asserting the first theme of the first movement, in augmentation and after the manner of a *cantus firmus*.

The thematic organisation of the Finale is also concerned with disintegration rather than consolidation: before the synthetic events of the coda, the material is presented in its most stable form in the exposition. Examples 2.7 and 2.8 summarise the main thematic content of the exposition. It is insufficient to characterise the thematic groups as concerned simply with stating the principal themes; rather, each group is in itself defined by a thematic

Example 2.6  Third Symphony (1873), Finale

Coda

Example 2.7  Third Symphony (1873), Finale

First-theme group – motivic content

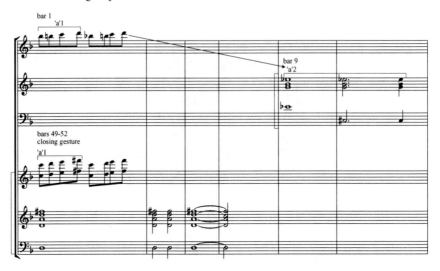

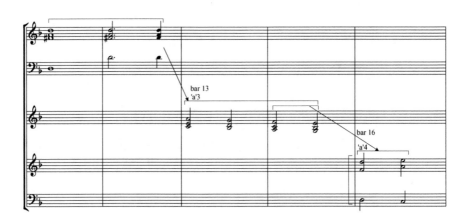

process. Bruckner's habit of introducing material as part of an ongoing process of thematic 'becoming', which numerous commentators have observed, and to which I shall return in Chapters 4, 5 and 6, is clearly represented here.[18]

[18] See for example Ernst Kurth, *Bruckner*, 2 vols. (Berlin, 1925); Werner Korte, *Bruckner und Brahms: Die spätromantische Lösung der autonomen Konzeption* (Tutzing, 1963); Stephen Parkany, 'Kurth's *Bruckner* and the Adagio of the Seventh Symphony', *Nineteenth-Century Music* 9 (1988), pp. 262–81; Korstvedt, *Bruckner: Symphony no. 8*, pp. 31–3.

Example 2.8  Third Symphony (1873), Finale

Second and third groups – motivic content

1. Second group
bars: 69

2. Third group
bars: 209

In the first group the main ideas, labelled a1, a2, a3 and a4 in Example 2.7, exhibit two levels of motivic activity. Motives a2, a3 and a4 do not appear discretely; a3 and a4 evolve out of a2 in a continuous syntagmatic chain of events. The accompanimental figure a1 forms a consistent background to this process until the concluding climax of bars 49 to 52, after which it is liquidated through augmentation in bars 60 to 62. Topical distribution in the group is in this way reinforced by the motivic structure. The motives associated with each component topic follow their own characteristic paths of development: a2, a3 and a4 comprise the 'heroic' first theme; a1 comprises the *Sturm und Drang* accompaniment.

A similar dualism arises in the second group. The chorale and the polka follow simultaneous, and reflexive, motivic processes. The two opening phrases of the chorale yield two basic ideas, b1 and b2, and b1 itself contains two smaller overlapping cells, the first of which forms the rhythmic basis of the continuation of b2. As was demonstrated in Example 2.2, b1 follows a process of motivic mutation, through which it is transformed into the *Liebestod* quotation, and ultimately into the first theme of the Second Symphony. After the transposed reprise of the group's opening from bar 161, the chorale is gradually fragmented, into two-bar units by bar 177, and into single-bar units by bar 181. Finally, the structure of b1 is retrieved at bar 193, and leads to an extended cadential continuation. The way the polka material maps onto this process is also traced in Table 2.1. The distribution of its three component motives, labelled as b3, b4 and b5 in Example 2.8, is varied with each strain of the chorale. At the same time, motive b5 consistently forms the basis of the accompaniment. Significantly, aside from the accompanimental form of b5, which persists until its liquidation by augmentation in bars 145 to 146, references to these motives become more diffuse with the appearance of the *Tristan* quotations. After the reprise at bar 161, which reinstates these motives in their original form, the polka departs even further from the motivic content of the statement. By bar 177, even the basis of the accompaniment in b5 has been abandoned in favour of free, rhapsodic material; by the eighth strain of the chorale the accompaniment based on b5 is removed altogether, and the first violin part completely gives up its motivic allusion.

Interaction of motivic content and topical discourse is different again in the third group. Here, changes of topic correspond to transformations of the two basic motives, c1 and c2. Thus both the main figure of the pastoral section and the string figures in the *Sturm und Drang* passage derive from the plainchant idea c1, whilst the brass parts of the *Sturm und Drang* passage allude to c2 (see Example 2.8).

In the exposition, the opposition of characteristic topics and their distribution is directly reflected in the motivic structure. The first and second groups are organised around distinct complexes of motivic processes, which are consistent within a given topic, but which are contrasted between topics. The third group departs from this pattern, instead deriving topical variety from the transformation of two basic ideas.

The three stages of the development involve either extension or combination of motivic figures. The first stage, bars 310 to 358, presents a variation of the exposition form of the first group. Framed by returns of a1 and a2 in bars 310 to 326 and the group's closing climactic gesture in bars 349 to 358, this passage sequentially spins out motives a3 and a4, almost after the manner of baroque *Fortspinnung*. This is not a process of development following the exposition statement of material, but a further elaboration of the syntagmatic processes already present in the first group. The second section, bars 359 to 421, takes this process a stage further, pursuing the combination of motives from the theme-groups, rather than their successive elaboration. Thus: bars 367 to 374 develop a2 sequentially; bars 375 to 398 combine a1 with a rhythmic form of c1; bars 399 to 414 combine a1 and b1; bars 415 to 418 combine a1 with c1. Once more, the topical discourse is supported by motivic processes: the conflict of topics is part of a coherent motivic process, which proceeds through two phases of expansion for the first-theme motives to a combination of first-, second- and third-group motives. And, just as the aftermath of the climax brings about textural and topical fragmentation, so it also signals a breakdown of the thematic process. The fragments of second- and third-group material in bars 419 to 432 try to assert a new stage of motivic elaboration, but persistently lapse into silence. Thematic treatment in the chorale-prelude section between bars 433 and 468 is as much a matter of texture as of motivic treatment: the division in the exposition – such that the strings take the polka and woodwind and horns take the chorale – is dissolved, the chorale material being passed between celli, horns and upper winds.

The structural insecurity of the recapitulation is similarly apparent in its thematic organisation. Whilst the main changes to the first group are harmonic, the truncation of the second group markedly affects its thematic structure. This is particularly clear in the polka material. The motivic treatment of b3, b4 and b5 accompanying the strains of the chorale in the exposition is completely absent in the recapitulation. The string texture in bars 558 to 580 is exclusively based on motive b5, and after bar 588 the motives of the polka play no part in the string accompaniment. The material appears drained of its developmental potential, rather than as stabilised in relation to the recapitulation or as providing a new level of thematic development. In contrast, the third group recovers a degree of developmental momentum, first of all in the pastoral section starting at bar 621, where the string accompaniment now supports the horn theme derived from the first half of c1 with a diminution of the second half of c1. Bars 637 to 674 carry this process a stage further, combining variants of c1, a2 and, from bar 641, the main theme of the first movement. The logical conclusion of the move towards material combination is provided in the coda, with the conflation of a1, a2, c1 and the main theme of the first movement in its complete form.

Clearly, topical synthesis in the coda is the result of a motivic procedure. Concentration on motivic features also clarifies the relationship between the conflation of topical elements and the response, in the thematic character of the recapitulation, to the structural collapse at the heart of the development. It is evident that this involves a gradual recovery of developmental potential. The return of material from earlier movements is crucial in this respect. The new combinations of motives in the third group and coda are organised around the introduction of thematic factors from outside the finale.

Topical and thematic elements work in close conjunction with the tonal strategies of the movement. The reduction given in Example 2.9 reveals that the exposition is organised around two large-scale semitonal pairings, embedded within a framing progression from D to F. The F sharp major tonality in which the second group begins turns out, at bar 151, to be a chromatic upper neighbour-note to F, and the D flat tonality of the third group can be read both as flat-IV of F in its immediate context, and on the larger scale as a lower neighbour-note to the tonic, D. F sharp is subsequently reinterpreted enharmonically as G flat at the climax in bars 273 to 277. The structure could also be understood as the interlocking of an underlying D–F with a I–V–I counter-structure in F sharp/G flat. More locally, the semitonal pairings are reflected, in a typically Brucknerian fashion, in the harmonic character of the first theme, which initially establishes a V–I cadence in E flat major, before E flat is reinterpreted as an altered dominant of D in bars 10 and 11.

The tonal structure consistently articulates the distribution of topics. On the very largest scale, the main divisions between theme groups, and therefore between topics, are underscored by unprepared tonal digressions, to F sharp at the start of the second group and D flat at the start of the third. Topical digressions are also tonally articulated at more regional levels of structure. The transformation of the chorale into the *Liebestod* motive in bars 134 to 146, and the ensuing temporary disruption of the chorale-prelude texture, coincides with the stabilisation around A major of the previously continuously mobile harmonic context. In the same way, tonicisation of

Example 2.9  Third Symphony (1873), Finale

Exposition – tonal strategy

F major marking the return of the second theme from bar 151 articulates the re-establishment of that material's recently liquidated topical context. Tonality also underscores the topical digressions of the third group. The pastoral material of bars 221 to 244 is introduced in C major without harmonic preparation, and the progression from G flat to F that concludes the exposition coincides with the sudden shift from *Sturm und Drang* to chorale.

Tonality is instrumental in guiding the topical narrative of the development in a similar sense. The differences of topical distribution between the first and second parts of the development – concentration on the first theme in the first part, and progression from the first theme to an attempted topical synthesis in the second – are supported by the tonal structure. The first part is circumscribed by a prolongation of C, whereas the second is tonally mobile, initially treating the first subject in sequence, before introducing the chorale in E flat at bar 399, and reaching D minor at the climax in bars 415 to 420. Thus, where no topical digression occurs, there is a single overarching key; where topical digression occurs, there is rapid harmonic progression. The choice of D minor as the key of the climax is also significant. In keeping with the Beethovenian struggle–victory archetype, the synthetic events of the coda are supported by a large-scale *tierce de Picardie*, and this is prefigured by the D major inflection of the first theme in the exposition. The D minor tonality of the development climax therefore supports a negation of the attempted topical synthesis with a negation of the tonic major. The fragmentation that ensues is the product of a negative tonal event – assertion of the tonic minor – as well as a failure to unite disparate topical elements.

Tonal strategy also assists the increased sense of disjunction pervading the recapitulation. In a turn of events reminiscent of late Schubert, the recapitulated first theme is more tonally unstable than its exposition counterpart. The first theme in the exposition is broadly circumscribed by D; in the recapitulation, it concludes on a G7 chord. The tonal pairing in the second group, which replaces the F sharp/F dualism of the exposition with A flat/A, exacerbates this instability, introducing a tritone relationship with the tonic. The remaining topical actions of the movement are similarly articulated by tonal events that delay rather than consolidate the tonic. The third group interjects, at bar 601, in B flat; from the return of the second theme to the beginning of the third group there is now a consistent semitonal ascent, A flat–A–B flat, in place of the F sharp–F–D flat progression in the exposition. Lastly, the references to prior movements in bars 675 to 688 are also given their own tonal space, through the temporary tonicisation of C major. As Example 2.10 demonstrates, the recapitulation gradually works towards D in the coda through a stepwise bass progression. The penultimate key of this ascent, C, is preempted at the end of the recapitulated first group: the G7

Example 2.10  Third Symphony (1873), Finale

Recapitulation – tonal strategy

Overall bass motion:

chord left unresolved at this point is taken up again between bars 655 and 674, and resolved as a dominant to C at bar 675.

Several points arise from this analysis. To begin with, the topical discourse evinces a complexity that renders the traditional classification of Bruckner's symphonies as wordless masses thoroughly inadequate. Although sacred elements are undeniably present, and perform a key structural function, to isolate them as the music's characteristic feature is simplistic. Rather, the sacred allusions stand within a complex of topical oppositions that are enmeshed not only in a web of religious signification, but in the topical vocabulary of the post-Beethovenian symphony. Neither is the discourse of the movement concerned, as Timothy Jackson has suggested as a general paradigm for Bruckner, with the redemption of the hero through faith.[19] The sacred and the heroic are presented in sharp opposition, and the means by which they are reconciled is not the assertion of sacred elements over their human antitheses, but the intervention of a deus ex machina, in the form of the quotations from earlier movements.

These features also indicate that Bruckner was far more engaged with the plot archetypes of the Beethovenian symphony than has been suggested, an issue that will be broached more extensively in Chapter 5.[20] The Finale is

---

[19] Although Jackson is quite right to link Bruckner's symphonic paradigms to the 'heroic' symphonic models of Beethoven, Berlioz and Liszt. See 'Bruckner, Anton', in *The New Grove Dictionary of Music and Musicians*, 2nd edn (London, 2001), vol. IV, p. 475.

[20] On the matter of Bruckner's relationship with the plot archetypes of the Beethovenian symphony, see Warren Darcy, 'Bruckner's Sonata Deformations', in *Bruckner Studies*, pp. 256–77.

profoundly teleological: any efforts at structural consolidation are systematically disrupted until the final approach to the coda. In this respect, the movement exacerbates rather than alleviates the condition of goal-directedness found in the Finales of Beethoven's Fifth and Ninth Symphonies. In both these examples, the Finale as a whole acts as a counterbalance to the negative conclusions of the first movement; in Bruckner's symphony, the Finale prolongs and even emphasises structural disjunction and irresolution, transferring the burden of resolution to the final stages of the work. There is no 'patient search for pacification' in Simpson's terms; rather, the symphony concludes with a triumphal synthesis that wrests resolution from the mounting threat of disintegration.

## Context

If the Finale can be viewed as a direct response to the imperatives of post-Beethovenian symphonic composition, it can also be placed within the philosophical, historical and social contexts of that tradition, as formulated by Adorno and others. The most obvious way in which social or philosophical circumstances are sedimented in the movement is through its topical narrative. The dialectic of the sacred and the human, which is played out as a structural process, signifies a historical context in a way that is markedly more complex than the standard assessment of Bruckner's music simply as embodying a *Vormärz* conservatism. The topical discourse does not present the narrative of pre-Enlightenment monarchic authoritarianism or Catholic dogma that one might expect from a composer allegedly seeking to reproduce in symphonic form the social structures of Austria before Metternich's fall and the 1848 revolutions. The expected symbols of such a representation – an unambiguous or fixed sacred content standing above human elements of the discourse, or a clear domination of the form by authoritarian allusions, for instance to martial topics or the Baroque material traits that Adorno associated with a pre-Enlightenment 'collectivity' – are consistently problematised by a greater complexity of topical or generic context. Thus in the second-theme group the conflation of chorale and polka humanises the sacred references as much as it sanctifies the mundane; the essence of the passage lies in an unreconciled dialectic through which the sacred is reflected by a human context and vice versa. The heroic first theme is similarly ambiguous, being beset by *Sturm und Drang* material in a way that does not permit the domination of one by the other.

The complexities of topical discourse are more reflective of the social conditions of Austria during the period of Bruckner's compositional maturity, and therefore of the political circumstances in which the Third Symphony was produced; that is to say, the period of reform under the Emperor

Francis Joseph beginning with the 'October Diploma' of 1860, embracing the *Ausgleich* of 1867 and the founding of the so-called 'dual monarchy' of Hungary and Cis-leithania in the wake of Austria's defeat in the Austro-Prussian War of 1866, and concluding with the decline of Viennese liberalism in the late 1890s. This period encompassed the Viennese form of late bourgeois ascendancy, from the early liberal government of von Schmerling to the defeat of the liberals in Vienna at the hands of Karl Lueger in 1896.[21] The Austrian liberals acquired power in a manner that was markedly different from the rise of the bourgeoisie in other countries, most strikingly in France, being more a product of the domestic expediencies of Austria's disastrous foreign policy than of the overthrow of the monarchic system. Consequently, liberal power was nuanced by a characteristically Austrian coexistence with the mechanisms of aristocratic and imperial authority: as Carl Schorske put it, 'the chastened liberals came to power and established a constitutional regime in the 1860s almost by default. Not by their own internal strength, but the defeats of the old order at the hands of foreign enemies brought the liberals to the helm of state.'[22] These developments provoked the belated emergence in Austria of the social phenomena generally associated with the post-revolutionary bourgeois age. Constitutionalism emerged, albeit problematically and at the instigation of the Emperor, as an antidote to feudalism. Rationalism consequently displaced Christianity, and specifically Catholicism, as the ideology of the politically ascendant parties. The trappings of market capitalism developed, with increasing pace after 1867: between 1867 and 1872 Austrian agriculture, industry and finance experienced unparalleled growth.[23] The constitutional reforms of the 1860s also established a greater degree of ethnic tolerance, towards the manifold ethnic groups comprising the Empire, and significantly towards its Jewish community, a development that carried implications for the growth of the Empire's financial markets.[24] In short, the era embodied the political domination in Austria, in Schorske's terms, of 'rational man'.[25]

---

[21] For general appraisals of this period in Austrian history, see for example C. A. Macartney, *The Hapsburg Empire 1790–1918* (London, 1968), pp. 495–585; Alan Sked, *The Decline and Fall of the Hapsburg Empire 1815–1918* (London, 1989), pp. 187–238; Steven Beller, *Francis Joseph* (London, 1996), pp. 80–117. For more focused consideration of political and cultural matters, see Carl Schorske, *Fin de Siècle Vienna* (New York, 1980); John Boyer, *Political Radicalism in Late Imperial Vienna* (Chicago, 1981).

[22] *Fin de Siècle Vienna*, p. 5.

[23] Macartney gives an account of the economic growth of the Empire after the Austro-Prussian war in *The Hapsburg Empire 1790–1918*, pp. 606–8.

[24] On the relationship between liberalism and Austria's Jewish community, see Steven Beller, *Vienna and the Jews 1867–1938* (Cambridge, 1989) and Boyer, *Political Radicalism in Late Imperial Vienna*, pp. 40–121.

[25] *Fin de Siècle Vienna*, p. 5.

Bruckner's Finale engages with these themes in a number of ways. The association of the principal subject with a Beethovenian thematic type links it directly with the musical model of the bourgeois subject as Adorno construed it.[26] This submits to an obvious historicist reading: the conflicted status of the principal theme in the movement's formal strategy embodies the ascendancy of the bourgeois subject in the face of absolute social forces, chiefly monarchy and religion. The chorale prelude comprising the second theme expresses this even more directly. Its conflation of high and low styles places religion – and in Bruckner's case we can safely assume Catholicism – in open conflict with a contemporary secular dance. The generic opposition of heroic first theme and sacred genre in the second theme reproduces the same dichotomy on a larger scale.

The conflicted status of the sacred elements is also more obviously redolent of the position of the Church in Austria during the liberal era than of its status during the *Vormärz*. Much of the energies of constitutional liberalism were directed towards restricting the authority of the Roman Church, which stood in opposition to bourgeois rationalism, and which was seen as an agent of monarchic absolutism; as Macartney remarks, 'the advance of the bourgeoisie was naturally accompanied by retreats on the part of its chief opponents, the aristocracy and the Catholic Church'.[27] The key event in this regard was the passing of the anti-clerical May Laws of 1868, which sought to assure the legal parity of religious denominations, and which imposed state control over marriage and education.[28] The effects of this legislation were far-reaching; as John Boyer observes:

> After 1867 the lower [Catholic] clergy faced a secular political regime which no longer pretended to affirm the older eighteenth-century or newer *Vormärz* versions of the Josephist compromise. It offered no political guarantee of the service mentality of the clergy; it even allowed its press to denigrate the very terms of that mentality . . . For clerics who did resist the new state's authority there was only humiliation and disgrace.[29]

[26] In this regard, see for example Theodor Adorno, *Introduction to the Sociology of Music*, trans. E. B. Ashton (New York, 1976), p. 209 [originally published as *Einleitung in die Musiksociologie: Zwölf theoretische Vorlesungen* (Frankfurt, 1962)]. Adorno's view of nineteenth-century music is not contained within a single work, but has to be pieced together from isolated sources. For a general overview of Adorno's philosophy of musical history, see Max Paddison, *Adorno's Aesthetics of Music* (Cambridge, 1993), pp. 218–62; for a specific study of Adorno's view of nineteenth-century music, see Rose Rosengard Subotnik, *Developing Variations* (Minneapolis, 1991), Chapter 2.

[27] See *The Hapsburg Empire 1790–1918*, p. 620.

[28] On this matter, see Beller, *Francis Joseph*, p. 102.

[29] See Boyer, *Political Radicalism in Late Imperial Vienna*, pp. 136–7.

Strikingly, the topical discourse of the development and recapitulation plays out just such a conflict; and, as we have seen, any synthetic accommodation of the two is emphatically deferred until the coda. The point of negation in the development, the climax in bars 415 to 420, therefore carries plain social significance: the failure of the chorale either to assert itself against the first-group material, or to be unified with it in a climactic gesture, expresses the uneasy relationship between the Catholic establishment and bourgeois liberalism that defined the work's historical context.

The process through which an overcoming of topical tensions is sought also seems more reflective of the relationship of Church and State in the liberal period than in the *Vormärz*. It is simply not the case that Bruckner imposes a straightforward solution reflecting a naively Baroque acceptance of the authority of religion. On the contrary, the failure of the development to resolve the dialectic of the sacred and the secular destabilises both the 'bourgeois' first theme and the sacred second theme in the recapitulation. Moreover, the final progression to the coda has nothing to do with the earlier sacred allusions, but looks beyond the Finale to the previous movements for a way out of the aporias generated by the prior attempts at resolution. When the *Sturm und Drang* material of bars 688 to 715 finally yields to the synthesis of topics in the coda, the moment of overcoming, although partly alluding to a chorale-prelude texture, does not privilege sacred over human elements, but combines all these aspects in an egalitarian texture giving no preference to its sacred components. If the coda can be read as an overcoming of dialectical tension, it is one engendering an accommodation of topical oppositions at a new level of discourse that eradicates their qualitative differences. Again, this looks more like a merging of the aims of the bourgeois secular subject and the Church than an imposition of Catholic dogma.

The quotations from *Tristan* in bars 134 to 146 complicate this discourse still further. Given Bruckner's famously naive conception of the plots of Wagner's operas and music dramas, it would be erroneous to assume a narrative intertextuality derived from the themes of transfiguration and Schopenhauerian negation that exercised Wagner. The quotations might at the very least signify a relation of the sacred to the transforming force of Wagner's musical style. The fact that the material passes from chorale, through the *Liebestod* motive to a symphonic self-quotation that also has strong liturgical overtones indicates a transcendent status for Wagner's style, through which the sacred might be equated with the symphonic, and thus through which the sacred might be reunited with the bourgeois secular subject. Yet significantly, this is not the means through which the movement finally asserts a synthetic conclusion. The *Tristan* allusions play no further part in the Finale, and are absent from the eventual preparation of the coda. Its isolation therefore indicates a restricted function for the Wagnerian influence. It is at the very most a component in a much broader discourse, and certainly it does not carry the enabling function suggested by the frequent claims of symphonic Wagnerism. This event is subsumed within the basic dialectic of secular and sacred and its social implications.

The dialectical tensions of the Finale – its constant struggle with the forces of structural disjunction and material disintegration – also make it a clear candidate for reading in negative dialectical terms, *pace* Adorno's own marginalisation of Bruckner. The topical discourse assists this, pointing to a contextual semiosis that is less heavily dependent on the kind of metaphorical interpretation of thematic process that Adorno employed, for example in his analysis of Berg's Op. 1.[30] Key elements of Adorno's view of the historical character of nineteenth-century music can be discerned in this movement: tensions between the rational and the mimetic, and between the developmental process of 'becoming' and the static state of 'being', and the unfulfilled urge towards an overcoming of these oppositions in a synthetic, quasi-universal symphonic style, are all apparent. They are given added clarity by the absence, in Bruckner's style, of the sort of 'false' concealment of artifice that Adorno identified as 'phantasmagoria' in Wagner's mature style, and which is evident in a different form in Brahms's music.[31] The discontinuities of the music are not concealed beneath a veneer of technique that protests a naturalness for the labour of production; rather, they are built into the work's structural process, through the opposition of rational, material development and its disruption by mimetic, 'static' gestures, principally in the form of abruptly imposed silences.

The topical discourse can be understood as reflecting Adorno's view that nineteenth-century music embodies with increasing clarity the failure of post-Enlightenment attempts to unite man as a free, rational subject and a concept of society as an objective totality that also engenders the bourgeois notion of subjective freedom. In short, the irreconcilable relationship of subject and object, which Adorno perceived as an emergent property in Beethoven's late music, is evident in Bruckner's Finale.[32] The dialectic of bourgeois subject (in the first theme) and religious absolute (in the second

---

[30] See Adorno, *Berg: Meister des kleinsten Übergangs* (Vienna, 1968), trans. Juliane Brand and Christopher Hailey as *Berg: Master of the Smallest Link* (Cambridge, 1991), pp. 40–6.

[31] 'Wagner's operas tend towards magic delusion, to what Schopenhauer calls "the outside of the worthless commodity," in short towards phantasmagoria.' See Adorno, *In Search of Wagner*, trans. Rodney Livingstone (London, 1981), pp. 85–96, this quotation p. 85.

[32] See in particular 'Alienated Masterpiece: The *Missa Solemnis*', trans. Duncan Smith, *Telos* 28 (1976), pp. 113–24.

theme) is persistently denied a moment of overcoming, leading instead to open contradiction and the breakdown of structural continuity. The extreme insecurity of the recapitulation is especially notable in this respect, since Adorno, following Hegel and others, perceived the recapitulation in the high-classical sonata form to be the musical embodiment of dialectical synthesis.[33] Its fragmentation in the Finale suggests a breakdown of the classical paradigm, and with it the idea that the conflicted aspects of the work's content can be reconciled by means of a generalised formal principle. The moment of synthesis in the coda could similarly be read dialectically as asserting a synthesis of oppositions at the level of the individual work, whilst sacrificing it at a more general level of style or formal convention. Whereas the classical recapitulation at least projects the illusion of being a generalised, or objective, formal strategy, Bruckner's synthetic coda only operates at the level of the individual work, and cannot be said to re-establish a general formal principle common to the late nineteenth century as a whole.[34] This is notwithstanding its relationship to other attempts to compose teleological symphonic finales. Although the 'finale problem' itself is endemic to the late nineteenth-century symphony, individual formal solutions do not coalesce into a consistent practice that equates to a universal stylistic substance in the classical sense. It is significant in this regard that Bruckner made three attempts at composing this ending. The problem of how to turn the combination of themes and topics into a gesture that is compelled by the dialectical logic of the material proved consistently insoluble. The last version seems considerably further from a solution than the first: the form is heavily truncated, and the coda thus appears even more to be grafted on as an imposed resolution.

Other categories of Adorno's thought are represented in the Finale. The opposition of an asserted rational control over content and a simultaneous mimetic regression, which Adorno considered to be critically apparent in Wagner's music, characterises the progress of the material in this movement at key points of the form.[35] This is particularly clear at moments of

---

[33] On this matter see Adorno, *Drei Studien zur Hegel* (Frankfurt, 1957) trans. Shierry Weber Nicholson as *Hegel: Three Studies* (Cambridge, Mass., 1993); Andrew Bowie, *Aesthetics and Subjectivity: From Kant to Nietzsche* (Manchester, 1990), pp. 123–7; Janet Schmalfeldt, 'Form as the Process of Becoming: The Hegelian Tradition and the "Tempest" Sonata', in Christopher Reynolds, ed., *The Beethoven Forum*, vol. IV (Lincoln, 1995), pp. 37–71.

[34] On this matter, see for example Rose Subotnik, 'Romantic Music as Post-Kantian Critique', in *Developing Variations*, pp. 112–40.

[35] On this matter see Adorno, *Aesthetic Theory*, trans C. Lenhardt (London, 1984), pp. 403–4 and *In Search of Wagner*, pp. 28–42. The point is appraised in Paddison, *Adorno's Aesthetic Theory*, pp. 140–3 and 243–4. For a recent analytical deployment of the idea, see Alastair Williams, '"Répons": Phantasmagoria or the Articulation of

disjunction in the development and recapitulation, where the music dissolves into silence in the absence of a successful reconciliation of antithetical elements. In both cases, the disruption of structural logic yields to a purely gestural event: the imposition of a caesura. The frustration of the formal goal of synthesis gives way to an abdication of rational control over the progress of the thematic material. Adorno's characterisation of such gestures in Wagner as 'pre-linguistic' has an obvious application here:

> [Wagner's] musical consciousness exhibits one peculiar instance of regression: it is as if the aversion to mimicry, which became increasingly powerful with the growth of western rationalisation and which played a by no means insignificant role in crystallising out the autonomous, quasi-linguistic logic of music, did not have complete power over him. His music lapses into the pre-linguistic, without being able to divest itself wholly of quasi-linguistic elements.[36]

Bruckner's response to the breakdown of the 'rational' symphonic process is recourse to precisely such 'pre-linguistic' gestures: the music gives up its symphonic discourse and lapses into silence. This carries social resonances: the breakdown of structural logic in favour of gesture embodies the failure of the work's bourgeois subject to assert rational control over the antithetical archaic elements of the music, chiefly its sacred aspects. Consistently, such events are attended by a fragmentation of material. The silences following the climax of the development in bars 415 to 420, and preceding the restatement of the second theme in bar 581 and the recapitulation of the first theme in bar 475, are either prefaced or framed by the fragmentation of the texture into disjunct motivic repetitions. The tonal and thematic structure consistently supports this reading. The dissociation of the recapitulation from any synthetic function is a product of its thematic and tonal insecurity: it results from the breakdown of the thematic structures of the exposition, and from pushing the tonal strategy to the limits of conflict rather than reconciliation through the introduction of the tritone relationship D–A flat.

Adorno's general context for western art music in the nineteenth and early twentieth centuries – the condition of alienation generated by the failure of the efforts of post-Enlightenment rationalism to re-establish a form of totality embodying Enlightenment concepts of subjective freedom, and its crystallisation in the fragmentation of structure in musical material – is schematically demonstrated in this movement, perhaps to a more blatant extent than in the music of any of Bruckner's contemporaries. Whilst Bruckner's

---

Space?', in Anthony Pople, ed., *Theory, Analysis and Meaning in Music* (Cambridge, 1994), pp. 195–210.
[36] *In Search of Wagner*, p. 34.

aesthetic and religious sensibilities militated against ultimate acquiescence in the impossibility of synthesis – it is almost an ideological imperative that his works should culminate in a moment of overcoming – the process through which this goal is reached nevertheless turns discontinuity into an overt formal principle.

In summary, the Finale can be read contextually on two levels. In one sense, the topical and structural narrative resembles a musical embodiment of the antithetical factors defining Austrian society in the second half of the nineteenth century, principally the transition from a feudal system to a constitutional monarchy, and the resulting antagonism between secular liberalism and Catholic absolutism. At the same time, the movement also engages with broader philosophical and social contexts. If we accept Adorno's contention that pieces of music, like all works of art, are 'the unconscious historiography of their epoch', then the conflicts in this movement between rationalisation and discontinuity, Beethovenian symphonic discourse and archaic sacred forms, synthesis at the level of the individual work and particularity at a general level of symphonic style, all indicate that it deserves a central place in the dialectically unfolding history of music as Adorno conceived it.[37]

## Conclusions

This analysis suggests various parallel paths of enquiry. Primarily, it argues for the inclusion of Bruckner within a line of critical contextual analysis from which he has traditionally been excluded. The motivation for this is twofold. First, if Bruckner's music is divested of its historical otherness and placed within the Beethovenian tradition of instrumental music, then this demands engagement with the philosophical and social contexts of modernity as well as the political climate of Bruckner's immediate or formative circumstances. Second, even a brief analysis shows that the technical characteristics of the symphonies far exceed the scope of the contextual categories habitually deployed. Terms like 'monumentality', 'symphonic Wagnerism' or 'redemption through faith' are both too superficial and too generalised to do justice to the complexities of structural and topical process that the works exhibit. At best they point to overall features of the music's affect; at worst they take isolated events and turn them into defining characteristics, much in the manner of Carolyn Abbate's 'moments of narration'.[38] The analysis

[37] See Adorno, *Aesthetic Theory*, p. 261, translated in Paddison, *Adorno's Aesthetics of Music*, p. 218.
[38] See Carolyn Abbate, *Unsung Voices* (Princeton, 1991), p. 29.

of the Finale of the Third Symphony makes this plain. The topical discourse is wide-ranging and articulated by a dense network of procedures in other parameters, and the end result is certainly not an emphasis on monumentality at the expense of technical detail, or on faith at the expense of the secular associations of the material.

The approaches adopted here are, from a number of perspectives, admittedly problematic. The relation of structure and context could be dismissed as naive without an acceptance of the irretrievably metaphorical nature of the endeavour. Even the topical strategy, which sets up social allusions having a lineage that of course long antedates Bruckner, is crucially dependent on the intervention of discourse as a way of rendering it socially meaningful. In semiological terms, the musical topic as signifier does not relate directly to a linguistic signified through which the material becomes comprehensible in social terms, but relies on the presence of a parallel, or substitutive, linguistic signifier, which enables connection to an extra-musical concept. As a result, the topical structure submits to a plurality of contextual interpretations, since it is always possible to posit more than one discursive intervention between musical material and historical context. No matter how plausible our historicist reading might be, it can thus never be verified absolutely as arising from an embodied property of a work's content. The point is made succinctly in Alan Street's appraisal of Abbate's notion of musical narrative: 'any attempt to read music as a speaking sequence amounts to nothing more than an act of ventriloquism: a manipulation of the figure of prosopopoeia for the sake of jumping the abysmal gap between word and work'.[39] The philosophical sleight of hand through which Adorno reconstrued the relationship of social context and musical content as a dialectic does not necessarily overcome this difficulty; it could still be argued that Adorno's social context resides at a level of discourse that is not of necessity immanent to a work's specifically musical properties.

These objections do not critically undermine the pursuit of a historically informed view of music. They do, however, indicate that the criterion for establishing the basis of such a perspective is not factual, but interpretative: it is based on an assessment of detail and plausibility, rather than any grounding in a veracity that can be pinned absolutely to the materials of a work. If such readings are to be undertaken, we are at least obliged to ground them in a thorough appraisal of the analytical evidence. Returning

---

[39] See Alan Street, 'The Obbligato Recitative: Narrative and Schoenberg's Five Orchestral Pieces, Op. 16', in *Theory, Analysis and Meaning in Music*, pp. 164–83, this quotation p. 183.

to Street's incisive critique, if 'under these terms . . . musical criticism returns to the question of its allegorical condition; to the inevitable divide which separates all modes of commentary from composition', then the goal of a historically founded analysis of Bruckner's music becomes the construction of interpretations that respect both the plurality of contextual readings and the technical complexity of the music's structure.[40]

[40] Ibid.

# 3 Right-wing cultural politics and the Nazi appropriation of Bruckner

## Reception history

*I*

In June 1937, Joseph Goebbels addressed the assembled members of the International Bruckner Society, officials of the Reichsmusikkammer and high-ranking National Socialists, including Hitler himself, as part of the Regensburg Bruckner Festival.[1] The speech effectively advanced an agenda for the appropriation of Bruckner's music, personality and biography as vehicles for Nazi cultural ideology and propaganda. Goebbels adeptly entwined biography, hermeneutics and politics in an effort to present Bruckner as an Aryan composer of the highest pedigree, and an icon of German culture. The composer's peasant origins and provincial education, apart from the influence of Viennese liberal intellectualism, were marshalled by Goebbels as evidence of racial and ideological purity. In consequence, Bruckner's music represented a cultural expression of the Nazi doctrine of blood and soil, the work of a 'rustic genius' whose pure Austrian lineage and close links with nature gave rise to an unsullied 'German musical creativity'.[2]

Inevitably, Goebbels associated critical hostility to Bruckner with the influence of Judaism. Bruckner's detractors, primarily Eduard Hanslick and the Brahmsian faction in Vienna, espoused ideologies that were un-German and complicit with the opposition of international Jewry. They valued superficial urban intellectualism over true education, the parasitic practice of art criticism (*Kunstkritik*) over any kind of genuine creativity, and dry formalism over the artistic 'inner consistency' (*innere Folgerichtigkeit*) discovered in Bruckner's music.[3] With considerable ingenuity, Goebbels fashioned the

---

[1] See *Goebbels Reden*, ed. Helmut Heiber (Düsseldorf, 1971), pp. 281–6. The speech is translated by John Michael Cooper as an appendix to Bryan Gilliam, 'The Annexation of Anton Bruckner: Nazi Revisionism and the Politics of Appropriation', *Musical Quarterly* 78 (1994), pp. 605–9. The article is reprinted in revised form in Paul Hawkshaw and Timothy Jackson, eds., *Bruckner Studies* (Cambridge, 1997), pp. 72–90. All subsequent references refer to the reprint. For a review of the Regensburg Festival, see Paul Ehlers, 'Das Regensburger Bruckner Erlebnis', *Zeitschrift für Musik* 104 (1937), pp. 745–8.

[2] See *Goebbels Reden*, p. 282.

[3] Ibid. Goebbels described Hanslick *et al.* as 'intellectual pirates' (*geistigen Freibeutern*). In place of art criticism, he advocated *Kunstbetrachtung* (art commentary), supposedly

evidence of Bruckner's life and the reception of his music into a microcosm of political ideology. Bruckner became a symbol of pure Germanic culture, embattled by elements of a supposed Judaeo-Bolshevik conspiracy, and ripe for deployment as an instrument of National Socialist propaganda.

Perhaps the most audacious aspect of Goebbels' address was his detachment of Bruckner from the influence of Catholicism, a tactic conflicting directly with biographical evidence. Again, Goebbels sought to bring Bruckner within the remit of party ideology, with which the composer's Catholic faith did not sit comfortably. In place of the traditional Christian denominations, the Nazis promoted instead the concept of *Gottgläubigkeit*, a generalised notion of 'belief in God' that was purposely distant from Christianity in any of its principal forms, inclining more towards a kind of pre-Christian mysticism.[4] Goebbels characterised Bruckner's mature faith in precisely these terms. The decisive factor in this respect was taken to be the influence of Wagner: as Bruckner came into contact with Wagner's music, his preoccupation with sacred composition fell away, and his symphonic ambition was born. With a single gesture, Goebbels related three key issues in Bruckner's artistic development – his Catholic faith, the Wagnerian influence, and his turn towards symphonic composition – in order to establish that his music embodied the highest ideals of Nazi culture *avant la lettre*.

Goebbels' arguments are not difficult to refute. Bruckner's contact with Wagner occasioned no retreat from Catholicism, as Goebbels claimed, and certainly the Wagnerian influence cannot be cited as motivating the shift from sacred to instrumental composition. Not only, as Bryan Gilliam observes, did Bruckner continue to write sacred music to the end of his life; there are also both strong sacred influences in the symphonies, and

---

a value-neutral descriptive practice evading critical judgement. For Goebbels' views on this matter, see 'Reichsminister Dr Goebbels zur Kunstkritik', *Zeitschrift für Musik* 104 (1937), p. 259, part of a general symposium entitled 'Musikkritik – Musikbetrachtung'.

[4] Michael Burleigh has argued for a view of Naziism itself as a form of 'political religion' that invested political and scientific ideas with pseudo-religious meaning; see *The Third Reich: A New History* (London, 2000), pp. 1–22 and 252–68. Christianity, which was incompatible with *völkischer* ideology, should therefore yield to *Gottgläubigkeit*, which as a concept of faith was integrated into Naziism's political aims. Burleigh's view has precedents: see for example Eric Voegelin, *Die politischen Religionen* (Munich, 1996), Jacob Talmon, *The Origins of Totalitarian Democracy* (London, 1952), Claus-Ekkehard Bärsch, *Die politische Religion des Nationalsozialismus* (Munich, 1998) and Robert Pois, *National Socialism and the Religion of Nature* (Beckenham, 1986). On Naziism's relationship with the Church, see O. D. Kulka and P. R. Mendes-Flohr (eds.), *Judaism and Christianity under the Impact of National Socialism 1919–1945* (Jerusalem, 1987) and Günter Lewy, *The Catholic Church and Nazi Germany* (New York, 1964). Gilliam considers this issue in 'The Nazi Annexation of Bruckner', pp. 81–7.

strong symphonic tendencies in the three great masses.[5] Aside from the widely used topoi of chorale and *stile antico*, there are obvious references to the masses in the symphonies: the Benedictus of the F minor Mass in the slow movement of the Second Symphony; the Miserere of the D minor Mass in the first movement of the Third Symphony and in the Adagio of the Ninth Symphony, to name but three.[6] Conversely, the main precursors of the D minor and F minor Masses are the masses of Haydn, Beethoven and Schubert, all of which are concerned with the cross-fertilisation of the sacred and symphonic genres. The idea that Bruckner shed his Catholicism under the influence of Wagner has no basis either in biography or in the nature of his compositions. Moreover the equation of hostility to Bruckner with, in Fritz Skorzeny's words, 'the fight [of international Jewry] against the German spirit', quite apart from its spurious historical basis, misrepresents the composition of the respective Viennese factions, which cannot be defined according to racial criteria.[7]

Rather, Goebbels' view is significant for two principal reasons. First, it is a key example of the Nazi manipulation of the arts to political ends, amplified in this instance by the fact that it carried the direct approval of Hitler.[8] Second, it is not historically isolated, but institutionalised a trope of reception originating in Bruckner's lifetime.[9] The politics of elements of the Brucknerian faction in Vienna, for whom Bruckner and his music became instruments of post-Wagnerian ideology, prefigured the cultural politics of the Nazi appropriation. Bruckner was made a symbol of the anti-Semitic nationalistic movements opposing the liberal Viennese establishment, and his links with

[5] See 'The Annexation of Anton Bruckner', p. 82.

[6] The Benedictus material occurs twice in the slow movement of the Second Symphony, first in bars 137–42, second in bars 180–3. The Miserere quotation in the first movement of the Third Symphony occurs in bars 260–7 in the 1873 version, in bars 231–41 in the 1877 version, and in bars 227–37 in the 1889 version (all references to the Leopold Nowak editions). The quotation in the Adagio of the Ninth Symphony appears as the principal motive of the second subject (bar 45, also in Nowak's edition), which is an inverted variant of this figure. Some of these quotations are noted by Robert Haas; see *Anton Bruckner* (Potsdam, 1934), p. 156.

[7] Fritz Skorzeny, 'Anton Bruckner im Lichte deutscher Auferstehung', *Die Musik* 30 (1938), p. 311. On the matter of the Brahms–Bruckner controversy and its political resonances, see Margaret Notley, 'Brahms as Liberal: Genre, Style and Politics in Late Nineteenth-Century Vienna', *Nineteenth-Century Music* 17 (1993), pp. 107–23.

[8] On Hitler's interest in Bruckner, see Hanns Kreczi, *Das Bruckner-Stift St. Florian und das Linzer Reichs-Bruckner-Orchester* (Graz, 1986), particularly pp. 52–4 and also Gilliam, 'The Annexation of Anton Bruckner', pp. 74–6.

[9] See Manfred Wagner, 'Bruckner in Wien', in *Anton Bruckner in Wien: Eine kritische Studie zu seiner Persönlichkeit* (Graz, 1980), pp. 9–74 and 'Response to Bryan Gilliam Regarding Bruckner and National Socialism', *Musical Quarterly* 80 (1996), pp. 118–31.

Wagner were emphasised, and frequently exaggerated.[10] Goebbels' equation of Bruckner, Wagner and anti-Semitism is abundantly represented in the work of Bruckner's biographer, August Göllerich, and appears with particular clarity in the remarks of the critic Josef Stolzing:

> The great German master is naive and kind as a man, his innermost being is so little founded on the influence of Jewish elements, that he even associates with Jews . . . in a friendly manner. Also he has no 'Judentum in der Musik', no 'Modern', no 'Erkenne dich Selbst' on his conscience. Anton Bruckner has been feuded over from the moment when he dedicated his Fourth Symphony [*sic*] to the master Richard Wagner. And woe to those Austrians who proclaim themselves as full-blooded Wagnerians, as Wolzogen so admirably names them![11]

These views were maintained in elements of the intervening literature: Max Auer, Alfred Lorenz, Karl Grunsky and his son Hans Alfred Grunsky all pre-empted key aspects of Goebbels' speech. Although Auer, who was president of the Bruckner *Gesellschaft* in the years immediately preceding the Second World War, did not share Goebbels' opinions on the influence of Wagner, other key aspects of Nazi cultural politics surface in his writings, in particular a resistance to the 'artistic Bolshevism' of modernism.[12] Lorenz directly foreshadowed Goebbels' location of Wagner as the catalysing influence in Bruckner's turn to the symphony: 'the gift of genius must often be awakened by external impetus . . . Wagner was, and remains,

[10] On Wagnerian appropriations of Bruckner, see Notley, 'Bruckner and Viennese Wagnerism', in *Bruckner Studies*, pp. 54–71.

[11] 'Der große deutsche Meister ist als Mensch naiv und liebenswürdig, sein innerstes Wesen wird so wenig von dem Einflusse jüdischer Elemente berührt, daß er sogar mit Juden . . . in freundschaftlicher Weise verkehrt. Auch hat er kein "Judentum in der Musik", kein "Modern", kein "Erkenne dich Selbst" auf dem Gewissen! – Anton Bruckner wurde von dem Zeitpunkt an so befedet, als er seine vierte Symphonie dem Meister Richard Wagner widmete. Und wehe denen in der Ostmark, die sich als Vollblut-Wagnerianer, wie Wolzogen so trefflich dieselben nennt, bekennen!' Quoted in Manfred Wagner, 'Bruckner in Wien', p. 65. Stolzing erroneously cites the dedication of the Fourth Symphony to Wagner, when he presumably intends the Third Symphony. Numerous reviews by Göllerich reveal his politics: see for example that of Brahms's Third Symphony in the *Deutsches Volksblatt* (28 March 1889), and his attempts to absorb Bruckner into the Wagnerian aesthetics of the symphony in August Göllerich and Max Auer, *Anton Bruckner: Ein Lebens- und Schaffensbild* (Regensburg, 1922–37), vol. I/1, pp. 14–29. Notley considers Göllerich's affiliations extensively in 'Bruckner and Viennese Wagnerism', quoting in particular from 'Anton Bruckner. Die beim Bruckner-Commers nicht gehaltene Festrede von August Göllerich', *Deutsches Volksblatt* 13 and 15 (1891).

[12] See Auer's remarks in Göllerich and Auer, *Anton Bruckner: Ein Lebens- und Schaffensbild* vol. IV/4, pp. 61–2.

the rouser of Bruckner's sublime genius'.[13] Lorenz's analytical method has also been considered pre-emptive of the hierarchical organisation of the Nazi state via the process of *Gleichschaltung* (coordination).[14] The journalist Karl Grunsky anticipated the Nazi doctrine of *Gottgläubigkeit* and the dissociation of Bruckner from Catholicism in his claim that Bruckner's mature faith most closely resembled medieval German mysticism, a view later echoed by Robert Haas amongst others.[15] Grunsky also stressed the affinities between Bruckner and Wagner, together with the idea that true appreciation of Bruckner is impossible for non-Germans, and especially Jews. Similar convictions are evident in the work of Karl's son, the philosopher Hans Alfred Grunsky, which in its advanced form amounted to nothing less than a National Socialist analytical methodology.[16] In general, the Nazi appropriation of Bruckner represented the culmination of a history of political annexation, the point at which this tendency became institutionally predominant.

## II

Recently, there has been considerable scholarly interest in this phase of Bruckner reception. Essays by Margaret Notley, Bryan Gilliam, Morten Solvik, Benjamin Korstvedt and Stephen McClatchie have traced the history and ideological contexts of the pre-war Bruckner discourse in some detail.[17] This research displays two common convictions: primarily, that the

[13] See Alfred Lorenz, 'Zur Instrumentation von Anton Bruckners Symphonien', *Zeitschrift für Musik* 103 (1936), pp. 1318–25, this quotation p. 1325.

[14] See Stephen McClatchie, 'Bruckner and the Bayreuthians: Or, *Das Geheimnis der Form bei Anton Bruckner*', in *Bruckner Studies*, pp. 110–21, and particularly, pp. 113–14. Gordon Craig defines *Gleichschaltung* as follows: 'Specifically, *Gleichschaltung* meant in its first stages the purging of the civil service, the abolition of the Weimar party system, the dissolution of the state governments and parliaments and of the old Federal Council . . . and the co-optation of the trade union movement'; see *Germany 1866–1945* (Oxford, 1981), p. 578. Clearly, the parallel must remain that of a metaphor for the structure of the state after *Gleichschaltung*, since it would be stretching credibility to suggest that Lorenz's method inflicts a kind of violence on the musical work akin to the brutal ethnic and political purge that the Nazis instigated. For a consideration of the cultural consequences of *Gleichschaltung*, see Hildegard Brenner, *Die Kunstpolitik des Nationalsozialismus* (Hamburg, 1963), pp. 35–43 and also Erik Levi, *Music in the Third Reich* (London, 1994), pp. 14–38.

[15] See Grunsky, 'Bruckner als Künder einer neuen Zeit', *Die Musik* 24 (1932), *Anton Bruckners Symphonien* (Berlin, 1908), *Anton Bruckner* (Stuttgart, 1922), *Kampf um deutsche Musik!* (Stuttgart, 1933). See also Haas, *Anton Bruckner*, p. 1.

[16] See Hans Alfred Grunsky, 'Form und Erleben', in *Bayreuther Festspielführer* (1934), and *Seele und Staat. Die psychologischen Grundlagen des nationalsozialistischen Sieges über den bürgerlichen und bolschewistischen Menschen* (Berlin, 1935).

[17] Notley, 'Bruckner and Viennese Wagnerism'; Gilliam, 'The Annexation of Anton Bruckner'; Benjamin Korstvedt, 'Anton Bruckner in the Third Reich and After: An

general tendency of post-war scholarship has been to deal with the right-wing annexation of Bruckner largely by ignoring it;[18] furthermore, that political, aesthetic and analytical concerns in the pre-war literature cannot easily be disentangled, and consequently that a failure to come to terms with right-wing appropriations has led to the unwitting reproduction of fascist ideology in subsequent scholarship. Gilliam assesses the matter as follows:

> Could one argue . . . that important post-war Bruckner interpretations (exemplified by slow tempi and lush harmonies) have unwittingly carried over this phenomenon of Bruckner as Nazi religious icon to the contemporary symphony hall or recording studio? Can we edit or analyse Bruckner today ignoring the fact that such words as 'authenticity', 'purity' and 'organicism' were encoded with distinct political meanings in Nazi-era Bruckner discourse?[19]

Korstvedt makes a similiar point:

> [A]s a result of the failure to tackle the Nazi appropriation of Bruckner head on, some of the subtler and more conceptually slippery dimensions of the traditions of reception fostered by National Socialism still haunt our engagements with Bruckner and his music . . . As a result, present-day understanding of Bruckner betrays a subtle – even subterranean – indebtedness to Nazi-era reception.[20]

Essay on Ideology and Bruckner Reception', *Musical Quarterly* 80 (1996), pp. 132–60 and '"Return to the Pure Sources": The Ideology and Text-critical Legacy of the First Bruckner *Gesamtausgabe*', in *Bruckner Studies*, pp. 91–109; McClatchie, 'Bruckner and the Bayreuthians'; Morten Solvik, 'The International Bruckner Society and the N.S.D.A.P.: A Case Study of Robert Haas and the Critical Edition', *Musical Quarterly* 83 (1998), pp. 362–82. See also Leon Botstein, 'Music and Ideology: Thoughts on Bruckner', *Musical Quarterly* 80 (1996), pp. 1–11.

[18] This point is stressed by Korstvedt: 'typically, [Bruckner scholars] have tried to move Bruckner reception onto new ground and to distance it from its immediate past, without explicitly mentioning National Socialism or the Third Reich'; see 'Anton Bruckner in the Third Reich and After', p. 147. Leopold Nowak's Bruckner bibliography for *The New Grove Dictionary of Music and Musicians*, ed. Stanley Sadie (London, 1980), vol. III, pp. 368–71, is telling in this respect; it more or less systematically omits much of the politically charged pre-war Bruckner discourse.

[19] See 'The Annexation of Anton Bruckner', pp. 89–90.

[20] See 'Anton Bruckner in the Third Reich and After', p. 148. These views have been challenged on historical grounds by Manfred Wagner. For Wagner, Goebbels' Regensburg address is simply one more appraisal of a view that was well entrenched in Germanic culture, rather than part of a distinct phase of Bruckner reception. More seriously, Wagner questions Gilliam's undifferentiated conflation of aesthetics and politics, citing 'a view of National Socialism which no longer accords priority to aesthetics over ideology' as one of the 'major problems that plague the history of the reception of Anton Bruckner'. See 'A Response to Bryan Gilliam Regarding Bruckner and National Socialism', p. 118. In this regard, see also Matthias Hansen, 'Die faschistische

These remarks broach an important issue that it is the principal aim of this chapter to address. Their basic contention is that fascism taints any methodology with which it comes into contact, so that subsequent applications, which on the face of it have no political agenda, in fact covertly reinstall Nazi cultural politics. Recent attempts to apply Schenkerian theory to Bruckner would therefore tacitly consort with Naziism, because the Schenkerian preoccupation with coherence resembles post-Wagnerian notions of organicism and the 'inner necessity' of music.[21] Commentators reading Bruckner's symphonies as quasi-religious experiences at odds with the 'heroic' Beethovenian symphonic model, among them Deryck Cooke and Robert Simpson, would by these terms fall prey to the same danger: they implicitly reinscribe, as Gilliam puts it, 'the phenomenon of Bruckner as Nazi religious icon'.[22] Such a view understands reception history in terms of broad discursive or ideological formations, the influence of which will be felt in a range of ostensibly disparate examples.

I have three main reservations about this approach. First of all, it assumes that ideology is an immanent property of a particular methodology or mode of discourse. Statements, for example about musical coherence, once inculcated with fascist aesthetics, then take on fascist politics as an incipient attribute. Significant developments in ideology critique have asserted the contrary view: that ideology is not a property of a particular statement, methodology or idea, but of its relation to a set of dominant or insurgent power interests within society. This has been expressed in Marxist terms by Louis Althusser, who considered ideology to be the means by which social and economic structures reproduce themselves, and more recently by Terry Eagleton, who has defined ideology in part as 'the relations between . . . signs and processes of political power'.[23] If this view holds, it follows that the ideological implications of a methodology or statement will change when its political context changes, a conclusion proving detrimental to the argument for the reproduction of right-wing ideology in subsequent Bruckner

Bruckner-Rezeption und ihre Quellen', *Beiträge zur Musikwissenschaft* 28 (1986), pp. 53–61 and Christa Brüstle, *Anton Bruckner und die Nachwelt: Zu Rezeptionsgeschichte des Komponisten in der ersten Hälfte des 20. Jahrhunderts* (Stuttgart, 1998).

[21] See for example Edward Laufer, 'Some Aspects of Prolongation Procedures in the Ninth Symphony (Scherzo and Adagio)', in *Bruckner Studies*, pp. 209–55.

[22] See Deryck Cooke, 'Bruckner, Anton', in *The New Grove Dictionary of Music and Musicians*, ed. Stanley Sadie (London, 1980), vol. III, pp. 352–66 and Robert Simpson, *The Essence of Bruckner* (London, 1967, repr. 1992). Timothy Jackson has recently reinforced this view; see 'Bruckner, Anton', in *The New Grove Dictionary of Music and Musicians*, 2nd edn (London, 2001), vol. IV, p. 475.

[23] Louis Althusser, 'Ideology and the Ideological State Apparatus', in *Essays on Ideology* (London, 1971), pp. 1–60; Terry Eagleton, *Ideology: An Introduction* (London, 1991), pp. 28–9.

scholarship. Second, understanding examples in the literature with reference to an encompassing ideological substructure inevitably raises a problem of specificity. The pervasiveness of ideology may not be supported by close reading of how politics, methodology and analysis interact in individual cases, and this might in turn affect more generalised accusations of political complicity. Third, concentration on general trends in reception history frequently produces a neglect of analysis. The analytical implications of Nazi annexation are broached in Gilliam's study of the matter only in brief concluding remarks. Korstvedt has sought more substantial solutions, grounding an analysis of the Eighth Symphony in late nineteenth-century symphonic aesthetics.[24] In so doing, he effectively replaces one ideological context with another: the Eighth Symphony is considered inseparable from the aesthetic context of its time, just as, for example, Lorenz's analytical technique could be considered inseparable from its political background, and we encounter a peculiarly postmodern notion of musicological historicism. The question of whether we can salvage techniques and analytical observations from the pre-war discourse, or whether a completely ideologically cleansed methodology is required, has not been extensively pursued.

Above all, engagement with these issues demands an investigation of whether generalised statements about the effects of the right-wing Bruckner discourse can be derived from close reading of individual examples in the literature. Taking as case studies Hans Alfred Grunsky's analysis of the first movement of the Ninth Symphony and Robert Haas's edition of the Eighth Symphony, I will attempt to identify the location and function of ideology in their work, and consequently to test the assumption that methodology becomes irreversibly infused with politics.[25] On the basis of these studies, I will suggest ways in which an ideologically aware mode of analysis might proceed.

## Hans Grunsky's analysis of the first movement of the Ninth Symphony

*I*

Grunsky's analysis provides a good starting point from which to consider these issues.[26] Although published in 1925, his essay conveys an ideological agenda that clearly pre-empts Nazi cultural politics, an association he

---

[24] See Korstvedt, *Bruckner: Symphony no. 8* (Cambridge, 2000), p. 9.

[25] Hans Alfred Grunsky, 'Der erste Satz von Bruckners Neunter. Ein Bild höchster Formvollendung', *Die Musik* 18, pp. 21–34 and 104–12.

[26] In his analysis, Grunsky used Ferdinand Löwe's edition of the symphony, published by Doblinger in 1903. Although Löwe substantially reorchestrated the work, deleting aspects of the texture and adding material embellishments as he saw fit, the changes

developed explicitly in the 1930s.[27] The article also invokes ideas placing it squarely within a line of development beginning with Göllerich and the Viennese Wagnerians.

Grunsky begins with a strident polemic directed both at detractors and at apologists who defend Bruckner by placing him in a special category. Critics levelling the common accusation of formlessness are denounced as 'frivolous and superficial' (*leichtfertige und oberflächliche 'Kritiker'*), whilst those claiming the symphonies to be orchestrated organ improvisations are charged with evading the matter in hand through recourse to 'empty clichés' (*Redensarten*).[28] These remarks have unmistakable political resonances. The attack on the complaint of formal incompetence is aimed once more at the Viennese liberals and their successors, whilst the disparagement of criticism prefigures Goebbels' hostility towards *Kunstkritik*. By rejecting the idea that Bruckner composed symphonic organ fantasies, Grunsky distances the symphonies from Bruckner's background as a church musician.[29] It is not difficult to see, in such associations with Viennese Wagnerism, and in the dissociation of the symphonies from Bruckner's experiences as an organist, a link with Goebbels' secularising of Bruckner through the invocation of Wagner.

The preoccupation with organicism that Gilliam notes as a predisposition of Nazi Bruckner discourse is also fundamental to Grunsky's study. His principal objection to the characterisation of the symphonies as expanded organ fantasies is that it evades the question of whether the music satisfies the criterion for membership of the canon of masterworks, and therefore confirms by omission the criticisms of Bruckner's detractors. And this criterion turns out to be the presence or absence of formal coherence: 'rather, there are from the start only two possibilities: either Bruckner's works possess a complete form, and therefore can justly be called masterworks, or this is absolutely not the case.'[30] For Grunsky, the notion of a formless artwork

---

to the first movement are not so drastic as to render the main points of Grunsky's analysis inapplicable to the editions published by the Bruckner Gesellschaft (Orel in 1932, Nowak in 1951).

[27] McClatchie cites a letter from Grunsky to the Kulturministerium, dated 5 May 1933, which makes his political affiliations plain; see 'Bruckner and the Bayreuthians', p. 120. Grunsky later undertook a full-length study of Bruckner's symphonies based on these principles, a project that never came to fruition.

[28] 'Der erste Satz von Bruckners Neunter', p. 21.

[29] This objection sets Grunsky apart from commentators like Max Auer, who stressed Bruckner's roots in church music. See Max Auer, 'Anton Bruckner, die Orgel und Richard Wagner', *Zeitschrift für Musik* 104 (1937), pp. 477–81.

[30] 'Es gibt vielmehr von vornherein nur zwei Möglichkeiten: entweder besitzen die Werke Bruckners eine vollendete Form und heißen deswegen mit Recht Meisterwerke, oder

(*ein Kunstwerk ohne Form*) is self-contradictory, since form and content are interchangeable concepts (*Wechselbegriffe*). Consequently, the true artwork should be considered an organism (*ein Organismus*), in which the coherence of the whole depends upon the relationships of its component parts.

In his analysis, Grunsky sets about defending Bruckner by demonstrating how the first movement of the Ninth Symphony fulfils the criterion of coherence. He contends that this can be achieved by applying Lorenz's analytical method, upon which he places a dialectical spin.[31] Lorenz's formal categories, the *Strophenform*, *Bogenform* and *Barform*, together with the new category of the *Gegenbar*, are considered by Grunsky to be syntheses of an underlying dialectical model, which he perceives as the basic musical *Urform*. In this way, he is concerned to show that Lorenz's formal types arise from the resolution of incipient dialectical tensions. This approach of course has wider philosophical implications. Grunsky in effect proposes a musical form of the Hegelian dialectic, in which the meaning of musical events

> [is] more clearly conceptualised in terms of the law that Hegel (and before him in particular Jakob Böhme) recognised as the great law of development in the realm of the spirit: thesis – antithesis – synthesis, that is, the development of a spiritual state of being through contrast, moving through struggle and tension to a higher, richer unity . . . If music is the most elemental expression of the spirit, it must of necessity follow the spirit's fundamental law.[32]

Music and ideology are related because they are both manifestations of *Geist*, the structure of which is dialectical.

Grunsky first divides the movement into two main *Hauptstrophen*, each of which is in itself a three-part *Bogenform*.[33] The first *Hauptstrophe*, as McClatchie observes, occupies the exposition space of a sonata form, whilst the second conflates development and recapitulation into a single *Bogen*.[34]

---

es ist mit ihnen überhaupt nichts.' See 'Der erste Satz von Bruckners Neunter', p. 21. This, of course, leads to the highly suspect conclusion that an organ fantasy, or works in general subscribing to this title, must be denied canonical membership or the status of a masterpiece.

[31] For a consideration of Grunsky's modifications of Lorenz, see Stephen McClatchie, 'Bruckner and the Bayreuthians', pp. 110–21.

[32] '. . . begrifflich genauer ausgedrückt in jenem Gesetz, das Hegel (und vor ihm besonders Jakob Böhme) als das grosse Entwicklungsgesetz im Reiche des Geistes erkannt hat: Thesis – Antithesis – Synthesis, d.i. die Entwicklung einer geistigen Wesenheit hindurch durch ihren Gegensatz, durch Kampf und Spannung zu höherer, reicherer Einheit . . . Wenn Musik die elementarste Äußerung des Geistes ist, so ist eine Notwendigkeit, das sie dem Grundgesetz des Geistes folgt.' See 'Der erste Satz von Bruckners Neunter', p. 23.

[33] Ibid., pp. 25–6.    [34] See 'Bruckner and the Bayreuthians', p. 118.

Table 3.1 *Ninth Symphony, first movement*

Hans Alfred Grunsky's formal synopsis

| Grunsky's Reading | Sonata-form Reading |
| --- | --- |
| First *Hauptstrophe* (bars 1–226) | Exposition (bars 1–226) |
| *Hauptsatz* – Barform (bars 1–96) | First-theme group (bars 1–96) |
| *Stollen* a (bars 1–18) | |
| *Stollen* b (bars 19–26) | |
| *Abgesang* (bars 27–96: *Höhepunkt* at bar 63; *Reaktion* in bars 77–96) | |
| *Mittelsatz* (bars 97–166) | Second-theme group (bars 97–166) |
| *Strophe* a (bars 97–130) | |
| *Strophe* b (bars 131–52) | |
| Coda (bars 153–66) | |
| *Hauptsatz* – Barform (bars 167–226) | Third-theme group (167–226) |
| *Stollen* a (bars 167–78) | |
| *Stollen* b (bars 179–90) | |
| *Abgesang* (bars 191–226: *Höhepunkt* in bars 211–14) | |
| Second *Hauptstrophe* (bars 227–516) | Development (bars 227–332) |
| *Hauptsatz* – Barform (bars 227–420) | |
| *Stollen* a (bars 227–64) | |
| *Stollen* b (bars 265–302) | |
| *Abgesang* (bars 303–420: *Höhepunkt* in bars 333–400; *Reaktion* in bars 401–20) | Recapitulation – First-theme group from *Höhepunkt* – (bars 333–420) |
| *Mittelsatz* (bars 421–58) | Second-theme group (bars 421–58) |
| *Hauptsatz* – Barform (bars 459–516) | Third-theme group (bars 459–516) |
| *Stollen* a (bars 459–66) | |
| *Stollen* b (bars 467–78) | |
| *Abgesang* (bars 479–516: *Höhepunkt* in bars 492–504; *Reaktion* in bars 505–16) | |
| Coda (bars 517–67) | Coda (bars 517–67) |

The points of contact between Grunsky's analysis and a sonata-form read-ing, which he purposely evades, are summarised in Table 3.1.[35] In the first *Hauptstrophe* each part of the *Bogenform* corresponds to a theme group. In the second *Hauptstrophe*, the point of tonal recapitulation occurs at the

[35] A similar clarification is provided by McClatchie; see 'Bruckner and the Bayreuthians', p. 119.

*Höhepunkt* of the first part of the *Bogen*, and the second and third parts corre-spond to the recapitulation of second- and third-theme groups respectively. The coda is treated as a separate section.

The way Grunsky perceived the dialectic to operate within the material can be clarified through a consideration of his analysis of the first *Hauptsatz* (bars 1–96), reproduced in Example 3.1. This comprises a bar form, in which the subdivisions *Stollen – Stollen – Abgesang* have the respective functions of thesis, antithesis and synthesis. These functions are for Grunsky embod-ied in the melodic, harmonic and rhythmic characteristics of the music. In melodic terms, the dialectic arises from the opposition of static and developmentally active material. In the first *Stollen* (bars 1–18), the devel-opmental potential (*Entwicklungsmöglichkeit*) of the material is contained by the circumscribing D pedal, which holds it in a state of initial repose. The second *Stollen* (bars 19–26) then supplies what the first has suppressed: a continuation that is both motivically developmental and harmonically mobile.

The dialectic is conveyed tonally by the opposition of two polarities: the D minor of the first *Stollen*; the C flat major that forms the climactic point of the second at bar 21, which Grunsky refers to as a counter-tonic (*Gegentonika*). Moreover, C flat is not considered to oppose D minor by itself, but as the centre of a field of tonalities focused on C flat and its enharmonic equivalent, B. This allows Grunsky to explain not only C flat but also the pivotal E flat 7 chord that starts the second *Stollen* as part of the same general area opposing the tonic. The opposition has structural consequences for the entire movement: 'we may, without being misunderstood, formulate the theorem thus: the harmony of the first movement of the Ninth Symphony rests on the tremendous tension between d and C flat'.[36]

The long *Abgesang* (bars 27–96) is then considered to have a synthetic function. In harmonic terms, it moves towards a *Höhepunkt* that conclusively reasserts the tonic in bars 63–75, whilst also restating the counter-tonic C flat in bar 70, now circumscribed by a prolongation of D. Because the *Abgesang* summarises the basic harmonic scheme of the thesis and antithesis within a single section, it consequently resolves the previously antithetical elements into a higher unity (*in höherer Einheit ... vereinigt*). Melodically, the *Abgesang* initiates a developmental ascent at bar 27 culminating at the climax in bars 63–75. For Grunsky, the effect of this climax is to overcome the opposition of rest and developmental motion standing between the first and second

---

[36] 'Dann dürfen wir, ohne mißverstanden zu werden, den Satz formulieren: *Die Har-monik des ersten Satzes der 9. Symphonie beruht auf der ungeheuren Spannung zwischen d und Ces*' [italics in original]. See 'Der erste Satz von Bruckners Neunter', p. 29.

Example 3.1 Ninth Symphony, first movement

First-theme group

*Stollen*, since it both releases the developmental tension generated by the opening, and also confirms the structural integrity of the first-theme group as a single formal unit. As a result, he considers the location of a single definitive *Hauptthema* to be misleading. The essence of the material resides in the initial dialectic itself, rather than in the character of the individual themes; the thematic statement at bar 63 should consequently be viewed as a 'developmental climax' (*ein Entwicklungshöhepunkt*). The transitional passage in bars 75 to 96 Grunsky calls a *Reaktion*, in which the moment of dialectical overcoming is necessarily balanced by a stable aftermath.

The dialectic is reproduced at each successive structural level. Subdivision of the component parts of the first *Hauptsatz* reveals smaller bar forms that are resolved into single sections at higher levels of analysis. In this way, we could see the entire movement as embodying a thesis–antithesis structure in the two main *Hauptstrophen*, which is resolved into a higher unity by the coda.

The relationship that Grunsky posited between this analytical method and the tenets of National Socialism in his work of the 1930s is clearly prefigured here. Because the analysis stresses participation in an unfolding dialectic over formal taxonomy, it emphasises a concept of form as dynamic process rather than architectonic pattern, and therefore privileges the experience of form (*Formerleben*) over its definition.[37] Grunsky came to see the artwork that betrays such characteristics as reflecting the life of the *Volk*: in short, it embodies the Nazi cultural identity. The appropriation of Hegel is crucial in this respect. Music, as an expression of *Geist*, reflects the spirit's dialectical structure. And, for Grunsky's purposes, *Geist* became indistinguishable from National Socialist consciousness.


*II*

Jean-François Lyotard's notion of the phrase regimen can be applied as a means of scrutinising the relationships between analysis, methodology and politics in Grunsky's essay. Lyotard identifies this concept as the basic sub-category of discourse; as he defines it: 'A phrase . . . is constituted according to a set of rules (its regimen). There are a number of phrase regimens: reasoning, knowing, describing, recounting, questioning, showing, ordering, etc.'.[38] For Lyotard, genres of discourse arise in the linkage of phrase regimens. This, however, frequently serves to emphasise their heterogeneity. Lyotard

---

[37] See Hans Alfred Grunsky, 'Form und Erlebnis'.
[38] See Jean-François Lyotard, *The Differend: Phrases in Dispute*, trans. Georges Van Den Abbeele (Manchester, 1988), this quotation p. xii.

is particularly concerned with instances of irreducible conflict between reg-imens, which he characterises via the legal notion of the differend, a 'case of conflict . . . that cannot be equitably resolved for lack of a rule of judgment applicable to both arguments'.[39] If, as McClatchie has it, Grunsky's article demonstrates 'the difficulty of separating the aesthetic from the political during the 1920s and 30s', such a condition of heterogeneity should not arise in the text.[40] The various regimens should merge together, so that the music-analytical evidence and the dialectical mode of reasoning become indivisible from the political agenda.

Three principal regimens are at work in the article. The dialectical method, preoccupation with coherence and the Lorenzian formal categories evince a rational mode of phrasing. These techniques are put to two basic ends: to interpret the analytical evidence of the work; to relate this interpretation to an extra-musical idea, namely the structure of *Geist*, and later the tenets of National Socialism. Both these intentions involve a second regimen: the acts of interpreting evidence to construct a music-analytic reading and an ideo-logical agenda are instances of ostension (showing). Consistently, however, this process is mediated by a third regimen. The dialectical reading is made possible by the employment of certain key metaphors, which consequently amount to a process of description. The text shuttles continuously between these three regimens: reasoning, description, ostension.

Throughout the analysis, there is a consistent problem with Grunsky's efforts to render the material ostensive of the dialectical method. Demon-stration of dialectic involves proving that a concept and its logical antithe-sis are embodied in the material as inherent properties. Grunsky does not achieve this; rather, the dialectical interpretation is enabled by his metaphor-ical language. In Lyotard's terms, ostension (showing that music reflects the extra-musical because they share dialectical properties) is made possible because Grunsky's descriptions support his mode of reasoning (dialectics). But the material evidence is not ostensive of a dialectical opposition apart from description. Instead, the dialectical readings of the thematic and tonal structure rely on a small repertoire of metaphors – tension and repose, the build-up and discharge of developmental potential, tonal conflict and reso-lution – which are imposed on the material. In the absence of proof that the *Gegensätze* are immanent to the material, the argument becomes circular. The descriptive language, chosen to represent the dialectical character of the music, ends up confirming the dialectical interpretation.

For example, although the second *Stollen* supplies a continuation in which it is possible to discern thematic traces of the first – bars 19–20 employ

[39] Ibid.    [40] 'Bruckner and the Bayreuthians', p. 121.

contracted forms of the dotted motive of bar 5, to which a new continuation is appended in the subsequent descending arpeggiation – these connections do not embody an antithesis in themselves, as a logical property. The thematic dialectic relies crucially on a descriptive account of other parameters of the music: rapid textural variations, abrupt changes of dynamic, sudden chromatic modulation and expansion of tessitura. Similarly, characterisation of C flat as a *Gegentonika* to D minor relies on the perception of a structural tension between the two keys, which amounts to the relationship thesis–antithesis. But there is no sense in which D minor and C flat necessarily stand in a relationship of logical contradiction.[41] Again, the dialectic is corroborated by an imposed metaphor, in this case the idea that the relationship between D minor and C flat generates a structural tension. In both cases, analytical evidence and mode of reasoning are linked through the mediation of description.

Grunsky's argument for the synthetic function of the *Abgesang* is similarly constructed. The relationship of tonalities implied in the first and second *Stollen* to the harmonic structure of the *Abgesang* is unambiguous, and it could scarcely be denied that the octave theme commencing at bar 63 acts as a point of culmination for the gradual intensification that precedes it. But restatement of the progression d–E flat–C flat does not necessarily prove its synthetic function. Once more, the dialectical overcoming is not an inherent quality of the harmonic or thematic structure, but depends on the intervention of metaphor: the descriptive account of the music's affect that mediates between the material and the dialectical reading.

The component regimens are thus not indissolubly linked in the way McClatchie suggests. To the contrary, the linkage of evidence, ideology and dialectics emphasises their heterogeneity. Grunsky cannot demonstrate dialectical properties as immanent to the material, only through recourse to metaphor, and therefore via the agency of description. As a result ideology – the notion of music as a reflection of Spirit, and ultimately National Socialist

---

[41] This can be asserted *pace* Hegel's own view on the dialectical character of tonal harmony, which likens the inception and resolution of dissonance, especially in the perfect cadence and the tonal structure of a sonata movement, to the structure of a dialectical proposition. The change of orientation between tonic and dominant, reciprocal between any two chords a fifth apart, bears much closer resemblance to the thesis–antithesis model than Grunsky's example. In the former case, the tonic identity of one is defined by the dominant identity of the other, and vice versa, and the two stand in an immediate relationship within the tonal system. D minor and C flat enjoy no such relationship: one is not instrumental in defining the tonic status of the other, since the two are chromatically related. See Georg Friedrich Hegel, *Wissenschaft der Logik* (Nuremberg, 1812–16) vol. I, p. 421. See also Andrew Bowie, *Aesthetics and Subjectivity: From Kant to Nietzsche* (Manchester, 1990), pp. 123–7.

consciousness – is not embedded in the analytical evidence, because this
evidence is not in itself ostensive of the dialectical method. The ideology
of the essay is rather located in its specific attempt to link regimens: not
in the analytical evidence, nor the dialectical method, nor the descriptive
language, but in the particular way in which they are combined to the end of
demonstrating an ideological position. Invoking Lyotard again: if 'genres of
discourse supply rules for linking together heterogeneous phrases, rules that
are proper for attaining certain goals', ideology in this case resides in the goal
of linkage, not in the regimens themselves.[42] This assessment corroborates
Eagleton's view that 'fascism tends to have its own peculiar lexicon . . . but
what is primarily ideological about these terms is the power interests they
serve and the political effects they generate'. Grunsky's political agenda is
consequently separable from his methodology, since 'exactly the same piece
of language may be ideological in one context and not in another'.[43]

We may consequently extract specific aspects of the analysis, provided
we detach them from Grunsky's 'goal of linkage', which leads to complicity
with National Socialism. In particular, Grunsky's 'counter-tonic' C flat plays
an influential role in the movement's tonal strategy. As Example 3.2 shows,
regions of the music shift continuously between the tonic D minor and C flat,
via the mediation of E flat and its relations. This is especially clear in the closing group of the exposition. Example 3.2 reveals that a counter-structure
centred on C flat/b is inserted within a circumscribing I–III in D minor.
The two structures are at first separated: a distinct region of D minor is
followed by a progression from C flat to G flat. At the climactic passage in
bars 207–19, they are condensed into a single progression: movement from
b to e overlaps with a ii–V–iv–I cadence in F. Note also that B is inserted as
a distorting melodic chromaticism against the final F major chord. In the
parallel section of the recapitulation, this structure is effectively reversed.
Here, an overall progression from B minor (enharmonic C flat minor) to
B flat minor alternates with a counter-structure centred on D minor. The
harmonic structure of the coda can be read as an attempt to resolve the opposition. A progression from a flat to F sharp via B is now embedded within a
prolongation of the tonic, and in the closing bars the E flat 7 chord, which
in the exposition had initiated the move towards C flat, now consistently
resolves back onto D minor.

The argument for the complicity of methodology and ideology is further
problematised by a consideration of the essay's philosophical precedents.
Although it is true that the lineage of right-Hegelianism can be traced to
National Socialism, it would be an act of bold essentialism indeed to argue

---

[42] See *The Differend*, p. xii.     [43] See *Ideology: An Introduction*, p. 9.

Example 3.2  Ninth Symphony, first movement

Deployment of d/C flat opposition

1. Exposition, first-theme group

2. Exposition, third-theme group

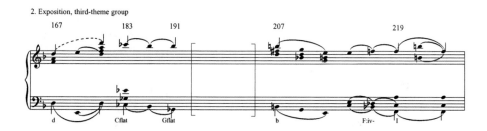

3. Recapitulation of third-theme group and coda

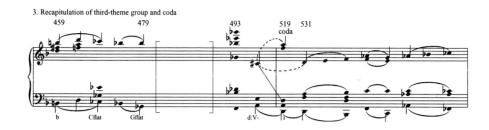

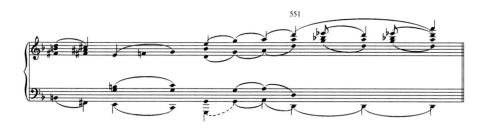

for the complicity of dialectical thought per se with Naziism, by which reasoning Karl Marx, Theodor Adorno, Arnold Schoenberg and Carl Dahlhaus
would all find themselves variously guilty either of pre-empting or reproducing Nazi cultural politics. The argument could be qualified by making
a distinction between left- and right-Hegelian tendencies. But in this case

we would effectively admit that methodology stands apart from its political appropriation, and therefore Grunsky's dialectical method is not of itself bound to his politics. The emphasis on process over statement in the thematic analysis in particular connects it with the work of other commentators in the post-Hegelian tradition who had no overt affiliations with Naziism, for example that of Ernst Kurth.[44] Neither is this issue specifically Brucknerian. As Janet Schmalfeldt has noted, considerations of formal process from A. B. Marx to Carl Dahlhaus emphasise the notion of dialectical becoming as basic to the post-Beethovenian sonata form.[45] Similarly, preoccupations with organicism and musical coherence link Grunsky with figures within this tradition who, for the Nazis, composed the most virulent forms of *entartete Musik*, chiefly the composers of the Second Viennese School.[46] If notions of coherence have proved enduring in post-war musicology, it is due at least in part to the legacy of Viennese modernism, rather than to the 'subterranean' influence of Nazi aesthetics.

In summary, the contention that politics, methodology and analysis are indivisible in Grunsky's article is hard to sustain. The various elements of his argument are not integrated seamlessly, but fragment on close examination. Taken apart from the political agenda, elements of analysis and methodology are relevant to an understanding of the piece, and derivative of wider tendencies in central European thought that are not necessarily orientated around right-wing ideology.

## Robert Haas and the Finale of the Eighth Symphony

Research into the Nazi appropriation of Bruckner has been closely involved with reappraisal of the first critical edition, and by extension with a resurgence of support for the versions of the symphonies published during and shortly after the composer's lifetime.[47] Scholars have traced the influence of

---

[44] See Ernst Kurth, *Bruckner*, vol. I (Berlin, 1925, repr. Hildesheim, 1971), in particular p. 279.

[45] See Janet Schmalfeldt, 'Form as the Process of Becoming: the Hegelian Tradition and the *Tempest* Sonata', in Christopher Reynolds, ed., *The Beethoven Forum*, vol. IV (Lincoln, 1995), pp. 37–71.

[46] On the concept of *entartete Musik*, see Erik Levi, *Music in the Third Reich*, pp. 82–123 and Gordon Craig, *Germany 1866–1945*, pp. 651–2.

[47] See Benjamin Korstvedt, *Bruckner: Symphony no. 8*, pp. 1–9 and 86–103, 'The First Published Edition of Anton Bruckner's Fourth Symphony: Collaboration and Authenticity', *Nineteenth-Century Music* 20 (1996), pp. 3–26, 'The Bruckner Problem Revisited (A Reply)', *Nineteenth-Century Music* 21 (1997), pp. 108–9 and '"Return to the Pure Sources"'. See also Morten Solvik, 'The International Bruckner Society and the N.S.D.A.P.' and Dermot Gault, 'For Later Times', *Musical Times* 137 (1996),

National Socialism on the principal editor of the first *Gesamtausgabe*, Robert Haas, and on the Internationale Bruckner Gesellschaft, under whose auspices the project was conducted. The aims of the edition became entangled with politics; the resurrection of Bruckner's autograph manuscripts became an instrument of Nazi propaganda.[48] Goebbels' Regensburg address not only consolidated Bruckner as a symbol of Nazi ideology, it also lent public support to this editorial project, and thus institutionalised its text-critical strategy.

That Haas's motivations were in part political has been clearly established. His interpretative responses to Bruckner's music frequently employed politically charged rhetoric, linking both the project of the *Gesamtausgabe* and the music itself to contemporary aesthetics and politics.[49] In his analyses he made consistent use of Lorenz's ideas, and in fact partly absorbed Grunsky's analysis of the first movement of the Ninth Symphony in his own commentary on the work.[50] The *völkisch* ideologies of nationalist mysticism and the concomitant distancing of Bruckner from Catholicism that surface in Goebbels' speech are both apparent in Haas's writing.[51]

His editorial strategy was similarly imbued with ideology. He was explicitly hostile towards systematic philology, which he associated negatively with Jewish liberal intellectualism.[52] For Haas, the textual problems attending the symphonies could not be resolved through the objective assessment of manuscript sources; rather, disentangling 'pure' Bruckner from the interventions of colleagues entailed 'the inner immersion in Bruckner's original

pp. 13–19. Support for the first published editions has a history both in central Europe and in Britain and America: see for example Emil Armbruster, *Erstdruckfassung oder "Originalfassung"? Ein Beitrag zur Brucknerfrage am Fünfzigsten Todestag des Meister* (Leipzig, 1946); Constantin Floros, 'Historische Phasen der Bruckner-Interpretation', in Othmar Wessely ed., *Bruckner-Symposium Bericht 1982. Bruckner-Interpretation* (Linz, 1983), pp. 93–102; Egon Wellesz, 'Anton Bruckner and the Process of Musical Creativity', *Musical Quarterly* 24 (1938), pp. 265–90; Donald Francis Tovey, 'Retrospective and Corrigenda', in *Essays in Musical Analysis VI: Miscellaneous Notes, Glossary and Index* (London, 1935–9), p. 144.

[48] This was recognised as early as 1942 by Geoffrey Sharp; see 'Anton Bruckner: Simpleton or Mystic?', *Music Review* 3 (1942), pp. 46–54.

[49] See for example the introduction to Haas's *Anton Bruckner* (Potsdam, 1934), and also his preface to *Anton Bruckner: Sämtliche Werke, Band VIII/8. Symphonie in C-moll (Originalfassung)* (Leipzig, 1939), which specifically links the publication of Bruckner's 'authentic' text with the recent *Anschluss*. The latter is quoted in Korstvedt, *Anton Bruckner: Symphony no. 8*, p. 8.

[50] See *Anton Bruckner*, pp. 154–5.   [51] See for example *Anton Bruckner*, p. 6.

[52] See Haas's critical comments in *Anton Bruckner: Sämtliche Werke, Band II/2. Symphonie in C-moll (Originalfassung)*, p. 66, translated in Solvik, 'The International Bruckner Society and the N.S.D.A.P.', p. 371.

mental, spiritual and sonic world', what Solvik describes as 'an inner empathy with Bruckner's spirit'.[53] Haas defended the decisions to mix sources in his editions on these grounds. Conflations became necessary when what he determined to be pure Bruckner could not be located in a single text. He was persistently defensive of these methods, styling the project as a struggle to bring about Bruckner's posthumous triumph over spiritually degenerate opposition. In Haas's philological, hermeneutic and analytical inclinations the imprints of Nazi cultural politics are plain: an emphasis on the spiritual over the intellectual, and a concomitant notion of textual 'purity'; a sense that this project was embattled by the forces of Jewish liberalism; a nationalist context seeing in Bruckner's music the embodiment of an unadorned 'German essence'.

The gravity of the political connotations in Haas's case has perhaps obscured the extent to which his philology affects the material content of a score, and consequently the extent to which politics changes the analytical reading of a work. Again, instead of interpreting Haas's editions in the light of his politics, we could examine how his editions evince ideology. This can be assessed through a comparison of Haas's score of the Finale of the 1890 revision of the Eighth Symphony with the ideologically less controversial Leopold Nowak edition, which was published in 1955.[54] If Haas's politics are endemic to his edition, their location should reveal itself in the material absent from the more positivistically motivated Nowak score. And this, in turn, should leave an analytical trace: shifts of political inclination producing a change in content will have analytical consequences that allow an assessment of the relationship between analysis and ideology.

The two editions are compared in Table 3.2, and related to the main divisions of the movement's sonata structure. Haas's score is one of the most extensive examples of his readiness to mix sources in the name of an idealised purity of intention. The passages absent in Nowak's edition represent cuts made by the composer during the process of revision. Haas repealed these excisions, in the belief that they were forced upon Bruckner by Hermann Levi and Josef Schalk, and the result is a conflation of the 1887 and 1890 scores. Moreover, not all of Haas's insertions are verbatim restorations of material from the earlier text. The material of bars 609–16 is not present in the 1887 version at all, but was composed largely by Haas himself, as Korstvedt has shown, as an elaboration of a flute part sketched by Bruckner in the margins of the revision. Haas's two guiding ideologies are plainly at work here. Text-critical decisions are justified by a belief that the spirit of the composer

---

[53] 'The International Bruckner Society and the N.S.D.A.P.', pp. 371 and 372.
[54] See *Anton Bruckner: Sämtliche Werke, Band VIII/2* (Vienna, 1955), pp. 105–71.

Table 3.2 *Eighth Symphony, Finale*

Comparison of Nowak and Haas Editions

| Haas | Nowak |
|---|---|
| Exposition | Exposition |
| First-theme group (bars 1–68) | First-theme group (bars 1–68) |
| Second-theme group (bars 69–134: transition in bars 123–34) | Second-theme group (bars 69–134: transition in bars 123–34) |
| Third-theme group (bars 135–230: passage from 1887 version inserted in bars 211–30) | Third-theme group (bars 135–214: passage from 1887 version omitted) |
| Codetta (bars 231–72: passage in bars 253–8 inserted from 1887 version) | Codetta (bars 215–52: insertion from 1887 version omitted) |
| Development (bars 273–458) | Development (bars 253–436) |
| Recapitulation | Recapitulation |
| First-theme group (bars 459–566) | First-theme group (bars 437–546) |
| Second-theme group (bars 567–616: passage from 1887 version inserted in bars 587–98; passage fabricated by Haas after material from the 1887 version inserted in bars 609–16) | Second-theme group (bars 547–82: passages from 1887 version omitted) |
| Third-theme group (bars 617–84: passage in bars 671–4 inserted from 1887 version) | Third-theme group (bars 583–646: passages from 1887 version omitted) |
| Coda (bars 685–747) | Coda (bars 647–709) |

cannot be represented by publishing a single text, together with a desire to protect Bruckner from the type of coercion that Haas perceived had inhibited the composer's cause. The effects of ideology seem unambiguous: an editorial policy affiliated with National Socialist cultural politics gives rise to a particular rendition of the source materials.

There are three discrepancies between the editions large enough to influence an analysis significantly. The first is located between the climax of the third thematic group and the closing section in the exposition. In Nowak, this is simply a four-bar link (bars 210 to 214) in which the timpani prolongs V of E flat. The insertion in Haas (bars 210 to 230) extends the link to twenty bars, and adds thematic material that is not adumbrated earlier in the movement. The second occurs in the recapitulation of the second theme, where the cut in Nowak omits bars 587 to 598 of Haas's edition, corresponding to the parallel section between bars 89 and 98 in the exposition. The third is the material devised by Haas in bars 609 to 616.

These differences can be assessed against a range of analytical criteria. None of them significantly affects an understanding of the form. The three-subject structure of the exposition is preserved in both editions, as are the locations of important events in the recapitulation. The truncated second-group reprise in Nowak admittedly alters the proportions of the recapitulation, although not to an extent that could be considered deformational of the overall scheme.[55] Usually, Haas's insertions prolong structural events that are presented in Nowak in a more economical form. For example, in the closing section of the exposition, the material reintroduced extends a structural dominant. Although inflected with local chromaticisms, principally E flat minor at bar 211 and G flat at bar 219, the underlying B flat pedal remains.

The insertion in bars 609 to 616 of Haas's score is more problematic. Although the material itself is spurious, Haas based its harmonic scheme on the parallel section of the 1887 score. The cut alters the immediate key relationship between the second and third groups: direct transposition from E to C minor in Nowak is softened in Haas by the addition of a dominant preparation of C minor. The comparison given in Example 3.3, however, reveals that both editions share the same basic tonal plan. Since the new dominant in Haas does not resolve to I at the start of the third group, but rather anticipates the dominant pedal underpinning the whole of this group that really only resolves at the start of the coda (bar 685 in Haas), the overall progression E–V of c–c obtains in both editions. Again, Haas's additions elaborate a progression that is preserved in Nowak, without affecting the deep structure of the music.

The discrepancies can be measured against other criteria. Several commentators have drawn attention to the structural importance for the symphony of the mixture of the modes of D flat/b flat and C minor adumbrated in the first theme of the first movement, and also set out schematically in the first theme of the Finale.[56] The tonal strategy of the last movement can be understood as working towards a resolution of this polarisation, by persistently subordinating the dissonant D flat/b flat elements to the immediate

---

[55] I use the term deformation here in the sense intended by James Hepokoski: the truncation or distortion of a theoretically normative sonata pattern. See James Hepokoski, *Sibelius: Symphony no. 5* (Cambridge, 1993), pp. 19–30.

[56] See for example Paul Dawson-Bowling, 'Thematic and Tonal Unity in Bruckner's Eighth Symphony', *Music Review* 30 (1969), pp. 225–36; William Benjamin, 'Tonal Dualism in Bruckner's Eighth Symphony', in William Kinderman and Harald Krebs, eds., *The Second Practice of Nineteenth-Century Tonality* (Lincoln, 1996), pp. 237–58; Dereck Watson, *Bruckner* (London, 1975, repr. Oxford, 1996), pp. 113–114; Julian Horton, *Towards a Theory of Nineteenth-Century Tonality* (Ph.D. dissertation, University of Cambridge, 1998), pp. 128–270.

Example 3.3 Eighth Symphony, Finale

Recapitulation of second-theme group – reductive comparison of Haas and Nowak editions

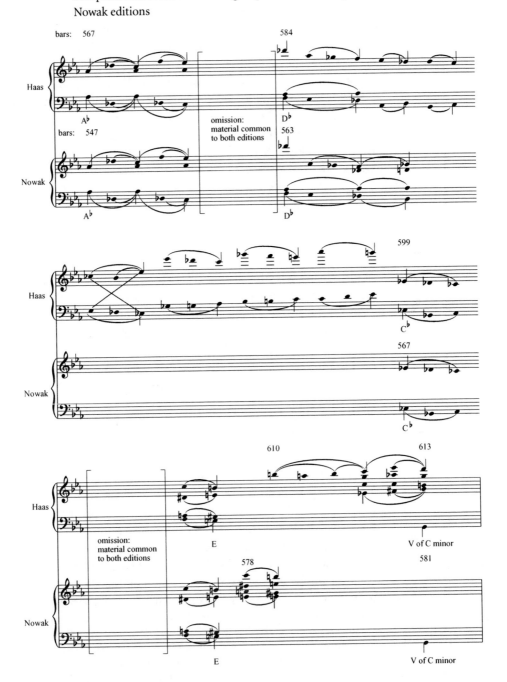

relations of c. Haas's alterations do little to affect the progress of this strategy. The passage inserted in the closing section of the exposition is revealing in this respect. Both editions effectively prolong a V–I cadence in E flat major at this point. The structural consequence of this is that B flat, which has been associated with the tonal polarity opposing C minor, is now forced to function as V of an immediate relation of c. Haas's revision does not jeopardise this resolution. The re-harmonisations of the B flat pedal, as $\hat{5}$ of e flat and $\hat{3}$ of G flat, in the inserted 1887 material act as a reminiscence of B flat's association with the D flat polarity, and therefore throw its circumscribing function as V of III into sharper relief. The other main points at which this process of resolution is carried out, the recapitulation of the first group and closing section, and the coda, are left untouched by Haas except for minute changes to the orchestration.

Neither is the thematic structure of the movement significantly affected. The passage inserted in the exposition has no direct precedents in earlier material, and no subsequent influence in the development, recapitulation or coda. Its excision in Nowak makes plain through direct juxtaposition the relationship between the passage culminating at bar 210 and the cadential section starting at letter P in both scores, a clarity of connection that is lost in Haas (both passages derive from the first subject). The first of Haas's insertions in the second-group reprise is similarly free of wider thematic consequences. This passage repeats the parallel section from the exposition until bar 594, after which a new five-bar continuation ensues. Since the second theme functions primarily as an interlude in both exposition and recapitulation, its truncation in Nowak does not affect the broader thematic process: its abbreviation does not compromise a motivic relationship that would otherwise be clarified.

Altogether, the comparison reveals that the effects of ideology are minimal in this case: a fundamental shift of politics and philological strategy has little more than a peripheral impact on the structure and analytical interpretation of the music. The only insertion for which there is no justification apart from Haas's ideology is the section he elaborated himself between bars 609 and 616; the other inserted sections were at least composed by Bruckner.[57] In realistic terms, the most substantial effect of Haas's politicised philology, in a movement of 747 bars, is the fabrication of a single seven-bar phrase. And the Eighth Symphony is one of the most extreme examples of divergence between Haas and Nowak. With the notable exception of the Second

---

[57] The issue of the extent of collaboration with respect to the other cuts is also debatable, turning on the interpretation of Bruckner's remarks to Felix Weingartner dated 27 January 1891. See Max Auer (ed.), *Anton Bruckner: Gesammelte Briefe* (Regensburg, 1924), pp. 237–8.

Symphony, discrepancies in the other symphonies are largely matters of expression, orchestration and tempo. Although, as Chapter 6 will investigate, the analytical ramifications of editorial policy can be complex and variable between works, the search for a material effect of Haas's political rhetoric produces a similar situation to that found in Grunsky's article: ideology does not proliferate to infect all aspects of the text, but becomes increasingly confined to the realm of politically interested discourse.

The problems arising in the relation of Grunsky's work to its historical precedents are also evident here. It would be misguided to condemn Haas's interventionist practice purely because of its political motivations. Such interventions became common practice amongst nineteenth- and early twentieth-century editors, as is evinced, ironically, in the first editions of Bruckner's symphonies, a body of publications that modern scholarship now partly embraces.[58] The practices of both Haas and the editors of the first editions are similarly at odds with positivist philological strategies, and can therefore be condemned or accepted for the same reasons, aside from their respective political milieux. Consequently the view, expressed most trenchantly by Korstvedt, that re-evaluation of the original publications should proceed because a preference for Bruckner's autograph manuscripts was associated with Naziism, conflates two separate issues. If we wish to reanimate the *Bruckner-Streit* of the 1930s and argue for the first publications, we should do so according to philological criteria. The fact that these questions became embroiled in politics is an essentially separate matter: the political spin placed upon an editorial decision does not undermine the idea that a particular source should be published. Comparison of the Haas and Nowak editions makes this clear. Nowak subscribed to the same basic policy of publishing the autograph manuscripts, despite his purposeful distance from Haas's politics and text-critical strategy.

These observations are not intended as an apology for Haas. Many of his editorial decisions are questionable by contemporary philological standards, and my feeling as an analyst is that the cuts retained by Nowak produce a more successful symphonic structure. Clarification of Haas's politics has however motivated an urge to condemn all aspects of his work before the material effects of ideology and their analytical consequences have been examined for each of his editions. Many of the issues raised by these editions deserve objective consideration apart from the aesthetics of National Socialism.

[58] Indeed, Korstvedt has argued in favour of the Schalk edition of the Eighth Symphony precisely because its editorial strategies are more historically 'authentic' than the positivist pursuit of textual accuracy, a historicist argument that could also be marshalled in defence of Haas's edition. See *Bruckner: Symphony no. 8*, pp. 86–103.

## Conclusions

My purpose in this chapter is emphatically not to defend the kind of ideological musicology practised within this line of Bruckner reception, nor is it somehow to legitimise its political affiliations. It is instead to try to escape from the generalised assumption that methodologies coming into contact with such dark political agendas inevitably become tainted by these affiliations, regardless of their broader historical context or evident applicability. The assumption of unavoidable complicity may itself incline towards a kind of essentialism. Notions of musical organicism, authenticity and the appropriation of dialectics do not have a single history linking them only with fascism, but appear in a plurality of ideological contexts: organicism as part of the aesthetics of modernism; dialectics as the philosophy of theoretical Marxism and left-Hegelianism; authenticity as a positivist textual strategy. To trace all applications back to a single trope in this history is to fall prey, as Pieter van den Toorn has put it, to 'the fallacy of synecdoche': the characterisation of the whole in terms of one of its component parts.[59]

The pervasiveness of politics can also be questioned within individual texts. In the two examples considered, ideology occupies a very specific location within the discourse. Grunsky's politics are not inherent to his methodology, nor to his formal analysis, nor even to his descriptive language; they become ideological in his specific attempt to render them politically meaningful. In the same way, Haas's edition of the Eighth Symphony does not in itself embody Nazi ideology; neither does the concept of a philological policy advocating editorial intervention at the expense of textual accuracy. Both edition and textual method are made ideological by the specifics of Haas's justificatory discourse, from which they may be detached through a process of critical analysis and reconstruction. In short, for these purposes, ideology resides in the linkage of methodologies with certain political power interests, specifically National Socialism.

This in turn suggests a means of answering the questions raised by Bryan Gilliam. Analytical and philological methods can be rescued if they are detached from the process of making them ostensive of right-wing political aims; in other words if they are reconstructed following a process of critical scrutiny. Taken out of context, some of the concepts appropriated allow engagement with crucial questions raised by Bruckner's music. The issue of the limits of material coherence, of the extent to which the symphonies integrate material and the extent to which they deconstruct such ambitions, has not been widely addressed, and will remain obscure if the concept of

[59] See *Music, Politics and the Academy* (Berkeley, 1995).

organicism itself is discarded on account of its past political affiliations. The dialectical method could likewise be a powerful tool both analytically and as a means of locating Bruckner's music historically. But if dialectics is irretrievably linked to its fascist appropriations, then this opportunity will be lost.

The concerns of this chapter clearly have wider ramifications. The issue of what we can salvage from the methodological abuses of National Socialism touches on matters of deep sensitivity, most obviously the misappropriations of science in the name of eugenics and ethnic cleansing. Whilst I do not wish to suggest that comparatively inoffensive matters of aesthetics and editorial practice deserve the same weight of consideration as developments that led to gross abuses of medical ethics and ultimately genocide, there are points of contact with respect to the relationship of means and ends. Michael Burleigh's remarks are instructive in this regard:

> Nazism invested natural laws with religious authority, so it is simple-minded to blame something so nebulously Hegelian as the 'spirit of science', or indeed the technocratic character of modern medicine, for the inhumane policies of Nazi Germany. Science, after all, cannot be reduced to hereditarian biology, so to criticise its 'spirit' seems sweeping.[60]

In the same way, concepts that arose within the general episteme of modernism – organicism, authenticity and especially dialectics – are not reducible to a single instance of misappropriation, however abhorrent the consequences may have been. It becomes a virtual imperative that we do not allow such misuses to damage fatally the propriety of the methods themselves. To do so would be to abdicate responsibility in the face of totalitarian misapplication.

---

[60] See Michael Burleigh, *The Third Reich: A New History*, p. 348. On the same matter, see also Burleigh, *Death and Deliverance* (Cambridge, 1994).

# 4 Bruckner and musical analysis

It is perhaps emblematic of Bruckner's location on the margins of musical analysis that current debate over the applicability of established theoretical models to his music should have developed at a time when their influence has waned in the face of postmodern or 'new' musicological critiques.[1] Belated realisation that the symphonies are, albeit problematically, susceptible to voice-leading analysis, or that they stand in an analytically profitable relationship with the topical and formal discourses of the Beethovenian symphony, has ironically coincided with a fundamental reappraisal of the aims and methods of analysis, amidst a general redefinition of institutional priorities. It is a further irony that the admission of Bruckner to the analytical canon has, at least partly, entailed critical reappraisal of the limitations of the theories applied. Debate attending the last-minute 'construction' of the symphonies via the mechanisms of formal analysis runs parallel with the critical 'reconstruction' of analysis in response to postmodern or post-structuralist hostility.

There are two related matters under scrutiny here: the question of whether Bruckner's practices are normative or marginal in themselves; the more general problem of whether the repertoire they occupy is part of, or extraneous to, a theoretically defined common practice. Both issues are present as text or subtext in a recent exchange between Edward Laufer and Derrick Puffett concerning the applicability of Schenkerian theory.[2] Laufer traces the marginalisation of Bruckner by Schenkerians to Schenker's famously

---

[1] Craig Ayrey has summed up this turn of events succinctly: 'it would appear that an awareness of the provisional and contingent nature of all statements about music, of all positions, is increasingly paralysing the impulse to analyse'. See 'Debussy's Significant Connections', in Anthony Pople, ed., *Theory, Analysis and Meaning in Music* (Cambridge, 1994), pp. 127–51.

[2] See on the one hand Edward Laufer, 'Some Aspects of Prolongational Procedures in the Ninth Symphony (Scherzo and Adagio)', in *Bruckner Studies*, pp. 209–55 and 'Continuity in the Fourth Symphony (First Movement)', in Crawford Howie, Paul Hawkshaw and Timothy Jackson, eds., *Perspectives on Anton Bruckner* (Aldershot, 2001), pp. 114–44. On the other hand, see Derrick Puffett, 'Bruckner's Way: The Adagio of the Ninth Symphony', *Music Analysis* 18 (1999), pp. 5–100, recently reprinted in *Derrick Puffett on Music*, ed. Kathryn Bailey Puffett (Aldershot, 2001), pp. 687–790. All subsequent references are to the *Music Analysis* version of the essay. For a critique of Laufer's analysis of the Ninth Symphony, see Julian Horton, review of *Bruckner Studies* in *Music Analysis* 18 (1999), pp. 155–70, and in particular pp. 164–5. Kevin J. Swinden

hostile reception of Bruckner as a composer for whom 'the art of prolongation was no longer attainable'.[3] Laufer's strategy is to refute Schenker's opinions through analysis: by demonstrating the existence of foreground linear
progressions that also emerge at deeper levels of structure, seminally in the
Scherzo and Adagio of the Ninth Symphony, and more recently in the first
movement of the Fourth Symphony. In the Adagio of the Ninth, he points
to third and fourth progressions that putatively underpin both the first and
second themes, which are composed out, admittedly by unorthodox means,
as the movement proceeds. In both this movement and the first movement
of the Fourth Symphony, he posits an overarching process involving the
gradual clarification of the initial *Kopfton* of the fundamental line, such
that the whole movement effectively prolongs an ascent to $\hat{3}$ culminating
in the coda. Laufer concludes that it is Bruckner's novel application of prolongational techniques that impeded Schenker, rather than their complete
absence.

Puffett takes issue with two basic points. First, he considers the detail of
the music consistently to frustrate linear analysis: 'I decided that I couldn't
analyse the Adagio [of the Ninth Symphony] from a Schenkerian perspective because I couldn't analyse the first eight bars.'[4] Second, an *Anstieg*
which only concludes at the end of a movement, and which is followed
by no structural descent of the *Urlinie*, is not a Schenkerian concept in
the orthodox sense, because the cadential formula basic to the *Ursatz* has
been evaded.[5] In other words, a Schenkerian analysis that demonstrates the
absence rather than the presence of an *Ursatz* is effectively self-negating.
Puffett's assessment of Laufer's analysis is emphatic: it is 'worthy of huge
admiration almost regardless of the result. It also seems to me fundamentally
misguided.'[6] His preferred solution, in part following Hugo Leichtentritt's
analysis of the Eighth Symphony, is to segment the Adagio into discrete periods, and to concentrate on the questions of harmonic and linear analysis

---

has deployed Schenker in a similarly critical fashion in 'Bruckner's *Perger* Prelude: A
Dramatic *Revue* of Wagner?' in the same volume, pp. 101–24.

[3] As reported by Oswald Jonas in 'Heinrich Schenker. Über Anton Bruckner', *Der
Dreiklang* 7 (1937), pp. 167–77. See also Laufer, 'Aspects of Prolongation', fn. 3,
p. 210.

[4] See 'Bruckner's Way', pp. 9–10.

[5] This emerges particularly in Puffett's critique of Laufer's interpretation of the coda of
the Adagio as gradually removing the multiple dissonances left unresolved at the climax
in bar 206, leaving a clear degree $\hat{3}$ of the fundamental line. Puffett responds: 'Achieving
this cleansing . . . means by-passing the dominant that, according to Schenker, is an
essential part of the cadential process. This does not invalidate the analysis, but it
certainly makes it questionable.' See 'Bruckner's Way', p. 11.

[6] Ibid., p. 9.

to which each period gives rise, without claiming a broader Schenkerian dimension.[7]

At first blush, the field of contention here is clear: Laufer absorbs Bruckner into the Schenkerian canon; Puffett excludes him. At a broader level of discourse, however, the claims of the two analyses converge. Both regard Schenkerian theory as synonymous with common-practice tonality; by applying Schenker in order to establish which elements of the music do not submit to linear analysis, Puffett still defines common practice in Schenkerian terms.[8] But what exactly is the status of works, or materials within a work, standing outside the Schenkerian 'index of common practice'? Do they inhabit a different, chromatic tonal practice? If they do not, then their position outside common practice implies that they are in some sense prescient of the emancipation of the dissonance, and the analysis thus tacitly confirms Schoenberg's evolutionary model of tonality engaged in an entropic slide towards atonality. On the other hand, if the non-Schenkerian aspects of the music form part of a different kind of tonal practice, then the question arises as to what the basis of this practice is, and we are left with the problem of theorising a common-practice chromatic tonality before we are fit to the task of analysing Bruckner's music. To be sure, this would not be a novel undertaking. Yet with the exception of William Benjamin's analysis of the Eighth Symphony, which situates Brucknerian treatment of modal dualism within a more general tonal 'second practice', analyses engaging with matters of tonality have not clarified this theoretical context.[9]

Laufer's concentration on motivic prolongation opens up similarly vexed questions of thematic analysis. His conviction that motivic coherence in Bruckner arises from the composing out of initially stated linear progressions contrasts sharply with the German-language literature from Kurth to Dahlhaus, and its more recent anglophone appropriations, which either consider thematic coherence in Bruckner to be a matter of rhythm rather than pitch or interval, or else emphasise thematic mutation, or 'becoming', as a guiding principle. Again, the underlying issue is that of what is normative for the Germanic symphony, and again Bruckner is variously pulled between margins and centre. Dahlhaus's adoption of Schoenbergian musical

---

[7] See *Musikalische Formenlehre* (Leipzig, 1911), translated as *Musical Form* (Cambridge, Mass., 1951).

[8] 'Schenker's methods might be used as a criterion or index of common practice, allowing what is unusual or distinctive in the music to stand out in relief.' 'Bruckner's Way', p. 8.

[9] See 'Tonal Dualism in Bruckner's Eighth Symphony', in William Kinderman and Harald Krebs, eds., *The Second Practice of Nineteenth-Century Tonality* (Lincoln, 1998), pp. 237–58. Another exception would be my own analysis of the Eighth Symphony in *Towards a Theory of Nineteenth-Century Tonality* (Ph.D. dissertation, University of Cambridge, 1998), pp. 128–270.

logic as the benchmark of normal practice ascribes normative status to an essentially Brahmsian concept, and Bruckner's techniques are consequently deemed exceptional. In contrast, the substantial differences of technique and philosophy separating Laufer and Kurth mask a common attempt to install Bruckner within a normative tradition: a dialectically unfolding history for Kurth; a Schenkerian canon for Laufer. The net effect is once more that the concept of a normative practice itself comes under scrutiny.

The problem of theoretical norms attends questions of form in a rather different way. The recent attempts by Warren Darcy and Timothy L. Jackson to understand Bruckner's sonata forms via the concept of 'deformation' proposed by James Hepokoski rely on the basic conviction that nineteenth-century composers more or less consciously distorted an established theoretical pattern, chiefly defined in the central European *Formenlehre* models of A. B. Marx, Carl Czerny and others, which ostensibly reduced a classical stylistic principle to a reified architectural plan.[10] By these terms, the formal habits of composers were increasingly orientated around a theoretical prescription that had come to be regarded as normative, derived primarily, although not exclusively, from the theorising of procedures found in Beethoven's early and middle periods. The widespread formal experimentation in the later nineteenth century is regarded as being enabled by the presence of this pattern. Sonata procedures should therefore be classified according to the way in which they distort, or 'deform', the *Formenlehre* model.[11] In this instance, the relationship of norm and exception is conceived more expansively as a relationship of theory and practice. And since deformation is common to the sonata-type music of the late nineteenth century, deformational works come to be classified, somewhat paradoxically, as a 'non-normative' repertoire.

The source of these problems is analytical theory, not Brucknerian practice. Bruckner emerges as analytically supplementary because the limits of theory, at least as they are defined in Anglo-American analysis, have arisen from an explicitly inappropriate context. Schenkerian and Schoenbergian models of structure, in particular, rely at base on highly selective music-historical attitudes, for which Bruckner was not central. The pertinence of

[10] See Warren Darcy, 'Bruckner's Sonata Deformations', in *Bruckner Studies*, pp. 256–77 and Timothy L. Jackson, 'The Finale of Bruckner's Seventh Symphony and the Tragic Reversed Sonata Form', in ibid., pp. 140–208. Jackson's work in this area differs from Darcy's in its relation of deformation to a Schenkerian concept of form, whereby the reversal or omission of formal regions is linked to the completion or otherwise of a proposed *Urlinie*.

[11] As Hepokoski puts it: 'These [deformational] structures cannot be said to 'be' sonatas in any strict sense: this would be grossly reductive . . . Still, as part of the perceptual framework within which they ask to be understood, they do depend on the listener's prior knowledge of the *Formenlehre* sonata.' *Sibelius: Symphony no. 5*, p. 5.

these models would be further jeopardised if procedures deemed to isolate Bruckner from a perceived mainstream could also be located in the
'normative' repertoire itself. Puffett's statement that 'when you look at any
Bruckner first movement and compare it with Brahms, it looks . . . motivically chaotic; it doesn't seem to hang together at all' consequently pinpoints a
problem that the negative application of Schenker is not going to resolve; the
Schenkerian context will still reinforce the non-normative status of features
standing outside a selectively Brahmsian concept of structural integrity.[12]
The idea of sonata deformation reproduces the same problem on a larger
scale. It tacitly confirms Charles Rosen's conviction that nineteenth-century
theory rendered sonata-type works ahistorical, by which terms Bruckner's
symphonies are part of a repertoire that is important chiefly because it
delineates the boundary between a living stylistic principle and its ossified
after-image.[13]

  In the present context, I do not propose anything so ambitious as a full-
scale re-theorising of thematic, tonal and formal principles for nineteenth-
century music, or even for the nineteenth-century symphony. Elements of
such a model can however be glimpsed by establishing analytical principles
in specific parameters (harmony, tonality, theme, form) that are consistent
to Bruckner's symphonic style, and by testing these principles against a range
of theoretical models, to the end of discovering a general analytical context
that treats nineteenth-century symphonic practices as norms of their time,
rather than as negative reflections of a reified common practice.

## Harmony

In the search for fresh authorities upon which institutionalised models of
tonal theory might be based, reanimations of Hugo Riemann's ideas have

---

[12] 'Bruckner's Way', pp. 14–15. Puffett's remarks return to the sentiments of the
Brahmsian faction in Vienna. See for example Eduard Hanslick's response to the
String Quintet: 'It remains a psychological puzzle how this gentlest and most peace-
able of all men . . . becomes, in the act of composition, an anarchist who pitilessly
sacrifices everything that is called logic and clarity of development and structural and
tonal unity.' Review in the *Neue freie Presse* (26 February 1885), trans. in Crawford
Howie, *Anton Bruckner: A Documentary Biography*, vol. II (Lampeter, 2002), p. 444.
Gustav Dömpke made similar comments about the Seventh Symphony: 'Bruckner
lacks the feeling for the basic elements of any musical structure and for the combination of a series of integral melodic and harmonic parts.' Review in the *Wiener
Allgemeine Zeitung* (30 March 1886), trans. in Howie, p. 508.

[13] As Rosen states: 'When sonata form did not yet exist, it had a history – the history
of eighteenth-century musical style. Once it had been called into existence by early
nineteenth-century theory, history was no longer possible for it; it was defined, fixed
and unalterable.' See *Sonata Forms* (New York and London, 1980), p. 292.

of late loomed large. The burgeoning interest in Riemann is of both ideological and music-theoretical origin. His thought is comparatively free from
the kind of overweening ideological rhetoric that Schenker attached to his
own analytical techniques. Consequently, it has escaped the critical oppro-
brium that has recently overwhelmed Schenkerian analysis. Moreover, the
expressly non-hierarchical orientation of both Riemann's functional theory
and his later *Tonnetz* representations of tonal relations points towards a post-
hierarchical notion of tonality resonating strongly with the postmodern
flight from the surface–depth, or conversely base–superstructure, metaphor
informing much modernist thought.[14] Riemann, in many ways, seems
the ideal foundation on which to erect a postmodern concept of tonality.

The harmonically problematic repertoire of the late nineteenth century
has proved central to the empirical development of neo-Riemannian principles. These developments have taken a variety of forms. Brian Hyer has
pursued David Lewin's suggestion that the advantage of Riemann's theoretical apparatus is its capacity for separating transformational grammar and
scale-degree function. He accordingly maps the categories of transformation
across an equal-tempered *Tonnetz*, whilst abandoning their functional contexts.[15] The result is a quasi-algebraic representation of triadic progressions,
in which modified versions of the voice-leading procedures through which
Riemann relates triads under the same function – chiefly the dominant,
parallel, relative and *Leittonwechselklang*, or (D), (P), (R) and (L) – are freed
from their moorings in a functional concept of tonality. As Hyer puts it:
'Riemann's functional transformations . . . integrate the twelve pitch classes
of the octave into a single abstract, multi-circular conceptual expanse, oblit-
erating the distinction between the diatonic and the chromatic.'[16] Hyer, in
other words, capitalises on what David Kopp has called the potential 'tonic
blindness' of Riemann's *Tonnetz* representations.[17] Kopp, in turn, has both

---

[14] On the question of post-hierarchical tonal theory and its postmodern contexts, see
Robert Fink, 'Going Flat: Post-Hierarchical Music Theory and the Musical Surface', in
Nicholas Cook and Mark Everist, eds., *Rethinking Music* (Oxford, 1999), pp. 102–37.

[15] See Brian Hyer, 'Reimag(in)ing Riemann', *Journal of Music Theory* 39 (1995), pp. 101–
38 and as a precedent David Lewin, 'Amfortas' Prayer to Titurel and the Role of D
in *Parsifal*: The Tonal Spaces and the Drama of the Enharmonic Cflat/B', *Nineteenth-
Century Music* 7 (1984), pp. 336–49.

[16] 'Reimag(in)ing Riemann', p. 135. Hyer in fact reverses the meanings of (R) and (P)
in Riemann's system. *Relative* for Riemann signified the major–minor change within
a single triad, and *parallel* the lower minor-third relation in major tonality and the
upper minor third in the minor. Hyer designates major–minor mode change as parallelism, and the minor-third relationships as relative.

[17] See *Chromatic Transformations in Nineteenth-Century Music* (Cambridge, 2002),
p. 141.

moderated and expanded Hyer's approach. Rather than jettisoning function as pertinent to either symmetrical or asymmetrical progressions, he
revises the concept of tonic identity to embrace common-tone as well as
fifth relationships, and thus installs major and minor third root motion as
tonic-defining within chromatic tonality. The result is the enlargement and
revision of Hyer's taxonomy of transformations to include six basic categories: dominant, fifth-change, mediant, relative, identity and parallel.[18]

Richard Cohn and others have alternatively placed greater emphasis on
the group-theoretic implications of Riemann's ideas.[19] Notably, Cohn has
transferred the neo-Riemannian reading of triadic progressions through
successive major thirds into a set-theoretical context.[20] He codifies the basis
of these practices in the hexatonic pitch-class set 6-20, formalises the parsimonious voice-leading operations through which triads in the system are
linked, and groups the relationships between transposed hexatonic systems
under the general rubric of the so-called 'hyper-hexatonic' system. Although
both Cohn and Hyer reject Riemann's theory of functional dualism, Cohn
extends this revisionism to a complete abandonment of Riemann's terminology, the sole point of contact being the derivation of the harmonic network
from the *Tonnetz*. Other theorists have proved more susceptible to functional
dualism. Daniel Harrison has proposed a dualistic model of mixed modality,
replacing Riemann's failed attempt to define minor tonality as the dialectical opposite of the major via appeals to its basis in the mythical 'undertone'
series with a conceptual opposition of major and minor that, for Harrison,
characterises the harmonic practices of the later nineteenth century.[21] Kopp
provides a more circumspect evaluation of dualism, distinguishing between
what he terms the 'essential dualism' arising for Riemann and others from
the oppositional relationship of major and minor, and the 'reciprocal dualism' evident in the inverse relationship of certain transformations within
the chromatic system.[22]

Bruckner's music stands directly within the harmonic practice that has
proved most amenable to these ideas. Many of his more advanced harmonic techniques exploit the symmetrical triadic progressions with which
neo-Riemannian theorists have been principally concerned. Moreover, these
progressions are frequently embedded within functionally tonal harmony

[18] See ibid., pp. 171–3.
[19] See for example Richard Cohn, 'Maximally Smooth Cycles, Hexatonic Systems
and the Analysis of Late-Romantic Triadic Progressions', *Music Analysis* 15 (1996),
pp. 9–40.
[20] See ibid., especially pp. 13–23. Cohn also responds to Lewin's work in this respect.
[21] See Daniel Harrison, *Harmonic Function in Chromatic Music* (Chicago, 1994).
[22] See *Chromatic Transformations in Nineteenth-Century Music*, pp. 181–6.

in such a way as to render their theoretical isolation problematic. In the ensuing analysis, two versions of the neo-Riemannian perspective, those of Hyer and Cohn, are applied to a passage from the Seventh Symphony, with the twofold intention of illuminating key features of Bruckner's harmonic practice, whilst potentially exposing the lacunae in the transformational model.

Example 4.1 gives a reduced score of the second-theme group of the first movement in its exposition form, as far as the transition to the closing group. As Graham Phipps observes, the group comprises a statement and four variants of the second theme.[23] The statement itself can be split into two components: the ascending diminished octave scale in bars 51 to 54, labelled 'a'; its descending complement in bars 54 to 59, labelled 'b'. The lower system in example 4.1 provides a harmonic synopsis of the same passage, onto which Hyer's transformational vocabulary has been mapped. It is immediately evident that the dissection of the statement into two parts reflects a division of harmonic, as well as thematic, labour. Each part employs a distinct distribution of transformations. In the progression B major–B minor–G major in bars 51 to 53, B major transforms into B minor under the parallel, or (P), which, as Hyer puts it, 'relates triads a perfect prime apart, maintaining a common perfect fifth';[24] the progression B minor–G major deploys the *Leittonwechsel*, (L), since they are 'two triads a major third apart' which maintain 'a common minor third'.[25] The progression can therefore be written $(B,+)(P)=(B,-)(L)=(G,+)$. In contrast, the sequence in bars 54 to 59 is constructed from the alternation of two fresh categories: the subdominant (S), or in Hyer's terminology the under-dominant $(D^{-1})$, and the parallel relative (PR). The progression underlying 'b' is therefore $(B\ flat,+)(D^{-1})=(F,+)(PR)=(A\ flat,+)(D^{-1})=(E\ flat,+)(PR)=(G\ flat,+)(D^{-1})=(D\ flat,+/C\ sharp,+)$.

Each subsequent variant either changes the distribution of the transformational categories, or else places the material of the statement in fresh harmonic contexts. The reharmonisation of the ascending diminished octave is crucial to this process. In bars 59 to 62, the motive is transferred into the bass, where it now supports the progression $(C\ sharp,+)(PR)=(E,+)(D)=(A,+)(PR)=(C,+)$. The modal parallelism with which the group began has yielded to a minor-third transposition operation, or in Hyer's terms the parallel relative, and the stepwise fourth at the centre of the motive swaps its original (L) for a rising dominant transformation.

[23] See Graham H. Phipps, 'Bruckner's Free Application of Strict Sechterian Theory with Stimulation from Wagnerian Sources: An Assessment of the First Movement of the Seventh Symphony', in *Perspectives on Anton Bruckner*, pp. 228–58.

[24] 'Reimag(in)ing Riemann', p. 109.     [25] Ibid., p. 108.

Example 4.1 Seventh Symphony, first movement

Second theme in exposition – rhythmic reduction and harmonic analysis

Example 4.1 (*cont.*)

Example 4.1  (*cont.*)

Example 4.1 (*cont.*)

The descending continuation returns, in transposition, to its original alternation of (PR) and $(D^{-1})$ in bars 62 to 66, now embellished with passing diminished sevenths; however, Bruckner subsequently adds an extended tail to this material, which first of all transforms A flat into D flat7 via (D), and then approaches the second-inversion chord of B major in bar 69 by way of the tritone progression D flat7–G7. The tail, in other words, can be read as (A flat,+)(D)=(D flat,+)(2PR)=(G,+)(LP)=(B,+). The tritone progression arises from a double application of (PR), from which the intervening minor-third transposition has been omitted: (D flat,+)(PR)=(E,+); (D flat,+)(2PR)=(G,+).

The second variant consists principally of two linked forms of 'a', as indicated in Example 4.1; 'b' is represented solely by the residual dotted figure in bar 72, through which these forms are connected. Again, some elements of the statement are retained and others altered. Motive 'a' recurs untransposed in bars 69 to 72; the harmonisation of the first two bars of the statement is likewise recalled, albeit with B major and B minor represented as second inversions and G elaborated to become G7 in its last inversion. The material diverges harmonically from the statement in bar 72: the second form of 'a' is linked to the first by the progression E dim.7–E flat7–G, which, if one considers the diminished seventh as an alteration of the E flat chord it precedes, reduces to $(G,+)(PL)=(E$ flat$,+)(LP)=(G,+)$. E flat7 returns in its last inversion in bars 75 to 76, resolving to C major for the start of the fourth variant in bar 77; bars 73 to 77 can thus be interpreted as $(G,+)(PL)=(E$ flat$,+)(RP)=(C,+)$. Observe also that in bars 73 to 76, 'a' for the first time encompasses a perfect, rather than a diminished, octave. The process of harmonic variation is thus closely bound up with a process of thematic mutation. The changes of harmonic context reflect the ongoing alteration of thematic content.

In sharp contrast, the third variant consists entirely of functional harmony prolonging C major and its relative. Self-evidently, and as Example 4.1 makes plain, this translates in transformational terms into a near-exclusive deployment of $(D)$, $(D^{-1})$ and their compound applications, either cadentially or sequentially. The significant exception arises from the need to supply the secondary dominant of A minor in bars 79 to 80, generating the progression $(G,+)(RP)=(E,+)(D)=(A,-)$.

The final variant in a sense balances the omission of 'b' that characterises the third variant. Motive 'a' recurs un-transposed in bars 89 to 92, after which bars 92 to 103 are concerned entirely with the sequential spinning out of 'b'. The harmony of 92 to 99, however, deploys $(D^{-1})$ and $(PL)$ in alternation, replacing the shifts between $(PR)$ and $(D^{-1})$ that characterised 'b' in the statement. The network of transformations in these bars emerges thus: $(B,+)(PL)=(G,+)(PR)=(B$ flat$,+)(D^{-1})=(F,+)(PL)=(D$ flat$,+)(D^{-1})=(A$ flat$,+)(PL)=(E,+)(D^{-1})=(B,+)(D^{-1})=(F$ sharp$,+)$. $(PR)$ is then restored to 'b' in bars 99 to 101, which can be read as $(F$ sharp$,+)(PR)=(A,+)(PR)=(C,+)(D^{-1})=(G,+)$. Finally, $(G,+)$ resolves onto $(B,+)$ in bar 103 under $(LP)$.

The prevalence in this passage of the transformations $(PR)$, $(LP)$ and their inverses urges reinterpretation from the set-theoretic perspective advanced by Richard Cohn. In particular, Cohn's formalisation of the properties of successive $(LP)$ transformations within a hexatonic generalised interval system

Example 4.2  Cohn's four hexatonic systems

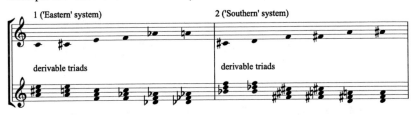

have clear applications in this example. The transformations (PR) and (RP), which are extensively deployed, can moreover be formalised as standing within an octatonic interval system in an analogous fashion.

The hexatonic and octatonic systems require theoretical elaboration before they can be applied analytically. In Cohn's terms, four hexatonic systems are possible, as explained in Example 4.2. The systems are classified as hexatonic because the materials of each derive from the four possible transpositions of the hexatonic set-class 6-20 [0,1,4,5,8,9]. Each transposition of the set yields three pairs of major and minor triads, related by successive major thirds. The four systems collectively exhaust the fund of major and minor triads derivable from the total chromatic; any progression through successive major-third relations arises from one of these four systems, regardless of whether it deploys major triads, minor triads or a mixture of the two. Cohn furthermore defines sub-categories of the systems, or 'co-cycles', which reflect the possible transpositions 'in hexatonic triadic space', and which are therefore described as T1, T2, T3, T4 and T5 respectively, as shown in Example 4.3. The four systems are further ramified by Cohn into a general hyper-hexatonic system, which maps not only the internal properties of each system, but also how they interact.

Triadic progressions arising from the octatonic set 8-28 [0,1,3,4,6,7,9,10] can be theorised in a similar way. Example 4.4 gives the total fund of major and minor triads arising from each of the three octatonic collections, and arranges them into analogues of Cohn's hexatonic systems. Transpositions within the systems are of course possible, yielding T1–T7 possible co-cycles,

Example 4.3  Hexatonic co-cycles

also charted in Example 4.4. Interaction of octatonic and hexatonic systems accounts for the total number of triadic progressions stemming from the symmetrical division of the octave by equal major and minor thirds. This manifestly does not exhaust the repertoire of progressions arising from symmetrical division; transposition by successive major or minor seconds is also common, and would require separate theoretical elucidation. The latter, in particular, is evident at least from the music of Berlioz onwards,

Example 4.4 Octatonic collections and co-cycles

Example 4.4 (*cont.*)

and was often deployed by Bruckner.[26] Extended semitonal transposition is most comprehensively theorised as a property of the total chromatic, a phenomenon that generates its own theoretical difficulties.

The harmonic structure of the second group in the first movement of the Seventh Symphony can be understood in terms of the interaction of hexatonic and octatonic systems with the asymmetric properties of diatonic chord functions. The differences between the statement and variants, which in Hyer's terms reflect the deployment and alteration of networks of transformations, can now be defined according to the specific distribution of hexatonic, octatonic and diatonic progressions. In the statement, the *Hauptmotiv* of 'a' arises from a T1 hexatonic co-cycle. It is, in fact, a fragment of the progression from Brahms's Double Concerto with which Cohn exemplifies this co-cycle, and also reproduces the harmonic structure of the 'Siegfried' motive from *Die Walküre*, which Hyer cites as a model for the application of (P) and (L).[27] The end of 'a' shifts to octatonic system 2, comprising either part of co-cycles T5b or T6a, and 'b' as a whole alternates diatonic progression with possible components of these two co-cycles from octatonic systems 3 and 1 respectively. The first variant exchanges the hexatonic head of 'a' for a consistent alternation of diatonic progressions and octatonic T5b or T6a segments, derived from systems 2, 1, 2, and 3. The tritonal progression in bars 67 to 68, explained in Example 4.1 as an

---

[26] I think particularly of bars 200–24 of the first movement of Berlioz's *Symphonie fantastique*. A Brucknerian example can be found in the Fifth Symphony, first movement, bars 446–52.

[27] See Cohn, 'Maximally Smooth Cycles', pp. 13–15 and Hyer, 'Reimag(in)ing Riemann', pp. 111–12.

application of (2PR), can now be construed as an octatonic T4 co-cycle. In contrast, variant 2 consists entirely of hexatonic co-cycles, with the single exception of the progression leading into variant 3, which consists of an octatonic T2a segment from system 1. After the diatonic interlude of the third variant, variant 4 furnishes the most diverse interaction of systems in the group. The succession of hexatonic and octatonic segments characterising 'a' in the statement is retrieved in bars 89 to 92, but the extended version of 'b' that follows freely mixes octatonic, hexatonic and diatonic fragments: (B flat,+) – (F,+) is diatonic; (F,+) – (D flat,+) is a T2 hexatonic fragment; (D flat,+) – (A flat,+) is diatonic; (A flat,+) – (E,+) is a T2 hexatonic fragment; (E,+) – (B,+) and (B,+) – (F sharp,+) are both diatonic; (F sharp,+) – (A,+) and (A,+) – (C,+) comprise a subset of a T6a octatonic co-cycle from system 1; (C,+) – (G,+) is diatonic; (G,+) – (B,+) is part of a hexatonic T4 co-cycle.

The two approaches deployed here have different limits of applicability. Hyer's transformational model encompasses triadic relationships in general, and is therefore indifferent to shifts between symmetrical and asymmetrical progressions. The result is that the whole of this passage appears as a continuous network of transformations, which coheres only through the algebraic connections between chords, as Hyer describes them, regardless of whether or not the music alludes to the practices of what might commonly be described as functional tonality. Cohn's approach is more selective. As his invocation of Carl Dahlhaus's appraisal of the challenge posed by the post-Wagnerian repertoire – as that of 'clarifying its position floating between a tonality that has been attacked by the weakening of the root progressions but not yet completely destroyed, and an atonality anticipated by the increased independence of semitonal motion' – suggests, the set-theoretical modelling of symmetrical progressions is designed as a complement to tonal function. Cohn consequently evades applying set-theoretical vocabulary outside the hexatonic context, despite the more wide-ranging implications of his conclusion that the triad's role as a pivot 'between diatonic and chromatic space' has relevance for music from Willaert to Schoenberg.[28]

In broaching Dahlhaus's comments, Cohn isolates a problematic historical context for the neo-Riemannian approach. Since his theoretical model seeks clarification of Dahlhaus's remarks as 'a standard for descriptions of Romantic harmony', it consequently adopts as its basis a specific conception of the historical development of tonality in particular, and by implication of western music in general. If post-Wagnerian practice stands on

[28] See 'Maximally Smooth Cycles', pp. 30–4.

the cusp of the late maturity of tonality and 'an atonality anticipated by the increased independence of semitonal motion', it behaves precisely as Schoenberg claimed: as the last stage of an inevitable historical process culminating in atonality. Despite its superficially post-hierarchical stance, Cohn's theoretical premises lend credence to what is perhaps the defining argument of musical modernism: the necessity of atonality and the historical dialectic of decay and innovation from which it arose. There is, however, no reason why this historical model should govern our theoretical approach to the late nineteenth-century repertoire. On the contrary, if the pervasive postmodernity of contemporary musicology is to be taken seriously, there is a positive onus to view such historical master narratives with considerable suspicion. Cohn's attempt to theorise continuity between late tonality and the emancipation of the dissonance could be regarded as bolstering the imposition of Schoenberg's pre-compositional discourse, rather than as systematising an objective 'fact' or imperative of music history.[29] This affiliation forces a wedge between the historical and theoretical means guiding Cohn's ideas: the *Tonnetz* model of triadic progressions engenders a post-hierarchical perspective that his governing notion of music history contradicts. But if atonality was only a necessity insomuch as the force of Schoenberg's discourse compelled it, then the harmonic phenomena Cohn identifies stand within a late nineteenth-century common practice, which, although it grows out of classical tonal practice, nevertheless exhibits a self-sufficiency for which the views of Cohn, and by extension Dahlhaus, cannot account.

If anything, the concept of the transformational network overcompensates for this deficiency. Its specific application to the nineteenth-century repertoire masks a broader historical indifference: the theory could, in practice, be applied equally to the music of Monteverdi, Beethoven or Debussy, and they would appear distinctive only in the specific distribution of transformations within the network for each piece. Triadic materials can also arise in a serial context; indeed there is no theoretical limitation on the composition of serial music that consists entirely of triads, and this would also submit to transformational analysis. But if the model is incapable of detecting a systemic shift as dramatic as that separating Monteverdi and serialism, it fails in a crucial historical duty. And what critically separates serialism from the *seconda prattica* is in no small measure a change of attitude towards tonic centricity.

---

[29] On this matter, see Lawrence Kramer, 'The Mirror of Tonality: Transitional Features of Nineteenth-Century Harmony', *Nineteenth-Century Music* 4 (1981), pp. 191–208.

These reservations are compounded by a series of specifically theoretical concerns, the most pressing of which is that of tonic blindness.[30] In the *Tonnetz* model, there is no essential difference, in terms of the effect upon the perception of chord identity, between applying (D) or (D⁻¹) and applying (PR) or (LP); they are simply particular ways of moving around the network, which have no distinct ramifications for the identity of the chords they connect, or for the relationship between a given triad and its formal context. Bruckner's Seventh Symphony is thus in no meaningful sense 'in E major'; to make such a claim is to ascribe tonic identity to (E,+), and therefore to accord it a position of hierarchical privilege. The fact that the piece begins and ends with (E,+) is not a confirmation of that triad's function, it merely reveals that the total transformational network is, so-to-speak, book-ended by a single chord. The fact that (E,+) may occasionally arise from the application of (D) is no more or less significant than any other transformation of this or any other triad.

Accepting this reading not only involves suppressing the general feeling that abandoning tonic function seems counter-intuitive in this instance amongst many others, it also requires us to overlook a fundamental theoretical inconsistency. The concept of transformation cannot exist independent of chord identity: the action of transformation, through which one chord becomes another, is meaningless without an anchorage in the possibility of non-transformation, as a result of which a chord remains unchanged. Lewin and Hyer are of course aware of this, and consequently introduce the category (I), or 'identity'(IDENT. in Lewin's terms): for example, $(C,+)(I)=(C,+)$.[31] All the remaining transformations are measured in relation to this: (D), (L) and (P) are meaningful insomuch as they involve one further step around the network than (I). And here we become entangled in a contradiction. In keeping with its mathematical ambition, the neo-Riemannian vocabulary posits (I) as another type of transformation; in effect, the transformation under which a triad remains untransformed. But how is this possible? How can non-transformation be categorised as

---

[30] And this is leaving aside the fact that the neo-Riemannian model has nothing to say about chord inversion, or about distinctions between melodic consonance and dissonance and their attendant issues of voice leading. Kopp's broadening of the definition of tonic identity to include common-tone relationships to an extent alleviates these difficulties, since it provides a means of including symmetrical divisions of the octave within a notion of tonic centricity. For a penetrating critique of neo-Riemannian theory from a Schenkerian perspective, see John Rothgeb, Review of Eytan Agmon, 'Functional Harmony Revisited', *Music Theory Online* 2 (2002).

[31] See Hyer, 'Reimag(in)ing Riemann', pp. 114–25.

a class of transformation, stasis as a form of motion? (I), in other words, is antithetically distinct from the other categories; but the model demands that it should be considered categorically equivalent, that is to say, that it should fall within the same class of phenomena.

This problem could be alleviated by redefining identity dialectically, as the antithesis of transformation: (I) defines identity; (D), (L), (R) and (P) are classes of non-identity, or difference. Yet acceptance of (I) as antithetical to (D), (L), (R), (P) and their combinations amounts to a readmission of chord identity as a distinct phenomenon. The various transformations act upon chord identity, but identity is not somehow also defined as a class of transformation. Once this is accepted, however, the hierarchical properties of tonality flood back into the system. (I) defines the triad itself; the transformations account for the relationships between triads. Therefore (I) is really no different from (T), or the tonic. And if (T) is necessarily regarded as a point of orientation against which relationships are antithetically measured, it must be hierarchically distinct from the triads produced under transformation.

A comprehensive response to these problems would comprise nothing less than a wholesale revision of the common-practice theory of nineteenth-century chromatic harmony, a project clearly exceeding the scope of this chapter.[32] More tentatively, the analytical perspective from which we view the above example from the Seventh Symphony could be shifted in order to accommodate some of these concerns.

First of all, it is plainly not the case that this music abandons any concept of a general point of tonal orientation. Excluding, for the moment, the third variant, which makes most extensive reference to eighteenth-century practices, some triads in the group nevertheless stand out from the network as a result of three related factors: frequency of recurrence; location at hypermetrical structural downbeats; articulation of decisive thematic events, usually the inception of a statement or variant of the second theme. Primarily, the statement, the second and fourth variants, and the transition to the third group all begin with B major triads, which gain emphasis because they

---

[32] Such a consideration would of course have to broach a substantial body of literature in addition to the neo-Riemannian perspective, including Gregory Proctor, *The Technical Basis of Nineteenth-Century Chromatic Tonality* (Ph.D. dissertation, Princeton University, 1978), Robert Bailey, 'The Structure of *The Ring* and Its Evolution', *Nineteenth-Century Music* 1 (1977), pp. 48–61 and the large body of literature that has grown up in response to the ideas of Bailey and Proctor, for example the essays collected in William Kinderman and Harald Krebs, eds., *The Second Practice of Nineteenth-Century Tonality*. For an extended elaboration of the ideas advanced in this brief analysis, see Horton, *Towards a Theory of Nineteenth-Century Tonality*.

each initiate thematic events and articulate significant hypermetrical junctures. These recurrences are not contextually indifferent; on the contrary,
a crucial feature of the group is the gradual revision of how (B,+) should
be contextually understood. In bar 51, its status is highly ambiguous. It is
preceded, in bars 49 and 50, by an augmented-sixth chord, which on the
larger scale reinforces the function of B major as the dominant of E.[33] The
immediate application of (P) and (L) in bars 52 and 53, however, does
not permit this function to settle. When (B,+) returns at the beginning of
variant 2, it has tentatively acquired a tonic function: it is now preceded
by an, albeit brief, augmented-sixth chord on G, and the application of
(P) that originally defined the first two bars of 'a' is absent. The tonic status of (B,+) is again inferred at the start of the fourth variant. (P) is once
more extracted from 'a', which is now additionally embellished by passing
dominant harmony. Finally, the transition to the third group essentially
comprises an expanded V(6-4)–V(5-3)–I cadence in B, the resolution at
bar 123 admittedly underplayed through the substitution of the parallel
minor.

In effect, the group is underpinned by the gradual revelation of B's tonic
status. This is not a result of prolongation in the Schenkerian sense, but of
a kind of directed evolution of tonal identity: the strategic disposition and
reinterpretation of a chord within a network, such that it accrues characteristics that change its functional identity. This process is not reflected, at
every stage, in the chord-to-chord detail of the network. There is no consistent, reflexive relationship of foreground and background of the sort posited
by Schenker. Instead, a gap opens up between the harmonic detail of the
music, which deploys practices that extend beyond the simple reinforce-
ment of cadential harmony, and an encompassing process of constructing a
tonic by articulating its evolving identity at key points within the network.
The result is not an abandonment of structural depth or hierarchical chord
function as analytically germane, but a change in the relationship between
foreground and background. The putatively organic formulation of this
relationship in classical practice gives way to a dichotomous formulation.
Viewed diachronically, the proliferation of symmetrical progressions renders impossible the maintenance of a hierarchical reading that considers all
chord relationships as reflective of a cadentially projected functional identity. Viewed synoptically, deep-structural properties reassert themselves in
the form of conceptually related apices or articulated events, the relationship
of which is only dependent upon the intervening material insomuch as it

---

[33] The augmented sixth is considered from a neo-Riemannian point of view in Kopp,
*Chromatic Transformations in Nineteenth-Century Music*, pp. 180–1.

supplies the network within which the moments of functional identity are suspended.

This perception does not render the transformational model redundant; it simply construes it as one half of a dualism that does not describe the relationship of major and minor functions or inverse transformational relationships, but the relationship of foreground and deep structure. The former becomes a harmonic field, defined by the specific distribution of types of progression; the latter maintains tonic identity, but only through the articulation of specific points within the field. It is furthermore possible to group the types of progression that constitute the field into broader categories. There is, for example, an essential difference between the triadic applications of (PR) that generate the chromatic continuation in bars 54 to 59 and the pivotal use of dominant-seventh and augmented-sixth chords in bars 67 to 69. The former, as part of a generalised interval system, constitute transposition operations. The latter treat dissonance pivotally, and are therefore not concerned with motion around a generalised interval system, but with the linking of triads via the parsimonious resolution of dissonant pitches. Transposition operations, in short, tend to involve triadic motion within hexatonic, octatonic or other symmetrical systems; pivotal resolution of dissonance enables the linkage of systems. The dissonances thus employed might, of course, themselves derive from symmetrical modal resources: diminished, half-diminished and dominant sevenths can, for example, all be traced to octatonic origins. Crucially, however, they are not necessarily derived from the same systems as the triads they connect. The diatonic materials stand within a third category, as representatives of an asymmetrical system and of a cadential harmonic context. A fourth category is also possible, of which Bruckner makes little use in this passage. Chromatic triadic relationships might be enabled not only by the pivotal deployment of dissonance, but also by the reinterpretation of functionally diatonic progressions to produce chromatic relationships. For instance, the progression $(B,-)(G,+)(C,+)$ exploits the dual functional identity of $(G,+)$ – as VI of $(B,-)$ and V of $(C,+)$ – to relate two triads a semitone apart.

A categorisation of background structures is also possible, defined not purely as cadential voice-leading models in the Schenkerian sense, but more broadly as possible tonal strategies arising from the chromaticised modal environment. This might involve the kind of implication–realisation model, to use Eugene Narmour's term, observed in the present example, or it might entail symmetrical division of the octave, in which case the hexatonic and octatonic systems of transposition operation are projected at the background, and Kopp's notion of common-tone tonality comes into play.[34] It might, in addition, comprise the cadential structures posited by Schenker, although by the late nineteenth century they have become a subset of a much-expanded system. It could also embrace Robert Bailey's concept of the double-tonic complex, as a background structure expressing two competing tonic orientations, and the notion of directional tonality, in which case we observe a progression from one possible background to another.

These ideas are applied to the second group in Example 4.5. The neo-Riemannian labels are now additionally grouped according to their membership of the above categories of progression, and the gradual realisation of the tonic status of (B,+) is represented in the deep structure by a beamed arrow. The foreground is now defined as a harmonic field, comprising a specific distribution and interaction of the four categories. The division into statement and variants demarcates changes in the distribution of categories, and therefore indicates a segmentation of the field into smaller units, where each unit comprises a specific harmonisation of 'a' and 'b'. The analysis also reveals a variety of voice-leading phenomena that are crucial to the structure, but which the neo-Riemannian perspective does not detect. In particular, it shows that chords articulated at the background are frequently the termination point for medium-range linear patterns. This is most clearly evinced in the second variant, the whole of which is underpinned by a chromatic descent from F sharp to C in the bass. C, in turn, forms a neighbour-note to the root-position B major triad at the start of the fourth variant. This develops out of an internal property of 'b' in the statement, the voice leading of which is guided by a linear chromatic descent from F in bar 54 to D flat in bar 59, and similarly by a descent from E to B in bars 60 to 68.

## Tonal strategy

The model developed above permits the analysis of a concept of tonal strategy that is common to the symphonies at least from the Fourth onwards, and which has been broached in passing in Chapters 1 and 3, but which has thus far escaped investigation as a general Brucknerian device. This is the embedding of chromatic properties within the first theme that come to control aspects of tonal structure across the symphony. This technique has three prominent formal effects. Primarily, theme groups do not unambiguously prolong a given key; instead, they expose a harmonic field, or 'dissonant

---

[34] See Eugene Narmour, *Beyond Schenkerism: The Need for Alternatives in Music Theory* (Chicago, 1977), and more recently *The Analysis and Cognition of Basic Melodic Structures: The Implication-Realization Model* (Chicago, 1990).

Example 4.5  Seventh Symphony, first movement

Second theme in exposition-analysis showing field structure, tonicisation of B and voice-leading properties

Example 4.5 (*cont.*)

Example 4.5  (*cont.*)

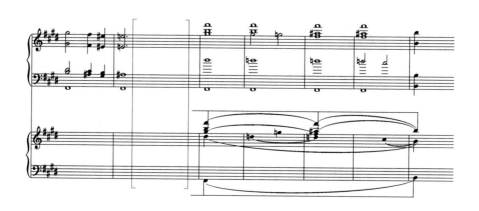

Example 4.6  Fourth Symphony, first movement, first theme

complex' as Korstvedt describes it, in precisely the sense suggested above, which comes to define the group within the form.[35] Consequently, non-tonic areas, for example the second-theme group in the exposition, do not simply introduce a tonal polarity opposing the tonic, but refer to a polarisation that is already present within the first group. On the largest scale, the tonal strategy will thus take on characteristics of a 'double-tonic' structure: it will move between overlaid tonal structures, frequently the ultimate tonic and a chromatically related counter-structure, to borrow Christopher Wintle's term.[36]

In the Fourth Symphony, the dissonant counter-structure is anticipated by the 5̂–flat-6̂–5̂ neighbour-note figure characterising the first theme of the first movement, given as motive 'a' in Example 4.6. This inflection becomes significant at various levels of structure. In the first place, as Laufer observes, 'a' reappears in various guises as a middleground motive in the Schenkerian sense.[37] An instance of this is given in Example 4.7, which provides a reduction of the first-theme group as far as the transition, bars 1–51. If we trace the progress of the upper voice across this passage, we see that 'a' frames the structure as a whole, via a process of registral transfer. Second,

[35] See Benjamin Korstvedt, '"Harmonic Daring" and Symphonic Design in the Sixth Symphony: An Essay in Historical Musical Analysis', in *Perspectives in Anton Bruckner*, pp. 185–205.

[36] The term 'double-tonic complex' is introduced by Bailey in his analysis of the *Tristan* Prelude. See 'An Analysis of the Sketches and Drafts', in Robert Bailey, ed., *Tristan und Isolde: Prelude and Transfiguration* (New York, 1985), pp. 113–46. Wintle's concept of the counter-structure is developed in 'Kontra Schenker: "Largo e Mesto" from Beethoven's Op. 10 no. 3', *Music Analysis* 4 (1985), pp. 145–82, and see also 'The Sceptred Pall: Brahms' Progressive Harmony', in *Brahms 2: Biographical, Documentary and Analytical Studies* (Cambridge, 1987), pp. 197–222.

[37] See 'Continuity in the Fourth Symphony (First Movement)'.

Example 4.7  Fourth Symphony, first movement

Bars 1–51

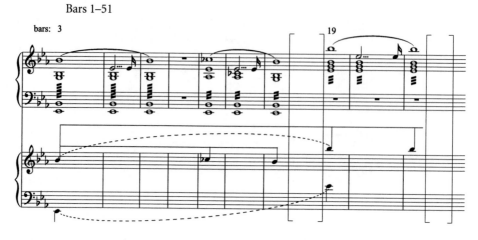

Example 4.8  Fourth Symphony, first movement

Bars 51–71

'a' almost immediately starts to generate local harmonic diversions. Bars
1 to 51 divide into two sections, the second being an extended variant of
the first. Harmonically, the second section is distinguished from the first
by the introduction of digressions that are either interpolated relations of a
putative counter-tonic C flat, or else exploit the neighbour-note associated
with 'a' to produce chromatic shifts.

Third, 'a' generates passing tonal events, and therefore inflects the middleground bass progression. The first instance of this occurs in the transition
from first to second themes in the exposition. As Example 4.8 demonstrates,
the modulation from I to V of V is bisected by a passing tonicisation of C flat.
Inflection of the bass progression with either complete or incomplete forms

Example 4.9 Fourth Symphony, first movement

Expansion of 'a', bars 469–86

of 'a' is a consistent feature of the articulation of structural downbeats within the movement. An instance of this is given in Example 4.9, which shows the transition from second to closing themes in the recapitulation. Here, C flat is temporarily tonicised, before being reinterpreted as a neighbour-note inflection underpinning the preparatory dominant in bars 479 to 485.

Fourth, 'a' is instrumental in guiding tonal structure at a deeper level. The synopsis of the exposition in Example 4.10 reveals that the embedding of D flat as the key of the second theme between V of V at the end of the first group and V at the start of the third arises from a large-scale projection of 'a': the D flat bass-note is an upper neighbour-note to degree $\hat{5}$ of F, and

Example 4.10  Fourth Symphony, first movement

Exposition – reduction

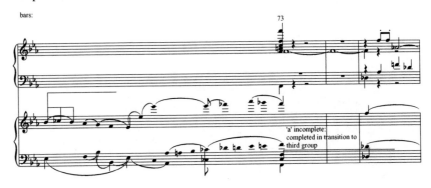

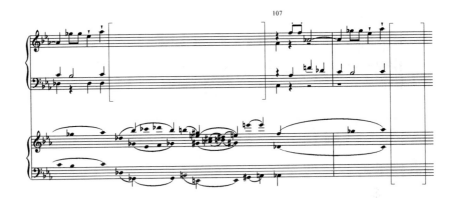

Example 4.10 (*cont.*)

Example 4.11 Fourth Symphony, first movement

Recapitulation – transition, second group and start of third group

effectively resolves as such in the dominant preparation of B flat in bars
115 to 118. Transposition of this progression in the recapitulation so that it
proceeds from E flat to B major has the effect of reintroducing 'a' at pitch:
the second theme now enharmonically tonicises the dissonant C flat of the
first theme, and the bass progression thus reinterprets C flat as a bass adjunct
to $\hat{5}$ (see Example 4.11). The coda introduces a second transposition of the
neighbour-note, demonstrated in Example 4.12. Since it begins in E major,

Example 4.12 Fourth Symphony, first movement

Coda

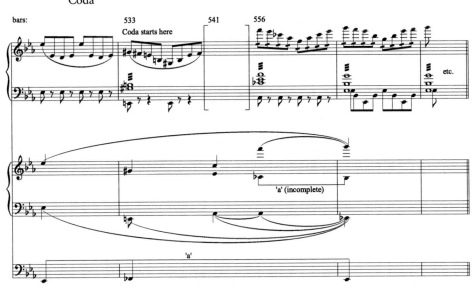

and is immediately preceded by E flat, the bass motion of the coda prolongs a large-scale 1–flat-$\hat{2}$–$\hat{1}$ figure.

In this way, C flat is not influential by itself, but as the centre of a network of tonal relationships collectively opposing the tonic and its relations. It is precisely this property that impedes the establishment of an *Ursatz*: because tonal structure is driven by the competition between chromatically related tonal polarities, rather than the simple prolongation in time of a cadential formula, the task of the closing cadence is not to confirm the structural force of the dominant, but to subsume elements of the counter-structure into the tonic *Klang*. This is what happens at the end of the movement. The final progression subordinates C flat to E flat by treating it as a minor inflection within a plagal cadence; the dominant is avoided because it affords no such opportunity. The choice of E flat minor as the central key of the development is also instructive in this regard. The minor modality brings both the tonic and the counter-structure within the ambit of the same *Stufe*; the movement pivots at its centre around a tonal event that straddles the competing tonal complexes.

Lastly, the dissonant complex becomes an issue across the symphony. Thus in the second movement, the governing C minor tonality is usurped by C flat at various levels of structure. As Example 4.13 shows, C flat forms a goal of modulation within the first theme, and recurs at key structural downbeats in the development and coda. The governing C minor tonality produces

Example 4.13  Fourth Symphony, second movement

Structural applications of 'a'

Example 4.13  (*cont.*)

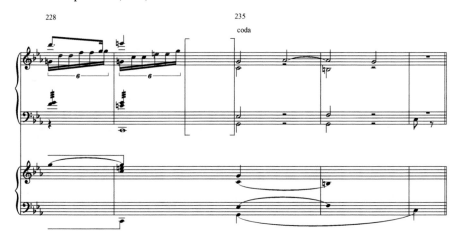

an inversion of the neighbour-note figure: $\hat{1}$–flat-$\hat{1}$–$\hat{1}$ replaces $\hat{5}$–flat-$\hat{6}$–$\hat{5}$. A transposed form of the figure is similarly influential in the Scherzo: again, the music shifts between relations of the tonic B flat and a flat-VI counter-structure. As Example 4.14 makes clear, the A section embeds a counter-structure centred around G flat/d flat within an overall progression from I to V. The music returns immediately to G flat at the start of the B section, and variation of A such that it concludes in the tonic in the reprise eliminates the original D flat inflections, leaving a clear I–flat-VI–I as governing bass progression. This is reproduced on a larger scale in the relationship between the Scherzo and the Trio: the Scherzo is in B flat, the Trio is in G flat. More remarkably, the tonal structure of the Trio encapsulates the G flat–B flat relationship in reversed tonal circumstances: the A section modulates from G flat to B flat, and before the reprise the B section traces the same progression on a larger scale (see Example 4.15).

The conflict of E flat and C flat is composed out extensively in the Finale. Again, C flat is introduced within the first theme, as Example 4.16 shows. The flat-VI relation recurs in transposed form in the third-theme group, in which G flat inflections are embedded within a prolongation of B flat. The recapitulation then conflates all the chromatic neighbour-notes arising from the C flat counter-structure into a single formal region. The second group enharmonically tonicises G flat as F sharp, and passes through E (enharmonic F flat) and D flat before the transition to the coda reinstalls C flat as a bass neighbour-note around V of E flat. The coda then sets up the E flat–C flat alternation as a governing bass progression, and at the end a bass descent from C flat culminates in a huge phrygian cadence through F flat onto the tonic (the coda is summarised in Example 4.17). Closure is

Example 4.14  Fourth Symphony, Scherzo

Structural applications of 'a'

Example 4.15  Fourth Symphony, Trio

Structural applications of 'a'

Example 4.16 Fourth Symphony, Finale

Elements of 'a' in first theme

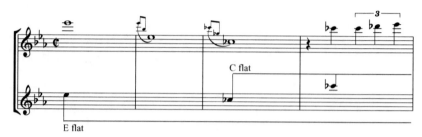

Example 4.17 Fourth Symphony, Finale

Coda

achieved precisely because the dissonant neighbour-note has finally been allowed to control the cadential structure, a resolution that would not be possible in the environment of a perfect cadence, and which has not been effected at any prior point in the form.

In later works, the dissonant complex in the first theme is introduced as a harmonic event rather than a voice-leading inflection. In the Fifth Symphony, the major–minor modal mixture engendered in the first theme of the first movement (Example 4.18) generates a move to G flat that subsequently gives rise to a complex of tonal relations around flat-VI opposing the tonic B flat and its near relations. The structure is complicated further in this instance by the addition of a third tonal polarity, D minor, as the key

Example 4.18  Fourth Symphony, first movement

Allegro, first theme

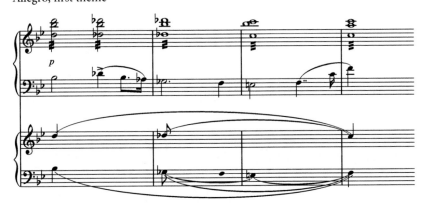

of the Adagio and Scherzo.[38] In a manoeuvre that owes something to the
first movement of Schubert's Ninth Symphony, these three polarities are all
either stated or implied in the symphony's introduction: as Example 4.19
makes clear, the opening contrapuntal passage introduces B flat and also
G flat as a bass neighbour-note inflection around V; the arpeggiated figure
at bar 15 introduces the chord of G flat; the ensuing brass chorale in bars
18–21 introduces D. In this way, the tutti restatement of the chorale in A
that immediately precedes the Allegro can be understood as a large-scale
dominant, left unresolved until the tonicisation of D minor in the second
and third movements.

The Finale accommodates these issues by reinterpreting them as part of
a contrapuntal complex, in which context the process of resolution involves
conflating the opposed tonal orientations of distinct fugue subjects through
contrapuntal combination (the form is a conflation of double fugue and
sonata). Thus the subject comprising the first theme (Example 4.20) inflects
a prolonged B flat with the neighbour-note C flat, whereas the development
fugue subject that eventually becomes the first theme's counter-subject initially treats G flat as a tonic, moving to F only at the subject's conclusion.
The process of combining the two subjects, begun in the tonic at bar 270
and developed thoroughly before being stated definitively at the recapitulation in bar 374, contains the dissonant start of the second subject within
the enclosed tonal context of the first. The two subjects therefore represent the polarities conflated into the first theme of the first movement. This

[38] The inner movements are also related by common thematic material: the Scherzo
starts with an accelerated version of the accompaniment that opens the Adagio, and
the theme introduced from bar 3 of the Scherzo fills in by diminution the melodic
contour of the Adagio's first theme.

Example 4.19 Fifth Symphony, first movement

Harmonic synopsis of introduction

is made even more explicit in the recapitulation of the third group, where Bruckner introduces the first theme of the first movement in counterpoint with the first subject of the Finale. The coda, summarised in Example 4.21, then restates the G flat/C flat counter-structure within an overall prolongation of the tonic. The polarisation is still articulated by the respective subjects: the coda opens with an augmentation of the start of the first subject in the bass; the first gestural goal of the coda is the entry of the second subject as chorale in C flat major at bar 583, restated on G flat from bar 591. A thematic feature of the closing bars emphasises the synthetic character of the coda: versions of the *Hauptmotiven* of the first themes from first and last movements are combined within a chord of the tonic, and therefore drained of the dissonant characteristics that had proved structurally potent.

Example 4.20  Fifth Symphony, Finale

Fugue subjects – combinations and tonal properties

Example 4.21  Fifth Symphony, Finale

Coda

A similar strategy is traced by Benjamin Korstvedt in the Sixth Symphony. Here, two factors predominate in the work's opening theme. First, its tonality is ambiguous; intimation of the tonic A is quickly compromised by the introduction of elements suggestive of D minor. Second, the theme as a whole comprises a harmonic field governed principally by chromatic-third relationships, rather than the prolongation of an overall tonic. Attempts to rid the theme of its subdominant inflection constitute a basic process in this movement. The ambiguity it creates persists until the final plagal cadence, which forces D minor into a cadential context establishing A as tonic. The overlaying of tonic major and subdominant minor also pervades the slow movement, and reappears in the Finale. In the latter, the transposition of the main theme from A minor to D minor at bar 19, and especially the B flat neighbour-notes in the bass in bars 27 and 28, inflect the A major tutti from bar 29 with a dominant character that is not entirely dispelled until the coda.

This technique is extensively deployed in the Eighth Symphony.[39] Again, Bruckner compresses a basic tonal opposition into the first theme of the first movement, and the result, more transparently than in any of the previous examples, is a first-theme group comprising a harmonic field in which the tonic emerges as a conflicted point of orientation rather than an encompassing premise. The influence of the D flat/B flat minor inflection in the first theme is extensive, and I restrict consideration here to some of its most striking manifestations. Its formal consequences in the first movement, as appraised in Example 4.22, are profoundly negative. At the point of thematic recapitulation, the underlying D flat/C duality is expanded rather than resolved. Because the central tonal opposition is present within the first theme, its recurrence reproduces a structural problem, rather than enabling its resolution. The result is a structural collapse. C minor is attained only over a $^6_4$ chord, and the structure of the first theme is only gradually regained, and moreover in a dissonant context. At the end of the movement, the conflict between C minor and the D flat counter-structure collides without satisfactory resolution. In the climactic progression in bars 381 to 385 the chord preceding the culminatory $i^6_4$ in C minor has a function in the context of either tonal polarity, since it could be interpreted either as V7 in D flat or

---

[39] All references are to the 1890 version, in the edition prepared by Leopold Nowak; see *Anton Bruckner: Sämtliche Werke, Band VIII/2. VIII Symphonie C-Moll. Fassung von 1890* (Vienna, 1955). This issue is relevant to the 1887 and 1890 versions, although the revision clearly affects its deployment. The most striking alteration is perhaps the end of the first movement. In the 1887 version, the movement concludes with a fortissimo tutti cadence built out of the phrygian inflection of the main theme.

Example 4.22  Eighth Symphony, first movement

Tonal properties of the first theme and their structural consequences

Example 4.22 (*cont.*)

tonal reprise

3. Third group and coda, bars 377–395

diminished third chord or
V6-4-2 of D flat (G flat enharmonically respelled)

Example 4.22 (cont.)

a diminished third in C minor. The coda compounds the instability attending this cadence, reorientating C as V of F minor.

In the Scherzo, both the A and A1 sections are conceived as harmonic fields vacillating between C minor and relations of the counter-structure centred around D flat, as Example 4.23 reveals. Strikingly, the tonal structure of this movement is in effect pulled inside-out: the most stable passage of tonic harmony occurs in the B section before the reprise, and the retransition in bars 127 to 134 prepares the dissonant complex rather than the tonic, via the build-up of a double-tonic sonority conflating elements of C minor, D flat major and B flat minor. This sense of structural inversion is taken further in the Adagio. The tonic is now D flat major, and C is present in the first theme as a dissonant inflection. In the same way, many of the structural tonal goals of the movement relocate relations of C within the context of D flat; so for example the *Höhepunkt* of the movement occurs on E flat, and its aftermath settles eventually on C major.

These matters are again worked out thoroughly in the Finale. The first theme, given in Example 4.24, lays out in progression the principal relations of both polarities. The process of resolution works by making C the goal of this progression in the recapitulation, and its encompassing tonic in the coda. In a move that harks back to the Finale of the Fifth Symphony, here there is also a process of draining the first theme from the first movement of its dissonant properties, and thus of rendering it structurally stable. In the preparation for the coda, it appears climactically over a dominant pedal, and finally in the closing bars it is present in a form arpeggiating a C major triad, and in combination with similarly 'diatonicised' forms of the themes from the other movements (see Example 4.25).

Lastly, an expansive form of the technique occurs in the first movement of the Ninth Symphony. As Grunsky quite rightly observed, the progression from D minor to C flat and E flat in the first twenty-six bars plays an

Example 4.23  Eighth Symphony, Scherzo

Reduction

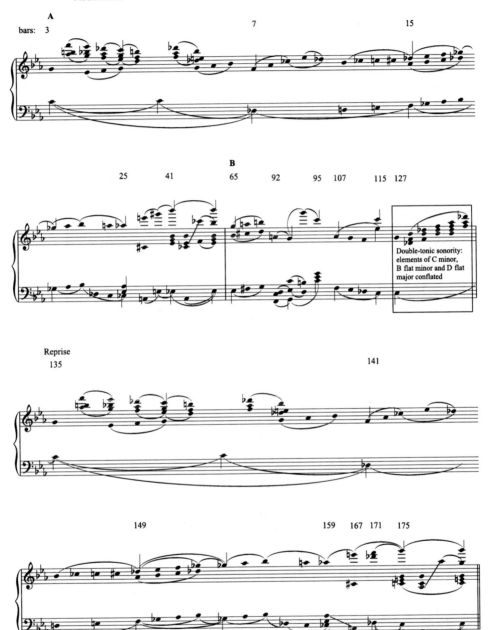

Example 4.24  Eighth Symphony, Finale

First theme

Example 4.25 Eighth Symphony, Finale

Culmination of third group reprise and coda

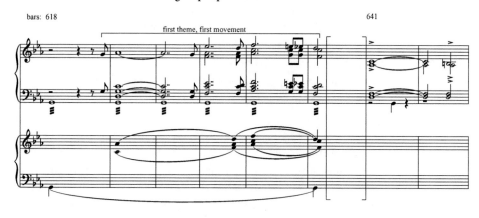

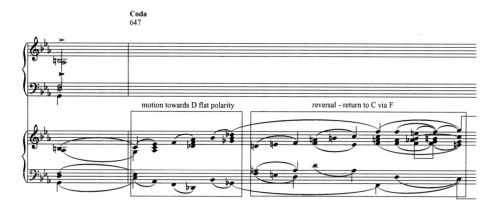

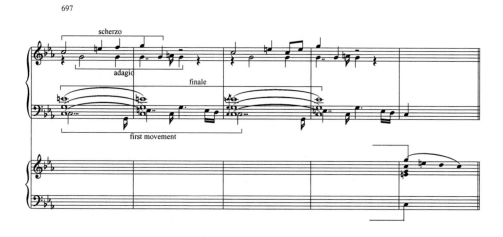

influential role in the movement's tonal strategy. As the analysis in Chapter 3 has already shown, motion between these two polarities via the intervention of E flat is a basic organising principle in this movement. Example 3.2 has identified this with respect to the first-theme group and third-theme group in the exposition, the third-theme group in the recapitulation and the coda. In each case, the tonal framework for the material derives from the initial D minor/C flat opposition. There are two main ways in which these relationships are distributed. In the first group and coda, elements of the C flat polarity are circumscribed by the tonic. In both forms of the third group, C flat and its relations are embedded within a directed tonal scheme. For the exposition form, this scheme is grounded in the tonic polarity, proceeding from d to F. The recapitulation form, in contrast, begins in B minor, and the directed scheme thus traces a progression from the enharmonic parallel of C flat to d. Although the reprise of the third group seems more dissonant than its exposition counterpart, in a sense it engenders an act of resolution. For the first time in the movement, C flat constitutes a point of tonal departure, and D minor behaves as a goal, which, once attained, is sustained.

Although Korstvedt has characterised these practices as a response to the problem of importing Wagnerian harmony into a symphonic context, they may have earlier precursors, and more general motivations. Three Beethovenian precedents spring readily to mind. In the first movement of the Sonata Op. 31, no. 1 in G, B major appears as the initial key of the second group, and the expected I–V relationship is conflated into the first theme. A more condensed form of the same procedure happens in the first movement of the 'Waldstein' Sonata, Op. 53. Tonicisation of E major as the key of the second group again leads Beethoven to compress the I–V relationship that normally spans the exposition into the first theme. In the opening of the 'Appassionata' Sonata, Op. 57, the F–G flat semitonal motion in bars 1 to 8 introduces a middleground progression that becomes influential both as a foreground motive and as part of the tonal strategy. In all cases, the result is an initial theme that expresses a progression rather than a stable prolongation. The balance of chromatic and diatonic elements in these examples takes two forms, both of which are also evident in Bruckner's music. Where a chromatic relationship obtains between first and second theme, the dissonant complex within the first theme is more diatonically conceived. Where the second theme tonicises a close relation of I, the dissonant complex expresses a more remote relationship.

Similar procedures can also be found in later music; indeed, the development of chromatic tonality renders inevitable the dissolution of prolongation as the unequivocal basis of thematic formal function. The concept of subject group as harmonic field is taken up, for example, in the outer movements of Schumann's Sonata, Op. 11 and Liszt's B minor Sonata. The first theme in the first movement of Brahms's G major Violin Sonata, Op. 78, encloses a progression to B major/E major within an overall prolongation of G, which proves influential at later points in the form, and the opening of the first movement of the C minor String Quartet, Op. 51, no. 1, embeds a dissonant complex around B flat minor within the context of C minor. All these examples respond to the same problem of how to incorporate the properties of an extended tonal system into the sonata design. Beethoven is certainly the source in this regard. Bruckner's practice is consequently not an isolated phenomenon, but a part of his reception of Beethoven that can be identified as a general practice in nineteenth-century music.

## Thematic analysis

Example 4.26 shows the opening theme group of the Eighth Symphony. This passage is of particular interest, since it exemplifies simultaneously the ideas on Bruckner's thematic technique of Korte, Kurth and Dahlhaus. The passage splits unambiguously into two sentence structures after Schoenberg's model, the second being a texturally expanded variant of the first. Thus bars 1 to 9 and 23 to 32 each constitute a statement and complementary repetition, bars 10 to 17 and 33 to 40 are both elaborations, and liquidation occurs in 18 to 22 and 40 to 43. In the second sentence, the liquidation is extended to accommodate the transition to the second group.

The first sentence provides the basic evidence for Korte's notion of motivic 'mutation'.[40] This process, which he represents in a fashion that is prescient of the semiological distribution of paradigms, is organised in a way that respects the divisions of the sentence structure. As Example 4.27 demonstrates, each stage in the process of thematic mutation corresponds to the discrete sections of the sentence, and the functions of these stages resemble those of the elements of a sentence as Schoenberg understood them.[41] The first stage states and variously restates the basic material; the second stage elaborates upon a maintained motivic characteristic of the first stage; the final stage liquidates a motivic residue of the process within a cadential context. Example 4.27 also traces the structure of the second sentence in this fashion. Korte, and more recently Dahlhaus and Korstvedt, considered this

---

[40] See Korte, *Bruckner und Brahms: Die spätromantische Lösung der autonomen Konzeption* (Tutzing, 1963), pp. 24–9.

[41] As for example in *Fundamentals of Musical Composition* (London, 1967), pp. 20–4 and 58–81.

Example 4.26  Eighth Symphony, first movement

First-theme group

process to involve the manipulation of pitch and interval content around a maintained rhythmic identity: rhythmic motivic characteristics provide a stable sub-structure around which pitch and interval are freely manipulated. This technique furnishes the evidence for Bruckner's departure from post-Beethovenian, and especially Brahmsian, norms, for which interval content is considered to be the basis of thematic identity. Thus, although the phrase structure and superficial outline of a Schoenbergian thematic

Example 4.26 (*cont.*)

technique are present, the mechanism of thematic process after the manner of Schoenbergian musical logic appears to have been up-ended.

On the face of it, this interpretation contrasts sharply with that of Kurth. Korte's concentration on the stage-by-stage alteration of an initial idea, the music's 'chaining structure' (*Kettenstruktur*) as he puts it, stands in opposition to the concept of dynamic unfolding stressed by Kurth.[42] Kurth's intention is not to deny the presence of a governing motivic logic or economy, but rather to locate these properties within strategies of intensification and the dynamic release of tension at various levels of structure. In the first sentence, he perceives the material to be organised around a single point of culmination, the dynamic and melodic climax of bars 17 and 18. For Kurth this moment, which corresponds to the beginning of the final stage of Korte's mutation process, is the apex of an initial dynamic wave. The detachment, at this point, of the triplet figure from the dotted motive that starts the piece is emblematic of a transition from intensification to dissipation, underscored by the removal of the previously consistent tremolando accompaniment,

[42] See Korte, *Bruckner und Brahms*, p. 27.

Example 4.27  Eighth Symphony, first movement

First-theme group – Korte's mutation process, with Schoenbergian categories overlaid

which Kurth described as 'a symbol of the growth impulse'.[43] At the same time, Kurth also considered this event to initiate a 'retrogression', since it leads, at the beginning of the second sentence at bar 23, to a reprise of the opening material in a texturally and dynamically expanded form. On the larger scale the process of intensification is here reinforced, and culminates more forcefully at the climax in bars 40 to 43, leading in turn to 'a much longer attenuative retrogression' that only really subsides with the entry of the second subject. As a result, Kurth viewed the whole group as 'an enormous double wave, the first constituent wave . . . being an antecedent, the second a consequent superseding the first'.[44] And this, of course, must also be located within the structure of the whole movement, in which context it functions altogether as an initial dynamic gesture. In short, Kurth's analysis is teleological, whereas Korte's is additive.

In fact these readings are far from incompatible. Korte's mutation process could be reinterpreted as the motivic means by which Kurth's wave forms are constructed, provided we are willing to abandon Korte's insistence on the 'self-contained' character of the initial motivic cell; the goal-directed process perceived by Kurth only opposes Korte's 'chaining' technique because the latter insists on a discrete status for the initial material. Within each sentence, the mutation process is directed towards the beginning of the liquidation, which in each case is also the apex of the wave in Kurth's analysis. The apex is articulated by a decisive thematic reorientation: detachment of the triplet figure from the initial *Hauptmotiv* lends the former the status of a distinct idea. On the whole, the group is defined by a conflict between the dynamic urge to transform the theme into its apex form, and the antithetical pull towards restatement of the opening, which asserts itself at the start of the second sentence. The dynamic effect of the climactic second liquidation in bars 40 to 43 resides in the achievement of escaping the centripetal urge to return to the original form of the first theme. After this event, the transition retains the apex triplet figure, which subsequently forms an integral part of the second theme. At a larger level of structure, as Kurth shrewdly observed, the developmental process in the first group is directed towards the start of the second group, in which context the whole mutation process becomes a 'pre-developmental' preparation of the second theme.

In effect, both Kurth and Korte approach the same idea from antithetical directions: they both describe a process of motivic *becoming*, but whereas Kurth perceived the form to hinge on the points of dissipation, the 'apices',

---

[43] See Lee A. Rothfarb, trans. and ed., *Ernst Kurth: Selected Writings* (Cambridge, 1991), p. 209.

[44] Ibid., p. 205.

before which prior events appear as preparatory, Korte emphasised the evolution of new ideas out of discrete earlier motivic forms. More broadly, it is the category of becoming itself that is fundamental to this passage. The theme group is in this way defined not by the exposition of ideas that are subsequently to be developed, but by the exposition of a concept of thematic process based on the teleological transformation of themes towards a defining event, the apex. The idea that these processes retain rhythm and vary pitch and interval is not entirely adequate in this context. Rather, pitch and interval content remain invariant at structural apices, and are freely varied during processes of mutation or intensification. In each liquidation, the duplet–triplet figure is stated and repeated with its pitch and interval character intact, and this is moreover held invariant between apices.

Superficially, the structure of the second-theme group resembles that of the first: both are bipartite structures, in which the start of the second part is marked by a reprise of the group's opening. Each part again conforms broadly to the sentence pattern, albeit more loosely than in the first group. Thus in the first part bars 51 to 58 comprise statement and complementary repetition, bars 59 to 66 the elaboration and 67 to 72 the cadential liquidation, and in the second part statement and complementary repetition appear in bars 73 to 80, the elaboration in 81 to 84 and the liquidation, which in turn leads to the transition to the closing theme, in bars 85 to 88. The underlying motivic process fits less comfortably into the model proposed by Korte. In the first place, there is a contrapuntal elaboration of material from bar 63, which in effect splits the developmental process of the first section in two, as shown in Example 4.28. Although the 'chaining' strategy can be followed in the upper part, the bass-line introduces an inverted variant of the subject in counterpoint with this process, such that the mutation of the theme sets off in two simultaneous directions. Furthermore, the division into retained rhythmic substrate and variable pitch and interval content is less convincing here. In bars 51 to 58 the process rather involves retention of the interval character of the first half of the theme, and free variation of its continuation. And although the material of bars 59 to 60 is evidently a free variant of bars 51 to 52, bars 59 and 66 deploy precisely the opposite technique: the interval pattern of this new variant is preserved, and its rhythmic character is changed.

Kurth's approach also requires qualification here. A wave pattern is again clearly visible: the first sentence builds to an apex at bar 69, and then dissipates towards the beginning of the second sentence at bar 73. This proves also to be the apex of the whole group: a less forceful climax occurs at bar 83, after which the motivic structure fragments, yielding to the transition preparing the closing group in bars 89 to 96. Yet characterisation of the

Example 4.28  Eighth Symphony, first movement

Second-theme group, excluding transition to third group

Sentence 1

Example 4.28  (*cont.*)

Sentence 2

group by means of the concept of teleological pre-development is problematic. The apex is constructed from a variant of the motive form introduced
in bar 59, and as such seems to be the consequence of development acting on
an initially stated *Grundgestalt*, an impression reinforced by the return of the
second theme in its original form at bar 73. The statement and restatement
of this motive articulates the structure of the group by presenting stable
forms of the theme which then generate distinct motivic processes. The stability of the original form is compounded by its tonal context: whereas the
tonality of the first subject is disrupted by an embedded chromaticism, the
second theme is grounded at the points of statement and restatement by a
root-position chord of G major. The apex of the group thus emerges as the
point of maximum distance from the stable thematic form, rather than as
an attempt to overcome an incipient instability.

In the development section, the conflict between these two forms of thematic process is intensified. Ostensibly, the first and second parts, bars 153 to
192 and 193 to 224, seem to be concerned with similar motivic procedures,
since in both parts the two themes are subjected to various contrapuntal
operations. Thus bars 153 to 192 employ augmentations and free inversions
of the first theme in sequence, whilst bars 193 to 224 are occupied with the
sequential treatment of the *Hauptmotiv* of the second theme in inversion,
combined from bar 204 with the anacrusic component of the first theme.
The functions of the two sections become distinct, however, when understood in relation to the exposition. The instability of the first theme in the
exposition lends the first part of the development the character of a new
stage in the process of pre-development, preparing the arrival of a putative
definitive form. On the other hand, the variants of the second theme relate to
a stable exposition form. The result is an exacerbation of the initial dialectic
of development and pre-development, rather than a simple succession of
new motive forms.

The climax initiated at bar 225, which overlaps with the point of thematic
(although not tonal) recapitulation, attempts a synthesis of this opposition.
The augmentation of the first theme in the bass supplies a potential definitive
form towards which the process of pre-development has been working, and
the simultaneous presence of a free augmentation of the second theme in the
upper strings and woodwind knits the antithetical themes together in such
a way as to suggest that a point of thematic overcoming has been reached.
This moment, however, turns out to be the beginning of another ascending
developmental sequence, culminating with the return of C minor at bar 249.
The fragmentary liquidation of motivic residues after this point emphasises
the categorical failure of bars 225 to 249 to effect a genuine synthesis, a
negation that is further underscored by the fragmentary character of the rest

of the recapitulation, to which I shall return below. In the closing section and coda, the absence of a definitive form for the first theme is starkly emphasised. The theme is reduced to its rhythm alone in the climactic passage of bars 368 to 390, and is successively broken up in the coda, until only a single motivic residue remains at the end.

Korte's mutation process is largely absent in the development. The manipulation of both first and second themes relies on the repetition, variation and combination of relatively discrete motive forms, rather than the evolution of one form out of another. Mutation plays a more substantial role in the recapitulation, with the return of the thematic structures of the exposition (first group from bar 279, second group from bar 311, third group from bar 341). These structures are however variously distorted or truncated, and the impression is again of a negation of their exposition counterparts. From this perspective, the movement unfolds a three-stage process: the setting up of types of mutation process in the exposition; isolation and manipulation of motive forms from these processes in the development; distortion of mutation processes in the recapitulation.

Again, these strategies are the mechanisms through which the broader Kurthian formal dynamic unfolds. Bars 153 to 249 comprise two successive waves, bars 153 to 192 and 193 to 249, the division corresponding to the shift from first- to second-theme material. The first major apex of the second wave occurs with the attempt to assert a stable form of the first theme and its combination with the second theme at bar 225, and the wave of course culminates with the return of C minor at bar 249. After this point, there is no 'attenuation' akin to that observed by Kurth at the end of the first group in the exposition, but the immediate initiation of a fresh wave. And since the mutation processes of the exposition are tied to their respective wave forms, the distortion of these processes in the recapitulation is part of a general recapitulatory revision of the wave forms of the exposition. This revision decisively emphasises the climax appended to the third group between bars 368 and 389, which functions as the culminating intensification of the entire movement, and which is followed by a dissipation, or attenuation, after which the dynamic momentum cannot be recovered. Underlying this structure is the attempted synthesis of the dialectic of development and pre-development set up in the exposition, and its subsequent negation.

## Issues in sonata form

The models of Bruckner's sonata practices established by Darcy and Jackson draw upon James Hepokoski's five principal categories of sonata deformation: the 'breakthrough deformation' or 'unforeseen inbreaking of a seemingly new . . . event in or at the close of the "development space"'; the 'introduction–coda frame'; the introduction of episodes within development space; the 'strophic/sonata hybrid'; the multi-movement form within a single movement.[45] Hepokoski considers these practices 'to have stemmed from key works of Berlioz, Mendelssohn, Schumann, Liszt and Wagner, although certain structures of Beethoven, Weber, Schubert and Chopin were by no means irrelevant'.[46] He also isolates five additional principles derived specifically from the symphonic models of Sibelius, which are more particularly concerned with material process: the content-based form or 'fantasia'; the 'rotational form' or 'multisectional strophe'; 'teleological genesis'; '*Klang* meditation'; and 'interrelation and fusion of movements'.[47]

Darcy adopts two of Hepokoski's categories as particularly germane to the Brucknerian context: teleological genesis and rotational form. He also provides three additional concepts – the 'rebirth paradigm', the 'alienated secondary theme zone' and the 'non-resolving recapitulation' – and fuses two of Hepokoski's ideas in order to characterise the Brucknerian coda, creating the concept of '*Klang* as *telos*'. These categories are located within the more general narrative context of a response to the 'redemption paradigm', which amounts to a redefinition of the Beethovenian 'struggle–victory' plot archetype. Darcy regards Bruckner's sonata deformations as negations of the demands of resolution imposed by this paradigm: 'Nearly all the sonata-form portions of Bruckner's first and last movements are constructed in such a way as to "fail" to solve the problems they pose. These "problems" usually stem from Bruckner's deformation of the so-called "redemption paradigm".'[48] The burden of resolution in Bruckner is almost always transferred to the coda, an area that Darcy considers to stand outside the action of the sonata form. In consequence, the moment of resolution becomes overtly transcendental: the coda 'must be understood as drawing its strength from *outside* the sonata form and, in a sense, must *transcend* that form in order to succeed'.[49] This has the additional effect of isolating, or 'alienating', the second-theme group. The *Gesangsperioden* tend to exhibit characteristics that indicate a 'suspension' of the sonata process, emphasising repetition or 'rotation' of material and non-tonic keys in both exposition and recapitulation forms.

Although these formal categories are plainly at work in Bruckner's symphonies, their status as deformations of a theoretical norm is questionable. In the first place, the notion of theory as cause and practice as effect runs

---

[45] *Sibelius: Symphony no. 5*, pp. 6–7.    [46] See ibid., p. 5.    [47] Ibid., pp. 19–30.
[48] 'Bruckner's Sonata Deformations', p. 258.    [49] Ibid., p. 259.

into difficulties of historical specificity. Bruckner's teacher Kitzler evidently took Ernst Friedrich Richter's *Die Grundzüge der musikalischen Formen und ihre Analyse* as a basic text, with minimal secondary input from Marx's *Die Lehre von der musikalischen Komposition*.[50] Assuming that Bruckner took any notice of these precedents when formulating his mature notion of sonata form, we nevertheless confront the problem that Richter's model differs in crucial aspects from that of Marx, as well as from the influential theories of Reicha and Czerny. Marx understood form as a product of dialectical tensions inherent in musical material, rather than simply as an architectural scheme. Sonata form is therefore a result, or effect, of content.[51] This notion is completely absent from Czerny's definition, which more straightforwardly traces the outline of the form and then establishes the function of its constituent parts. Richter diverges from Marx, and leans more clearly towards Reicha, in defining the sonata as a bipartite, rather than a tripartite structure.[52] At the same time, he reflects Marx's progression from 'musical idea' (*musikalische Gedanke*) to form via intermediate phrase structures, without Marx's expressly dialectical formulation.[53] Deformational theory therefore encounters the difficulty that there is no single, fixed definition around which distortions of the form might orientate themselves. At best, we would have to identify theoretical sources for each composer, and show how deformations relate specifically to these models, rather than to a generalised *Formenlehre* pattern. At worst, the *Formenlehre* model is pieced together as the average of various divergent theories, and therefore becomes an abstraction of an abstraction.

There is furthermore a significant gap between the theoretical sources against which deformation is measured, and the sources in compositional practice that Hepokoski cites. Given that the earliest example of a consensus model of sonata form is usually taken to be that of Marx's treatise of 1845–7, how is it possible that the main deformational procedures have their foundations in the music of Chopin, Mendelssohn and Schumann, and especially Beethoven, Weber, Schubert and Berlioz? Although some of the later sonata-type music of Mendelssohn, Berlioz, Schumann and Chopin is contemporary with Marx's work, it is scarcely credible to suggest that these composers either consciously or unconsciously designed their compositions as

---

[50] Ernst Friedrich Richter, *Die Grundzüge der musikalischen Formen und ihre Analyse* (Leipzig, 1852); A. B. Marx, *Die Lehre von der musikalischen Komposition* (Leipzig, 1837–47).

[51] On this matter, see Scott Burnham, 'The Role of Sonata Form in A. B. Marx's Theory of Form', *Journal of Music Theory* 33 (1989), pp. 247–72.

[52] See *Die Grundzüge der musikalischen Formen und ihre Analyse*, pp. 27–48.

[53] Ibid., p. 1.

distortions of Marx's theory. We could reorientate their music around earlier theories, for example Reicha's *Traité de haute composition musicale* of 1826, but the earliest sonata movements of Berlioz, Chopin and Mendelssohn, all of which contain apparently deformational procedures, predate even this text. Tracing the idea back to Beethoven and Schubert is even more tendentious; can we really assert that the variety of sonata structures in their music arises from the deformation of theoretical norms? If their practices are deformational at all, it is in response to the principles of the classical style itself, which both composers partly inhabited. The concept of deformation therefore rests on an incompatible duality: on the one hand, it responds to a vaguely defined theoretical norm; on the other hand, it is traced to the expansion and variation of classical precedents undertaken by Beethoven and Schubert.

The notion of deformation is part of a tendency that is endemic to our theoretical and analytical discourse about the nineteenth-century repertoire, which is a consistent reticence to read its structures as distinct stylistic, formal or systemic norms. Although the formal categories observed by Hepokoski predominate in the repertoire he cites to the virtual exclusion of the normative model, and although he admits them as 'norms within the first, active phase of liberal-bourgeois modernism', the possibility that these practices should be theorised as normative apart from the distortion of theoretical precedents is not pursued. Instead, we could understand deformational practices as part of a general process of post-Beethovenian diversification: it is not so much that nineteenth-century sonata practices fall within the shadow of perfected or theorised high-classical forms that they can only distort, but that the Beethovenian achievement enables a diversity of formal procedures that the relative homogeneity of the classical style constrains. This progression is of course aesthetic and social as well as formal. The increased plurality of practices within the generic remit of sonata design is a function of the liberating effects of the emergence of a radical concept of autonomy unconstrained by social function and the subordination to text, for which Beethoven's music came to be regarded as prototypical, together with the transition from the philosophical and aesthetic rationalism of the eighteenth century to the idealism of romantic aesthetics and post-Hegelian philosophy. Sonata procedures are reinvented to accommodate a fresh set of social, aesthetic and expressive demands: they are therefore not deformations, but rather reformations of the classical principle.

By these terms, what appears to be distortion is really the normative basis of practice; theory represents a parallel effort to codify the structures of the sources of influence acting on practice. Regardless of the extent to which theory feeds into composition (and generally this relationship is obscured by a morass of historical particularities), theory is not itself an index of practice, but another part of the esthesics of the Beethovenian symphony and its extra-musical contexts. Nineteenth-century symphonic forms are therefore in essence dialectical: they simultaneously acknowledge and supersede the Beethovenian model, whilst presenting the result as a synthetic whole that attempts to be more than the sum of its antithetical parts. The dialectic is the norm of its time; Hepokoski's deformations are its individual manifestations.

Bruckner's symphonic first movements from the First to the Ninth Symphonies attest to these points. Each movement contains practices that might in some sense be regarded as deformational, but which are both consistent in Bruckner's case, and also frequently present in the music of his contemporaries and predecessors. Casting the net more broadly than Darcy, these practices can be grouped into four basic categories: expansion, teleology, negation and discontinuity. The categories are not exclusive, but interact, such that one is often assisted by the application of another. Generally, they underpin Hepokoski's deformations; they are the cause, of which the types of deformation are the effect.

The most frequently noted example of expansion, which is already fully developed in the First Symphony, is the increased delineation of second group and closing section, to the extent that the closing section becomes a third group in itself. Here, Bruckner goes some way beyond the obvious precedents in the symphonies of Beethoven, Schubert, Mendelssohn and Schumann in terms of clarity and consistency of execution.[54] The means by which the third theme is made distinctive are of four types. In the First and Second Symphonies, the third group is prepared as a tonal and gestural goal by a cadential phrase that is also integral to the structure of the second group. In the Third, Fourth, Sixth and Seventh Symphonies, the two groups are connected by an appended, cumulative intensification. This type invokes the category of teleology: the third group is established as the outcome of motivic and harmonic intensification, which in turn forces a structural reorientation through which the first and second themes appear as preparatory. This practice is complicated in the Fourth and Sixth Symphonies by the harmonic relationship between the second group and the preparation of the third. In the former, the transition to the third theme resumes and resolves the dominant preparation of V interrupted at the end of the first group. In the latter, the gestural force of the arrival of the third theme is compromised by its harmonic function as an interrupted cadence. In both examples, teleology and discontinuity interact. The Fifth and Ninth Symphonies deploy

---

[54] I have in mind the first movements of Beethoven's Ninth Symphony, Schubert's Ninth Symphony and Mendelssohn's Third Symphony.

discontinuity without teleology: the second theme is liquidated, the texture dissolves into silence and the third theme is introduced in a new, unprepared tonality. In both examples, teleological intensification is reserved for the end of the third group. The Eighth Symphony combines elements of the previous two types at this point. The transition between second and third groups comprises a thematic liquidation that also prepares the tonality of the third theme, and the moment of teleological intensification is transferred to the end of the exposition in the same manner as the Fifth and Ninth Symphonies.

The concept of negation, which Darcy describes more specifically as 'sonata process failure', tends to involve a redeployment of teleology and discontinuity in the recapitulation, such that the expected continuity of tonal context and material presentation is disrupted. Negation is a feature of the first movements from the Fifth Symphony onwards. In the Fifth and Sixth Symphonies, this results from the location of the reprise of the first theme as the goal of the movement's most extensive intensification process thus far: a protracted dominant preparation in the Fifth; a false recapitulation and its rectification in the Sixth. The result in the former example is a fragmentation of the first group and an expansion of the teleological intensification in the third group. In the latter, the intensification preceding the third group is removed and replaced by liquidation and discontinuity: there is no tonal or gestural preparation of the third group at the end of the second, but a reduction of texture and repetition of a single motive, which is interrupted by the tutti, fortissimo third theme. The recapitulation in the first movement of the Seventh Symphony is even more extensively denuded of the points of intensification characterising the exposition. The first two apices of the exposition – the fortissimo form of the first theme in bars 25 to 40 and the dominant preparation of the third group – are removed. The conclusive passage of the reprised second group, bars 351 to 362, carries no preparatory function, and the third group begins over an interrupted cadence.

An even more emphatic example occurs in the first movement of the Eighth Symphony. The functions of development and recapitulation here overlap to their mutual detriment. The reprise at pitch of the first theme in augmentation in the bass constituting the gestural goal of the development at bar 226 is simultaneously a thematic recapitulation and part of an ongoing developmental process that presses towards the climactic recovery of the tonic C minor at bar 249. The return of the first theme can sustain neither a stable point of thematic return, being part of a continuous process of developmental intensification, nor a stable return to the tonic, being harmonically oblique and part of an ascending sequential progression.

Conversely, the return to the tonic cannot support a thematic reprise, since the necessity of tonic prolongation is compromised by the first theme's harmonic instability. The antithetical demands of thematic presentation and tonal stability provoke a negation of recapitulatory function.[55] In the space between this climax and the return of the second theme, bars 249 to 310, a structural gap opens up in which the expected first-group reprise is replaced by the sequential repetition of motivic residues. The phrase structure of the group is obliquely reassembled in bars 282 to 302, but this is undercut at bar 303 by a chromatic interruption leading to the second group. As with the Sixth and Seventh Symphonies, the relationship of second and third groups is now changed from one of preparation to discontinuity. The second group culminates on an unresolved diminished seventh, and the third group enters after a caesura. Bruckner again compensates for this disjunction by placing a more forceful teleological intensification at the end of the third group. In this instance, there is no attempt to balance this climax with a synthetic coda; as noted above, the movement ends with a profound structural fragmentation.

The Ninth Symphony, which is concerned in many ways with expanding the structural procedures presented in a relatively concise form in the first movement of the Eighth Symphony, takes the clash of recapitulatory and developmental functions a stage further. On the largest scale, the first movement plays out a conflict between bipartite and tripartite conceptions of sonata form. The second and third groups are reprised in varied but more or less complete forms, but the tonic return of the first group from bar 333 is again elided with the end of the development. In this instance, the recapitulated first-group material is not the initial subject, but the climactic subordinate theme from bar 63. Since the development has been concerned chiefly with the initial material of the first group, the whole of the development and recapitulation can be read as a single formal unit, consisting of a developmental expansion of the first group, and varied reprise of the second and third groups. The return of the tonic D minor at bar 333 is thus caught between the competing structural demands of development and reprise, between intensification and resolution. Bruckner's response to this problem once more turns on the distribution of teleological intensification and discontinuity. Like the Eighth Symphony, the restatement of first-group material at pitch is part of a chromatic sequence, which yields at bar 355 to a new passage of developmental intensification leading to the movement's most substantial climax to this point, over F minor, in bars 387 to 398. The subsequent relationship of second and third groups also resembles the

[55] Darcy describes this as 'a serious recapitulatory crisis'. See 'Bruckner's Sonata Deformations', p. 275.

strategy adopted in the first movement of the Eighth. The discontinuity between groups is exacerbated rather than resolved, and the intensification process at the end of the third group is concomitantly expanded.

As Darcy observes, negation of recapitulatory function transfers a burden of resolution onto the coda. In the Fifth, Sixth and Seventh Symphonies, the coda responds positively to these demands, supplying a cumulative intensification in the tonic major. In the Eighth Symphony, Bruckner adopts the opposite strategy, closing the first movement with an exacerbation of the recapitulatory crisis. The first movements of the Third and Ninth Symphonies tread a middle path between these two extremes: the coda supplies a final teleological intensification, which emphatically negates the possibility of a synthetic minor–major tonal trajectory. In cases where negation is sustained at the end of the first movement, the responsibility of synthesis is placed more heavily on the finale. At the same time, Darcy's association of 'sonata process failure' primarily with the absence of a 'redemption from minor to major or the purging of minor elements from the major mode' is perhaps too limited.[56] Negation also results from an inability to accommodate the conflicting demands of teleological intensification and recapitulatory stabilisation, and the redistribution of teleology and discontinuity that results.

Expansion, teleology and discontinuity also underpin Bruckner's use of the 'breakthrough deformation', as Hepokoski describes it. Brucknerian examples tend to reflect some of the properties of the breakthrough noted by Hepokoski and violate others. A clear example occurs in the first movement of the First Symphony. The climax of the third group in the exposition at bar 94, which follows a protracted process of intensification, is marked by the tutti intervention of new material, whose resemblance to the pilgrims' music in *Tannhäuser* has been frequently noted.[57] Hepokoski's definition of the breakthrough as 'an unforeseen inbreaking of a seemingly new . . . event' is appropriate here, although its context has shifted from the end of the development to the end of the exposition. The new theme introduces a point of thematic discontinuity with the preceding material, which grows out of an accompanimental figure from the first group. It falls to the development to work the *Tannhäuser* figure more fully into the symphonic discourse. An example that conversely appears within development space but expands an existing theme rather than introducing a new one can be found in the first movement of the Third Symphony. In all three versions of this movement, the development is punctuated by a climactic tutti statement of the first

---

[56] Ibid., p. 274.    [57] See for example Simpson, *The Essence of Bruckner*, p. 32.

theme in the tonic D minor.[58] The moment of breakthrough reverses the intensification process that opens the exposition. In the exposition, theme a1 participates in the teleological build-up, and the subordinate figure a2 constitutes the telos of the intensification. The climax of the development turns this thematic relationship on its head: the *Hauptmotiv* of a2 forms the preparatory intensification, and a1 constitutes the telos. This has the additional effect of aligning a1 with the assertion of a functional tonic. When the movement's opening returns at the recapitulation, and a1 is again located at the start of an intensification, it is referentially imbued by the development climax with a functional security that was absent in the exposition. This example will be considered in more detail in the next chapter.

## Conclusions

The techniques identified here might easily fall through the gaps of a common practice predicated on Schenkerian or Schoenbergian norms. Although the music reveals a prolongational concept of motive to a certain degree, there is also a relationship between motivic detail and deep structure involving the generation of conflicts between large-scale counter-structures out of an initial dissonant complex, rather than the elaboration of a diatonic *Ursatz* through diminution. Schenker was therefore in a sense correct to note in Bruckner the collapse of prolongation into progression. What Schenker failed to observe is that it is precisely this phenomenon that gives rise to the dissonant complex, and therefore to a rather different notion of the relationship between detail and deep structure. In fairness, Schenker's comments require contextualisation: they were part of his general hostility towards Wagnerian and post-Wagnerian tonality. But this renders the basic point even more urgent: Bruckner's habits may stand within a normative late nineteenth-century practice for which we have no generally accepted theoretical model. Neither can rehabilitations of Riemann's theories entirely fill this space, since their post-hierarchical concentration on tonal networks is incapable of representing the large-scale consequences of the techniques that Bruckner employs.

Similar problems attend the analysis of theme and formal design. In this respect, German-language literature has been more accommodating than Anglo-American analysis. Dialectically minded commentators like Kurth were quite happy to include within a normative symphonic practice Bruckner's emphasis on thematic 'becoming' over statement and

---

[58] Bar 387 in the 1873 version, bar 343 in the 1877 version and bar 341 in the 1889 version.

development. The formal consequence of this technique, a notion of formal process based on the concept of 'teleological genesis', has also appeared as normative to post-Hegelian commentators and 'deformational' to Anglo-American analysts, standing as they do within a tradition of understanding sonata forms dialectically that encompasses Hegel, A. B. Marx, Theodor Adorno and Carl Dahlhaus.

These various responses demonstrate acutely the problems of matching up analysis as reception history and analysis as a measure of compositional practice. And this leads inevitably to the fundamental question of whether analysis, relying as it does on established theoretical principles and therefore on a type of discourse to ground its observations, can ever represent properties of a work and their music-historical context without simply magnifying the discursive conditions of pre-analytical theory. Certainly, the extent to which Bruckner's music has been considered unified or incoherent, mainstream or peripheral, is at least as much a measure of aesthetic, philosophical and even political circumstances as it is an assessment of the music's dichotomous properties. Yet I would categorically resist a postmodern retreat from the work into a consideration of discourse as the only worthwhile focus of enquiry. Avoiding the kind of canonical exclusion from which Bruckner has suffered simply requires sensitivity to the relationship between theoretical norms and the prevalence of practices for which these norms cannot account, and a willingness to modify the theoretical foundations of analysis accordingly. If we allow our theoretical strategies to expand until they become mistaken for a general 'index of common practice', then the propensity for marginalisation on the one hand, and for allowing analysis to be swamped by discourse on the other, will inevitably increase.

# 5  Bruckner and the construction of musical influence

The question of which influences acted upon the development of Bruckner's symphonic style has been frequently addressed and yet sparsely analysed. At every stage of the works' reception history, commentators have hastened to locate the symphonies within various lines of development, generally without extended analytical qualification, and often in the service of interpretative, music-historical or even political agendas. At the same time, musicologists concerned with questions of musical influence have been slow to recognise the rich territory offered by the symphonies for the elucidation of theoretical problems in this area. Diverse attempts to bring literary critical models of influence to bear on musical repertoires have largely ignored Bruckner, despite exploration of their relevance for the nineteenth-century symphony in general.[1] A study that brings these two fields of enquiry together could be beneficial to an understanding both of Bruckner and of the notion of musical influence in general.

In the early reception of the symphonies the perception of Wagnerian affiliations was pervasive. Viennese critics of hostile and apologetic persuasions cited more or less superficial Wagnerisms as grounds for classifying Bruckner's music as a symphonic after-effect of the 'artwork of the future'. Conflicting contemporary responses to the Seventh Symphony make this abundantly clear. Hans Merian's review of the first performance of the work in Leipzig noted the Wagnerian association with displeasure: 'The work is shot through with numerous reminiscences of Wagner's compositions, an almost unavoidable feature of Wagnerian imitations.'[2] It consequently gave the impression of 'a free-fantasia on well-known themes which are developed and interwoven without any purpose'.[3] Bernhard Vogel, responding to the same performance, turned this perception into a virtue, observing:

---

[1]  I think particularly here of Mark Evan Bonds, *After Beethoven: Imperatives of Originality in the Symphony* (Cambridge, Mass., 1996).

[2]  Review in the *Leipziger Tageblatt und Anzeiger* (1 January 1885), trans. in Crawford Howie, *Anton Bruckner: A Documentary Biography*, vol. II: *Trial, Tribulation and Triumph in Vienna* (Lampeter, 2002), p. 428.

[3]  Ibid.

a genuine, natural empathy with Berlioz, Liszt and, above all, Wagner by virtue of which he stands out like a giant above the crowd of those pygmies who believe that they have achieved something splendid when they repeat parrot-fashion what these composers have already said more strikingly and powerfully.[4]

Vogel explicitly distanced Bruckner and his precedents from Beethoven: the Seventh was not absolute music in the Beethovenian mould, but a series of 'musical tone pictures' that profited from the convergence of Wagner and Liszt's symphonic poems.

Performances in Munich, Hamburg, Berlin and Vienna elicited similar responses: Bruckner either invoked Wagner in order to bypass Beethoven, or else refracted Beethovenian models through Wagnerian style and allusion. Whether or not he was considered successful in this respect turned on the extent to which Wagnerian elements were deemed appropriate to a symphonic context, a judgement also bound up, of course, with the reception of Brahms's symphonies. Hanslick portrayed this relationship with characteristic sarcasm: 'In a letter to me, one of Germany's most respected musicians describes Bruckner's symphony as the chaotic dream of an orchestral musician overtaxed by twenty *Tristan* rehearsals. That appears to me to be apt and to the point.'[5] Max Kalbeck noted the convergence of Beethoven and Wagner with equal distaste, describing the Adagio as 'a scrupulously schematic copy of the Adagio of Beethoven's Ninth with the free use of Beethovenian and Wagnerian melodies'.[6] Such views contrast markedly with that of Joseph Sittard, for whom Bruckner 'has not copied the advances for which we have the composer of *The Ring* to thank, but simply accepted the greater wealth of expressive means acquired by music in the last fifty years, transferred them to symphonic form and developed them in a completely independent way'.[7]

Claims of symphonic Wagnerism have persisted in a number of forms and ideological contexts, from Alfred Lorenz's politically charged observation of Wagnerian influence as a function of orchestration to the synthetic master narratives of Halm and Kurth. Most recently, it has been reanimated in Benjamin Korstvedt's conviction that the ramification of Beethovenian

---

[4] Review in the *Leipziger Neueste Nachrichten* (1 January 1885), trans. in Howie, *Anton Bruckner: A Documentary Biography*, vol. II, pp. 426–7.

[5] Review in the *Neue freie Presse* (30 March 1886), cited in Göllerich and Auer, *Anton Bruckner. Ein Lebens- und Schaffensbild* (Regensburg, 1922–37), vol. 4/2, p. 436.

[6] Review in *Die Presse* (3 April 1886), trans. in Howie, *Anton Bruckner: A Documentary Biography*, vol. II, pp. 509–12, this quotation p. 510.

[7] Review in *Hamburger Correspondent* (20 February 1886), cited in Göllerich and Auer, *Anton Bruckner. Ein Lebens- und Schaffensbild*, vol. 4/2, pp. 417–20.

and Wagnerian elements offers the basis of a historicist analysis, since it is rooted in a compositional problem that was widely felt in the late nineteenth century. The challenge to the Wagnerian view has come not from a reorientation around Beethoven, Schubert or other nineteenth-century precedents, but from a concentration on atavistic, pre-classical or sacred motivations. In all this, the precise nature and function of Beethovenian and particularly Schubertian models remains somewhat amorphous. A detailed analytical and theoretical investigation of the ways in which Bruckner reads, or perhaps misreads, specific Beethovenian and Schubertian precedents is conspicuous by its absence. Often, the Beethovenian influence either becomes a matter of vague stylistic or gestural imitation (the opening of the Ninth Symphony, for example), or else is re-routed into generalised concepts of thematic and formal substance or narrative process (Halm's dialectic of musical 'cultures', for instance, or Darcy's invocation of the struggle–victory archetype). The dialectical models of Halm, Kurth and Bloch aside, the theoretical foundations of this enterprise have also largely evaded analytical scrutiny. The problem of precisely how the mechanisms of influence operate and leave analytical traces is both crucial and under-theorised in Bruckner's case.

## Theories of influence

Carl Dahlhaus has offered a clear position from which to approach this issue. For Dahlhaus, Bruckner's idiosyncratic participation in the reception history of the Beethoven paradigm stands within a general tendency that is historically problematic: 'to speak of the symphony after Beethoven is not to refer to a chronological truism but to point out a problem for the historian ... arising from the fact that later examples of the genre relate directly and immediately to models left by Beethoven, with intermediate stages playing only a minor role'.[8] In consequence, 'to prove himself a worthy heir of Beethoven, a composer of a symphony had to avoid copying Beethoven's style, and yet maintain the same degree of reflection that Beethoven had reached in grappling with the problem of symphonic form'.[9] Dahlhaus's observations are at once historical and analytical. As a point of history, he isolates an almost Foucauldian disjunction in the development of the genre. Before Beethoven, the symphony develops through a linear historical process. The symphonies of the Mannheim composers, Mozart's late symphonies, Haydn's 'London' symphonies and Beethoven's early examples are moments in a continuous

---

[8] See Carl Dahlhaus, *Nineteenth-Century Music*, trans J. Bradford Robinson (Berkeley, 1989), p. 152.
[9] Ibid., p. 153.

narrative incorporated into the evolution of the classical style as a whole. After Beethoven, the prevalence of Beethovenian models induces a kind of historical stasis, or 'circumpolarity', as Dahlhaus puts it.[10] Symphonists from Mendelssohn to Mahler feel Beethoven's influence in equal measure, and thus chronology is no longer a measure of the progress of the genre. The late eighteenth and nineteenth centuries consequently appear as discrete *epistèmes*, to use Foucault's term: the former defined by linearity, the latter by circularity. The analytical consequence of this argument is that formal and material procedures in post-Beethovenian symphonies will always reveal a Beethovenian model at some level of structure, no matter how radically original they appear to be.

Dahlhaus's analytical demonstration of this is characteristically dialectical. In the symphonies of Schubert, Berlioz, Mendelssohn, Schumann, Brahms and Bruckner he defines the Beethovenian influence principally as a matter of the relationship between theme and form. The practical legacy of Beethoven's symphonies is a concentrated concept of theme that conditions formal design through the execution of goal-directed developmental processes. The question that exercised composers of the post-Beethovenian generation was that of how to unite this idea with an essentially non-symphonic influence: the self-contained, rhapsodic melodic style of the Lied. For Dahlhaus, Schubert's 'Unfinished' Symphony, Berlioz's *Symphonie fantastique*, Mendelssohn's 'Scottish' Symphony and Schumann's 'Spring' Symphony represent more or less successful attempts to synthesise vocal and thematic melodic styles in a way that preserved the integrity of the inherited symphonic forms. In the later nineteenth century, this dialectic putatively extends to encompass music drama, but the essential antithesis of thematic and rhapsodic elements persists: the difference between the Schubertian conflation of symphony and song and Bruckner's engagement with Wagner is one of degree, not of kind. The Beethovenian models of formal design are specific to each composer – the 'Eroica' and the 'Pastoral' for Berlioz, the Fourth and Seventh Symphonies for Schumann, the Ninth for Bruckner – and these features may or may not be attended by more general concepts associated with Beethoven's symphonies – monumentality, the expansion of form, and so forth. But Dahlhaus's essential distinction pits classicism as a 'culture of theme', to appropriate August Halm's term, against romanticism as a 'culture of song' throughout, within the formal constraints of the symphonic genre.

Whilst it is difficult to contest the music-historical appeal of Dahlhaus's view, its analytical application is insubstantial in key respects. He is, in truth,

---

[10] Ibid., p. 152.

highly selective in his choice of the analytical parameters that betray these influences: they are either a matter of thematic process, or generalised formal or aesthetic concepts like monumentality. Influence may however be evident in any possible parameter, and may involve the straightforward appropriation or quotation of materials, the adoption and distortion of processes or formal precedents, or the rather more amorphously defined appropriation of texture, and we cannot assume that parameters will act cooperatively, or that influences apparent in one parameter will appear in another.[11] Moreover, the pleasing binary structure of the argument masks a pluralism that it struggles to contain. For composers of Bruckner's generation – the 'second age of the symphony' as Dahlhaus describes it – the polyphony of secondary influences increases dramatically, and the reading of processes in any given parameter as evincing influence becomes concomitantly more complex. In Bruckner's case, the Beethovenian source is filtered not only through Wagnerian notions of harmony, melodic style and dramatic gesture, but also thematic, formal and tonal procedures borrowed from Schubert, together with Schumannesque, Mendelssohnian and Lisztian influences acquired during his period of study with Otto Kitzler. And this is to say nothing of the pre-Beethovenian 'historicism' that pervades much of his work, which would include Renaissance and Baroque polyphony and archaic devices derived from the Catholic liturgy as contributory sources.

Dahlhaus is furthermore vague about the extent to which his analyses draw upon intention as an authority. Assertions such as the following strongly indicate that the veracity of the analysis is rooted in the composer's intentions:

> [I]t is no paradox to claim that Schubert has used [in the 'Unfinished' Symphony] Beethoven's devices to solve a problem that Beethoven himself never confronted – or, in other words, that Schubert, having 'poeticised' his music . . . drew on Beethoven to satisfy the axioms that Beethoven himself had posed for large-scale symphonic form.[12]

Similarities of process in the works he considers are taken collectively as evidence for a general post-Beethovenian *Zeitgeist*, understood as the sum of conscious responses to the Beethoven paradigm. But this issue renders influence even more multivalent, since we must not only parse the multiple strands detectable through analysis, but also distinguish between influence as an analytically defined facet of the text, influence as a matter of verifying

---

[11] The re-composition of textural devices is basic to Charles Rosen's view of the relationship between Brahms and his classical sources. See 'Influence: Plagiarism and Inspiration', in *Nineteenth-Century Music* 4 (1980–1), pp. 87–100.

[12] *Nineteenth-Century Music*, p. 154.

links biographically, and influence as arising from the 'spirit of the age' in a broadly Hegelian sense.

The concept of influence is perhaps better served by a more pluralistic approach. And this leads, inevitably, into the territory of literary theory, which has anticipated the problems inherent in Dahlhaus's model at a considerable distance. Mikhail Bakhtin, Harold Bloom and Julia Kristeva, amongst others, offer models of literary influence that prove musicologically inviting precisely because they sidestep the binary logic of Dahlhaus's argument.

In an attempt to embrace these authorities, Kevin Korsyn has reformulated the question of musical influence as a problem of the relationship of text and context, or 'the threshold where the individual composition meets the surrounding world'.[13] Modernist models of musical history habitually read this relationship dualistically, as the process of connecting the properties of autonomous works (the domain of analysis) to those of other autonomous works (the domain of history), and as such trap musical research within a self-perpetuating binary structure, the hierarchical nature of which will always insist on the domination of one component by the other.[14] Complicit with this model is the whole arsenal of concepts, suspicion of which formed an essential preoccupation of the 'new' musicology of the 1990s: the notion of formal unity; the validity of the bounded, autonomous text; the assumption of its place within a historical canon revolving around a geographical and aesthetic centre; an attendant baggage of analytical and hermeneutic metaphors, which fail to recognise their origins in social and ethical prejudices.

Korsyn styles the dialectic of text and context as a conceptual aporia, a crisis which condemns musical scholarship to the eternal migration between two contradictory, but dependent, polarities. Solutions to this problem are forthcoming for Korsyn in the recent discourses of post-structuralism, whose radical consequences for historical musicology have, in his view, not been adequately understood.[15] Drawing on the collective authority of Bakhtinian dialogics, Derridean deconstruction, Kristeva's concept of intertextuality, Bloomian notions of poetic misprision and Foucauldian archaeology, he seeks to replace the text/context opposition with the analysis of

---

[13] See Kevin Korsyn, 'Beyond Privileged Contexts: Intertextuality, Influence and Dialogue', in Nicholas Cook and Mark Everist, eds., *Rethinking Music* (Oxford, 1999), pp. 55–72, this quotation p. 55. Korsyn has elaborated these ideas more extensively in 'Towards a New Poetics of Musical Influence', *Music Analysis* 10 (1991), pp. 3–72.

[14] Korsyn takes his cue from Derrida here; see *Margins of Philosophy*, trans. Alan Bass (Chicago, 1982), p. 329.

[15] 'Beyond Privileged Contexts', p. 56.

'relational fields', in which pieces of music are understood as 'relational events or nodes in an intertextual network'.[16] At base, his approach suggests nothing less than the complete abandonment of any unified conception of the musical work. If the post-structural notion of texts collapsing under deconstruction into 'inter-texts' has validity for the history of music, then the integrity of the work as text is fatally compromised. They should rather be understood as open-ended documents standing in complex dialogic relationships with other inter-texts as points in a relational network. Influence, in these terms, is the process through which one inter-text acts on another; measuring influence becomes a matter of isolating the points of contact between inter-texts, the moments when works reveal their permeable nature by making plain their embodiment of preceding 'relational events'.

The vocabulary we deploy for describing this process changes depending on which authority we invoke. In Bakhtinian terms, influence appears as the dialogue of 'heteroglossia', of 'socially stratified languages', within and between texts.[17] In Kristeva's view, a text is essentially 'a mosaic of quotations' in which 'several utterances, taken from other texts, intersect and neutralise one another'.[18] If we choose to couch the argument in Harold Bloom's terms, the same relationships become a matter of *misprision*, of texts revealing the way they misread precedents:

> Let us give up the failed enterprise of seeking to 'understand' any single poem as an entity in itself. Let us pursue instead the quest of learning to read any poem as its poet's deliberate misinterpretation, *as a poet*, of a precursor poem or of poetry in general.[19]

[16] Ibid., p. 59.

[17] Korsyn refers especially to Mikhail Bakhtin, *Speech Genres and Other Late Essays*, trans. Vern W. McGee, ed. Caryl Emerson and Michael Holquist (Austin, 1986), and *Problems of Dostoevsky's Poetics*, trans. and ed. Caryl Emerson and Michael Holquist (Austin, 1984).

[18] See Julia Kristeva, 'Word, Dialogue and Novel', in Toril Moi, ed., *The Kristeva Reader* (Oxford, 1986), pp. 34–61, this quotation p. 35.

[19] See Harold Bloom, *The Anxiety of Influence* (Oxford, 1973), p. 43. Bloom defines misprision, or *clinamen*, as the process through which 'a poet swerves away from his precursor, by so reading his precursor's poem as to execute a clinamen in relation to it. This appears as a corrective movement in his own poem, which implies that the precursor poem went accurately up to a certain point, but then should have swerved, precisely in the direction that the new poem moves.' See ibid., p. 14. Bloom's six 'revisionary ratios', or categories of misreading, are taken up by Joseph Straus as a model for understanding inter-textual relationships in Stravinsky's neo-classical music. See *Remaking the Past: Musical Modernism and the Influence of the Tonal Tradition* (Cambridge, Mass., 1990) and also 'The Anxiety of Influence in Twentieth-Century Music', *Journal of Musicology* 9 (1991), pp. 430–47. See also Richard Taruskin, review of Korsyn, 'Towards a New Poetics of Musical Influence' and Straus, *Remaking the Past*, *Journal of the American Musicological Society* 46 (1993), pp. 114–38.

If these ideas are transplanted into the domain of history, they imply the breakdown of narrative continuity, since 'the historical counterpart of the autonomous text is the ideal of continuous history',[20] and we find ourselves in the territory of Foucauldian archaeology, which construes history as comprising discontinuous discursive formations, or *epistèmes*.[21]

Demonstrating the heteroglossic nature of influence through analysis requires the quasi-deconstructive progression from unity to plurality. Considering the Beethovenian influences on Brahms's Quartet Op. 51, no. 1, for example, Korsyn proposes that Brahms 'dismantles the Beethovenian hierarchy' without providing any subsequent resolution.[22] In this context, the processes demanded by the Beethovenian model and the elements of post-Beethovenian style are not antithetical forms of the same concept, but heteroglossia: intertextual voices demanding no resolution into a unified whole. The historical meaning of the work depends precisely upon its failure to assimilate its precedents as a synthetic whole. Any attempt to read Brahms's quartet as a unified response to Beethoven will misrepresent not only its structure but also its music-historical context, ascribing to it a stylistic unity that it cannot project.

The most substantial attempt to apply these ideas to the nineteenth-century symphony has come from Mark Evan Bonds, who effectively redefines Dahlhaus's proposals in the terms of a Bloomian anxiety of influence.[23] Circumpolarity, in other words, is an effect, the cause of which is an anxiety of influence akin to that with which literature is critically burdened after Shakespeare. Bonds thus expands the analytical categories advanced by Dahlhaus into classes of misprision. Composers of symphonies must simultaneously accept and reinvent the concepts of monumentality, teleological structural narrative, thematic integration, conflation of programmatic and absolute tendencies, and the ramification of vocal and instrumental elements that Beethoven consolidated, or risk either historical irrelevance or slavish imitation. And although Bonds turns to Mendelssohn, Brahms and Mahler for analytical verification, the relevance of these categories to Bruckner's music is self-evident.

The authorities cited by Bonds and Korsyn carry their own agendas, which are more or less germane to the present context, and concerning which

---

[20] 'Beyond Privileged Contexts', p. 65.

[21] See Michel Foucault, *The Order of Things* (London, 1970) and its theoretical counterpart *The Archaeology of Knowledge*, trans. A. M. Sheridan Smith (London, 1972).

[22] '[Brahms] dismembers and disarticulates Beethoven's procedures... Rather than collapsing into a synthesis, these historical modes fail to coalesce. The non-convergence, the abrasion, of discourses seems to me more essential than any dialectical resolution.' See Korsyn, 'Brahms Research and Aesthetic Ideology', *Music Analysis* 12 (1993), pp. 89–103 this quotation pp. 98–9.

[23] See *After Beethoven: Imperatives of Originality in the Symphony*.

Korsyn and Bonds are accordingly selective. The invocation of Foucault brings with it the archaeological method through which 'we no longer relate discourse to the primary ground of experience, nor to the *a priori* authority of knowledge; but . . . seek the rules of its formation in discourse itself', a context not easily subsumed within Korsyn's text-critical strategy.[24] Bloom is likewise not always benign to Korsyn's cause. On the one hand, Bloom's notion of anxiety provides a methodological basis for escaping 'the tyranny of privileged contexts' that Korsyn is quick to embrace.[25] The idea of originality as evasion born of anxiety permits the replacement of the model of continuous history with a concept of influence as discontinuity, since misreading entails an oppositional relationship with the source of influence. On the other hand, Bloom is concerned with a means of determining canonical membership that sits uncomfortably with Korsyn's agenda. Misreading is a capability of 'strong' poets; the anxious evasion of precedents thus becomes a criterion for admission to the canon:

> Weaker talents idealise; figures of capable imagination appropriate for themselves. But nothing is got for nothing, and self-appropriation involves the immense anxieties of indebtedness, for what strong maker desires the realisation that he has failed to create himself?[26]

The two strands of Bloom's argument converge in the figure of Shakespeare, who embodies both the source of anxiety and the benchmark of canonical status: 'to say that Shakespeare and poetic influence are nearly identical is not very different from observing that Shakespeare is the western literary canon'.[27] This focus on a consciously, and indeed unapologetically defined canon of 'strong' figures jars with Korsyn's emphasis on heterogeneity and the context of anti-canonical discourse that it invokes.

The concept of antithetical influence is also less tractable than it might seem. For how do we define 'what is missing . . . because it has been excluded' in a musical text? How do I establish, for example, what Bruckner's Third Symphony represses? At worst this work, like any other, may exclude the entire repertoire that it does not invoke by material, generic or stylistic quotation or inference. The 'dark matter', as Korsyn puts it, that invisibly attends texts may thus be every other conceivable text, and 'antithetical influence' reduces to a mere historical truism. Moreover, if absent texts are to be selected, then what are the criteria of selection? In the literary domain, the problem of absence is obviated by a specifically linguistic concept of

---

[24] See Michel Foucault, *The Archaeology of Knowledge*, p. 79.
[25] See 'Beyond Privileged Contexts', p. 70.
[26] *The Anxiety of Influence*, p. 5.     [27] Ibid., p. xxviii.

signification and its location within a multi-dimensional discursive space. Kristeva characterises 'the status of the word' as the investigation of 'its articulations (as semic complex) with other words in the sentence', which is then expanded to encompass 'the same functions or relationships at the articulatory level of larger sequence'.[28] Following Bakhtin, she consequently distinguishes three 'coordinates of dialogue', 'writing subject, addressee and exterior texts', and extends the geometric metaphor, situating these coordinates on two levels: a horizontal level (as the domain of writing subject and addressee); a vertical level (the orientation of text 'towards an anterior or synchronic literary corpus').[29] The concept of intertextuality arises from this multi-dimensional construal of signification; it is enabled by the conception of 'the word as minimal textual unit' that 'turns out to occupy the status of *mediator*, linking structural models to cultural (historical) environment, as well as that of *regulator*, controlling mutations from diachrony to synchrony, i.e., to literary structure'.[30] Bloom's notion of misprision is well served by this idea: it is in effect another way of describing the 'vertical' condition of the word, through which the relationship with an 'anterior or synchronic literary corpus' is regulated.

But how, specifically, does this model translate into a music-analytical method? Clearly, the analysis of relationships between musical intertexts requires assessment of the possibility of establishing an equivalent 'minimal textual unit' of music. Korsyn does not identify what this might be, but even if he did, the guiding premise – that the basic paradigm of musical structure is analogous to that of the literary intertext – would be far from self-evident, for by what means might this parity be determined? How could it be the case that an established minimal unit of music mediates between 'structural models' and 'cultural environment' in the same way as the word? With slight modification, this proposition starts to look like Adorno's structure-as-metaphor argument; but any pull towards Adorno's theory of musical material is a return to precisely the dialectical formulation of text and context from which Korsyn seeks to escape.

These observations are not intended simply to strike a blow for a reanimated formalism. They do however suggest that the intertextual reading of music is condemned to a level of generality that can be overcome in literature. Bloom identifies evaded literary 'others' with precision because he can draw upon the word as a minimal textual unit; and the absent 'other' of a linguistic signifier is, by some terms, not merely tractable but essential to its identity.[31] This relationship of difference simply does not obtain

---

[28] See Kristeva, 'Word, Dialogue and Novel', p. 36.    [29] Ibid., p. 37.    [30] Ibid.
[31] For example in Saussurian terms.

for music. If, for example, we accept the thematic paradigm as the minimal unit of text, it would nevertheless not stand within a family of omitted
paradigms in relation to which its identity is secured, since the paradigms
omitted would amount to nothing less than the sum of all pitch collections
other than the paradigm itself. In short, musical influence can only be determined by first establishing what is partly present in the text at various levels
of structure; a theory of absence alone collapses into nothing. Bruckner's
Third Symphony might, for example, be understood as evading the model
of Beethoven's Ninth on the largest scale, since it swerves away from the
precedent of a choral finale. But this observation is only relevant because
the Third Symphony embodies other elements that seem to accept the precedent of Beethoven's Ninth: the tonality of D minor and a range of generic,
textural and material procedures that underpin Bruckner's compositional
decisions. Without the presence of Beethoven's Ninth, its absence is no more
relevant than that of any other symphonic model, or indeed of any other
work that is not Bruckner's Third Symphony.

The progression from unity to heterogeneity gives rise to another methodological dilemma: in practice, the heteroglossic, permeable nature of the
work is undemonstrable without the formalist analytical techniques it seemingly supplants. If heterogeneity relies on the deconstruction of unity, it
must, as Korsyn acknowledges, also rely on the demonstration of unity, in
which case it is negatively dependent on the techniques it opposes. It is not
just that we should move from unity to heterogeneity, but that heterogeneity
depends upon unity. The source of this problem is philosophical: the open-
ness, or plurality, at which deconstruction aims cannot be attained simply
by refusing to close the circle, by leaving a binary opposition open-ended at
the point where the initial thesis has collapsed, because the two halves of the
opposition remain dialectically related. In other words: homogeneity and
heterogeneity are antithetical forms of the same concept, and therefore progression from the former to the latter does nothing to reduce their mutual
dependence. In concrete analytical terms, we have travelled no distance at
all; if I take an organicist model, and watch its results proliferate to the detriment of its guiding premise, the result is not a new methodology, but an
old methodology in a new rhetorical guise. And this reinforces a point that
Korsyn does not address: deconstruction is often understood as standing
outside rational discourse altogether, as exchanging reason for rhetoric.[32]
He is therefore open to the accusation that his concept of influence detaches

---

[32] As Jürgen Habermas puts it, '[the] transformation of the "destruction" into the
"deconstruction" of the philosophical tradition transposes the radical critique of reason into the domain of rhetoric and thereby shows it a way out of the aporia of
self-referentiality. Anyone who still wanted to attribute paradoxes to the critique of

music-analytic discourse from any basis in rationality, and consequently from any firm criteria for judging its validity.

## Analysis

These various speculations can be tested analytically through investigation of the 1873 version of the first movement of the Third Symphony, a work in which generalised 'dialogic moments' revealing the multiple influences on Bruckner's style can be observed with exemplary clarity at various levels of structure and semiosis. The work yields a dense network of influential voices; and although Bruckner seems to aim at a symphonic style that synthesises divergent strands, most frequently they compete for attention without resolution into a higher, organic totality. The axes of writing subject and anterior corpus intersect at four main junctures: Bruckner's symphonic style is conditioned by a primary angle of relation to the influences of Beethoven and Schubert, and secondarily to Wagner and to pre-classical sacred and strict topoi.

Tracing influence at the level of intention – of the 'writing subject' – is also compelling in Bruckner's case. Reports of his self-confessed relation to past and to contemporary models are readily available, and seem especially to corroborate a Bloomian anxiety of influence. Carl Hruby's estimation of the central place accorded to Beethoven by Bruckner is emphatic: 'Beethoven! Beethoven! For Bruckner he was the incarnation of everything lofty and sublime in music. He connected that hallowed name with all the twists of fortune in his own life, and at crucial moments he often asked how Beethoven would have behaved in the same situation.'[33] The conversation Hruby reports after a performance of the 'Eroica' Symphony is especially significant, and bears extended quotation:

> After he had spent a while sunk in thought . . . he suddenly broke the silence: 'I think, if Beethoven were still alive today, and I went to him, showed him my Seventh Symphony and said to him, "Don't you think, Herr von Beethoven, that the Seventh isn't as bad as certain people make it out to be – those people who make an example of it and portray me as an idiot –" then, maybe, Beethoven might take me by the hand and say, "My dear Bruckner, don't

metaphysics after this transformation would have misunderstood it in a scientistic manner.' See Habermas, *The Philosophical Discourse of Modernity*, trans. Frederick Lawrence (Cambridge, Mass., 1987), p. 190. The point is reinforced pejoratively by John Ellis, who regards deconstruction as maintaining a veneer of rationality that is in fact meaningless; see *Against Deconstruction* (Princeton, 1989).

[33] See Carl Hruby, *Meine Erinnerungen an Anton Bruckner* (Vienna, 1901), p. 19, trans. in Stephen Johnson, *Bruckner Remembered* (London, 1998), p. 158.

bother yourself about it. It was no better for me, and the same gentlemen who use me as a stick to beat you with still don't really understand my last quartets, however much they may pretend to." Then, I might go on and say, "Please excuse me, Herr von Beethoven, if I've gone beyond you . . ." (Bruckner was referring to his use of form!) ". . . but I've always said that a true artist can work out his own form and then stick to it.'"[34]

There is a strikingly Bloomian anxiety in these remarks. Beethoven is singled out as an overarching authority, to be invoked as a defensive source of validation, but to whom one must also apologise when the limits of authority have been transgressed. It is not difficult to read in this passage a self-justification for the act of misprision. Whatever intervening influences find their way into the music, Hruby's reminiscence pins Bruckner's symphonic ambitions fundamentally to the misreading of Beethoven.

It is harder to isolate Schubertian precedents in this way. Bruckner undoubtedly had access to Schubert's Lieder, and to various chamber and sacred works, from the time of his first employment at St Florian onwards, but reconstruction of his reception of the symphonies is more conjectural. Accounts of Bruckner's engagement with Schubert generally fail to document specific symphonic sources in the way that the 'Eroica' and the Ninth Symphony are cited as Beethovenian models. The extent of conscious symphonic influence is further problematised by the delayed transmission of Schubert's symphonies. Nevertheless, the two clearest precedents, the 'Unfinished' Symphony and the 'Great' C major, can be more or less circumstantially linked to Bruckner. The latter was first performed in 1839, forming the sole canonical representative of Schubert's mature symphonic style until the 1860s, and it is conceivable that Bruckner may have encountered it either during his period of tuition under Kitzler, or else in his early years in Vienna. The former received its first performance in 1865 under the direction of Johann Herbeck, and was published the following year. As Stephen Johnson speculates, Bruckner may very well have come to know the 'Unfinished' through Herbeck, who had secured both Bruckner's first position at the Vienna Conservatory and his first Viennese symphonic premiere.[35]

Contemporary reports of Bruckner's attitude to the music of his own time place an almost exclusive emphasis on Wagner. The point is summed up by Anton Meissner:

[34] Ibid., p. 160. Timothy Jackson has recently marshalled these remarks as evidence for the Beethovenian influence on Bruckner's sonata designs. See 'The Adagio of the Sixth Symphony and the Anticipatory Tonic Recapitulation in Bruckner, Brahms and Dvořák', in *Perspectives on Anton Bruckner* (Aldershot, 2001), p. 207.

[35] See *Bruckner Remembered*, p. 157.

[Bruckner] was completely wrapped up in Wagner. He did once say to me that Chopin was 'extremely interesting'. Unfortunately he used this stereotypical and often sarcastic expression to describe the work of Liszt. As far as I know, he liked only the Gretchen movement from the *Faust Symphony*. In 1895 he also dismissed Richard Strauss's *Till Eulenspiegel* as 'extremely interesting'. But he admitted to me, after the first performance of the work by the Philharmonic . . . that he had snoozed a little.[36]

Meissner's comments are corroborated by Franz Marschner, who claimed that 'apart from Wagner . . . [Bruckner] told me that no other contemporary composer had impressed him. Included in this damning judgement was Liszt.'[37] These remarks contextualise the more generalised affiliation of Bruckner and the 'New German School' that abounded in contemporary criticism. When Bruckner reported to Marschner that Anton Rubinstein's *Nero* was deficient because 'the new direction is being completely avoided', or when Marschner extrapolated the conclusion that 'in speaking of music which "gripped," he was obviously thinking of the new school' from Bruckner's remark that 'anyone who wants to listen to music in order to relax will enjoy the music of Brahms; but anyone who wants to be gripped by music cannot be satisfied by his works', the scope of the term 'new school' is tacitly restricted to Wagner and, at the very most, Bruckner himself.[38]

These fragmentary traces of anterior corpus in the biographical evidence translate tangibly into analytical evidence in the Third Symphony. The first movement, especially in its 1873 form, generously betrays Bruckner's attempts to accommodate and 'go beyond' these models.[39] It was composed at a time when he was consolidating the principal sources of his symphonic style: by the time the first version was completed in 1873, he had encountered Beethoven's Third and Ninth Symphonies at the very least, Wagner's *Tannhäuser*, *Der fliegende Holländer*, *Tristan und Isolde*, *Das Rheingold* and *Die Walküre*, and in all probability the late symphonies of Schubert.[40] In terms of texture, thematic process, form and harmonic

---

[36] Ibid., pp. 155–6.     [37] Ibid., p. 156.     [38] Ibid., p. 154.

[39] All references in the following analysis are to the 1873 version of the Third Symphony, in the 1977 Bruckner Gesellschaft publication edited by Leopold Nowak. Comparison with parallel points in the 1877 and 1889 versions will be annotated where necessary. For a detailed study of the versions of this work, see Thomas Röder, *Auf dem Weg zur Bruckner Symphonie: Untersuchungen zu den ersten beiden Fassungen von Anton Bruckners Dritte Symphonie* (Stuttgart, 1987) and more recently 'Master and Disciple United: the 1889 Finale of the Third Symphony', in *Perspectives on Anton Bruckner*, pp. 93–113.

[40] Questions of chronology need clarifying here. Bruckner first heard Beethoven's Ninth Symphony in 1866, the year in which he completed his own First Symphony. Bruckner's first encounter with Wagner's music is usually taken to be Kitzler's performance of

vocabulary it draws simultaneously on Beethovenian, Schubertian and Wagnerian sources, whilst elaborating a highly original concept of symphonic design. Perhaps more clearly than any other work by Bruckner, its boundaries as an autonomous work seem permeable, and consequently susceptible to location within an intertextual network.

The interaction of Beethovenian and Schubertian influences is immediately evident in the first-theme group. Most superficially, and as is frequently observed, the texture and gestural character of the opening passage, bars 1 to 46, resembles that of Beethoven's Ninth Symphony in its trajectory from pianissimo tremolando string texture to fortissimo unison tutti theme.[41] The first theme of Schubert's 'Unfinished' Symphony is also invoked, and perhaps more literally. Bruckner's tremolandi, like Schubert's, establish a distinctive thematic pattern emphasising the tonic triad, whereas Beethoven supplies an athematic dominant fifth A–E. Bruckner's opening both absorbs and supersedes these precedents. In Beethoven's model, the climactic unison theme from bar 16 is adumbrated in the preceding build-up, such that the theme coalesces out of preparatory motivic fragments. In Schubert's movement, the first theme appears as a distinct entity above the initial tremolandi, and the climax in bars 35 to 38 introduces neither a definitive form of the theme nor a significant new figure, but rather an isolated climactic gesture. Bruckner in effect fuses these two precedents together. Like Schubert, he supplies a distinct form of his first theme over the gathering tremolando,

*Tannhäuser* in Linz on 13 February 1863; Kitzler subsequently gave performances of *Der fliegende Holländer* and *Lohengrin* in Linz around this time. Bruckner's first experience of *Tristan* can be traced to a performance in Munich in 1865. Sources for his first contact with *Das Rheingold* and *Die Walküre* are harder to pin down. Although *Der Ring* was first performed in its entirety at Bayreuth in 1876, a performance that Bruckner attended, the references in the Third Symphony to *Die Walküre* betray prior familiarity. Excerpts from *Das Rheingold* and *Die Walküre* were performed in concert versions under Wagner's baton in Vienna on 26 December 1862, although Bruckner only moved to Vienna in 1868. The vocal score of *Das Rheingold* was first published in 1861, and the full score in 1873, the year Bruckner completed the first version of the Third Symphony; the vocal score of *Die Walküre* appeared in 1865 and the full score in 1874. It is therefore entirely plausible that he had access to both well before the composition of the Third Symphony. The chronology of Bruckner's reception of Schubert's symphonies has been considered above.

[41] Simpson assesses this parallel in *The Essence of Bruckner*, pp. 66–7. Hans-Hubert Schönzeller's remarks are also characteristic: 'Sonata form as it had come down to him from the Viennese classics and especially Beethoven and Schubert (and of these two composers it was particularly the former's Ninth and the latter's 'Great' C major which exerted strong influence on him) was for him a mere starting point, which he filled out, moulded and fashioned to suit his own particular requirements.' See *Bruckner* (London, 1970), p. 150.

which is unrelated to the material of the climax; like Beethoven, his climactic theme is of considerable importance for the symphonic design.

An additional feature is built into this opening that further complicates the reading. In functional harmonic terms, Beethoven establishes a prolonged V–I over seventeen bars, and although Schubert's harmonic context is more varied, it also presents the first theme against functional harmony establishing the tonic. Bruckner, however, treats D minor as a static *Klang* over a forty-six-bar tonic pedal, rather than as part of a cadential fortification of I. This effect is exacerbated in the harmony approaching the climax, in which elements of I and V are overlaid above the pedal point. The obvious precedent is the opening of *Das Rheingold*, which of course deploys E flat major in a similar fashion. In the first forty-six bars alone, there is a dense network of associations. The passage effectively conflates Beethovenian, Schubertian and Wagnerian influences; or rather, Bruckner establishes a textural, harmonic and stylistic milieu for a symphonic first theme, which refracts Beethovenian and Schubertian models through a Wagnerian harmonic device. The originality of Bruckner's opening derives in part from the overlaying of these three sources in a symphonic context, and in part from the fact that each source is in some sense refashioned, or inflected with properties from another: in other words, each source is purposefully misread.

There are two further factors conditioning Bruckner's misreading of his models. First, and most obviously, the proportions of the first-theme group massively expand those of Beethoven and Schubert: Bruckner's group is 134 bars long, Schubert's occupies forty-one bars, Beethoven's occupies seventy-nine bars. Second, unlike Beethoven and Schubert, Bruckner constructs the texture of his opening by filling in the rhythmic space between two durational extremes with strata of discrete rhythmic values, a technique I have elsewhere related to the overlaying of diminutions above a *cantus firmus* in species counterpoint.[42] Thus the trumpet theme entering in bar 5 occupies the first level of diminution above the sustained semibreves in the woodwind, and the strings supply four further levels of diminution from the minim pulse of the double basses to the viola semiquavers. The blending of symphonic and Wagnerian influences is in this way grounded in a pre-Beethovenian technical procedure. The tremolando device derived from Beethoven and Schubert is part of a texture constructed through a means deployed by neither precedent, and the polyphony of heteroglossia increases to four.

---

[42] See 'Bruckner and the Symphony Orchestra', in John Williamson (ed.), *The Cambridge Companion to Bruckner* (in press).

The model of Beethoven's Ninth is also present at a more general level of harmonic planning. Example 5.1 compares the structure of Beethoven's first-theme group with that of Bruckner. Both groups have an essentially binary structure, augmented by a transition. In both examples, the second part is a variant of the first. Beethoven answers the preparation over V and the tonic climactic theme of the first part with a tonic version of the preparation and a submediant form of the tutti in the second. After a more extended aftermath to the first climax, Bruckner instigates a dominant form of the initial build-up in bars 79 to 118, which also leads to a submediant reharmonisation of the climax at bar 119. In turn, Bruckner's transition is in effect an expansion of Schubert's example. Unlike Beethoven, who elides first and second groups by means of a dominant preparation, Bruckner follows Schubert in pivoting around a sustained pitch/chord of initially indeterminate harmonic identity: $\hat{3}$ of B minor becomes $\hat{5}$ of G in Schubert's case; chord V7 of C flat becomes an augmented sixth in F in Bruckner's case. In consequence, the material continuity of Beethoven's transition is supplanted by a much more typically Schubertian delineation of formal regions, a habit that Schubert deployed again in the first movement of the Ninth Symphony, and of which Bruckner made extensive use.[43]

The relationship of theme and form in this movement could also be viewed as an extended misreading of these two symphonic precedents. The key feature in this respect is the concept of 'teleological genesis' addressed in Chapter 4. Both the first movement of Beethoven's Ninth and of Schubert's 'Unfinished' are concerned, in different ways, with the teleological construction of thematic material. In Beethoven's case, this is not just a question of the establishment of a dialectical thematic substance that points towards a later moment of synthesis, a technique Dahlhaus considered representative of Beethoven's 'second' style in general, but of the literal goal-directed adumbration of themes leading to a 'definitive' form. The application of the technique in the first movement of the Ninth is limited. The *Grundgestalt* of the first theme is reached by bar 17, and subsequent processes are concerned either with its reconstruction, as is the case in the second part of the first group and more expansively in the coda, or else fragmentation and development. Schubert's example is more complex. The first movement of the 'Unfinished' is based not on a dialectic of Lied and symphonic theme, as Dahlhaus proposes, but on an open conflict between two antithetical types of thematic process. Thus the first and second themes in the

---

[43] See for example the transition between first and second themes in the exposition and recapitulation of the first movement of the Fourth Symphony (bars 73–5 and 435–7, 1878/80 version).

Example 5.1 Beethoven, Ninth Symphony, first movement and Bruckner, Third Symphony (1873), first movement

Comparison of first-theme groups

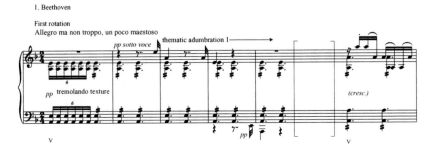

### Example 5.1  (*cont.*)

Example 5.1  (*cont.*)

79
Second rotation

118

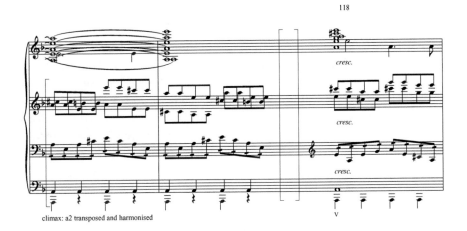

climax: a2 transposed and harmonised

Example 5.1 (*cont.*)

exposition occur initially in a stable form, which is subsequently developed within their respective subject groups. The development and coda,
on the other hand, are concerned almost exclusively with the introductory
bass theme. The definitive form of this theme is reached with its fortissimo
tutti statement in E minor at bar 171, and the whole of the development
as far as this point can be understood as an intensificatory adumbration.
The theme is subsequently broken up and developed contrapuntally, as
Example 5.2 shows. In the coda, the figure returns, and is ultimately liquidated in the closing cadence. The movement thus operates on two opposed
levels of thematic activity, which remain strictly compartmentalised within
their allotted formal regions.

Again, Bruckner overlays aspects of both precedents. Because, after
Beethoven's example, the thematic significance of the first climax in the
first group is preserved by Bruckner, Schubert's dialectic of teleology and
development is contracted into the first group: the trumpet theme, labelled
a1 in Example 5.2, is an adumbration; the climactic subsidiary figure a2 at bar
37 has the character of an initial *Grundgestalt*. The way in which a1 evolves
owes much to Schubert's example. Its definitive form is also supplied in the
middle of the development, from bar 377, and this is similarly conceived
as a fortissimo tutti statement that clarifies a1's adumbratory character in
the exposition. The intensification preceding this event is considerably more
involved than Schubert's analogous passage.[44] The development as far as bar
377 comprises two sections, each fulfilling a distinct thematic function. The
first, bars 285 to 332, sequentially spins out inversions of a1's *Hauptmotiv*

---

[44] This passage also perhaps owes something to the development of the first movement of Mendelssohn's Fifth Symphony. Compare with bars 209–67 in Mendelssohn's
movement.

Example 5.2 Schubert, 'Unfinished' Symphony, first movement and Bruckner, Third Symphony (1873), first movement

Comparison of developmental processes

Example 5.2 (*cont.*)

2. Bruckner
development from start of second section

beneath its accompanying quaver figure in the violins, and each sequential paragraph concludes with an inverted, diminished form of a2. The second, bars 333 to 376, abandons a1 and develops a2 extensively over free variants of a1's quaver accompaniment. In this way, the two thematic types interact, whilst pursuing opposed trajectories: a1 develops towards its definitive form; a2 develops out of its exposition form. Observe also that the intensification towards bar 377 involves the progressive contraction of a2, from the prime form set periodically against its diminution in bars 333 to 372, to a combination of diminution and double diminution in bars 373 to 376. Theme a2 is in effect liquidated as the definitive form of a1 approaches.

The treatment of a1 from bar 377 onwards misreads Schubert more blatantly. As the comparison in Example 5.2 shows, both proceed from an octave statement to a motivic splitting up of the theme above continuous string figurations. Furthermore, both passages clarify the theme's functional harmonic identity. Schubert places what was initially an unharmonised octave bass theme into a cadential assertion of the subdominant, E minor. Bruckner more radically locates a1 within a cadential establishment of D minor, and therefore bisects the development with a forceful statement of the tonic. Whereas in the exposition, a1 emerges from the tonic *Klang*, in which context the functions of I and V are conflated or blurred, here D minor is sharply defined. The conventional correlation of first theme and tonic key in the exposition space is thus problematised by the presence of an initial conflict: the theme that is definitively established in the first group, and which functionally consolidates D minor, is not the principal subject; the principal subject is consequently forced into a preparatory role. Bruckner compensates by recovering a definitive form and assertive tonic identity for the first theme outside exposition space, subordinating a2 to the preparation of this event in the process. The presence of D minor in the middle of the development does not arise from an incompetent handling of sonata form, as Robert Simpson suggested, but from an attempt to accommodate a dialectic of 'being' and 'becoming' that was alien to the mechanisms of the classical sonata principle.[45]

---

[45] See for example Simpson's *The Essence of Bruckner*, pp. 69–71, in which he cites the tonic statement of the theme at this point as an indication that 'the problems of momentum in a sonata movement on this scale and with this kind of slowness have defeated the composer at this stage in his development' (p. 70). Simpson misunderstands the relationship between theme and form here, making no provision for any notion of thematic process other than the statement of a *Grundgestalt* and its development. Although in later editions of the book Simpson claimed his reservations had been dispelled by encountering the 1873 version of the symphony, it is significant that neither in this version nor in any of the revisions does Bruckner change or remove the tonic statement of the theme in the development.

Two other passages in the movement constitute obvious 'dialogic moments': the retransition preparing the recapitulation, and the coda. The former differs from the other instances considered here in its use of literal quotation: the *Liebestod* from *Tristan* in bars 463 to 468; Bruckner's own Second Symphony in bars 469 to 476; the *Schlafakkorde* from *Die Walküre* in bars 479 to 488, reproduced in Example 5.3. Unlike the intertextual references considered so far, which concern formal, thematic, harmonic and textural models and which are consequently introversive, the function of these references is decisively extroversive: they point beyond the misreading of structural procedures and suggest a moment of external semiosis.[46]

The procession of quotations seems to disrupt, rather than to contribute to, the preparatory function of the retransition. Harmonically, they work against the dominant pedal in the timpani that circumscribes the passage. Although the *Liebestod* references are contained within the ambit of the dominant, the harmony breaks free from this context with the appearance of the opening theme of the Second Symphony at bar 469, and a series of chromatic modulations ensues: the Second Symphony references pass through F sharp, A flat and E; the *Schlafakkorde*, although circumscribed by F major, comprise sequential chromatic third and minor second transposition operations. The timpani pedal concomitantly drops out, reappearing only after the quotations have ceded to the reassertion of V from bar 489. The detachment of the passage from the sonata design is also thematic and gestural. There is no sense in which the quotations are either related to the principal material or grow out of it through a process of motivic mutation. On the contrary, the *Liebestod* allusion arrests the symphonic discourse, emerging after the sequential development of the second theme has broken down over a diminished seventh and yielded to a general pause in bars 459 and 460. Similarly, the retransition recovers its preparatory function only after the quotations have ceased, and therefore its harmonic function is not articulated by a thematic strategy related to the exposition material.

The quotations are better understood first of all as overtly invoking an external, non-symphonic authority, and secondly as relating that authority, through allusion to the Second Symphony, to the broader context of Bruckner's symphonic project as a whole. Yet it is significant that the Wagner quotations should be functionally isolated. Bruckner admits Beethovenian and Schubertian models as structural as well as material influences, and as a result largely refrains from direct quotation. But the Wagnerian influence is

---

[46] I use the terms introversive and extroversive semiosis in the sense intended by V. Kofi Agawu. See *Playing with Signs* (Princeton, 1991). The Wagner quotations were removed in the later versions, but the self-quotation was retained.

Example 5.3  Bruckner, Third Symphony (1873), first movement

Wagner quotations and self-quotation in retransition

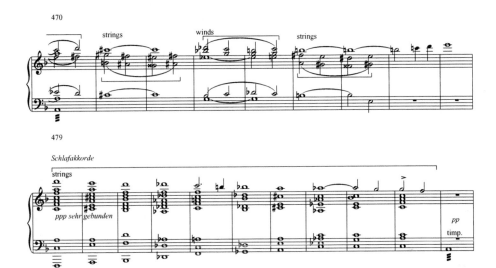

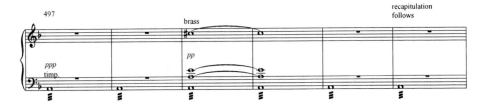

mainly restricted to the foreground, through discrete quotation, harmonic vocabulary and the local appropriation of texture. As the analysis in Chapter 2 suggested, the *Tristan* quotations are worked more thoroughly into the design of the Finale, but even in that context they bring about a temporary disruption, and again play no structural role comparable to the thematic and topical examples of Beethoven and Schubert. Moreover, within the retransition Bruckner misreads both Wagner and himself, since each quotation is placed into a topical context with which it originally had no affiliation. The *Liebestod* figure is treated in imitation, and thus invokes the learned style, whilst the opening theme of the Second Symphony and the *Schlaffakkorde* both resemble *cantus firmi*, and so similarly imply an archaic, sacred topic, an association that is also developed more fully in the Finale. There are therefore two levels of extroversive semiosis in play. Bruckner's open association with music drama in fact localises the Wagnerian influence as non-structural and hence external. Simultaneously, the Wagnerian materials are specifically linked to archaic and sacred topics; an association with 'the artwork of the future' becomes an emblem of pre-Beethovenian artifice.

The coda is, in turn, the closest Bruckner comes to the specific quotation of Beethoven's Ninth Symphony.[47] Example 5.4 shows the parallel: both codas are constructed from the gradual accumulation of forms of the movement's *Hauptmotiv* over a bass ostinato comprising a chromatic descent from $\hat{8}$ to $\hat{5}$. The points of misprision are also clear. The counterpoint of motives above the ostinato, and their textural distribution, is more complex in Bruckner's case. Beethoven's coda amounts to a final 'reconstruction' of the first subject: motivic fragments in the winds and brass coalesce at the climactic moment into a cadential tutti version of the first theme. The strings only participate thematically from the climax; before this they are restricted entirely to the ostinato. Bruckner, however, constructs his coda around the interplay of three motives: the *Hauptmotiv* of a1; a diminished form of a2; a1's accompanying violin quaver figure. The allocation of material within instrumental groups is changed concomitantly. The string parts are both thematic and accompanimental, the forms of a1 and a2 appear exclusively in the brass, and the winds play no thematic role.

The thematic process underpinning Bruckner's coda is in many ways the effective reverse of Beethoven's: whereas Beethoven directs his coda towards a fully formed statement of the first theme, Bruckner is principally concerned with liquidation. The first theme is represented only by a motivic residue, which is contracted by diminution from bar 692, and further reduced to a repeating, freely derived fragment of the theme from bar 697. This gradual

---

[47] The parallel is again identified by Simpson; see *The Essence of Bruckner*, p. 71.

Example 5.4 Beethoven, Ninth Symphony, first movement and Bruckner, Third
Symphony (1873), first movement

Comparison of codas

Example 5.4 (*cont.*)

liquidation is compounded by the imitation at successively diminishing rhythmic intervals between trumpets and trombones: a distance of two bars in bars 677 to 684; a single bar articulated at the half bar from bar 685; and half a bar articulated on the upbeat from bar 692. Key stages of this process are also emphasised by the distribution of a2. The repetitions of a2 in the horns increase in frequency from bar 685, and all thematic references aside from the residue of a1 in the trumpets drop out from bar 692, concomitant with the abandonment of the bass ostinato.

The harmonic structure of Bruckner's coda also misreads its Beethovenian precedent. For Beethoven, reconstruction of the first theme is part of a teleological process of cadential consolidation; in Bruckner's coda, the liquidation of the first theme articulates a disruption of tonic stability. By the climax in bars 705 to 709, the cadential function of the coda appears to have been disabled: the texture ceases abruptly over a diminished seventh, and the momentum is only retrieved after the disjunctive intervention, in bars 710 to 730, of the cadential continuation of a2 from bars 41 to 44. This provides only a slender dominant preparation for the closing section from bar 731. In consequence, the clear teleology of Beethoven's precedent is emphatically disrupted; the result is an exacerbation of the 'struggle–victory' narrative archetype. In Beethoven's case, this is conveyed by the work's minor–major tonal trajectory, and there is no ambiguity surrounding the cadential consolidation of D minor at the end of the first movement. Bruckner, however, introduces disruptive structural elements even at this late stage, which have a deleterious effect on the structural integrity of the tonic, and which thus transfer a burden of cadential consolidation to the Finale, in addition to the resolution of D minor onto D major.

## Conclusions

The distance between a dialogical and a dialectical reading of this movement may not be as great as Korsyn's deconstructive agenda suggests. Walter Benjamin's Hegelian statement of method, which furnished the starting point for Adorno's *Philosophy of Modern Music*, is instructive in this regard:

> The history of philosophy viewed as the science of origins is that process
> which, from opposing extremes, and from the apparent excesses of
> development, permits the emergence of the configuration of an idea as a
> totality characterised by the possibility of a meaningful juxtaposition of such
> antitheses inherent in these opposing extremes.[48]

---

[48] Walter Benjamin, *Ursprung des deutschen Trauerspiels* (Frankfurt, 1955), vol. I, p. 163, quoted in Theodor Adorno, *Philosophy of Modern Music*, trans. Anne Mitchell and Wesley Blomster (London, 1973), p. 3.

The foregoing analysis raises precisely the question of whether the dichotomy of innovation and tradition in nineteenth-century music, embodied here in the distinction between 'writing subject' and 'anterior corpus', attains the synthesis, the 'configuration of an idea as a totality', of which Benjamin speaks, and which Korsyn denies in Brahms's Op. 51.

Ostensibly, Bruckner's symphonic style seems not to be conceived as contradictory within itself. On the contrary, its preoccupation with generic consistency (the establishment of thematic, textural and formal types that are retained from work to work) and the resolution of teleological processes (in a culminating synthetic act) implies the installation of a new symphonic style as ramified totality, in which the heteroglossia of Kristeva's vertical axis fuse into a whole that is greater than the sum of its parts. There are, however, two ways in which the analysis calls this synthesis into question. First, the dialogue with the anterior corpus is not a consistent, unified phenomenon. There is no sense in which the movement engages each respective model for its duration, such that threads of Beethovenian, Schubertian and Wagnerian discourse are discernible as continuous narratives at every point and at every level of structure. Rather, Bruckner's precedents emerge and recede in specific regions in the form: they are sometimes coincidental, as suggested in the first-theme group, but never ubiquitous. In effect, the movement exemplifies Kristeva's 'mosaic of [misread] quotations', comprising a sequence of dialogic fragments that contribute to the structure without governing it. This is emphasised further by the respective functions of the models appropriated, which operate at different levels of structure and semiosis: concepts of thematic process derived from Schubert link first theme and development, without necessarily engaging other areas of the form; overt invocation of Wagner prompts the identification of an extroversive semiosis that is quite separate from the processual and stylistic precedents drawn from Beethoven and Schubert. The second-theme group is especially problematic in this regard. It suggests no single precedent that might enable an integrated reading of the whole form, and therefore appears to stand outside the dialogue established by the first group, development and coda altogether.

Second, the synthetic event towards which Bruckner's symphonies often progress only functions as such at the level of the individual work at best: it may effect an integration of the competing structural forces within the piece, but it does not thereby transcend these antinomies and engender a universal symphonic style. Bruckner's misreading of Beethoven in the coda marks this point acutely. By exacerbating the teleological drive of Beethoven's model to the point where it destabilises the coda's structural integrity, Bruckner forces an intolerable manifold burden onto the Finale, which must take on simultaneously the integration of its own material strategies and those of the whole symphony, as emblems of the 'writing subject', together with a fusion of the heteroglossia of the anterior corpus into a generalised, and at the same time individual, symphonic *lingua franca*. Each of Bruckner's symphonies becomes locked in the repeating struggle to overcome this problem. In the Third Symphony, the coda of the first movement constitutes the decisive point at which the goal of synthesis is revealed, through deferral, as unattainable, and the dialogic fragments are left tangibly related, but essentially separate.

The analysis also raises the matter of whether it is really justifiable to see these various processes as evidence for an anxiety of influence. Although Bruckner's own reported comments corroborate this idea, it provokes wider questions of the historical status and condition of the symphony in the late nineteenth century that potentially conflict with evidence traced at the level of intention. The concept of circumpolarity strongly resembles Charles Rosen's opinion that classical sonata-type works constitute a living, historically 'active' repertoire expressing the development of a general style, whereas sonata-type works of the nineteenth century are irrelevant to the development of style and therefore historically static.[49] In these terms, the symphony persists through the prestige of the Beethovenian precedent, rather than through its immanent value as a form or relevant mode of expression. In fact, this order of priority is largely arbitrary. There is no reason why the symphony, or any other sonata-type genre, should be accorded historical validity when it can be subsumed within the development of a style, and should relinquish this status as soon as style and form appear discontinuous. Instead, we could construe the nineteenth-century symphony as significant insomuch as it embodies the development of a dialectical mindset, in which sense it reflects a more general movement in the history of ideas. The discontinuity noted by Dahlhaus consequently describes part of an epistemic shift from the empirical rationalism of the eighteenth century to the dialectical idealism of the nineteenth century. The prestige of the symphony arises less from the pressure of the Beethovenian influence itself, more from the suitability of the genre as a dialectical mode of expression.

Put this way, Beethoven is not the cause, of which 'the symphony after Beethoven' is the effect; the post-Beethovenian anxiety of influence is really the projection of a dialectical *Zeitgeist*. Beethoven's symphonies, whilst maintaining a link with their classical precedents, encapsulate an emerging mode of thought of which they are one specific cultural example. Thus when Hegel isolated the sonata principle as a musical expression of

[49] See *Sonata Forms* (New York, 1980), pp. 292–3.

dialectic, he pinpointed a specific effect of a phenomenon he considered basic to artistic creation in general:

> And even if artistic works are not abstract thought and notion, but are an evolution of the notion out of itself, an alienation from itself towards the sensuous, still the power of the thinking spirit (mind) lies herein, *not merely* to grasp *itself only* in its peculiar form of the self-conscious spirit (mind), but just as much to recognise itself in its alienation . . . in its other form, by transmuting the metamorphosed thought back into definite thoughts, and so restoring it to itself. And in its preoccupation with the other of itself the thinking spirit . . . comprehends both itself and its opposite. For the notion is the universal, which preserves itself in its particularisations, dominates alike itself and its 'other', and so becomes the power and activity that consists in undoing the alienation which it had evolved. And thus the work of art in which thought alienates itself belongs, like thought itself, to the realm of comprehending thought . . .[50]

The parallel between this conception of artistic production and the processes of Beethoven's sonata-type works was taken up by Adorno: 'Music of Beethoven's type, in which ideally the reprise, the return in reminiscence of complexes expounded earlier, should be the result of development, that is, of dialectic, offers an analogy [to Hegel's system] that transcends mere analogy.'[51] The implications for the nineteenth-century symphony are equally clear: the 'preoccupation with the other of itself' as a result of which 'the thinking spirit . . . comprehends both itself and its opposite' in post-Beethovenian symphonies marks out the distinction between writing subject (as self) and anterior corpus (as other); the 'universal, which . . . dominates alike itself and its other' corresponds to the attempted synthesis of writing subject and anterior corpus into a generalised symphonic style. The simple formulation of a post-Beethovenian symphonic repertoire is therefore thoroughly inadequate; rather, we need to distinguish between two conceptions of symphonic form: a quasi-synthetic conception, evident in the eighteenth century, in which the relationship of style and form obviates the progression towards a moment of overcoming; a dialectical conception, the 'work of art in which thought alienates itself', evident in the nineteenth century, in which the teleological resolution of antitheses forms the basis of formal process. Beethoven sits on the cusp of these two models.

The fact that the conflicting discourses in the first movement of Bruckner's Third Symphony do not coalesce into a unified stylistic or formal totality

---

[50] See Hegel, *Introductory Lectures on Aesthetics*, trans. Bernard Bosanquet (London, 1993), p. 15.
[51] See Adorno, *Hegel: Three Studies*, trans. Shierry Weber Nicholsen (Cambridge, Mass., 1993), p. 136.

does not endanger this context. Bruckner may fail in the effort to construct a universal style that 'dominates alike itself and its "other"', but the 'meaningful juxtaposition of antitheses' remains central to the work and its philosophical context. Adorno is again close to the surface in these observations. Progression towards an increasingly acute condition of irresolution, which is nevertheless caught within a dialectical teleology, manifestly invokes Adorno's negative dialectics. Recovery of this context, which effectively reverses Korsyn's deconstruction of binary logic, has the crucial advantage of anchoring the nineteenth-century symphony in general, and Bruckner in particular, within a historical context. Without this, the pluralistic techniques favoured by Korsyn paradoxically appear hegemonic. To say that Bruckner engages in heteroglossic dialogue with his precedents without recognising the dialectical context of nineteenth-century idealism is to impose a decidedly un-Foucauldian model of history, to return to one of Korsyn's authorities. We have not allowed the nineteenth century to supply its own structural premises, but have imposed an ideological agenda of our own. The techniques derived from Kristeva, Bloom or Bakhtin are not positioned 'beyond privileged contexts'; they simply replace the binary ideology of modernism with the pluralist ideology of postmodernism.

# 6 Analysis and the problem of the editions

Cliff Eisen and Christopher Wintle prefaced a recent study of Mozart's C minor Fantasy, K.475, with the following remarks:

> Turn-of-century scholarship . . . faces a dilemma. On the one hand, division of labour has necessarily created an ever-higher degree of specialization in each musicological field; on the other hand, each field, by virtue of this specialization, stands in need of other fields to furnish an appropriate range of approaches and to help resolve its problems responsibly.[1]

The disciplinary convergence Eisen and Wintle have in mind involves the beneficial cooperation of philology and analysis. The sources and editions for K.475 reveal discrepancies, the interpretation of which is, as they put it, 'crucially dependent . . . on analysis'.

This dilemma is nowhere more pressing than in the field of Bruckner scholarship. The textual discrepancies highlighted by Eisen and Wintle, although by no means analytically insignificant, are small in comparison with the variations present in the editions of Bruckner's symphonies. Increasingly specialised philological research into these matters has generated an array of problems that philology is quite simply incapable of resolving.

A significant proportion of these problems concern the relationship between textual scholarship and analysis. Whilst it may well be the case that analytical engagement with Bruckner's music has been impeded by the textual situation, the more or less covert reliance of textual scholarship on analysis has been no less evident. In truth, analysis forms a troublesome supplement to much of the literature ostensibly concerned with textual issues. Leopold Nowak's almost moral disapproval of Haas's decisions is frequently attended by remarks inviting analytical rather than philological solutions. The following passage from his preface to the Second Symphony makes this clear:

> The present edition has eliminated passages that do not belong to the 1877 version and replaced them by those that do, so that we now have a complete

---

[1] Cliff Eisen and Christopher Wintle, 'Mozart's C minor Fantasy, K.475: An Editorial "Problem" and its Analytical and Critical Consequences', *Journal of the Royal Musical Association* 124 (1999), pp. 26–52, this quotation pp. 26–7.

final version of the Second Symphony. For technical reasons . . . the passages
marked 'vi-de' in the first version . . . have been retained, although obviously
in a performance making claims to a faithful reproduction of the 1877 version
they would have to be left out. This of course entails the loss, particularly in
the Finale, of a number of passages that one is loath to omit, and this in turn
poses a series of problems that defy a universally satisfactory solution.[2]

Two subtexts underpin these comments. Nowak's regret at jettisoning the
music included by Haas is in one sense aesthetic: the omitted material,
although philologically untenable, is aesthetically successful. But when he
characterises this loss as part of 'a series of problems that defy a universally
satisfactory solution', he passes from an aesthetic to an analytical mode of
phrasing. The cuts become a formal matter; the implication is that they
compromise the music's structure. As a result, Nowak is confronted by an
open conflict between philology and analysis: in the interests of authenticity,
he is forced to make editorial decisions that seem structurally questionable.
Haas, of course, was also alert to this problem, but felt less anxiety about
resolving it by abandoning philological rectitude.

The same conflict resurfaces in the debate over the editions of the 1890
version of the Eighth Symphony. Again, Nowak's comments mingle analytical dissatisfaction with an adoption of the musicological moral high ground.
On the one hand, he rebukes Haas for his loose philological standards: 'a
complete critical edition must not mix its sources: the result would be a
score that would not tally with either version and would certainly not be in
accordance with Bruckner's wishes'.[3] On the other hand, Nowak once more
laments the analytical price of philological rectitude: 'in the second version
the thematic balance [of the recapitulation in the Finale] is impaired, but
as the decision was Bruckner's own nothing can be done about it, especially
as Bruckner's cuts are confirmed by his metrical "figures"'.[4] Nowak tacitly
acknowledges the structural good sense behind Haas's editorial philosophy,
but he cannot square this with its tendentious musicological basis.

Subsequent contributors to this debate have invoked analysis in a similar
way. Deryck Cooke's rather premature claim to have simplified the textual
situation relied in no small measure on judgements that have little to do
with philology. His dismissal of Nowak's edition of the 1890 version of the
Eighth Symphony as formally nonsensical pedantry condones an order of
priority that would find scant support in contemporary textual scholarship.

---

[2] See Leopold Nowak, Foreword to *Anton Bruckner: Sämtliche Werke Band II. II Symphonie C-moll, Fassung von 1877* (Vienna, 1967, repr. 1997).

[3] See Leopold Nowak, Preface to *Anton Bruckner: Sämtliche Werke Band VII/2. VIII Symphonie C-moll, Fassung von 1890* (Vienna, 1955).

[4] Ibid.

For Cooke, Haas's edition should be preferred because it makes formal sense, a view that is of course grounded in Cooke's own analytical understanding of the work's structure. The radical conclusion of this argument, which is only selectively embraced by Cooke, is that textual accuracy should be subservient to analysis. If an edition conforms to a notion of structural sufficiency, it should be accepted; if not, it should be rejected, regardless of the extent to which it represents faithfully the manuscript sources.

Commentators less willing to pursue this end have nevertheless come up against the difficult equation of analysis and philology. William Carragan's work on the sources for the Second Symphony invokes analysis at critical junctures.[5] Whilst his underlying argument – that our perception of the piece has been impeded by the fact that neither Haas nor Nowak published the first version of 1872 – is uncontentious, his support for this version frequently moves beyond a philological defence of the *Urfassung*. His consideration of the order of movements is a case in point:

> Sometime in the late summer or early fall of 1872, a very peculiar thing happened: every one of the parts was cut apart and rearranged in the order first movement – Adagio – Scherzo . . . [T]he fact that the Scherzo was composed before the Adagio, and further, that in that order, the last note of each movement is the first important note in the next, plead strongly for the early order. All through the months of composition, Bruckner conceived of the Scherzo as preceding the Adagio; only in that sequence can we be reasonably sure that we are hearing Bruckner's own conception without any influence from other people such as Herbeck.[6]

Carragan's preference for the initial order of composition invokes the type of philological argument according privilege to the *Urfassung* over the *Fassung letzter Hand*. But when he adds weight to this conviction by noting that 'the last note of each movement is the first important note of the next', he imports an (essentially organicist) analytical concept: we should prefer the first version because it possesses a continuity that later versions lack. Finally, philology and analysis are backed up by an appeal to intention. The 1872 score reveals 'Bruckner's own conception'; in later sources authorial intention is variously compromised.

Carragan calls upon analysis to lend credence to other textual judgements. His critique of Haas's importing of material from the 1872 coda of the first movement into the 1877 version is analytical as much as it is philological: 'performing [this passage] in conjunction with music from

[5] William Carragan, 'The Early Version of the Second Symphony', in Crawford Howie, Paul Hawkshaw and Timothy L. Jackson, eds., *Perspectives on Anton Bruckner* (Aldershot, 2001), pp. 69–92.

[6] Ibid., pp. 73–4.

1877 is anachronistic and ultimately unethical, as the 1877 has its own logic which stems from the composer, not from an editor'.[7] Again, intention is deployed as an arbiter of textual authority, but the perception of a compositional 'logic' is an analytical interpretation of Carragan's own devising as much as it is a property of Bruckner's compositional methods.

Assessments of the publications edited by the Schalk brothers and others, which on the face of it rely even more crucially on biographical and textual evidence, still court the authority of analysis. Thomas Röder's defence of the abridged 1889 Finale of the Third Symphony frankly pursues these matters into analytical and hermeneutic territory.[8] Röder takes earlier commentators (in particular Simpson) to task for judging the Finale adversely for its departures from the perceived orthodoxies of sonata form: 'the assumption that there is a sonata form to be "spoiled" takes for granted that Bruckner composed from an orthodox formal position'.[9] In terms both of formal strategy and the authenticity of the text, he concludes that there is no basis for argument: 'a defence of the abridgements is not necessary. There is nothing to defend; Bruckner accepted all the cuts; he did so with consideration, and no abridgement was really quite new to him.'[10] For Röder, it is the plasticity of Bruckner's material that facilitates these changes. If we wish to impose value judgements on this version, we can consequently only do so from an aesthetic or analytical position: 'One cannot resolve this critical dilemma by defending one's favourite version with philological arguments.'[11] Ultimately, he considers the revision an example of 'the untamable desire of the composer's disciples to unite with their adored master', rather than a bowdlerisation that often dispensed with the composer's approval.[12]

Röder here invokes precisely the dilemma raised by Eisen and Wintle. In the case of the Third Symphony, philology quite easily supports three distinct versions: two by Bruckner; one resulting from the collaboration with Franz Schalk. If Röder's defence of the 1889 score is maintained, then at no stage can the editions of this piece be assessed relatively on the basis of textual arguments. As a result, we cannot dispose of the problem of the first publications by arguing that single authorship should always take precedence over collaboration, since this order of priority is not based fundamentally on philological grounds.[13] A preference for single, rather

---

[7] Ibid., p. 86. The passage in question is bars 488 and 519. Nowak is aware of the problems created by this interpolation, but 'for technical reasons connected with the engraving' he left this and other similar passages in his edition as optional, but recommended, cuts.

[8] Thomas Röder, 'Master and Disciple United: The 1889 Finale of the Third Symphony', in *Perspectives on Anton Bruckner*, pp. 93–113.

[9] Ibid., p. 99.    [10] Ibid.    [11] Ibid.    [12] Ibid., p. 108.

[13] Paul Hawkshaw has advanced this idea; see 'The Bruckner Problem Revisited', *Nineteenth-Century Music* 21 (1997), pp. 96–107.

than dual, authorship invokes a kind of musicological common sense, not a concrete textual authority. And this difficulty extends into the Haas–Nowak debate. Even if some of Haas's conclusions can be rejected out of hand, this does not hold for all the discrepancies between his editions and those of Nowak. The critical issues raised by Nowak, Carragan and Röder are at once essential components of an engagement with the textual situation, and also insoluble from within that field of scholarship. In consequence, any attempt to reduce the quantity of possible texts ends up relying on critical, aesthetic or analytical value judgements.

This, of course, is not so radical a conclusion; textual scholarship has been fighting a rearguard action against the combined forces of critical musicology, the performance-practice movement and the widespread discrediting of the Urtext mentality for some time. As Philip Brett wryly observes, recent circumstances presage a situation in which 'the editor will be lucky to find employment running the copying machine and brewing the herbal tea'.[14] Neither has Bruckner scholarship been immune to the pluralism that inevitably results from a loss of faith in philology's capacity for resolving critical issues definitively, or from the widespread discrediting of the ideology of the Urtext. Benjamin Korstvedt deploys precisely these arguments in support of the collaborative first editions, attacking the first *Gesamtausgabe* in part for its reliance on an Urtext mentality.[15] At the same time, relatively little effort has been devoted to following up the analytical observations generated by the editions of the symphonies in the sort of detail in which Eisen and Wintle consider Mozart's C minor Fantasy. Questions of structural insufficiency, material continuity and the fulfilment or disruption of compositional 'logic', once raised as adjuncts to textual scholarship, require extended analytical clarification before their role in parsing editorial decisions can be thoroughly evaluated.

## Analysis

### I

Rather than attempt a general overview of the editions and their related analytical dilemmas, it is perhaps more productive to focus on the analytical

---

[14] See Philip Brett, 'Text, Context and the Early Music Editor', in Nicholas Kenyon, ed., *Authenticity and Early Music* (Oxford, 1988), pp. 83–114, this quotation p. 84. See also James Grier, *The Critical Editing of Music: History, Method and Practice* (Cambridge, 1996) and 'Editing', in Stanley Sadie, ed., *The New Grove Dictionary of Music and Musicians*, 2nd edn, vol. VII (London, 2001), pp. 885–95.

[15] See Benjamin Korstvedt, '"Return to the Pure Sources": The Ideological and Text-Critical Legacy of the First Bruckner *Gesamtausgabe*', in *Bruckner Studies* (Cambridge, 1997), pp. 91–109, and especially pp. 108–9.

implications of isolated discrepancies in a single movement on which changes of editorial policy have had a profound effect: the Finale of the Second Symphony. Divergences between the Haas and Nowak editions of this work can be traced to the fundamental differences of editorial ideology broached in Chapter 3. Haas subscribed to the view that none of the available versions embodied, in themselves, an ideal response to the formal challenges posed by the material. Bruckner's revisions improved some aspects of the structure, but rendered others insufficient. This difficulty could be overcome by conflating sources: the structural gaps generated by revision could be filled by importing earlier material. As we have seen, Haas was prepared to sacrifice scholarly rectitude in this way because he believed Bruckner's artistic spirit was not best served by the literal results of philological research. The task of the editor was therefore to furnish ideal solutions where none was unambiguously forthcoming from the composer. Haas's conflations are thus in the broadest sense analytical. The formal dilemmas they are designed to remedy cannot be assessed without the intervention of analysis.

In the Second Symphony, Haas's solutions entailed integrating materials from opposite ends of a complex process of revision. His edition is for the most part a reproduction of the 1877 version, although this is in itself a ramification of numerous changes entered into the copy scores and parts in 1872, 1873 and 1876, together with a further reappraisal undertaken in 1877.[16] At key stages in the first movement, Adagio and Finale, he restored material

[16] The principal sources are as follows: composition score, dated 1872–3 (Austrian National Library, Music Collection, Mus.Hs.19.474); copy score by Carda, dated 1872, revised 1873 and 1877 (Austrian National Library, Music Collection, Mus.Hs.6034); copy score by Tenschert/Carda, revised 1872, 1873, 1877 (Austrian National Library, Music Collection, Mus.Hs.6035); orchestral part, dated 1872–3 (Austrian National Library, Music Collection, Mus.Hs.6061); pages extracted from Mus.Hs.6035 (Austrian National Library, Music Collection, Mus.Hs.6060); pages extracted from Mus.Hs.6034 (Austrian National Library, Music Collection, Mus.Hs.6059); piano reduction of Mus.Hs.6059 by Stradal (Austrian National Library, Music Collection, Mus.Hs.6095); amendments to the Adagio, dated 1877 (Austrian National Library, Music Collection, Mus.Hs.6023); holograph pages, comprising revisions to the first movement and Finale (privately owned when Haas had access to them, and unknown to Nowak, now Austrian National Library, Music Collection, Mus.Hs.39.744); copy score, dated 1877 (City and Provincial Library, Vienna, M.H.6781); pages removed from Mus.Hs.6034 and Mus.Hs.6035 (Stift Kremsmünster, Regenterei 56,8); orchestral part, copied by Carda and others in 1872 (Stift St Florian, Archiv 19/13). There is an additional source ('L') seen by Haas, which is now lost. There are four principal editions: first edition of 1892, edited by Cyril Hynais, published by Doblinger; Haas's edition for the first Gesamtausgabe, 1938, which mixes 1872 and 1877 scores; Leopold Nowak's edition of the 1877 score for the second Gesamtausgabe, 1965; William Carragan's edition of the 1872 version for the second Gesamtausgabe, 2001. A chronology of composition and revision, together with a synopsis of the sources, is offered by Carragan; see 'The Early Version of the Second Symphony', pp. 70–2.

from the 1872 score that Bruckner himself had removed. In the first movement, he reinstated a thirty-one-bar passage near the end (Haas/Nowak,
bars 488 to 519), which has the formal consequence of rendering the coda
a tripartite rather than a bipartite structure. He also subtracted a bar's rest
added to the movement's final cadence, reducing it from a five-bar to a four-
bar phrase. In the Adagio, Haas retained a varied repetition of the second
theme between bars 48 and 69, the removal of which reduced the second
group from a two-part to a one-part form, and also restored the 1872 coda,
which Bruckner later revised and in places reorchestrated. In the Finale,
Haas restored two key passages: bars 540 to 562, which repeat the reference
to the Kyrie of the F minor Mass found in bars 200 to 209; the first part of the
coda, bars 590 to 655, complete with its fragmentary allusion, in bars 640 to
649, to the opening of the first movement. As Carragan points out, in order
to render the Kyrie quotation compatible with the preceding material, Haas
was obliged to insert his own first violin part in bars 541 to 543.[17] Nowak's
1965 edition responds to these interventions in a variety of ways. The extra
bar at the end of the first movement is simply restored, whereas the coda of
the Adagio from the 1877 version is reinstated, but placed alongside its 1872
counterpart. The major insertions in the first and last movements, and in
the second-theme group of the Adagio, are retained in Nowak's edition, but
framed by cautionary 'Vi-De' markings.

Two key questions arise here. First, what is the precise nature of the
formal problem to which Haas responds? Second, what are the effects, in
terms of formal and material process, of removing the 1872 sections? These
questions are clearly related: if Haas was right to perceive structural difficulties resulting from revision, then excising his 'solutions' should render
the problems analytically visible. A comparative approach considering the
structural effects of omission in a variety of parameters could both clarify
and tentatively resolve these matters.

The two inserted passages in the Finale betray structural affinities, whilst
also raising analytical issues that are essentially distinct. The most obvious
matters arising concern the proportions of the movement and the related
question of whether the balance of the form is impaired. The first passage
separates the climax of the third group in the recapitulation from the transition to the coda. Its omission in Nowak reduces the group from ninety-seven
to seventy-four bars, balancing a third group in the exposition of eighty-
four bars' length. This truncation, however, is not in itself a problem that
demands rectification. In fact, the first and second groups are also abbrevi-
ated in the recapitulation: the first group is reduced from seventy-five bars

---

[17] See 'The Early Version of the Second Symphony', p. 87.

to forty-four; the second group from seventy-two bars to sixty-one bars. Removal of the Kyrie material thus brings the third group in line with a general principle of recapitulatory truncation, which Haas's amendments transgress. Moreover, this device is common to Bruckner's sonata forms in general. A brief survey of the relative proportions of theme groups in the first movements of the nine numbered symphonies (taking the Linz version of the First, the 1873 version of the Third, the 1878 version of the Fourth and the 1890 revision of the Eighth) shows that truncation is the norm in the vast majority of cases. Omitting the recapitulated first groups of the Eighth and Ninth symphonies, which are highly ambiguous with respect to position and function, for the rest there are only two examples of recapitulatory expansion (the third groups in the First and Second symphonies), and only one example in which a group remains the same length (the second group in the Second Symphony). In some instances, truncation is drastic: in the Fifth Symphony, the first group is reduced from fifty to eighteen bars, and the third group from sixty-four to twenty-eight; in the Third Symphony, the first group is contracted from 134 bars to sixty; in the Ninth Symphony, the second group is reduced from seventy bars to thirty-eight. If Haas believed that his policy of lengthening the third group in the recapitulation conformed to a general Brucknerian compositional principle, he was mistaken.

Detailed comparison of the third group in the exposition and recapitulation yields more equivocal results. In the exposition, the group is composed of four hypermetrical units, bars 148 to 165, 166 to 181, 182 to 199 and 200 to 231, occupying eighteen, sixteen, eighteen and thirty-two bars respectively. The sections are delineated by specific thematic, harmonic and topical characteristics. The first essentially performs two successive functions: assertion of the relative major, via a restatement of the climactic theme from bars 33 and 34 of the first group, in bars 148 and 149; sequential intensification of this material culminating on V of E flat in bars 150 to 165. The second section develops this first-group material, against continuous quaver figurations, through sequential modulations leading to G flat in bars 175 to 177. The third part, initially articulated by a general pause, resumes the intensification process, deploying the quaver figure introduced in the previous section, and rising to a climax in bars 190 to 197 over E flat and C, which also reintroduces a dotted duplet–triplet figure derived from the first movement. The final section, which contains the Kyrie allusion, functions as a closing section and abruptly dissipates the preceding climax.

In the recapitulation, the elements of this structure are reworked into revisionary counterparts of their exposition forms, and a further section, the pizzicato march of bars 563 to 589, is supplied as a transition to the coda. The first section, bars 493 to 512, is again composed of statement and intensification leading to a dominant, but here the harmonic relationship of these components is revised: the start of the group interrupts the preceding dominant preparation of C minor with E flat; the intensification reinstates V of c. Bars 513 to 520 offset the modulating sequence of bars 166 to 181 with an analogous sequence passing from c to G flat via f. Similarly, the climactic intensification in bars 521 to 539 balances that of bars 182 to 199, although the thematic construction is here more complex. The climax from bar 529 overlays both triplet and duplet quaver patterns, together with the dotted duplet–triplet figure from the first movement in the first and third horns, and briefly tonicises C flat major, before a slender V of C minor is recovered in bar 539. The inserted 1872 material, bars 540 to 562, then has three distinct parts, distinguished by harmonic function. The second contains the Kyrie allusion in its original key of G flat, and the surrounding phrases facilitate modulation from C minor to G flat and back. The lengths of the five sections of the group are now twenty, eight, nineteen, twenty-three and twenty-seven bars respectively.

This comparison ostensibly makes a stronger case for Haas's edition, since inclusion of the Kyrie reference supplies an analogous passage in the recapitulation for each section of the third group in the exposition, onto which the march linking the group to the coda is then grafted. Moreover, the proportions of the respective parts of the group form an arithmetic pattern in the exposition that is consistently distorted in the recapitulation; the 1872 material does not compromise this process. Thus: in the exposition, the first and third parts are the same length, the fourth part is twice the length of the second, and each part comprises an even number of bars; in the recapitulation, the sections increase in size irregularly from the second to the fifth, and the third, fourth and fifth parts are of uneven length.

Yet again this argument is not equally persuasive for all parameters, and particularly with respect to harmonic function. In the exposition, the Kyrie passage functions cadentially; the tonicisation of G flat links the climax on C major in bars 194 to 197 with the plagal cadence in III that closes the exposition. The same material in the recapitulation performs no such function. On the contrary, the dominant secured by the march section is also the last chord before the 1872 material begins. Bars 540 to 562 delay the prolongation of a perfect cadence by chromatic interpolation, whereas the same section in the exposition enables the consolidation of the relative major. If bars 540 to 562 do perform a vital function, it is not the contribution of a structural cadence. Again, at this level of scrutiny the analytical argument does not indicate a structural absence. In effect, the march passage substitutes for the structural function of the Kyrie in its exposition form: the latter consolidates the concluding key of the exposition; the former prepares the tonic for the coda.

## II

The 1872 material also occupies a place in the broader tonal scheme of the movement; and in this context its inclusion is more analytically constructive. Example 6.1 gives a reductive appraisal of the tonal strategy of the exposition. It elaborates a four-key scheme. The overall bass motion from c to E flat is augmented by two more local tonicisations: A major at the start of the second group; G flat as a climactic tonality of the third. The second and third groups are thus contrasted not only with respect to tonality, but also in terms of how key relationships are organised within the groups: the second employs a directed tonal scheme, whereas the third embeds G flat within a prolongation of III. Consequently, although the deep structure is governed by the diminished seventh C–E flat–G flat–A, the progression from C minor to E flat major is not a simple matter of arpeggiation through successive equal third relationships, but pits the tritone A–E flat (in the second group) against the third relationship E flat–G flat–E flat (in the third group). Moreover as Example 6.1 also shows, at the climax of the third group, immediately preceding the Kyrie quotation in G flat, E flat is temporarily usurped by C, so that the tritone C–G flat is inserted before definitive resolution onto the relative major is permitted. The tonal narrative of the exposition therefore concerns two means of deploying the structural potential of the diminished seventh. The complementary tritones A–E flat and G flat–C are embedded within a system of larger third relationships.

The way we understand the response to this structure in the recapitulation depends crucially on whether or not we admit the 1872 material. Without it, the whole of the reprise effectively prolongs the tonic. Interruptions such as the brief E flat major at the start of the third group, the climactic V–I in C flat in bars 531 to 536 and the local chromaticisms inflecting the second group are consistently subordinate to the tonic cadences in bars 388, 432 and 513, an effect that is reinforced by the extended dominant pedal supplied by the march material of bars 563 to 589. Readmission of the Kyrie allusion untransposed alters the complexion of this structure. The tritone C–G flat is now re-established at a critical juncture. The security of the dominant approaching the coda is concomitantly weakened, not only because the Kyrie places G flat between V in bar 539 and V in bar 561, but also because

Example 6.1  Second Symphony (1877), Finale

Summary of exposition

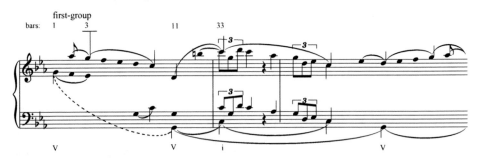

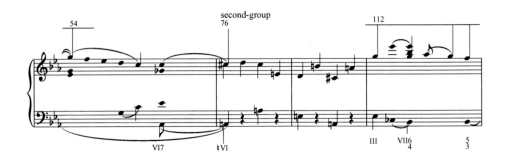

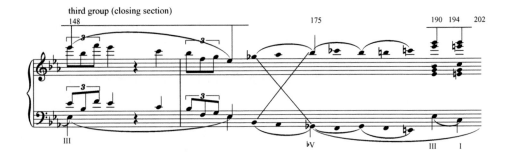

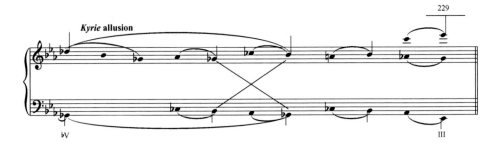

Example 6.2  Second Symphony (1877), Finale

Exposition – distribution of third relationships/tritones

the brief dominant of bar 539 is now sandwiched between C flat and G flat, as semitonal 'shadows' of the real i–V axis. This structure is summarised in Example 6.2.

Haas's edition thus exacerbates the teleological character of the movement. The presence of the tritone opposing C in the reprise of the third group introduces a late composing-out of an issue that is confined to the exposition in Nowak's edition. This, in turn, has a bearing on Haas's second appropriation from the 1872 score, bars 590 to 655. The increased complexity of the reprise, and the diminished force of the tonic, renders the final peroration potentially inadequate, a problem remediable by supplying the minor-key complement to the concluding V–I, contained within the 1872 material in bars 611 to 624.

These features coexist with a second issue, the resolution of which is an essential preoccupation in the recapitulation and coda. In the first-theme group of the exposition, the tonic is represented in the bass progression for the most part by a dominant pedal, not by a prolonged C. Bars 1 to 32 altogether prolong a registral transfer from g1 to G in the bass, to which local V–i resolutions are consistently subordinated. Although there is a strong resolution onto $i_3^5$ with the climax at bar 33, the prevailing G is resumed almost immediately as an internal voice in the horns from bar 34, and more forcefully as the structural bass-note from bar 40. As Example 6.1 reveals, the transition, beginning at bar 52 with the return of the movement's opening, then elaborates the semitonal bass progression G–A flat–A: A flat, as an unresolved dominant or augmented sixth, supplants the original G from bar 61; A major is asserted unequivocally at the start of the second theme, bar 76.

The recapitulation persistently seeks to subordinate the G pedal to the prolongation of a C *Stufe*. The first attempt proves insubstantial. Because the reprise of the first group starts at bar 388 with the climactic material from bar 33, the resolution of the preceding 40-bar dominant preparation is brief. V is reasserted by bar 395, and C remains caught between two much larger prolongations of G in the bass. This situation persists at the start of the second group, bar 432. Bruckner's strategy for removing the exposition's semitonal ascent to A is to resolve the A flat7 chord concluding the first group as an augmented sixth, as a result of which the second theme now begins in the tonic major over a second inversion. A flat is turned into a complete upper neighbour-note to G, but the unequivocal root-position declaration of the tonic is again deferred. This declaration is also either thwarted or undermined at key stages in the third group. Resolution of the dominant at the end of the second group, bar 492, is not fulfilled until bar 513, and again the tonic is then rapidly abandoned, yielding to G flat by bar 521.

As the comparative reduction in Example 6.3 makes plain, the addition of the 1872 material has a critical impact on the way this issue is ultimately decided. The Kyrie quotation disrupts what would otherwise be a simple prolongation of V and as a consequence delays the arrival of a sustained C *Stufe*. The additional passage in the coda pushes this deferral a stage further. The large-scale i–V–i elaborated between bars 590 and 620 prepares a chromatic ascent in bars 620 to 638 culminating on an unresolved diminished seventh, rather than a period of unambiguous tonic harmony, and the fragmentary allusions to the first movement and the second theme of the Finale in bars 640 to 655 hardly establish C minor with any degree of stability. The 1877 cuts simplify this process considerably. The transitional march supplies a final dominant preparation of C minor without interruption, after which the coda simply asserts the elusive i–V–I, sustaining the conclusive C *Stufe* over twenty-two bars. Again, Haas's editorial policy increases the movement's teleological drive. Both additions prolong the tendency to represent C minor most substantially by its dominant.

In this context, the argument turns on the perception of sufficient resolution. Taken by itself, the recapitulation of the 1877 Finale presents a relatively straightforward solution to the problems posed in the exposition, especially with respect to the tritonal key relationships, which are simply omitted. If these strategies form part of a general struggle–victory narrative informing the symphony, then the moment of overcoming may seem disproportionately brief in Nowak's edition. Haas's interpolations both respond to this problem, introducing a reprise and resolution of the C–G flat tritone, and an expansion of the conclusive cadential process. Of course, it could be argued that, beyond the basic requirement of supplying a structural cadence, the notion of sufficient resolution is nebulous at best. As Röder remarks: 'How hard should it be to attain the conclusion in order to project a dignified

Example 6.3  Second Symphony, Finale

Recapitulation and Coda – reductive comparison of Haas and Nowak

"per aspera ad astra" narrative?'[18] Yet we do not have to resolve this question in order to recognise its relevance for the matter in hand. In terms of tonal strategy at least, Haas's decisions are structurally grounded. Whether we accept the gravity of the difficulties they address or not, their structural function is clear.

[18] See 'Master and Disciple United', p. 99.

*III*

Similar arguments attend the thematic structure of the Finale. Carefully distributed processes of thematic intensification, dissipation and allusion articulate the characteristics identified above, into which the 1872 passages are inserted at critical junctures. This, in turn, demands a broader analytical comparison of the thematic structure of the exposition and recapitulation, against which the insertions in the recapitulation might be understood.

Thematic techniques observed in Chapter 4 are again helpful in this context. The concept of thematic mutation and the opposition of 'being' and 'becoming' as a means of articulating form are particularly crucial to the structure of the exposition. The redeployment or variation of these processes is central to the recapitulation and coda, and this is accordingly affected by inclusion or omission of the 1872 material. In the exposition, the first-theme group is characterised by a process of thematic mutation, taking place in three stages: bars 1 to 32, 33 to 51 and 52 to 75. The first stage opens up a structural problem, the resolution of which is a principal concern of the recapitulation. Two important figures, marked 'a' and 'b' in Example 6.4, are introduced immediately, but their status as self-sufficient thematic units is compromised by participation in a broader process of intensification culminating with the introduction of a new figure, described in Example 6.4 as 'c', at the start of the second stage, bar 33. The opening, in short, is simultaneously expository and preparatory. Moreover, 'a' immediately links the Finale to a broader thematic narrative, since it constitutes a free double diminution of the first theme of the first movement, a connection made more explicit in the development section.[19] The means by which the intensification proceeds is essentially circular: motive 'b', which is initially distinct from 'a', mutates back into an augmentation of 'a' by bar 20. The point at which 'b' becomes 'a' is also the moment at which the melodic ascent of the material towards bar 33 is arrested. The resolution onto the tonic at bar 33 is enabled thematically by a further mutation of 'a', through which the neighbour-note $\hat{6}$–$\hat{5}$ is allowed to resolve upwards as A–B flat–B–C.

Following the climactic statement of 'c', a second intensification process gathers momentum from bar 35 that relies on a different mutation technique. Here, an extended form of 'c', sequenced to create a seventeen-bar linear ascent, is first of all rhythmically contracted from a two-bar to a one-bar form at bar 39. From bar 48, the first half of the motive, including the characteristic triplet figure, is removed, leaving the residual consonant skip F–A flat. The third stage of the group, beginning at bar 52, initially reprises

---

[19] Bars 264–89 juxtapose the two forms of the theme: the Finale form principally as accompaniment; the first-movement form variously as *rectus* and *inversus*.

Example 6.4  Second Symphony, Finale

Thematic structure of first group

the first stage, but the intensificatory ascent is modified from bar 60, becoming a transitional dissipation. Motive 'b' becomes an augmentation of 'a' by bar 60, and the rest of the transition is a development out of this motive form. Each stage of the group presents a variant of the same organising principle: the material is defined not primarily by its identity at a given moment, but by its participation in an ongoing process of thematic mutation, which at each stage points beyond the group to a later moment of fulfilment or cessation.

In contrast, the second group chiefly comprises the largely unvaried repetition of a principal motive, identified as 'x' in Example 6.5, set against

Example 6.5 Second Symphony, Finale

Thematic structure of second group

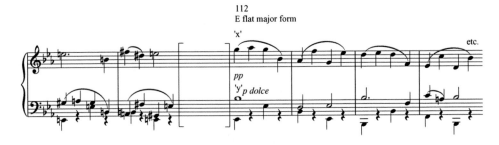

the free variation of a subsidiary theme 'y' introduced in the first violins
from bar 80. The two main tonal areas occupied by the group – A major
and its relations from bar 76 to 111 and E flat major from bar 112 to 147 –
are articulated by a simple change in the way 'x' is treated. The concluding
part of the first section, bars 100 to 111, dispenses with the second half of
'x' and sequentially repeats the first half. Conversely, with the exceptions of
the momentary recovery of the complete form of 'x' at bar 134 and again
ten bars later, in the second section the first half of 'x' is discarded after
bar 124, leaving only free variants of the second half. In a version of the
strategy we have already encountered in the Eighth Symphony, the second
group is distinguished not by a continuous process of becoming, but by a
condition of thematic 'being', centred on the statement and repetition of a
stable motive form.

The third group takes up and extends processes introduced in the first
group. Initially, the development of 'c' is reworked. Thus bars 148 to 162
comprise a transposed variant of bars 33 to 51, in which the contraction
process of bars 35 to 51 is modified: the single-bar form of 'c', introduced
at bar 150, is contracted in bars 156 to 162, such that the triplet figure
is retained and the consonant skip is abandoned, rather than vice versa
(see Example 6.6). In bars 166 to 171, this residual triplet is combined loosely
with the contour of 'b', leading to a continuous linear descent in the lower

Example 6.6  Second Symphony, Finale

Third group – primary thematic process

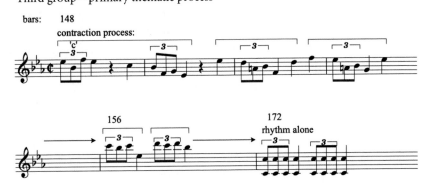

Example 6.7  Second Symphony, Finale

Third group – secondary thematic process

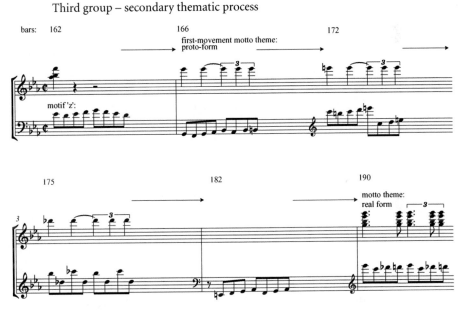

strings and eventual liquidation of the motive, now reduced to its rhythmic characteristics alone, in the trumpet in bars 178 to 181. After this point, 'c' plays no further part in the group. Against this, Bruckner counterpoints two further motivic processes, which follow distinct paths and deploy fresh material. From bar 150, the winds are given a duplet–triplet figure, which eventually becomes the dotted duplet–triplet motto theme from the first movement at the climax in bars 190 to 197. At the same time, a continuous quaver figure, defined as 'z' in Example 6.7, emerges in the cellos and basses from bar 162, replacing 'c' as the basic constituent of the string texture from bar 182. Altogether, the group as far as bar 197 plays out the liquidation of the first-theme material and its replacement by 'z' and the motto theme. Bars 166 to 182 effectively constitute a junction in the thematic structure, where all three figures are present simultaneously: 'c' moving towards its liquidation; the motto still in its preparatory form.

The sharp gestural and harmonic disjunction separating the Kyrie allusion introduced at bar 200 from the rest of the group also articulates a discontinuity of thematic process. The closing section makes no reference to the preceding material. Instead, a simple mutation process unfolds: the neighbour-note figure concluding the quotation in bars 204 to 205 first of all forms the basis of a rising sequence in bars 208 to 214; from bar 216 this merges into two interlocking augmentations of 'a'. Continuity with the body of the third group is sacrificed in order to establish a wider connection: first of all with the opening of the movement; more generally with the theme opening the whole symphony, of which 'a' is a variant. The result, however, is the exacerbation of a general formal problem. The return to a kind of 'becoming' as a governing principle in the third group does not lead, at the end of the exposition, to a decisive, synthetic event, but to a breakdown in the continuity of the symphonic discourse. The conclusion of the exposition is detached from a process spanning the first and third groups; the general pause in bars 197 to 199 in effect forces a rift between the thematic narrative and the structural demand for closure.

The reprise of the first-theme group at bar 388 is decisive in some respects and inconclusive in others. Truncation of the group so that the first part is omitted eliminates the dichotomy between exposition and preparation surrounding motives 'a' and 'b' in the exposition. Preparatory intensification is now the province of the retransition, which accumulates forms of the second theme over a forty-bar dominant pedal, and the return of 'c' at bar 388 is simultaneously a point of culmination and the start of the group. Similarly, 'a' and 'b' now constitute the aftermath of 'c', appearing only in their transitional forms from bar 407 onwards. In other respects, the dialectical relationship with the second group is maintained. Omission of the first section notwithstanding, the processes of thematic becoming associated with the first group are reprised almost without variation; the second group, although modified, adheres to its original principle of statement and embellished repetition.

When the third group returns, it consequently confronts two structural problems. The discontinuities characterising its exposition form conflict directly with its expected function in the recapitulation as an arbiter of closure. The group also carries the burden of resolving the conflict of thematic process between first and second themes. The mutation of themes

Example 6.8  Second Symphony, Finale

Third group, recapitulation – thematic process

in the first group points towards the attainment of a definitive, stable motive form, which would nullify its processual difference with the second theme. Yet again, resolution of these issues is deferred; instead, the processes evident in the exposition undergo a further stage of development, traced in Example 6.8. The statement of 'c' that opens the group in the exposition

Example 6.8 (*cont.*)

becomes a four-bar sequence in bars 493 to 497, after which a process of contraction reduces 'c' to its triplet component alone by bar 510. Bars 513 to 520 then furnish a reduced analogue to bars 166 to 181: the three motive forms – 'c', 'z' and the motto theme – characterising the group are again present simultaneously, the motto reappearing in its preparatory form, 'z' again appearing as bass-line. The subsequent progress towards the climax in bars 533 to 539 however differs markedly from the analogous passage in the exposition. All three motives are in different ways liquidated as bar 533 approaches: 'c' is once more reduced to a residual triplet; the preparatory form of the first-movement motto is dispersed completely in bars 521 to 528, before its full form is reintroduced and liquidated in the brass and (latterly) the winds between bars 529 and 538; 'z' is consistent to the bass-line until 523, but is removed after bar 533. The consequence of this climax is again fragmentation. The disjunctive gestures of bars 536 to 539 disperse the motivic residues of bars 533 to 535, and we appear irremediably distant from a synthetic thematic event.

And here we come again to Haas's insertions, both of which sit between this disjunction and the conclusive point of resolution. The synthetic thematic event evaded in the reprise is ultimately supplied in the coda, through two principal means. First, 'c' and 'b' are integrated from bar 680 into a single cadential figure, within an unvaried C major *Klang* constructed from repetitions of the first-movement motto (see Example 6.9). The terminus of the process of becoming is a new motive form combining first-group motives that were linked syntagmatically in the exposition and recapitulation, but never fused into a single paradigm. Second, in the preceding ascent 'a' is unequivocally preparatory, being in effect liquidated as part of the dominant build-up of bars 656 to 679. In Nowak's edition, these events are separated from the end of the third group only by the transitional march

Example 6.9  Second Symphony, Finale

Coda – distribution of material

of bars 563 to 589, which consists entirely of 'b' in various forms. In Haas's edition, the unravelling of thematic conflicts is considerably augmented by the addition of bars 590 to 655. The combination of 'c' and 'b' is pre-empted in bars 620 to 638. The moment of overcoming at bar 680 is thus reinforced by the fact that an earlier minor-key statement of this synthetic motive form had failed to articulate a conclusive gesture, leading instead to a further disjunction over a diminished seventh in bars 638 and 639. The fragmentary allusions to the first movement and the second theme in bars 640 to 655 then supply a cathartic gesture similar to the succession of quotations we have already observed in the 1873 version of the Finale of the Third Symphony. Again, this compounds the sense of overcoming at bar 680, since it now stands in close proximity to the extraction, by isolation, from the symphonic discourse of the work's opening theme (as the source of motive 'a') and the second theme of the Finale (as the stable motive form opposing the first theme).

The inserted Kyrie allusion in bars 540 to 560 contributes to the same process of catharsis, and by the same means. The mutation into 'a' characterising this material in the exposition is abruptly cut short at bar 556, leaving the quotation isolated by parenthetical general pauses. The means by which closure was obtained at the end of the exposition is thus emphatically negated, and the role of thematic process in the articulation of closure is brought sharply into focus. This again contributes to the synthetic force of the coda, which compensates for this absence and as a result invites direct comparison with the end of the exposition. The removal of the quotation in the 1877 score withdraws this connection. The conclusive drive towards a synthetic thematic event is an immediate response to the breakdown of texture at the end of the third group; the resolution of other structural issues is evaded.

*IV*

Finally, the 1872 passages participate in the movement's topical and expressive discourses; and again, comparison of exposition and recapitulation is essential to an understanding of their structural consequences. The response in the recapitulation and coda to the exposition's distribution of topics is crucially altered by the revisions in the 1877 version, and this in turn affects the articulation of tonal and thematic processes. Insertion of the 1872 passages also has wider expressive implications. The topics deployed by Bruckner link the Finale to its post-Beethovenian symphonic heritage, and are vital to the unfolding of the struggle–victory narrative informing the entire work. Furthermore, the topical discourse conveys extroversive meanings of a more contemporaneous or personal nature, playing out conflicts between secular and sacred influence in a manner prescient of that already observed in the Finale of the Third Symphony.

The first-theme group is dominated by martial or pathetic topical allusions. At the beginning, the *agitato* sigh figure 'a' combines with the processional march conveyed by 'b' and its variants. The entry of motive 'c' at bar 33 establishes a direct engagement with the rhetoric of Beethoven's so-called 'C minor mood', particularly in its association of C minor with a consistent octave texture.[20] In the group's two climactic intensifications, the material acquires *Sturm und Drang* resonances, most plainly in bars 27 to 32, where the textural accumulation over V is assisted by the addition of a tremolando string figure. The topical progression in the second and third groups involves both the reinterpretation of these affiliations, and the introduction of two opposing topical categories. The texture of the second theme strongly resembles a polka, evinced most persistently by the continuous pizzicato bass part. The Kyrie reference at the end of the exposition introduces both *stile antico* and sacred elements into the discourse, reinforced in this instance by its direct link with the F minor Mass. Before this, the third group's preoccupation with revisiting first-group material conveys a modification of affect: reinterpreting this material in the predominant context of E flat major produces a shift from pathetic to heroic modes of Beethovenian symphonic rhetoric.

[20] The obvious examples are of course the first movements of the Third Piano Concerto, the Fifth Symphony and the Sonata, Op. 111. Beethoven in turn draws on precedents in Mozart's Concerto K.491, Fantasy K.475 and Sonata K.457, as well as Haydn's Symphony no. 95. For consideration of this issue, see Michael Tusa, 'Beethoven's C minor Mood: Some Thoughts on the Structural Implications of Key Choice', in Christopher Reynolds, Lewis Lockwood and James Webster, eds., *The Beethoven Forum* (Lincoln, 1993), pp. 1–27.

As with the Finale of the Third Symphony, so here also the expressive trajectory of the exposition is far more complex than the commonplace idea of Bruckner as sacred symphonic composer might allow. The sacred reference is purposefully detached from the preceding material. It articulates closure, but only after the dialogue with the Beethovenian style has failed to achieve the same result, coming to an abrupt halt over the tonic major in bar 197. For the most part, the exposition unfolds a discourse of high and low secular styles: pathetic and heroic connotations frame a dance type.

Variations of material in the recapitulation produce concomitant inflections of the topical discourse. Initiation of the recapitulation with motive 'c' places a greater structural emphasis on the Beethovenian pathetic affiliation, and the martial elements with which the movement begins are now restricted to the articulation of the transition. In the second group, the polka elements dissipate at key points in the form. The characteristic bass-line is absent until the fifth bar, and in bars 481 to 484 the invasive reference to the rhythm of 'c' in the trumpets introduces a topical feature from the first group that contributes to the complete dispersal of the dance type in the bars immediately preceding the third group. The tonal scheme of the third group, which feints towards E flat before C minor is established at bar 513, exposes the dual nature of 'c', as a signifier of pathetic and heroic styles, within a single formal region.

Both 1872 passages change the way these topical conflicts contribute to the final stages of the struggle–victory narrative. Bruckner's later extraction of the first passage radically alters the complexion of the discourse. In Nowak's edition, the recapitulation and coda are entirely concerned with secular types and styles. As a result, the Kyrie quotation in the exposition retrospectively becomes an apostrophe in the rhetorical sense: it is a topical digression, which does not impinge on the later progress of the form.[21] Haas's restoration revives the sacred style at a critical juncture, and therefore reanimates its structural potential. Even if we regard this as a moment of dissolution, during which the sacred materials are expunged from the form, it nevertheless supplies a key stage in the progression from pathos to resolution. The greater structural integration of the sacred component is also emphasised by its connection with the preceding climax. Although the Kyrie reference in the recapitulation is again apostrophised by rests, the transition from *Sturm und Drang* climax in bars 533 to 539 to sacred style after bar 547 is now mollified by a topical overlap in the intervening bars,

[21] See Leonard Ratner, *Classic Music: Expression, Form and Style* (New York, 1980), pp. 91 and 93.

the string texture of the previous bars being liquidated against the sustained semibreves of the winds.

The contribution of the second passage is twofold. First, the parallelism between bars 590 to 638 and 656 to the end directly juxtaposes a return to the pathetic C minor mode (at bar 620) and its eventual overcoming (at bar 680), each climax being the outcome of an intensification deploying the same material, and therefore the same topic. Haas's edition enhances the effect of the final resolution to C major not only because it literally takes longer to reach the movement's goal, but also because it exposes two possible results of the same expressive device in close proximity. Second, the isolated references to the first movement and the second theme of the Finale in bars 640 to 655 add an extra dimension to the dialogue with Beethoven, recalling the apostrophised allusions to earlier movements with which the Finale of the Ninth Symphony opens. The fragmentary return of the second theme in particular carries an analogous topical function to that of the restored Kyrie reference. This could also be read as a topical dissolution, which prepares the conclusion by excising topics that obscure the transformation of the pathetic materials into their final, triumphant form. As in the Finale of the Third Symphony, so here also this idea of catharsis through quotation is deployed much later in the structure than in its Beethovenian precedent. Beethoven's model of teleological symphonic process is thus both invoked and reconceived. Once more, the point of overcoming is deferred until the last possible moment.

## Conclusions

The issues surrounding the convergence of analysis and editorial policy in Bruckner's music are complex, and cannot be disposed of through passing appeals to compositional logic, or to the evident structural integrity of one editorial decision over another in relation to a normative formal type. It is not only, as Röder rightly asserts, that a preference for Haas over Nowak, or for the *Gesamtausgabe* over an edition of Franz Schalk, is erroneous if it relies on the assumption that Bruckner was trying to emulate an orthodox notion of symphonic form, whatever that might be. Even if we accept a generalised formal prescription as grounds for measuring editorial policy, it is highly doubtful that this can accommodate the nuances of structural effect arising from material discrepancies between editions in all parameters with equal sensitivity. In the foregoing analysis, the thematic consequences of adding the 1872 passages are not the same as the tonal or topical consequences. The interaction of parameters is frequently cooperative or similar – thematic and topical processes often articulate tonal strategies – but the ramification of all these elements within a single, global model of structural sufficiency applies a blunt instrument to a delicate and manifold operation. In some instances, processes specific to a given parameter openly oppose those apparent in another. Comparison of the proportions of the third group in the exposition and recapitulation, for example, gives scant grounds for accepting Haas's inclusion of the Kyrie reference as a putative response to a structural problem, whereas analysis of the tonal strategy, or of the topical discourse, provides a much clearer basis for comprehending Haas's decisions.

For this reason, it is difficult to reach decisive conclusions about the more extensive discrepancies between editions without the assistance of detailed analysis: our understanding of the effects of editorial differences will remain inadequate until a comprehensive analytical survey of the music has been undertaken. In this sense, the foregoing analysis is little more than a preparatory sketch. It considers only two examples of editorial divergence, and their location within the broader structural narrative of the movement is highly selective, isolating specific functional correspondences between exposition and recapitulation to the virtual exclusion of the development. And this is to say nothing of the parameters that remain untouched, most obviously the hypermetrical structure, upon which the inserted passages would have an evident impact. Elements of the Finale also interact with processes spanning the entire work, not only through thematic cross-referencing and an encompassing symphonic narrative but in terms of the relative deployment of tonal strategies and the comparative distributions of affects, topics and expressive devices. This leads in turn to the more general matter of the implicit dialogue with the Beethovenian legacy, and to the extra-musical connotations of topical affiliations. All these factors have a bearing on how we understand Haas's interventions on the broadest scale.

The aim of this chapter is categorically not to mount an analytical defence of decisions that are philologically indefensible, as if analysis could somehow circumvent the bald fact that editors have frequently acted with scant regard for philological rectitude. At the same time, Carragan's dismissal of Haas's score on the grounds of anachronism, whilst philologically unproblematic, assumes a clear separation of analytical concerns on text-critical grounds, as if the versions of the symphony can be compartmentalised analytically because they can be classified chronologically. But this is not the case. The versions of the work are not distinct, bounded entities; they are rather multiple responses to the structural problems posed by the same material. As such, they court a heterogeneity that is at once essential to their comprehension and also unapproachable from an uncontentious text-critical position. Haas's edition is valuable because it opens up a window on this issue. His conflation of sources makes concrete the heterogeneity of the 1872 and 1877 versions, and thereby renders visible a compositional problem that is in a sense greater than the sum of its individual manifestations, a problem we cannot hope to understand without the aid of analysis.

Rejection of the homogeneous conception of a given version returns us to the text-critical issues broached at the start of this chapter, and in passing in Chapter 1. Jerome McGann's complaint that the ideology of the Urtext 'has the effect of desocializing our historical view of the literary work' spawns a model of the text as social product, which for Korstvedt 'renders untenable any categorical assertion that Bruckner's intentions can be represented only by private, manuscript sources'.[22] Editions, in other words, are instances of reception history, and reception history is essential to the understanding of music as a social, historical or cultural phenomenon. But analysis, in a general sense, is also a key part of this process: any omission or retention of material that does not literally reproduce the manuscript sources is likely to have involved decisions of a structural, and therefore analytical, nature. If, on these grounds, we widen the field of acceptable resources to include the first editions, we thus open up an array of analytical problems, the resolution of which will be essential to an understanding of the 'historical view of the work' that McGann describes.

This text-critical ideology and the heterogeneous conception of the work point towards the same basic conclusion: in both cases, we are compelled to abandon the illusive belief that a Bruckner symphony is necessarily and in all instances a single, self-contained composition. The multiple versions of a given symphony are not discrete, self-sufficient works; neither are they susceptible to the sort of instrumental judgements that isolate one as 'authentic' and discard the rest. They are, no matter how chronologically distant, multiple responses to the problems generated by a commonality of material and its expressive and generic connotations. Editorial differences of opinion, whether concerning the collaborative input of Bruckner's colleagues or the mixture of manuscript sources, simply add to the complexity of this situation, and concomitantly increase its analytical density.

[22] See Jerome McGann, *A Critique of Modern Textual Criticism* (Chicago, 1983), p. 121; Korstvedt, '"Return to the Pure Sources"', p. 108.

# 7 Psychobiography and analysis

In 1956, Donald Mitchell published a review of Hans Redlich's *Bruckner and Mahler*.[1] Mitchell noted with approval Redlich's skill in the enlightening presentation of biography, and was struck especially by the revelation of the composer's neurotic behaviour, which unseated his prevalent image of mystical detachment: 'Many English readers will be astonished, as I was, at the "seraphic" Bruckner's neuroses.'[2] Mitchell, however, neglected to appraise the full extent of Redlich's agenda, which, in a manoeuvre that places *Bruckner and Mahler* squarely within a persistent trend of reception history, went beyond the exposition of evidence to its psychological explication. For Redlich, the paradoxical aspects of Bruckner's character betrayed vaguely Freudian origins: 'his is a case of sexual inferiority complex, in need of powerful compensatory satisfactions. Indeed, the peculiarities of Bruckner's psychology and the entanglements of his emotional life can all be traced back to that cause.'[3] Redlich freely applied notions of obsession as a means of clarifying Bruckner's recurrent manias. The composer's 'obsessional urge' to count objects and his 'unhealthy interest in corpses' constituted pathological obsessions that replaced the 'intellectual penetrations into other spheres of human interest' evident in a healthy psychology.[4]

The task of explaining Bruckner's neuroses psychoanalytically has subsequently been taken up more systematically by the psychiatrist Erwin Ringel, who has gone so far as to suggest that Bruckner suffered from a lifelong mental disorder.[5] Ringel detected an entrenched neurosis, which manifested itself in a variety of symptoms. Problems that arose in Bruckner's early childhood remained unresolved in later life, resulting in a state of arrested development that gave rise to the supposedly infantile aspects of his personality. The composer consequently provoked in his colleagues the desire 'to tend

---

[1] Donald Mitchell, review of Hans Redlich, *Bruckner and Mahler* (London, 1955, repr. 1963), *Musical Times* 97 (1956), pp. 303–4.

[2] Ibid., p. 303.   [3] See *Bruckner and Mahler*, p. 27.

[4] Ibid., p. 30. As I hope to show below, Redlich fundamentally misuses the concept of obsession as it is clinically defined. The manias he identifies are more properly understood as compulsions, that is to say as compensatory responses to obsessional thoughts.

[5] See Erwin Ringel, 'Psychogramm für Anton Bruckner', in Franz Grasberger, ed., *Bruckner Symposion Linz 1977* (Linz, 1978), pp. 19–26.

to him, to give him a helping hand' that sustained a condition of childlike dependency. This issue worked in tandem with a fundamental insecurity. Bruckner's greatly diminished sense of self-worth generated an inflated view of the authority of others (Wagner would be an obvious example) that distorted his interpersonal relationships.

More recently, this tendency to make psychoanalytical capital out of Bruckner's life has been persistently attacked. Ringel's ideas have been vigorously contested by Constantin Floros, primarily on the grounds that they do not take adequate account of the biographical evidence.[6] In particular, the publication in 1991 of Renate Grasberger's and Erich Partsch's *Bruckner-skizzierte. Ein Porträt in ausgewählten Erinnerungen und Anekdoten* made available a wealth of information that contradicts Ringel's diagnosis, and to which he did not have access. Floros cites the issue of insecurity as a case in point, drawing attention to remarks of Franz Marschner, Franz Schalk and Josef Kluger that all attest to Bruckner's strength of character and pragmatism.[7] The composer's infantility is questionable for similar reasons: the perception that he was at best childlike, at worst a rural fool, breaks down on full consideration of the evidence. Numerous commentators, among them Alexander Fränkel and Friedrich Klose, noted a keen practical intelligence in Bruckner.[8] Floros concludes that there is no basis for reading the specific focus of Bruckner's intellectual attentions as evidence of infantility:

> In contrast to Hugo Wolf, Gustav Mahler, and many of his self-educated students, he had no interest in European literature and philosophy. Heated debates about Arthur Schopenhauer and Friedrich Nietzsche left him cold. Some of his students drew the conclusion that he 'had hardly any intellectual needs' – a totally misleading and incorrect claim which was hopelessly confused with a 'lack of intelligence'.[9]

Floros's critique in effect traps Ringel between two schools of thought for which his ideas appear equally unpalatable. On the one hand, observation of mental illness offends the sort of uncritical championship of Bruckner often discovered in older Germanic literature. On the other hand, Floros's

---

[6] See 'On Unity between Bruckner's Personality and Production', in Crawford Howie, Paul Hawkshaw and Timothy L. Jackson, eds., *Perspectives on Anton Bruckner* (Aldershot, 2001), pp. 285–98.

[7] See Grasberger and Partsch, *Bruckner-skizziert. Ein Porträt in ausgewählten Erinnerungen und Anekdoten* (Vienna, 1991), and Floros, 'On Unity between Bruckner's Personality and Production', pp. 287–8.

[8] See for example Fränkel in Göllerich and Auer, *Anton Bruckner. Ein Lebens- und Schaffensbild*, vol. IV/2, pp. 14–25, quoted in Grasberger and Partsch, *Bruckner-skizziert*, pp. 30–2 and also in Johnson, *Bruckner Remembered*, pp. 34–6, 108 and 161; Friedrich Klose, *Meine Lehrjahre bei Anton Bruckner* (Regensburg, 1927).

[9] See 'On Unity between Bruckner's Personality and Production', pp. 289–90.

objections contribute to the revisionist biographical tendency that gained force with Manfred Wagner's 1983 monograph, through which Bruckner was reconstrued as a pragmatic social climber. In a field of research for which the debunking of received prejudice has become a virtual first principle, the clinical diagnosis of psychological instability seems especially unhelpful.

The dismantling of Ringel's psychoanalysis also has implications for musical analysis: if we wish to understand the music biographically, we cannot proceed from the assumption that it is reflective of tendencies that are at best neurotic, at worst irrational. Floros proposes instead that Bruckner, reflecting the anthropocentric age in which he lived, conceived his music as a forum for subjective confession. Usually, this involved the attempt to inscribe biographical meanings by programmatic means.[10] Thus Floros understands the Adagio of the Second Symphony as Bruckner's hymn of thanks on recovering from his nervous breakdown. The quotations in this movement from the Benedictus of the F minor Mass, the inspiration for which allegedly brought the composer back from the brink of insanity in 1867, reveal for Floros a web of personal significations that problematises the symphonies' interpretation as 'the classic example of "absolute" music'.[11] Ultimately, he perceives Bruckner's music in general as an example of Goethe's notion of artworks as 'fragments of a large confession'.

There is, however, a sense in which Floros also presents a one-sided biographical reading. Although the evidence he cites can scarcely be ignored, there is a body of evidence testifying to modes of behaviour that, at the very least, appeared abnormal to many of Bruckner's contemporaries, which cannot be explained away as mere contemporary misunderstandings, or as fictions of reception history. Whether one accepts Ringel's diagnosis or not, his aim of securing a clinical basis for the understanding of these traits is laudable. Yet although concerns about Bruckner's mental health have formed a consistent thread in the secondary literature, attempts to ground them in the related psychoanalytic literature remain scarce. Redlich's remarks invite precisely such an investigation, since they freely deploy the diagnostic language of psychoanalysis, whilst making no effort to clarify their clinical or theoretical foundations. And this raises afresh the question of how psychology conditions composition, and of how the conclusions of psychoanalytical speculation translate into analysis.

Two matters are particularly germane in this context: Bruckner's compulsive behaviours and obsessions, perhaps most notably his perceived

---

[10] For a contrasting appraisal of the convergence of biography and analysis, see Mathias Hansen, 'Persönlichkeit im Werk. Zum Bild Anton Bruckners in der Analyse seiner Musik', in *Bruckner-Symposion Linz 1992* (Linz, 1995), pp. 187–93.

[11] 'On Unity between Bruckner's Personality and Production', p. 293.

numeromania; his sexual attitudes, which, if not infantile in character, were at least markedly adolescent for the duration of his adult life. It is possible that all these traits are consistent with a single condition; specifically, Bruckner may have suffered from a species of obsessive-compulsive disorder. Rather than try to pin the biographical and analytical evidence to a particular definition of obsessive-compulsive disorder, it is perhaps more productive to test it against a range of psychoanalytical views.

## Bruckner and obsessive-compulsive disorder

*I*

This label commonly embraces two distinct, but related, components: obsessions are 'persistent, ritualised thought patterns' that are intrusive upon, and distressing to, the subject; compulsions are 'persistent, ritualised behaviour patterns' that the subject deploys as 'parrying actions', to use Freud's term, in an effort to combat or control the intrusion of obsessions.[12] Obsessions may be unwanted thoughts, persistent and frequently repulsive images, or impulses that are anti-social, disruptive or redundant, but on which the subject is compelled to act. They take a wide range of forms; often, they involve preoccupations with disease and hygiene, death or unwanted impulses towards aggression and violence, morality and religion, sexual matters, or else trivial and meaningless ideas that nevertheless demand an active response. Compulsions, in turn, are ritualised repetitive behaviours that check or neutralise the influence of the obsession.[13] Thus compulsive hand-washing might respond to obsessional thoughts or images concerning contamination or hygiene.[14] Compulsions can be overt or covert: they might be motor rituals, checking or counting procedures, washing

---

[12] See Leon Salzman, *The Obsessive Personality* (New York, 1968), p. 10; Sigmund Freud, 'A Case of Obsessive-Compulsive Neurosis (the "Ratman")', in *The Wolfman and Other Cases*, trans. Louise Adey Huish (London, 2002), pp. 125–202, this reference p. 132. It should be noted that the division into obsession and compulsion as distinct entities was not recognised by Freud, who simply deployed the term *Zwangsneurose* to define both aspects of the condition. In part, later division into these elements has arisen from divergent attempts to translate *Zwang*, either as compulsion or as obsession. On this distinction, see Graham F. Reed, *Obsessional Experience and Compulsive Behaviour: A Cognitive-Structural Approach* (Orlando, 1985), p. 8, and also S. Rado, 'Obsessive Behaviour: A. So-called Obsessive-Compulsive Neurosis', in S. Arieti, ed., *American Handbook of Psychiatry* (New York, 1974).

[13] See Padmal de Silva and Stanley Rachman, *Obsessive-Compulsive Disorder: The Facts* (Oxford, 1992), p. 12.

[14] See Reed, *Obsessional Experience and Compulsive Behaviour*, pp. 34–43.

activities, or behaviours through which objects are repeatedly ordered and reordered; alternatively, they might be mental procedures, which deflect the intruding obsession through the repetition of an internal mantra or mental discipline.[15]

The origins, classification and theoretical basis of obsessive-compulsive disorders have generated diverse views. For Freud, obsessions comprised symbolic representations of repressed adverse responses to childhood sexual experiences: they were 'reproaches that have been repressed but now return transformed, always related to a sexual act from childhood that brought pleasure when carried out'.[16] The originary experience, in other words, passes into the unconscious, but leaves behind 'residues' that, symbolically reconstrued, constitute the obsession. In these terms, compulsive behaviours amount to defensive measures that protect the subject from the resurgent childhood memory. Thus, in the case of the so-called 'Ratman', Freud chronicles a history of repulsive thoughts pertaining to the death of the patient's father, which were consistently intrusive upon his sexual relationships, and which provoked elaborate defensive counter-measures. Analysis led Freud to the following conclusions:

> I ventured to reconstruct the possibility that as a child of six [the patient] had committed some sexual misdemeanour relating to masturbation and received a painful beating from his father. His punishment . . . had left him . . . with an ineradicable grudge against his father and fixed him for all time in the role of an intruder upon sexual pleasure. To my great astonishment the patient now told me that his mother had recounted such an incident from his early childhood on many occasions, and that it had obviously not been forgotten because it had such remarkable associations. He, on the other hand, had retained no trace of it in his memory.[17]

The repressed formative experience asserted itself in later life as an obsessive preoccupation linking anger at the patient's father, manifest in the wish that he might die, with anxiety over the forming of long-term relationships. The childhood memory itself, although essential to an understanding of the obsession, is displaced through a process Freud called 'elliptical distortion', and must be inserted before the patient's condition can be comprehended.[18] In this way, Freud reads the obsession 'if I marry [my partner], something terrible will happen to my father' thus:

---

[15] See De Silva and Rachman, *Obsessive-Compulsive Disorder*, pp. 6–7.
[16] See 'Weitere Bemerkungen über die Abwehr-Neuropsychosen', cited in 'A Case of Obsessive-Compulsive Neurosis', p. 179.
[17] See 'A Case of Obsessive-Compulsive Neurosis', p. 163.     [18] Ibid., p. 183.

> If my father were still alive my intention to marry . . . would make him as
> furious as he was in that childhood scene long ago, so that once again I would
> be overcome with fury towards him and would wish every kind of evil upon
> him, and because of their omnipotence my wishes would come true.[19]

Subsequent clinical approaches have revised and extended Freud's view.
Leon Salzman expands the definition to encompass a general anxiety of
control:

> The obsessive-compulsive dynamism is a device for preventing any feeling or
> thought that might produce shame, loss of pride or status, or a feeling of
> weakness or deficiency – whether such feelings are hostile, sexual or
> otherwise. I see the obsessional maneuver as an adaptive technique to protect
> the person from the exposure of any thought or feeling that will endanger his
> physical or psychological existence.[20]

In these terms, obsessional mechanisms respond to a fundamental anxiety born of an inability to accept the fact that the individual cannot have
absolute knowledge of, and therefore control over, the external world. This
instils a crippling indecisiveness in the subject, for which she or he compensates by enacting rigid, repetitive procedures supplying the comforting
illusion of omniscience or omnipotence.[21] Salzman observes three stages of
the condition: 'normal obsessional behaviour', which serves 'constructive
and adaptive purposes in human functioning' without provoking compulsive defensive measures; the 'obsessional personality', in which compulsive
behaviours are apparent, but the ability of the subject to function within
society is maintained; finally, 'obsessional neurosis' is evident when compulsive rituals become so pervasive that they render the subject maladapted
to the everyday world.[22]

More recently, systematic taxonomies of compulsive behaviour have
been undertaken. Graham F. Reed's cognitive-structural approach groups
such behaviours into eight categories: checking; motor rituals; avoidance
behaviour; arrangement of objects; washing and cleaning; counting and
numbering; tics and stammers; miscellaneous behaviours lying outside the
main taxonomy.[23] He classifies the general facets of the obsessive, or as
he terms it 'anankastic', personality in a similar fashion, identifying thirty-
three common traits, many of which relate to the issue of control noted
by Salzman, arranged within seven broader classes.[24] Thus anankasts may
exhibit excessive discipline, conscientiousness, or aspiration, and place a

---

[19] Ibid.      [20] See Salzman, *The Obsessive Personality*, pp. 13–14.
[21] Ibid., p. 21.      [22] Ibid., pp. 86–103.
[23] See *Obsessional Experience and Compulsive Behaviour*, pp. 34–43.
[24] Ibid., pp. 44–56 and 220–1.

high value on routine and systems of rules, which tend to be rigidly applied. They may be overly methodical and pedantic, categorise objects or tasks to an extreme extent, and insist on levels of precision and persistence beyond normal social conventions. Conversely, they may be plagued by doubt and indecision, and given to an inability to 'experience a sense of completion', as Reed puts it.[25] Often, anankasts measure their behaviour harshly against an idealised or even ritualised moral code, and this tends to be coupled with persistent doubt over the rectitude of decisions or actions.[26] The diagnosis of obsessive-compulsive disorder has been systematised in a similar way. The 'Maudsley Obsessive-Compulsive Inventory', for example, comprises thirty questions, designed to measure the extent of compulsive behaviour; more substantially, the 'Leyton Obsessional Inventory' consists of sixty-nine questions, which systematically monitor both compulsive behaviour and obsessive personality traits.[27]

The anankastic personality can also be understood in Lacanian terms. For Lacan, obsessive neurosis is defined by a specific ordering of the relationship between subject position, object and other within the structural discourse of neurotic behaviour.[28] This definition is clarified by Bruce Fink:

> Most simply stated, the obsessive's fantasy implies a relationship with an object, but the obsessive refuses to recognise that this object is related to the Other. Though the object always arises, according to Lacan, as that which falls away or is lost when the subject separates from the Other, the obsessive refuses to acknowledge any affinity between the object and the Other.[29]

Obsession thus involves a simultaneous denial of and dependence upon the other: '"Everything for the other," says the obsessive, and that is what he does, for being in the perpetual whirlwind of destroying the other, he can never do enough to ensure that the other continues to exist.'[30]

The Lacanian view also places an emphasis on control as a key factor in the anankast's psychological make-up. The discourse of the obsessive responds

---

[25] Ibid., p. 48.    [26] Ibid., pp. 53–5.

[27] These inventories are briefly discussed in De Silva and Rachman, *Obsessive-Compulsive Disorder: The Facts*, pp. 84–7. The Maudsley Inventory is reproduced as an Appendix in ibid., pp. 108–12.

[28] Bruce Fink defines neurosis as the effective opposite of the hysteric's discourse: 'hysteria and obsession can be defined as radically different subject positions implying opposite relations to the other and to the object' [italics in original removed]. See *A Clinical Introduction to Lacanian Psychoanalysis* (Cambridge, Mass., 1997), pp. 117–27, this quotation p. 121.

[29] Ibid., p. 118.

[30] See Jacques Lacan, *Seminar VII: The Ethics of Psychoanalysis* (London, 1992), p. 241.

to the problem of ontology through an association of being and thinking: secure knowledge of self-existence is guaranteed by placing an excessive emphasis on conscious thought.[31] This arises from a fear of the loss of control that the intervention of the unconscious brings. Sexual relationships are thus especially difficult, since they necessarily entail an abdication of control, and therefore an admission of the influence of the unconscious. The negation of the other is schematically evident here: the obsessive retreats from sexual relations because he or she is unwilling to facilitate the other's desire, in this case that of the sexual partner. The sexual act forces the subject to relinquish, or at least to subordinate, conscious control to the demands of the other.[32] Obsession consequently precludes desire, since the admission of desire entails an opening up to the other that threatens the obsessive with what Lacan termed 'aphanasis', the dissolution of his or her subject position.

This leads, in turn, to the role of *jouissance* in obsessive neurosis. The obsessive thought is not simply repellent to the subject; rather, it at once provokes revulsion and a subconscious 'libidinal satisfaction', which might be defined in Lacan's terms as jouissance.[33] As Dylan Evans observes, the eponymous obsessive fantasy that plagued Freud's Ratman appeared subconsciously pleasurable: Freud noted that '[a]t all the more significant moments of his narration a very strange compound expression is visible on his face, which I can only interpret as *horror at the pleasure he does not even know he feels*' [italics in original].[34] Ratman experienced, in Charles Melman's words, 'a jouissance in horror, a jouissance in the committing of a crime'.[35] In the context of sexual relations, the obsessive's mentality simultaneously denies and preserves the jouissance of the other. On one level, the demand for control results in a refusal 'to be the cause of the Other's *jouissance*'.[36] More fundamentally, the possibility of the other's jouissance remains essential in defining the obsessive's subject position; his or her attitude therefore 'takes on the transcendental function of ensuring the Other's

---

[31] See Fink, *A Clinical Introduction to Lacanian Psychoanalysis*, pp. 121–3.

[32] Fink, for example, associates orgasm with the abdication of conscious thought, with 'a brief end to thinking'; see ibid., p. 124.

[33] See Dylan Evans, 'From Kantian Ethics to Libidinal Experience: An Exploration of Jouissance', in Dany Nobus, ed., *Key Concepts of Lacanian Psychoanalysis* (London, 1998), pp. 1–28, and especially pp. 18–19.

[34] 'A Case of Obsessive-Compulsive Neurosis', p. 134, and see also Evans, 'From Kantian Ethics to Libidinal Experience', p. 19.

[35] See Charles Melman, 'On Obsessional Neurosis', in Slavoj Žižek, ed., *Jacques Lacan: Critical Evaluations in Cultural Theory* (London, 2003), pp. 117–24, this quotation p. 118.

[36] See Fink, *A Clinical Introduction to Lacanian Psychoanalysis*, p. 128.

jouissance'.[37] The condition is in this way underpinned by an essential dialectic: that which the obsessive resists also feeds a libidinal enjoyment upon which he or she depends.

## II

The evidence for Bruckner's obsessive-compulsive behaviour ostensibly stems from a small number of reminiscences and letters. The most frequently noted tendency, which clearly falls within Reed's taxonomy of compulsions, is his oft-cited counting mania.[38] This is most plainly evinced in a letter to August Göllerich of 1889, in which Bruckner demanded the classification of specific architectural features in Bayreuth:

> Excuse me, one more request: I'd so very much like to know the material
> from which the two pointed finials above the cupola of the two municipal
> towers . . . are made. Next to the cupola is a) the pommel: then b) the
> weathercock with ornament, isn't it? then . . . c) a cross?? and a lightning
> conductor, or what else? Is there a cross?
>
>   What is on the tower of the Catholic church? I believe only a weathercock
> without a cross?
>
>   Many apologies, and many thanks in advance. Please, write it all down; in
> the autumn I shall ask for clarification . . .[39]

Several instances of counting rituals are recalled by Max von Oberleithner. On arrival in Berlin in May 1891, he reports that

> Bruckner wanted to see the historic corner window on Unter den Linden in
> the Palace of the Crown Prince. It was then that I realised for the first time
> that Bruckner could not retain the appearance of a room in his memory,
> because he ran back several times and in the end he counted the windows,
> so as to keep the image in his mind.[40]

Oberleithner claimed that similar behaviour plagued Bruckner during his cure at Bad Kreuzen in 1867: 'even [at Bad Kreuzen] he found no peace. He

---

[37] See Lacan, 'Subversion of the Subject and Dialectic of Desire in the Freudian Unconscious', in *Ecrits*, trans. Alan Sheridan (London, 2001), pp. 323–60, this quotation p. 358.

[38] See Reed, *Obsessional Experience and Compulsive Behaviour*, p. 39.

[39] The letter is dated Vienna August 12th, 1889. See Max Auer, ed., *Anton Bruckner. Gesammelte Briefe. Neue Folge* (Regensburg, 1924), p. 225, translated in Redlich, *Bruckner and Mahler*, p. 31. Crawford Howie also alludes to the letter, and to Redlich's relating of it to numeromania, in *Anton Bruckner: A Documentary Biography*, vol. II (Lampeter, 2002), pp. 580–1. The original is lost.

[40] See Johnson, *Bruckner Remembered*, p. 63.

counted flowers on the women's summer dresses (the same mania for counting that I had noticed during our visit to the historic window in Berlin)'.[41]

Karl Waldeck recalls similar preoccupations from the time of Bruckner's
nervous breakdown:

> Bruckner suffered a great deal from mental disturbances, depressions,
> fixations etc. For instance, during a walk he would stand next to a tree in order
> to count its leaves. On one occasion he came into my house without knocking
> at the door or introducing himself, sat down at the piano, and played for a
> while. When I asked him what he was playing, he said 'the Kyrie of my new
> [F minor] Mass'. Most people were amused by his behaviour, but I took the
> unfortunate man under my wing and provided him with as much company
> as I could. When I wished to leave him late at night, he begged me to stay with
> him because, left on his own, he would be troubled by his fixations.[42]

Waldeck's account is of particular significance, because it describes not only
the compulsion or parrying action, which is the counting mania, but also
the underlying obsession that it was designed to deflect. The fixations that
Bruckner's plea for company sought to ward off constitute the unnamed
obsessions, whilst his counting of leaves represents the compulsive response.
The Göllerich letter, on the other hand, only reveals the compulsion. The
classificatory act is present, but there is no evidence of the causal obsession.

Bruckner's habit of counting bars beneath his scores and ordering them
into numerical groups is often regarded as the most visible compositional
effect of numeromania. This linkage has been made most straightforwardly
by Deryck Cooke:

> Insecurity was basic to Bruckner's life, and explains certain strange,
> unconsciously motivated features of his personality. His numeromania . . .
> was a compulsion to reduce a worrying multiplicity to order by accounting
> for it exactly. It even had a musical repercussion: in the autographs of the
> symphonies, the bars are numbered carefully throughout, in groups of four,
> eight, etc.[43]

Timothy Jackson has challenged Cooke's view, arguing that it misrepresents
the evidence of the sources.[44] If the metrical grid was a form of compulsive behaviour, then it should be evident most extensively during periods
of extreme mental duress, in particular in the late 1860s. This, however, is

---

[41] Ibid., p. 65.

[42] See Franz Gräflinger, *Anton Bruckner, Bausteine zu seine Lebensgeschichte* (Munich,
1911), p. 116 and also Johnson, *Bruckner Remembered*, p. 46.

[43] See Deryck Cooke, 'Bruckner, Anton', in *The New Grove Dictionary of Music and
Musicians*, ed. Stanley Sadie (London, 1980), vol. III, p. 359.

[44] See Timothy L. Jackson, 'Bruckner's Metrical Numbers', *Nineteenth-Century Music* 14
(1990), pp. 101–31.

not the case; rather, numberings are either limited or else entirely absent in the works from this period. Jackson concludes that '[a] *causal* relationship between the counting mania of 1867 and the metrical numbers is therefore out of the question'.[45] Instead, he contends that they represent a systematic theoretical principle, which had its roots in Bruckner's study with Simon Sechter, and which served the aim of demonstrating 'metrical correctness' through analysis. The technique became systematic in the late 1870s, seminally with the revision of the Second Symphony.

Although Jackson's critique of Cooke is well founded, his conclusions do not preclude a relationship between the metrical numbers and the diagnosis of an obsessive personality. As Jackson himself opines, the desire to systematise metrical structure may have been a response to social or practical pressures that only arose after the composer had moved to Vienna.[46] The hostile critical reception of the Third Symphony, and the rejection by the Vienna Philharmonic of the first version of the Fourth, initiated a negative relationship with the Viennese musical establishment that Bruckner may have sought to counteract by demonstrating to himself the theoretical rectitude of his music. The external forces that provoked the mental collapse of 1867 did not include a sustained critical attack on his music in this manner, and therefore they did not demand a parrying action that justified his compositional practice. The central place allocated to the accusation of formlessness by many Viennese critics adds further weight to this hypothesis. Again, many aspects of this phenomenon are consonant with psychoanalytical models of the obsessive personality. The insecurity or doubt that critical hostility engendered, and the recourse to systematisation and theoretical routines as a means of assuaging doubt, are, as we have seen, commonly observed symptoms. Moreover, the association of metrical numbering and obsessive behaviour does not necessarily entail a rejection of the numbering systems on the grounds of irrationality. Numerous commentators observe that compulsive tendencies can be channelled productively at the milder end of the disorder's spectrum; that is to say, they can serve an adaptive function, especially with respect to the systematisation of work.[47]

---

[45] Ibid., p. 102. Jackson draws upon Paul Hawkshaw's investigation of the sources from the Linz period to consolidate this view; see Paul Hawkshaw, *The Manuscript Sources for Anton Bruckner's Linz Works: A Study of His Working Methods from 1856 to 1868* (Ph.D. dissertation, Columbia University, 1984).

[46] See Jackson, 'Bruckner's Metrical Numbers', p. 103: 'this remarkable development of a "metrical consciousness" has nothing to do with emotional problems ten years earlier'.

[47] See for example Salzman, *The Obsessive Personality*, p. 93: 'It is clear that obsessional behaviour can increase one's efficiency and effectiveness in performing certain tasks. The tenacity which characterizes the obsessional often enables him to pursue his tasks with single-minded dedication.'

The commonplace assumption that a fundamental insecurity caused Bruckner repeatedly to revise his music, and to allow his students and colleagues to participate in the revision process, needs to be tested against the spectrum of obsessive-compulsive personality traits in a similar way. In view of the complexity of his working methods, both in his own revisions and in his collaboration with the Schalks and others, it is plainly inadequate to reduce this process to the simple expression of an obsessive doubt. At the same time, insecurity as an obsessive characteristic is not only a matter of doubting one's decisions; it is, as Reed observes, linked to a fundamental inability to experience completion.[48] And this, potentially, readmits the obsessive basis of revision. Formal alterations, changes to the metrical and periodic structure, reassessments of voice leading and orchestration may all have conformed to theoretical principles that Bruckner felt grounded his music in a type of artifice, but the root of the problem remains that he was sometimes incapable of regarding the completion of a version as synonymous with the completion of a work.

Other features of Bruckner's behaviour have also been understood as compulsive. The methodical recording of religious observances in his diaries and notebooks has been perceived both as the expression of a compulsion and as the simple recording of an everyday habit.[49] Leopold Kantner considered them reflective of an 'additive, mathematical piety' designed to combat the fear that 'an imperfection . . . could render the prayer ineffectual'.[50] Elisabeth Maier regards their psychological pertinence more sceptically: for her, they simply 'bear witness to the same comprehensive discipline which Bruckner applied to his studies and his composing'.[51] Maier concedes that elements of an obsessive personality may have been residual in Bruckner following his nervous breakdown; however, she regards this in itself as an inadequate explanation of the prayer records, which like the metrical numberings were a much more consistent feature of his life.[52]

In view of the clinical models considered above, this position is hard to sustain. In fact, the regulation of religious experience in this way conforms to a number of anankastic traits. The ritualistic coordination of prayer could

---

[48] Reed defines this phenomenon as 'inconclusiveness'; see *Obsessional Experience and Compulsive Behaviour*, p. 48.

[49] The prayer records form part of Redlich's psychoanalytical reading; see *Bruckner and Mahler*, p. 28.

[50] See Leopold M. Kantner, 'Der Frömmigkeit Anton Bruckners', in *Anton Bruckner in Wien: Eine kritische Studie zu seiner Persönlichkeit* (Graz, 1980), p. 250.

[51] See Elisabeth Maier, 'A Hidden Personality: Access to an "Inner Biography" of Anton Bruckner', in Paul Hawkshaw and Timothy L. Jackson, eds., *Bruckner Studies* (Cambridge, 1997), pp. 32–53, this quotation p. 45.

[52] Ibid., p. 46.

be understood as a compulsive act of control: Freud, indeed, regarded obsessional acts as pathological analogues of the actions of religious ritual, whilst Salzman goes so far as to regard all religious ritual as an institutionalised attempt to compensate for humanity's impotence in the face of the external world by systematising the comforting illusion that it might be influenced by internal thought processes.[53] More generally, the obsessive's concern for routine, 'scrupulosity', the application of rules and the adherence to clear moral codes are all manifest in Bruckner's prayer records.[54] Reed's description of the interaction of scrupulosity and religion clarifies this point:

> Until relatively recent times the content of anankasts' scrupulosity was commonly of a religious nature. The patients of both Janet and Freud were very often concerned with whether their moral views and behaviour were strictly in accord with their religious dogmas.[55]

At times of particular mental strain or exertion this scrupulosity simply became more intrusive. Salzman's remark that '[u]nder conditions of stress . . . these personality characteristics may congeal into symptomatic behaviour which will then be ritualized' appositely characterises this change. As Maier herself observes, the number of pages in Bruckner's calendars devoted to the recording of observances increased dramatically between 1889 and 1895: nineteen pages of prayers as against sixteen pages of notes in 1890–1; sixty-five pages of prayers compared with thirteen pages of notes in 1891–5.[56] And this corresponds precisely to the final decline in the composer's health and the extended revisions of earlier works that slowed his progress on the Ninth Symphony.

The rejection of a connection between the metrical numberings, the prayer records and an underlying neurosis on the grounds of their essential consistency is therefore erroneous, since it relies on the basic misconception that Bruckner's symptoms betrayed a condition that was only spasmodically present. Obsessive neurosis, however, is the extreme end of a spectrum of characteristics that collectively define the obsessive personality. By these terms, it is not so much that Bruckner's nervous breakdown left behind residual compulsions, but rather that an obsessive personality was pushed, in 1867, towards a fully fledged obsessive-compulsive neurosis. Following his treatment at Bad Kreuzen, the neurosis receded, but the underlying

---

[53] See Freud, 'Obsessive Actions and Religious Practices', in *Standard Edition of the Complete Works of Sigmund Freud*, vol. IX (London, 1907), pp. 117–27 and Salzman, *The Obsessive Personality*, pp. 55–7.

[54] Scrupulosity is Reed's phrase; see *Obsessional Experience and Compulsive Behaviour*, pp. 54–5.

[55] Ibid., p. 55.     [56] Maier, 'A Hidden Personality', p. 49.

personality type is unlikely simply to have disappeared. Instead, we might regard this as a shift from the second to the third of Salzman's stages of obsession: the nervous breakdown represents a transition from compulsive behaviour that is adaptive within society to compulsive behaviour that is maladaptive and threatens the subject's ability to function within normal social parameters. The cure, in turn, marks a return to the adaptive, second stage.

At least as controversial is the composer's apparent preoccupation with corpses and the paraphernalia of death. Carl Hruby's account of Bruckner's reaction to the exhuming of Beethoven's corpse in 1888 is particularly well known:

> The day Beethoven's remains were exhumed, Bruckner invited me to go with him to the old Währinger *Ortsfriedhof.* Those who participated in the ceremony will no doubt remember the unforgettable scene when, just as the coffin was being lifted up and solemn silence had descended all around, a nightingale suddenly launched into its sobbing song from a nearby tree – as if in a final greeting to the great musician. The profound effect was soon spoiled when the representatives of the city of Vienna began squabbling about whether the coffin should be opened in the cemetery or later, in the chapel. In the end, they decided on the first option. Bruckner stood in front of me and stared into the coffin, deeply moved.
>
> On the way home, his mood was very serious. The gloomy solemnity of the occasion appeared to have shaken him to the core . . . Suddenly he noticed that one of the lenses had fallen out of his pince-nez. 'I think', he said, brimming over with joy, 'it must have fallen into Beethoven's coffin while I was leaning over.' It delighted him to know that his eye-glass was buried with Beethoven.[57]

[57] 'Am Tage der Erhumirung der Reste Beethovens wurde ich von Bruckner eingeladen, mit ihm auf den alten Währinger Ortsfriedhof hinauszufahren. Theilnehmer an jener Feier werden sich gewiß noch jener unvergeßlichen Scene erinnern, da just in dem Augenblick, als der Sarg gehoben war und ihm Kreise ringsum unwillkürlich feierliches Schweigen herrschte, von einem nahen Baume eine Nachtigall plötzlich, – gleichsam als der letzten Gruß an den Großen Sänger, – ihr schluchzend Lied anzuheben begann. Der tiefe Eindruck wurde zwar sofort wieder dadurch verwischt, daß die delegirten Vertreter der Stadt Wien vor dem Sarge darüber zu zanken anfingen, ob dieser am Friedhofe selbst oder erst in der Kapelle geöffnet werden solle. Endlich einigte man sich für's Erstere. – Bruckner stand vor mir und starrte tief ergriffen in den Sarg hinein.

Beim Nachhausefahren war er in sehr ernster Stimmung. Der duster-erhabene Act mochte ihn in seinem Tiefinnersten aufgerüttelt haben . . . Plötzlich bemerkte er, daß ihm aus seinem Zwicker ein Augenglas fehle. "I' glaub'," meinte er mit freudiger Rührung, "das is m'r in 'n Sarg von Beethoven 'neingefall'n, wia i' mi' so stark vor'beugt hab'." Er war ganz glücklich darüber, sein Augenglas im Sarge von Beethoven zu wissen.' See Carl Hruby, *Meine Erinnerungen an Anton Bruckner* (Vienna, 1901), pp. 20–1.

Numerous commentators have cited Bruckner's letter to Rudolph
Weinwurm of January 1868 as an instance demonstrating the exacerbation
of this compulsion during the period of his nervous breakdown:

> Even during my illness this was the only thing that was dear to my heart: it
> was Mexico, Maximilian. I would gladly pay any price to see the body of
> Maximilian. Be so good, Weinwurm, as to dispatch a completely trustworthy
> person into the imperial palace; perhaps best inquire at the office of the
> Imperial Chamberlain, if the body of Maximilian is likely to be on view, either
> open in a coffin or visible in a glass frame, or if only the closed coffin will be
> visible. Please inform me kindly by telegram, so that I may not come too
> late.[58]

Although attempts to connect this issue to a latent necrophilia are, as
Maier suggests, plainly ridiculous, it is possible that it falls within the domain
of an obsessive-compulsive disorder.[59] The central obsession for Freud's
Ratman concerned images of death and decay. Most of his obsessional
thoughts centred on the death of his father, to the extent that Freud diag-
nosed a condition of 'pathological mourning' as a driving force behind the
illness:

> [The patient] cites the fact that his illness has been so enormously aggravated
> since his father's death, and I agree with him inasmuch as I recognise that
> mourning for his father is the principal source of the illness's intensity. His
> mourning has found pathological expression, so to speak, in his illness.
> Whereas the course of mourning is normally completed in twelve months to
> two years, pathological mourning like his can last for an unlimited length of
> time.[60]

Bruckner's interest in corpses could stem from a similar source. From early
childhood, he suffered the burden of loss to a very considerable extent: he was
the eldest of eleven children, only four of whom survived infancy; his father
died when he was thirteen, and his cousin and guardian Johann Baptist Weiss
committed suicide when he was twenty-six, an event that evidently caused

---

[58] 'Auch während meiner Krankheit war dieß das Einzige, was mir so am Herzen lag; es
war Mexico, Maximilian. Ich möchte um jeden Preis gerne die Leiche Maximilians
sehen. Sei doch so gut, Weinwurm, und sende eine ganz zuverlässige Person in die
Burg, am sichersten: lasse im Obersthoffmeisteramte fragen, ob der Leichnam Maximilians zu sehen sein wird, also offen im Sarge oder doch durch Glas, oder ob nur der
geschlossene Sarg zu sehen sein wird. Laß es mir dann gütigst telegrafisch anzeigen,
damit ich nicht zu spat komme.' See *Anton Bruckner: Briefe 1852–1886*, p. 78.

[59] See Maier, 'A Hidden Personality', p. 51. Howie adopts a similarly defensive attitude
towards this issue, ascribing it simply to the 'high regard' Bruckner had for Beethoven
and Schubert. See *Anton Bruckner: A Documentary Biography*, vol. II, p. 567.

[60] See 'A Case of Obsessive-Compulsive Neurosis', pp. 148–9.

Bruckner a great deal of distress. It is entirely conceivable that these experiences generated obsessional thoughts that demanded a parrying action,
which took the form of an urge to have contact with, and therefore to grasp
or control mentally the physical residues of death. In short, his mourning
could, as Freud puts it, 'have found pathological expression . . . in his illness'.
Maier's claim that Bruckner was personally expressing 'the veneration of
relics in the Catholic Church' can easily be absorbed into this reading.[61]
The connection between religious ritual and obsessive behaviour is suffi-
ciently close to permit the appropriation of the former in the service of the
latter.

In light of the above considerations, more elements of Bruckner's personality can be brought into the diagnosis. His famously abortive sexual life,
which comprised, until an advanced age, a procession of failed marriage
proposals and pursuits of young girls who evidently had little reciprocal
intent, could be interpreted in terms of the commonly observed patterns of
obsessive relationships. The superficial desire to find a partner evinced by
Bruckner's flirtations could easily mask the sort of distancing from com-
mitment, or from the abdication of self, that marks the obsessive's stance in
relationships. The attribution of his frequent haste in proposing marriage,
which often acquired a sadly comic character, to the requirements of his
Catholic faith indicates the establishment of an unrealistic standard that, by
its exorbitance, protected Bruckner from the genuine possibility of a relationship. As Stephen Johnson has put it: 'Bruckner found it more convenient
to fall for the unattainable.'[62]

A letter to Moritz von Mayfeld of 6 November 1885 is illuminating in this
respect:

> As far as marriage is concerned, I still to date have no bride; if only I could
> find a really suitable love flame! Certainly I have many female friends; recently
> many of the fairer sex have been pursuing me, and they believe they have to
> act idealistically. It is terrible, when one is unhappy! Totally forsaken![63]

Bruckner's optimistic conclusion that his female friends remained distant
out of a sense of idealism implies both a justification for his own failure
and a transference of his scrupulosity onto the object of desire. In Lacanian

---

[61] See Maier, 'A Hidden Personality', p. 51.     [62] See *Bruckner Remembered*, p. xiv.
[63] 'Was meine Heirath betrifft, so habe ich bis dato noch keine Braut; könnte ich doch
eine recht passende liebe Flamme finden! Wohl habe ich viele Freundinuen; denn in
letzterer Zeit setzen mir die Holden sehr viel nach, u. meinen idealisch [sic] handeln zu
müssen! Schreklich ists, wenn man unwohl ist! Ganz verlassen!' See Andrea Harrandt
and Otto Schneider, eds., *Anton Bruckner: Sämtliche Werke, Band 24/1. Briefe, Band
1: 1852–1886* (Vienna, 1998), p. 278. I am grateful to Wolfgang Marx for clarifying
aspects of the meaning of this letter.

terms, Bruckner was concerned in an extreme way with the simultaneous dependence upon, and denial of, the other. The fulfilment of the desire to find a bride threatens aphanasis, the slipping away of the self, and therefore cannot be attained; but the possibility of fulfilment sustains a libidinal enjoyment that also defines the composer's subject position. On the rare occasions when his advances yielded a positive response, his idealism offered a convenient means of escape. Crawford Howie's ascription of the failure of Bruckner's reputed engagement to the Berlin parlour maid Ida Buhz to 'the fact that she was a Protestant and not prepared to convert to Catholicism' isolates precisely this point.[64]

The connection of these issues to Bruckner's general psychological condition was pre-empted by Max von Oberleithner, who went so far as to suggest that a tension between his 'powerful masculine urges' and the discipline of composition was the root cause of his nervous breakdown.[65] This conflict occasionally drew startlingly frank admissions from Bruckner:

> At this point I should mention a peculiar experience during our time in Berlin. I had to help Bruckner pack so that we could get to the station on time. Amongst his effects was a huge pair of swimming trunks. In answer to my enquiring glance he explained, 'You see, I suffer from wet dreams, and I put these on at night so that no-one will find anything on the bed-linen.' – And this was a man of sixty-seven![66]

Oberleithner consequently identified the classifying rituals as symptoms of an inability to reconcile libido and the self-imposed routines of work. In this way, he comes very close to relating the sexual and habitual facets of Bruckner's personality within the diagnosis of an obsessive-compulsive disorder. And this returns us to the Freudian view of the roots of obsession as a response to childhood sexual repression: the dichotomy between libido and discipline implies a formative, causal event, as a result of which the coexistence of sexual desire and work became problematic.

Furthermore, following Freud's ramification of Ratman's attitudes towards sex and death within a general obsessive condition, we can

---

[64] Crawford Howie, *Anton Bruckner: A Documentary Biography*, vol. II, p. 682, and see also pp. 627, 651, 664 and 680. An account of Bruckner's relationship with Buhz, which stemmed from the first of his visits to Berlin in 1891, is also given in Göllerich and Auer, together with a reproduction of some of her letters to Bruckner. See *Anton Bruckner. Ein Lebens- und Schaffensbild*, vol. IV/3, pp. 160 and also 377.

[65] See Max von Oberleithner, *Meine Erinnerungen an Anton Bruckner* (Regensburg, 1933). Oberleithner devotes a chapter to the issue of Bruckner and women, which is translated almost in its entirety in Stephen Johnson (ed.), *Bruckner Remembered*, pp. 62–8, this reference, p. 65.

[66] Max von Oberleithner, *Meine Erinnerungen an Anton Bruckner*, p. 65, trans. in Stephen Johnson, *Bruckner Remembered*, p. 67.

speculatively do the same for Bruckner. Possible evidence of this connection is glimpsed in a letter to another of his potential 'love flames', Maria Demar:

> Heartfelt thanks for your marvellous picture! The beautiful, trusting eyes! How frequently it comforts me! This relic [*Reliquie*] will be dear and precious to me to the end of my life. And with what joy have I so often looked upon it![67]

The choice of the word *Reliquie* is striking and most unusual in this context, since it literally, and most commonly, signifies relics in precisely the Catholic, ritualistic sense.[68] Certainly, it is quite distinct from the more appropriate *Andenken*, which would simply imply a memento. Bruckner's attitude towards the photograph thus seems subconsciously tied to his curiosity about the relics of death. The compulsion that controls obsessional thoughts of death by grasping its physical relics finds a parallel here in the attempt to contain a fear of loneliness by assigning an almost religious value to the mementos of a potentially reciprocated desire.

It is even possible that the evidence of ambition, pragmatism, discipline and self-assurance that has been marshalled to defend Bruckner against the traditional claims of vacillation and insecurity can be understood in these terms. For example, all these features fall within the seven behavioural categories through which Reed defines the compulsive personality. Doubt, indecision and scrupulosity occupy the first category; thoroughness, concentration and precision occupy the second; aspiration, conscientiousness, perfectionism and persistence occupy the third.[69] The revisionist assertions that Bruckner was ambitious, pragmatic, gregarious and intelligent in no sense conflict with the diagnosis of an obsessive disorder. On the contrary, aspiration, diligence and conscientiousness coexist with doubt and insecurity in the anankastic personality.

## Analysis

### I

Again, and for the final time, we return to the fundamental question: how do these speculations impact upon the analysis of the symphonies? The

---

[67] 'Herzlichsten Dank für ihr herrliches Bild! Die treuherzigen schönen Augen! Wie trösten sie mich oft! Bis zum Ende meines Lebens wird mir die Reliqui[e] theuer u. kostbar sein. Und welche Freude bei so oftmaligem Anblicke!' See *Anton Bruckner: Sämtliche Werke, Band 24/1. Briefe, Band 1: 1852–1886*, p. 260. Howie briefly considers this relationship in *Anton Bruckner: A Documentary Biography*, vol. II, p. 466, although he does not cite this letter.

[68] I am grateful to Wolfgang Marx for clarifying this point.

[69] See Reed, *Obsessional Experience and Compulsive Behaviour*, pp. 114–16.

linkage of obsessive-compulsive disorder and analysis can be made most persuasively via the issue of control. It is plausible to regard the music as susceptible to the same desire to exert control over the world that motivates taxonomic or numeromaniacal impulses in the obsessive personality. Bruckner's metrical annotations and their consequences for revision afford the obvious opportunity to explore this connection. This practice can be understood as an attempt to exert a posteriori control over musical material and its structural realisation.

The First Symphony lays a strong claim on our attention in this regard. It was completed in 1866, the year before Bruckner's mental breakdown. Along with the E minor and F minor Masses, the works that it immediately precedes, it is the most substantial composition from this period. Its first performance on 9 May 1868 in many ways marked Bruckner's recovery, as well as his move from Linz to Vienna, which was finally undertaken in September of that year. Moreover the second revision of the symphony, completed in 1891, was one of the major projects of the period following Levi's rejection of the Eighth.[70] Work on the piece thus coincided directly with the two phases of Bruckner's life in which obsessive-compulsive symptoms were most pronounced. Analysis of the metrical annotations in the first movement of the 1891 version, and of their relationship to the revision process, offers suggestive parallels with the habits of compulsive control identified above.

Table 7.1 provides a synopsis of the movement's form, onto which Bruckner's numerical annotations have been mapped.[71] The annotations are for the most part unproblematic: there is a clear single layer of numbering for the entire movement, with the notable exception of bars 68 to 75, where the composer vacillates between description of the passage as a single eight-bar unit, and a second level of analysis subdividing it into a two-bar and a six-bar segment. The number beneath bar 94 is obscured by dense harmonic annotations, but the presence of a three is easily inferred from the surrounding numbers, which are two and one respectively.

The numberings exert theoretical control over the structure in three senses. First, as Jackson contends, they indicate a metrical dimension to the compositional process, imposing a hypermetrical grid onto the music, which distinguishes between structural downbeats and the metrical space

---

[70] I am aware that the first, so-called 'Linz' version as published by Nowak is actually based on a revision made in 1877. In the interests of clarity, and to avoid cumbersome epithets like 'first Vienna version' or '1866/77 score', I will refer below to this score simply as the Linz version.

[71] The surviving source is Mus.Hs.19.473 in the Austrian National Library, available as *Studienfilm* MF593.

Table 7.1 *First Symphony (1891), first movement*

Summary of metrical numberings

---

*Exposition*

*First group (bars 1–43)*
[1–2][1–8][1–7][(letter 'A')1–8][1–2][(letter 'B')1–8][1–8 (transition)]

*Second group (bars 44–64)*
[(letter 'C')1–8][1–4][(letter 'D')1–9]

*Third group (bars 65–104)*
[1–3][two readings here: either 1,2,3,4,5,6,7,8 or 1,2/1,2,3,4,5,6][1–4][1–6][1–6]
[(letter 'F', *Tannhäuser* theme)1–3][1–4][1–6]

*Development (bars 105–98)*
[(letter 'H')1–4][1–10][(letter 'J')1–3][1–3][(letter 'K')1–7][(letter 'L')1–3]
[(letter 'M')1–3][1–3][(letter 'N')1–12][letter 'O')1–8][1–4][(letter 'P')1–3][1–3]
[1–4][(letter 'Q')1–8][1–8][1–8][1–8]

*Recapitulation*

*First group (bars 199–239)*
[(letter 'R')1–2][1–8][1–7][(letter 'S')1–8][1–4][(letter 'T')1–8][1–4]

*Second group (bars 240–56)*
[(letter 'U')1–7][1–10]

*Third group/coda (bars 257–345)*
[(letter 'V')1–4][1–8][1–6][(letter 'W')1–10][1–16][(letter 'X')1–8][1–8][1–4]
[(letter 'Y')1–3][1–3 (letter 'Z' in last bar of unit)][1–6][1–4][1–9]

---

that the intervening material occupies. These downbeats always coincide with significant structural junctures. On the largest scale, the start of each subject group in the exposition and recapitulation is demarcated as a fresh metrical unit. Major points of articulation within the groups are also identified as the beginning of a new unit. Letter 'A' in the first group, bar 18, initiates the first climactic tutti, exposes two important subsidiary themes, and is consequently marked as the start of an eight-bar unit. The repetition of the second theme commencing at bar 56, which effectively bisects the second group, similarly coincides with the beginning of a nine-bar unit. In the third group, the climactic *Tannhäuser* allusion at bar 93 is read as the start of a three-bar unit, and Bruckner isolates the six-bar phrase appended to the *Tannhäuser* theme at the end of the exposition as a separate metrical segment. Despite alteration of the material, the annotations preserve these downbeats at parallel moments in the recapitulation.

The clear points of metrical articulation in the development and coda are identified in a similar way. The return of the *Tannhäuser* theme at bar 119 is also the start of a three-bar unit; the passage in bars 141 to 174, concerned with the development of first-group material, is framed by an eight-bar and a four-bar unit, and the retransition consists of three eight-bar units. All the main structural downbeats in the coda are located as the start of a metrical group: the tutti assertion of C minor at letter 'X'; the tentative allusion to the first theme following the hiatus in bars 15 and 16; and, allowing for the anacrusis in the second half of bar 332, the climactic linear descent to the final cadence articulated at bar 333. In this sense, the numberings behave precisely as Jackson has suggested for earlier annotations: as a means of assuring 'metrical rectitude by correctly identifying all downbeat measures and by causing them to fall in the "right" places'.[72]

Second – and this again confirms Jackson's interpretation – the metrical grid clearly influences the way in which the material of the earlier version is revised, and therefore allows control over the process of recomposition. Frequently, the addition or omission of material brings the music into line with the hypermetrical analysis. Bars 153 to 160, for example, differ from the equivalent passage in the Linz version, bars 156 to 162, through the addition of a bar: specifically, bar 160 in the earlier version is repeated. This affects the hypermetre: a seven-bar unit becomes an eight-bar unit. In the same way, the amendment of bars 261 to 270 of the Linz version in bars 261 to 268 of the Vienna version compresses a ten-bar unit into an eight-bar unit. In both instances, an uneven hypermetre is 'regularised'. The revision is not always directed towards achieving such regularity; Bruckner is often happy to retain irregular phrase lengths, as Table 7.1 makes clear. He is, however, concerned to monitor the structural consequences of irregularity. In each of the passages considered above, the material is engaged in a gradual linear ascent, the culmination of which constitutes a significant local structural highpoint. The revisions critically alter the pacing of the ascent, elongating it in bars 153 to 160 and condensing it in bars 261 to 268. Perhaps the most striking example of this occurs in bars 333 to 336 of the Vienna version. Again, Bruckner adds a bar in the revision, expanding the original into a four-bar unit and repeating the previous bar's minor-seventh linear descent onto middle C. The decisive arrival on the tonic in the next bar gains extra emphasis in the 1891 version through revision of the hypermetrical structure.

Third, the annotations trace the phrase structure of the movement, and as a result impose control over the relationship between material and form. The segmentation is not only a matter of isolating downbeats, but of marking

---

[72] See 'Bruckner's Metrical Numbers', p. 103.

out distinct melodic and harmonic regions according to criteria of statement, repetition, continuation and interruption; in other words, the means
by which the material is made formally meaningful. Thus the eight-bar unit
in bars 3 to 10 constitutes an antecedent–consequent phrase that exposes
the first theme. The ensuing seven-bar segment comprises an extended liquidation, which exploits melodic residues of the first theme. When the first
theme returns in varied form in bars 28 to 35, it is again isolated in the
metrical grid as an eight-bar antecedent–consequent phrase. The second
group is analysed in an identical fashion. The first eight-bar unit contains
the theme; the four-bar unit that follows furnishes a distinct continuation dwelling upon residues of the theme; the final segment restates, varies
and extends the first segment. Segmentation of the same material in the
recapitulation rigorously observes these criteria. In the development and
coda, where phrase analysis according to the principles of statement and
continuation becomes inappropriate, Bruckner relies on changes in the thematic process. For example, the segmentation of bars 141 to 174 demarcates
six stages of thematic treatment involving first-group material: development of the first theme; combination of this theme with the triplet figure,
first introduced in bar 18; inversion of this texture; extended treatment of
the triplet figure, and simultaneous liquidation of the first theme; persistence of the triplet figure alone; climax, with residues of the first theme
reintroduced.

Relating the metrical grid to phrase analysis furthermore suggests a possible grounding in Bruckner's compositional training. In particular, the
principle of segmentation employed here closely resembles the notions of
phrase developed in Richter's *Die Grundzüge der musikalischen Formen und
ihre Analyse.*[73] Richter considered the period to be the essential interme-
diary stage between the musical idea (*der musikalische Gedanke*) as the
smallest structural component, its presentation in cadential harmony (as
the *Satz*), and the construction of musical forms. The various types of
period permit the realisation of the three stages through which, in Richter's
view, the musical idea should proceed: beginning (*Anfang*), continuation
(*Fortführung*) and conclusion (*Schluss*). And just as the period represents
a large-scale expression of the consequences of the idea, so musical forms
for Richter result from the interaction of the various phrase types. In the

[73] For a consideration of the relationship between Richter's text and Bruckner's compositional process, see Stephen Parkany, *Bruckner and the Vocabulary of Symphonic
Formal Process* (Ph.D. dissertation, Berkeley, 1989), pp. 146–57. Paul Hawkshaw treats
the issue more cautiously; see 'A Composer Learns his Craft: Bruckner's Lessons in
Form and Orchestration, 1861–3', in *Perspectives on Anton Bruckner*, pp. 3–29, and
especially pp. 21–4.

sonata principle, the exposition comprises two *Periodengruppen* linked by *Verbindungsperioden* and concluded with a *Schlusssatz*. The recapitulation consists of a varied repeat (*Wiederholung*) of this material, and the development contains developmental periods (*Durchführungsperioden*), leading into the recapitulation via *Verbindungssätze*. Bruckner's numberings dissect the structure in precisely this way. In the first theme group, each hypermetrical unit corresponds to one of Richter's phrase types. After the initial two-bar upbeat, bars 3 to 20 present an *Anfangsperiode*, whilst bars 11 to 17 are a *Fortführungsperiode*. Bars 18 to 25 expose new material, and therefore constitute an *Anfangsperiode* for subsidiary ideas. Bars 26 and 27 furnish a *Verbindungssatz*, bars 28 to 35 comprise a varied *Wiederholung* of the initial period, and the final eight-bar unit functions as a *Verbindungsperiode* linking the group to the second theme.

In a revision of Jackson's view, it is possible to regard the oscillation between 'intuitive and analytical modes of thought' he detects in the numbering systems as a complex compositional response to the anxiety of control that is central to the obsessive personality. Each of the procedures considered here attempts a level of control over material, so to speak, after the event. Bruckner seems concerned to check or regulate the progress of musical ideas, which, as products of inspiration, do not arise systematically. In other words, the numberings respond to the fear that the material is never entirely subservient to conscious control, since there is always a moment of blindness or uncertainty inherent in its conception.

Bruckner's solution is to apply theoretical means that regulate or systematise the way in which the material gives rise to larger structures. In one sense, this involves the invocation of a didactic authority: the organisation of the material is justified because it can be segmented according to the criteria laid down in Richter's *Formenlehre*. However bold the initial inspiration might be, its validity can be assured through a demonstration of its grounding in a didactic text, which 'proves' that the elaboration of ideas conforms to a normative precedent. This approach has the additional benefit of supplying a metrical dimension to the compositional process. If the music yields the phrase structures from which sonata forms are of necessity constructed, then large-scale structural downbeats will inevitably coincide with the inception of fresh periods, since the form's principal junctures are by definition points at which new periods are initiated. The regulation of hypermetre is therefore really an attempt to consolidate theoretically the relationship between phrase and form.

This procedure is taxonomic in precisely the sense intended in Reed's categorisation of compulsive behaviours: it seeks to classify the component parts of the work, and in so doing to impose control over phenomena – the musical ideas – that have their origins in inspiration, and therefore in a temporary abdication of conscious control. This is not necessarily tied to a specific personal cause, for instance to Bruckner's nervous breakdown, but emerged as a consistent compositional procedure that allowed regulation of a fluctuating, but nonetheless ever-present, obsessive state. Other elements of the compositional process also conform to this reading. Bruckner's extensive harmonic annotations could be regarded as responding to the need to ground innovative practices in theoretical premises in a similar way. In this case, the authority invoked is Sechter, Bruckner's teacher in strict composition. The analyses extend Sechter's fundamental bass theory in order to exert a theoretical control over potentially promiscuous, chromatically motivated harmonic progressions; the underlying problem, however, remains that of how intuition can be systematically regulated.

This view also resonates with Freud's definition of obsessive-compulsive behaviour as systematic action regulating products of the unconscious. If composition is not uniformly a matter of conscious action, but engages a dialogue between inspiration and rationalisation, then it closely resembles the systematic compensation for obsessive thought that defines compulsive behaviour. This, of course, requires immediate qualification: *pace* Freud's view of artistic creation as a product of sublimation, it is not my intention to posit anything so sweeping as a general psychological theory of composition as obsessive act. It is rather to suggest that the levels of a posteriori control in Bruckner's case imply unease with the unmediated condition of the material that prompts parallels with the relationship between obsessive thought and compulsive action. I would be similarly reticent to trace the argument as far as Freud's diagnosis of the root cause of *Zwangsneurose*. This would entail construing the creative musical act in Bruckner's case as the metaphorical transformation, via the unconscious, of paternal punitive measures taken against childhood sexual behaviour. Since Bruckner's father died when the composer was thirteen, we would be obliged to posit a combination of repressed sexual memory and pathological mourning as the source of the composer's musical imagination. Such a reading makes connections demanding a suspension of disbelief considerably in excess of that required in the linkage of compositional process and biography via the issue of control.

Importing the Lacanian perspective is tendentious for the same reasons. A connection could be made between the numbering systems and the obsessive's denial of the jouissance of the other. The musical work, although created by the subject and therefore constitutive of a subjective expressive desire, becomes an object in its own right once created. In other words, it comes to occupy a position of alterity in relation to the composer. Just as the obsessive finds the association of object and other difficult, so Bruckner evidently found the objective identity of the work hard to tolerate; it gave rise to a level of independence, and consequently to a proliferation of meanings and interpretations, that escaped subjective control. The metrical grid could be understood as an attempt to deny, or at least limit, this proliferation by imposing such a control on the work's objectified materials. And this limitation parallels the denial of the jouissance of the other that arises from the obsessive's anxiety of control in sexual relations. The post-compositional symbolic promiscuity of the music is checked by the application of a systematic device that restricts the quantity of available interpretations within a specific structural parameter. This reading is suggestive, but highly speculative, relying as it does on the considerable assumption that all creative acts are part of a symbolic economy reflecting the discursive structure of the unconscious in an essentially similar way. This view seems excessively reductive. We can accept Bruckner's actions as psychologically evidential, without claiming that the relationship of composer and work is no different from that existing between composer and the sexual object of desire.

## II

If circumspection is necessary in relating the metrical grid to the anankastic personality, a much greater degree of caution is required in pursuing obsessional traits into the music's motivic, harmonic or tonal strategies. Redlich's assertion that 'the mania of counting inanimate objects was really a mania of repetition, i.e. a musical obsession [finding] its creative reflex in Bruckner's predilection for the frenzied repetition of short motives' is, to say the least, analytically evasive.[74]

Leaving aside the fact that Redlich has misunderstood the concept of obsession here (he in fact describes compulsive behaviour), and assuming that the simplistic analogy between motivic repetition and the counting or classifying of objects is tenable, it is nevertheless inadequate merely to identify instances of repetition as evidence of compositional compulsion. Given that the repetition of themes is a basic trait of western art music, it would be necessary to show that Bruckner's repetitions are in some sense excessive. And this depends on the existence of a norm of acceptable repetition, against which Bruckner's music might be measured. But how might such a norm be determined? How might we identify the point beyond which repetition becomes irrational or redundant within any given work. Would this benchmark therefore allow us to assert that relatively similar or greater

[74] Redlich, *Bruckner and Mahler*, p. 31.

quantities of repetition in another piece by another composer indicate that he or she was an obsessive-compulsive? On balance, the first movement of Beethoven's Fifth Symphony repeats its initial motive within the movement's structural framework more exhaustively than in any comparable movement by Bruckner. Does this mean that Beethoven exhibited obsessive personality traits? Even if this issue is resolved, we still face problems of aesthetic and historical limitation. Specifically, how widely can the chronological and cultural terms of comparison be defined before the results become historically or aesthetically meaningless? Is the comparison of Brahms and Bruckner, for example, more meaningful than that of Bruckner and Beethoven?

The difficulty arises here because Redlich has allowed the biography of an individual to be identified with a general compositional device. Repetition and monothematicism are technical options available to any composer; the counting of leaves or prayers is a specific facet of Bruckner's mindset. But even if we orientate the argument purely around Bruckner, the identification of compulsive thematic writing becomes no easier; we are still faced with the problem of locating a boundary of redundancy specific to Bruckner's style.

Looking again at the first-theme group in the first movement of the First Symphony, there is a density and insistence of thematic working that could easily be regarded as thorough to the point of compulsion. Example 7.1 reproduces the group itself; Example 7.2 traces the various motivic links within the principal material. The initial statement itself yields a complex network of relationships. In one sense, the two halves of the first phrase in bars 2 to 4 are complementary: the second is a free variant of the first, related by a consistency of rhythmic identity. Closer inspection reveals numerous more detailed relationships. The two neighbour-note figures comprising the *Hauptmotiv*, marked 'a' in Example 7.2, are clearly related: the G–A flat over the barline rhythmically extends the preceding anacrusic D–E flat. The varied repetition in bars 3 to 4 redeploys 'a' to create a $\hat{5}$–$\hat{2}$ linear descent, in which context it is twice freely inverted. The cadential tail in bars 4 to 6 then combines the two forms of 'a': the ascending neighbour-note appears transposed as B natural–C; the $\hat{3}$–$\hat{2}$ straddling bars 3 and 4 is contracted in bars 4 and 5 such that it is rhythmically identical to the opening of the whole theme, and then revised again through the descent of the minim D onto C in bar 6. The complementary repetition in bars 6 to 10 repeats this structure with one small modification. Bars 11 to 17 subsequently furnish an extended liquidation dwelling insistently on the cadential form of 'a', which is successively reduced by two means. First of all, its central minim is contracted to a crotchet from bar 13 onwards; secondly, its anacrusic semiquaver is removed from bar 14. This process of contraction yields to

Example 7.1 First Symphony (1891), first movement

First-theme group in exposition

veiled augmentation in the double-octave linear ascent of bar 17, which registrally displaces the neighbour-note G–A flat, and fills in the gap with an ascending scale. The whole passage thus far is purely concerned with the development of 'a' in a variety of forms. It even comes to dominate the accompaniment; from bar 11, the woodwind texture takes up the rhythm

Example 7.1 (*cont.*)

of 'a', supplying free variants of the motive's contour that contract to the repetition of a single pitch in bar 17.

The subsidiary material entering from bar 18 is no less thoroughly worked out. The two principal motives, bracketed as 'b' and 'c' in Example 7.2, are contrapuntally developed in two ways: they are loosely invertible, a property exploited in the relationship between bars 18 to 21 and 22 to 25; the inversion of parts is marked by an inversion of the contour of 'b', in the first violins in bars 22 to 24. Moreover, even after the relentless liquidation of 'a' in bars 11 to 17, its presence is still felt: as Example 7.2 shows, the contour of the *Hauptmotiv* is built into the middle of 'c'. A second process of liquidation then links this material to the varied reprise of 'a' that comprises

Example 7.2  First Symphony (1891), first movement

Thematic process in first-theme group

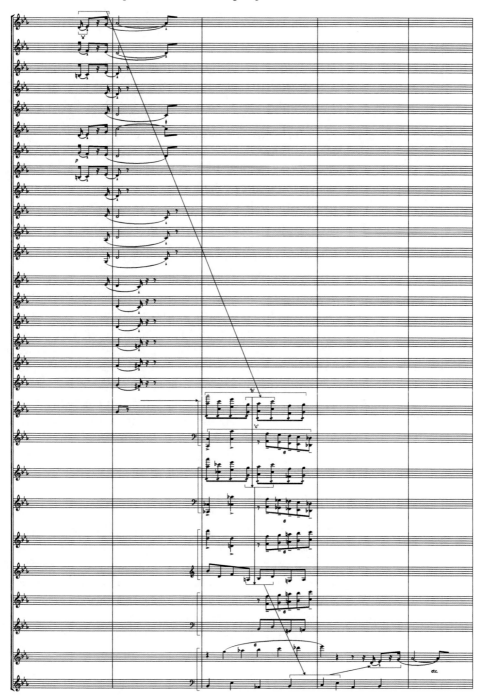

the transition. From bar 26, the second halves of 'b' and 'c' are detached and simultaneously augmented, as a result of which 'b', now in the bass, mutates into the crotchet accompaniment that opens the movement, over which 'a' returns. The transitional variant of the opening then brings with it a fresh development of 'a'. The process of contraction guiding bars 11 to 17 yields to the repetition of the motive's minim form, residues of which initiate the final phrase of the group leading into the second theme in bars 36 to 43.

This process is rigorous by any standard. Bruckner generates manifold relationships from a very limited repertoire of ideas, and the result is a conscientious thematicism that would not be out of place in a movement by Brahms. But identifying a moment at which conscientiousness becomes excess or redundancy is highly conjectural. The most obvious contender for such an assessment would be the liquidation in bars 11 to 17, which seems, in its insistent contraction of 'a', to evince precisely the 'mania of repetition' noted by Redlich, particularly in bars 11 to 14, where the cadential form of 'a' is simply repeated at the very point where the phrase structure appears to demand elaboration or digression. Yet as the reduction in Example 7.3 reveals, the repetitions are held in place by a clearly defined voice-leading strategy. The circumlocutory first violin part in bars 11 to 14 accompanies a chromatic turn around V in the bass, and the ensuing treatment of 'a' in the violins elaborates a chromatic ascent to $\hat{5}$, concluding over the structural dominant at bar 17. This responds to the voice leading of the statement and complementary repetition, which altogether prolongs a $\hat{3}$–$\hat{2}$–$\hat{1}$ descent. In general, the motivic design of the group fulfils evident formal duties at each stage, pertaining to the functions of thematic and tonal presentation and transition, or to the ornamentation of goal-directed linear patterns.

The concepts of tonal and harmonic redundancy are even more nebulous. Certainly, motivic repetition often sustains the prolongation of a single chord in Bruckner's music, most frequently enabling dominant preparation or tonic consolidation. The long retransitional dominants in the Finale of the Second Symphony and the first movement of the Fifth (bars 348 to 387 and 348 to 362 respectively), the dominant perorations at the centre of the development in the first movement of the Fourth Symphony and linking the second and third groups in the first movement of the Seventh, and the expansive regions of I and V in the first-theme group of the first movement of the Third constitute obvious examples. Again, revealing an excess of repetition in these instances would require a demonstration of their formal redundancy. Since the presence of the chord itself cannot be considered non-structural – all the above examples secure either the tonic or a related key that is essential to the tonal design – we would have to

Example 7.3  First Symphony (1891), first movement

First-theme group in exposition – voice-leading properties

assume that they exhibit redundancy through over-emphasis, by providing preparatory or consolidatory excess.

The problem of establishing firm theoretical criteria once more proves obstructive here. The most obvious basis for determining redundancy would be to assert that the proportions of the passages in question are bloated relative to the overall dimensions of the form. Yet all these cases occupy a fraction of their respective movement's total duration that in no sense seems disproportionate. Consistent internal procedures are apparent that also deflect this accusation. For example, bars 348 to 387 in the Finale of the Second Symphony, bars 79 to 118 in the first movement of the Third (1873), bars 217 to 252 in the first movement of the Fourth (1878/80) and bars 103 to 122 in the first movement of the Seventh all execute processes of phrase contraction. In each case, regular phrase lengths are established, which first of all contract arithmetically until their constitutive melodic units have reduced to sub-tactus dimensions, and then diminish to the point where a single motivic residue occupies the whole texture. The moment of resolution or climax always follows the maintenance of this texture for a phrase unit that is a regular subdivision of the passage's total length. These arguments, however, rely on the assumption that the harmony thus prolonged would become structurally over-extended if its duration were increased. But on what criteria is this judgement founded? Would the example from the Seventh Symphony become redundant if its final phrase were to be doubled in size? In the 1873 version of the Third Symphony especially, the long periods of static harmony contribute to a deliberate aesthetic of monumentality: the repetitions are designed to stretch the dimensions of symphonic form. Yet there are scant theoretical grounds for determining that further expansion would produce an excess that undermines this project.

In examining Redlich's proposition, we encounter a barrier over which psychoanalysis does not easily travel. The metrical numberings are themselves analytical annotations, and as such represent an *ex post facto* link between composer and work, making them an ideal conduit through which psychology might feed into analysis. The material processes of the works themselves afford no such mediation, and we are therefore obliged to supply our own theoretical terms in order to connect psychoanalysis and analysis. Inevitably, this connection is only ever as secure as its theoretical foundations: if the boundary between sufficiency and excess cannot be established absolutely, then neither can the numeromaniacal basis of Bruckner's thematic or harmonic practices. As we have seen, there are very often circumstantial grounds for asserting the structural good sense of Bruckner's repetitions; but this in itself courts a more fundamental problem: analysis is intrinsically concerned with the ways in which music makes sense. It will thus habitually construct the music, and will consequently always fall short as a tool for detecting redundancy or phenomena that have irrational motivations. A mode of analysis that compensates for this difficulty would amount to nothing less than a music-analytical discourse of unreason. And this would render the project of exposing redundancy impossible, because the exposition of irrationality is unavoidably its rationalisation: paraphrasing Derrida, analysis is unavoidably 'an organised language, a project, an order, a sentence, a syntax, a work'.[75] If there is a moment in Bruckner's music at which structure cedes to excess, reason to neurosis, it is destined to remain analytically inaccessible.

## Conclusions

The foregoing is decisively not offered as a systematic psychoanalytic study, a project that would require the scrutiny of a great deal more evidence, and a much more extensive account of the underlying psychoanalytical models. Neither has the aim been to regard Bruckner's personality and music as a whole in terms of the characteristics of obsessive-compulsive neurosis. There is at once biographical evidence that falls outside the diagnosis, aspects of the obsessive personality that Bruckner did not appear to exhibit, and remaining evidence supporting the diagnosis that has not been considered.

Instead, the study emphasises three basic points. First, arguments about Bruckner's psychological profile should refer, in at least a cursory way, to the psychoanalytic theories implied by their diagnostic vocabulary. Too often, concepts such as obsession, compulsion, numeromania and neurosis are invoked with no regard for the psychiatric or psychoanalytic background from which they arise. In this respect, Ringel's brief article is to be applauded, because it clarifies psychoanalytic issues on which other studies are tacitly dependent. Second, making this background overt allows a wide range of evidence to be considered symptomatic of a single condition. Not only the obvious checking rituals and counting manias, but also the composer's attitudes towards death, sex, relationships and religion can all be viewed as symptomatic of an obsessive-compulsive disorder. And, given the necessary space, the net could be thrown wider, encompassing attitudes towards cleanliness, the way Bruckner handled the significant transitions in his life (most obviously his move from Linz to Vienna), the routine of daily life and the pursuit of academic and professional recognition. Third, the defensive dismissal of all such diagnoses and the systematic dismantling of clichés

---

[75] Derrida refers critically to Foucault's *Histoire de la Folie*; see 'Cogito and the History of Madness', in *Writing and Difference*, trans. Alan Bass (London, 1978), p. 35.

that has been prominent in recent biographical work threaten to ignore or misrepresent evidence that strains to be encompassed by a revisionist account.

The transition from psychoanalysis to analysis is more problematic. The fact that analysis, or indeed any organised discourse on music, proves potentially at odds with the revelation of compositional irrationality leads on to general questions of how art and unreason intersect. For Michel Foucault, this relationship changed fundamentally in the nineteenth century. In the eighteenth century:

> there existed a region where madness challenged the work of art, reduced it
> ironically, made of its iconographic landscape a pathological world of
> hallucinations; that language which was delirium was not a work of art. And
> conversely, delirium was robbed of its meagre truth as madness if it was called
> a work of art. But by admitting this very fact, there was no reduction of one
> by the other, but rather . . . a discovery of the central incertitude where the
> work of art is born, at the moment when it stops being born and is truly a
> work of art.[76]

This productive exchange, which makes visible 'the space of indecision through which it is possible to glimpse the original truth of the work of art', gave way in the nineteenth century to an absolute antithesis.[77] Thus 'Nietzsche's last cry . . . is not on the border of reason and unreason . . . it is the very annihilation of the work of art, the point where it becomes impossible and where it must fall silent'.[78] Madness, in other words, begins at the point where art stops: it is 'the exterior edge, the line of dissolution, the contour against the void'.[79]

Viewed from this perspective, Bruckner's irrationality is invisible in the musical material not only because analysis, as the lens through which it is observed, converts it endlessly into a rational, sensible form. Rather, irrationality is the constitutive other of the post-Enlightenment work of art.[80] Compulsion is not manifest in thematic, tonal or harmonic elements of the music because composition is entirely circumscribed, so to speak, by the space of reason. Obsession and compulsion can, of course, appear in Bruckner's pre- and post-compositional discourse, of which the metrical

---

[76] Michel Foucault, *Madness and Civilization*, trans. Richard Howard (London, 1967), pp. 285–6.
[77] Ibid., p. 287.     [78] Ibid.     [79] Ibid.
[80] Foucault goes on from this point to assert that it is the very fact of this impossibility that conditions the perception of art in the modern world: 'by the madness which interrupts it, a work of art opens a void, a moment of silence, a question without an answer, provokes a breach without reconciliation where the world is forced to question itself'. Ibid., p. 288.

grid is a primary example. But in Foucault's terms, Bruckner's symphonies can only be works of art at all by virtue of their segregation from the types of systematic behaviour that have, through excess, become compulsion. Otherwise, paraphrasing Foucault, they 'no longer afford [music] but psychiatry'.[81] Analysis is thus a mode of rational discourse that constructs a phenomenon that is itself rational: it is reason observing reason. And this may also define the outer limit of the project that has underpinned this book. Ultimately, the boundary that in the end cannot be crossed is that separating analysis and unreason.

[81] Ibid.; Foucault's original phrase refers to Nietzsche: '[. . .] his texts are no longer philosophy but psychiatry'.

# 8  Epilogue: Bruckner and his contexts

The aim of this study has categorically not been simply to set up and resolve various components of the 'Bruckner problem' one after the other, as if these problems, and in fact those accruing to the life and work of any composer, simply dissolve under interdisciplinary scrutiny. Neither has it been to assert that such matters are in all cases irremediable except from an interdisciplinary, or broadly critical, perspective. Rather, it has been to point out the benefit to our understanding of Bruckner's symphonies of allowing them to act as the focus for a variety of methodological debates. This responds to a fundamental tendency to perceive contentious issues as methodologically self-contained: the idea that editorial and textual dilemmas demand exclusively philological solutions, or that biographical clichés will disperse if the appropriate biographical evidence is marshalled. It may, instead, be productive to view such problems as points of disciplinary convergence: editorial disagreements arise as much from analytical perceptions or from trends in reception history as they do from textual difficulties; biography becomes entangled in hermeneutic, analytical or historical agendas.

Developing this approach has involved maintaining a dual perspective. On the one hand, wide-ranging methodological debates have been engaged as vehicles for conceptualising Bruckner's music. On the other hand, Bruckner's music has served as a platform for the assessment of pressing issues in contemporary musicology: post-hierarchical concepts of tonality; the convergence of psychoanalysis and analysis; historicist models of analysis and hermeneutics; the relationship between analysis, politics and ideology; how reception history conditions analytical understanding; post-structural concepts of musical influence; editorial policies and their analytical ramifications. The conclusions arising in each case fall into two reflexive and mutually illuminating categories. The fact that the symphonies respond so readily and productively to such a broad range of approaches speaks eloquently of their analytical, historical, hermeneutic and expressive density and sophistication. This concomitantly offers responses to questions pertinent to a multiplicity of musicological contexts.

In the first place, many of the conclusions reached here plead for a more concerted effort from anglophone scholarship to consolidate Bruckner's music-historical position. Unfashionable though the historical grand designs of Kurth, Halm and Bloch might be, the confidence with which they locate Bruckner pivotally in a historical narrative suggests a canonical security that is both richly deserved and yet still precarious in current transatlantic musicology. And we do not have to resort to domineering historical master narratives to accord Bruckner his due significance. As, it is hoped, the foregoing studies have shown, his status can be asserted on a number of more specific criteria. In terms of musical influence, it is rapidly apparent that the symphonies constitute one of the most extensive and complex responses of their time to the Beethovenian legacy. The example considered in Chapter 5 provides a representative sample of a dialogue with Beethovenian and Schubertian precedents that Bruckner combined in each symphony with pre-Beethovenian and Wagnerian elements to produce an intricate network of misprisions. On these grounds alone, we are surely obliged to accord him a pre-eminent position. As an attempt to synthesise the diverse inheritance of the Austro-German tradition within a single genre, the symphonies have few contemporaneous parallels of such scope and sophistication. Past efforts to detach Bruckner from this legacy are at once neglectful of the analytical evidence and ultimately impede music-historical evaluation.

These claims are reinforced by the social resonances of the symphonies. As Chapter 2 sought to demonstrate, the conviction that they were somehow anachronistic in late nineteenth-century Vienna does justice neither to the wealth of topical and expressive references they contain, nor to the complexity of their implied social commentary. It is hard to see how one could encounter the manifold topical tensions at work, for example, in the Finale of the Third Symphony, and conclude that they simply embody an unreflective, quasi-medieval expression of Catholic dogma. At the very least, the extraordinary gestural and structural disjunctions in this movement distort any sense of an unproblematic continuity of symphonic discourse with an immediacy that surely unseats simplistic, monothematic conceptions of the music's social, philosophical or theological perspective. And these tensions are by no means restricted to this example; on the contrary, they are a basic stylistic principle from the First Symphony onwards. It is a supreme irony of reception history that music of such shocking, disruptive modernity should have been reduced, at least in its British reception, to a condition of pre-modern passivity, whilst the purposeful continuities of Brahms's music became integral to the discourse of *fin de siècle* Viennese modernism. The dialogue between sacred and secular elements is crucial in this respect. Bruckner's music often plays out with startling force the conflicts between subjectivity and faith, bourgeois secularity and religious authority, traditional artifice and radical innovation that define their time. It is perhaps the very rawness of this dialogue that rendered the music so indigestible to contemporary audiences. Again, it is hasty indeed to marginalise music that seems so fruitfully to express 'the unconscious historiography of its age'.

If Bruckner's symphonies are both music-historically vital and, in the broadest sense, representative of their time, their subsequent reception history embraces ideological, philosophical and political questions, the importance of which can scarcely be underestimated. Abhorrent though the Nazi appropriation of Bruckner as a symbol of political and racial identity undoubtedly was, it nevertheless exposes questions about the abuse of art and methodology in the name of political power interests that cannot be ignored. The fact that this music was ideologically absorbed via a more or less systematic process of misrepresentation, however, demands more than a reconstruction of the way in which this happened; it requires us to identify as carefully as possible the point at which the use of an idea, technique or phenomenon becomes its abuse. Without this endeavour, we become powerless to develop mechanisms for preventing the recurrence of such abuses. At a time when the manipulation of ideas or information in order to justify aggression and the prosecution of political power presses freshly upon the world, the question of what we can learn from the totalitarian manipulation of Bruckner's symphonies in particular, and of art in general, acquires a renewed urgency. The hostility towards Bruckner in Britain, which in many ways looks like the obverse of his fanatical elevation in the Third Reich, is in its own way as culturally revealing. Just as the presence of the symphonies offers a window onto the cultural politics of National Socialism, so their absence in Britain delineates an anti-idealistic mindset that preferred to view the Austro-German tradition through a selectively formalistic concentration on a line of development from Beethoven to Brahms. This, in turn, provokes assessment of how musical perceptions are conditioned by the history of ideas, and of how clearly this conditioning is circumscribed by national philosophical traditions. In both cases, Bruckner becomes the locus of questions that are fundamental to the cultural history of Western art music.

The symphonies are no less significant from an intra-musical point of view. Their formal, thematic, tonal and harmonic strategies operate at the very limits of technical capacity within the context of the late nineteenth-century tonal system and the generic demands of the symphony, and systematically expose the shortcomings of the entrenched theoretical models through which we have habitually understood this repertoire. Schenkerian theory, Schoenbergian concepts of motivic logic, *Formenlehre* models of sonata design and their distortion, and functional conceptions of chromatic harmony all buckle under the strain of encompassing Bruckner's symphonic style. With a number of honourable exceptions, analysis has often responded to this predicament either by ignoring Bruckner altogether, or else by attempting to squeeze his music into theoretical constraints that cannot contain it. Regrettably, the most substantial development in the theory of nineteenth-century tonality of recent years, namely neo-Riemannian theory, has almost completely bypassed Bruckner as a vehicle for exemplifying its theoretical terms.[1] Moreover significant Brucknerian practices, for instance that of compressing chromatic tonal oppositions into the first theme of a movement, have theoretical implications for late nineteenth- and early twentieth-century music that neo-Riemannian theory struggles to explain. The thematic techniques Bruckner developed urge the self-critique of analysis in a similar sense. If the concepts of thematic becoming that are central to the symphonies can also be detected in repertoire that has been regarded as representative of Schoenbergian notions of thematic coherence, then a wholesale reappraisal of what is thematically normative for 'music of Beethoven's type', as Adorno described it, is required. These considerations also feed back into the music-historical assessment of Bruckner, since they also force a reorientation of his place within the general development of tonality and symphonic technique after Beethoven.

The issue of doing historical justice to Bruckner impacts directly on the two areas that have above all formed the core of his problematic status: the editorial question, and the composer's biographical image. In these fields, more than in any of the others addressed in this book, it would be presumptuous indeed to claim to have furnished decisive solutions. At the same time, it is clear that these matters have needlessly hampered analytical, historical and interpretative assessment. With regard to the problem of the editions, the source of the difficulty has been a refusal to accept a condition of textual plurality. Once we accede to the impossibility of being able, in all cases, to clear the ground philologically before we approach the music analytically, then analysis is not only enabled; it becomes essential to the process of differentiating texts and versions. Analysis, in other words, becomes a vital comparative tool, which works in cooperation with textual scholarship. And since the products of analysis feed into diverse areas of enquiry, the comparative study of texts is connected, via a productive inter-disciplinarity, to historical musicology, and to the process of situating the symphonies philosophically and hermeneutically.

The adverse effects of psychobiographical perceptions can be reduced to the irrational prejudice that compositional greatness, significance or even competence is a function of a very specifically defined cultural intelligence.

---

[1]  Daniel Harrison's *Harmonic Function in Chromatic Music* (Chicago, 1994) is an honourable exception.

In one sense, the fact that Bruckner seemed unconcerned with contemporary poetry, literature and philosophy offended a crucial nineteenth-century conception of the artistic personality, for which the cross-fertilisation of the arts was central. Early twentieth-century views of Bruckner were substantially influenced by this notion. Tovey's vision of the composer as 'a helpless person in worldly and social matters; a pious Roman Catholic humbly obedient to his priest, and at ease neither in Zion nor in the apartments the Emperor of Austria assigned to him in his palace in Vienna' blatantly conditioned his opinion of the music:[2] no composer evincing such a striking lack of cultural education could hope to compete with figures like Schumann, Wagner, Liszt and Brahms, for whom cultural *Bildung* was a defining characteristic. The presence of recurring mental instabilities only compounded the problem. Naivety now went hand-in-hand with irrationality, and Bruckner accordingly disappeared off the music-historical map. Subsequent revisionism has deflected these criticisms in a way that has to an extent only reinforced their underlying premises. Reconstruction of Bruckner as pragmatic, intelligent, self-promoting and mentally secure puts in place the foundations of the cultural intelligence that was previously lacking, and the composer's reputation is concomitantly salvaged. *Bildung* is, however, not a prerequisite of symphonic greatness; neither is freedom from psychological problems. Bruckner's significance as a symphonist has to be established through the relation, by means of analysis, of compositional practice and its poietic and esthesic contexts. Biographical evidence has to be assessed on its own terms, and mindful of its psychoanalytical implications; it should certainly not be used as a stick with which to beat music that resists immediate comprehension.

Conversely, it has hopefully become clear that the use of the symphonies as a methodological testing ground has fulfilled two related and persistent agendas. First, each case study has in some way scrutinised the boundary between modern and postmodern approaches. Consistently, the simple appropriation of modern or postmodern authorities as methodological means has been evaded in favour of a comparative critical attitude that seeks to expose the lacunae in any one given strategy. If this approach appears in itself to be markedly postmodern in its critical pluralism or relativism, it should be noted that its results have frequently endorsed viewpoints that would find scant support in a radically postmodern context. In particular, the value of dialectical method as a means of comprehending Bruckner has been

---

[2] Donald Francis Tovey, 'Bruckner: Romantic Symphony in E flat Major, no. 4', in *Essays in Musical Analysis, Vol. I: Symphonies (II), Variations and Orchestral Polyphony* (London, 1935), p. 69.

consistently reiterated. This is perhaps most overt in Chapter 5, where a concerted attempt was made to narrow the gap between negative-dialectical and dialogical or heteroglossic conceptions of influence, to the end of situating the theory of musical influence within a more historically specific philosophical context. The retrieval of dialectics is also a preoccupation of Chapter 3, in which Lyotard's notion of the phrase regimen is applied partly as a means of rescuing dialectics from the clutches of Nazi misappropriation, and in Chapter 4, where it is suggested that dialectical conceptions of symphonic process allow us to dissolve the distinctions through which Bruckner's practices have become marginalised. The critique of neo-Riemannian theory in Chapter 4 is also dialectically motivated, both in its reading of the theory of transformational networks and in its putative suggestion of an alternative. These reanimations are not aimed at unleashing afresh the kinds of totalising historical master-narratives against which much postmodern thought has reacted so strongly. Instead, they either operate, to invoke Jürgen Habermas's terms, at the level of communicative rather than instrumental rationality and thus as productive vocabularies for understanding Bruckner's music, or else they furnish a way of locating Bruckner epistemologically, that is to say within a structure in the history of ideas.[3]

The second underlying agenda is an attempt to reclaim a central musicological role for analysis. The governing assumption throughout has been that the evaluation of historical and textual issues will remain insufficient unless they are linked interpretatively to the musical material via analysis. This is motivated not only by the conviction, expressed already, that we will remain distant from any accommodation of the problems surrounding the symphonies so long as we regard analysis as extraneous to their comprehension, but also by a general opposition to the type of recent musicological reasoning that has largely eliminated analysis in favour of the study of discourse or historical and philosophical contexts, on the grounds that 'the music itself', or any notion of a work amenable to analytical scrutiny, is little more than a modernist fiction. On the contrary, none of the problematic issues in philology or reception history broached here have any meaning or substance unless they pertain to constitutive objects that are the Bruckner symphonies. And if this is accepted, then it must also be admitted that considerations operating at the level of history or discourse are in some sense reflected in the works' musical materials, and consequently accessible to analytical scrutiny. This position can be maintained without clinging to simplistic notions of the unity of the work, or of the work concept as historically invariant. Pieces of music may be plural, multivalent or complex

---

[3] I have in mind Jürgen Habermas, *A Theory of Communicative Action* (Boston, 1984).

objects; they may stand in an intricate relationship with the analyst, editor or historian, and may require hermeneutic or analytical investigation before their content is made meaningful or accessible. But they are objects nonetheless.

The considerable scholarly impetus that has built up behind Bruckner in recent transatlantic musicology is long overdue, and it is hoped that the present study adds further momentum to this trend. If, however, this scholarship is founded on a belief that we somehow possess the objectivity with which to resolve problems that earlier generations have simply compounded through an inability to disentangle methodology and self-interest, then a note of caution needs to be sounded. Whilst scholarly detachment is of course to be sought, the cycle of revisionism that has sustained Bruckner scholarship, and which is, in a sense, the most deep-rooted and persistent 'Bruckner problem', owes much to the conviction that a real, uncontentious Bruckner will emerge if only the right criteria can be established. We cannot break this cycle by repeating calls for reassessment and placing faith in our own self-evident impartiality, to paraphrase the terms of Stephen Johnson's call to arms. Unless our approach is guided by synoptic, comparative and broadly critical strategies, the tendency for the agendas implicit in our methodologies to engulf specifically Brucknerian concerns will persist.

Perhaps the most imminent current danger is that of methodological institutionalisation. The laudable goal of according Bruckner his due status within our historical and analytical conception of nineteenth-century music will be undermined if this is achieved by forcing the symphonies to accord with institutionalised theoretical norms. The application of Schenkerian theory requires particular care in this regard. It is productive if applied in a limited, comparative and critically self-aware fashion. But if our aim is to show that Bruckner really composed in a Schenkerian manner after all, then we have simply succeeded in forcing him to submit to the hegemony of a single, encompassing theory. The current conditions of Anglo-American musicology are both advantageous and restrictive in this respect. The 'new musicology' of the 1990s has left in its wake a contemporary insecurity enabling a methodological freedom from which Bruckner scholarship can undoubtedly benefit, whilst also compelling the establishment of fresh institutional norms, the imposition of which may perpetuate the ongoing cycle of revisionism.

Ultimately, avoiding such pitfalls may entail abandoning the pursuit of an empirically determined 'authentic' Bruckner, conceived of in philological, biographical, hermeneutic or analytical terms: there is no accessible 'essence of Bruckner', to use Simpson's phrase. There are instead multiple contexts for Bruckner, each arising from a particular convergence of disciplines, circumstances, techniques and ideologies, and each demanding its own contextually sensitive response. The fact that such an abundance of meanings, questions and controversies has arisen around the symphonies is in these terms far from regrettable. On the contrary, such complexity is perhaps the most compelling evidence for their quality and significance. It is precisely this diversity that should be embraced and made productive if we are to do justice to this remarkable composer.

# Bibliography

Abbate, Carolyn, *Unsung Voices* (Princeton, 1991).

Abraham, Gerald, *A Hundred Years of Music* (London, 1938).

Adorno, Theodor, *Philosophie der neuen Musik* (Tübingen, 1949), trans. Anne Mitchell and Wesley Blomster as *Philosophy of Modern Music* (London, 1973).

    *Versuch über Wagner* (Frankfurt, 1952), trans. Rodney Livingstone as *In Search of Wagner* (London, 1981).

    *Drei Studien zur Hegel* (Frankfurt, 1957), trans. Shierry Weber Nicholsen as *Hegel: Three Studies* (Cambridge, Mass., 1993).

    *Einleitung in die Musiksociologie: Zwölf theoretische Vorlesungen* (Frankfurt, 1962), trans. E. B. Ashton as *Introduction to the Sociology of Music* (New York, 1976).

    *Berg: Meister des kleinsten Übergangs* (Vienna, 1968), trans. Juliane Brand and Christopher Hailey as *Berg: Master of the Smallest Link* (Cambridge, 1991).

    *Ästhetische Theorie*, ed. Rolf Tiedemann and Gretel Adorno (Frankfurt, 1970), trans. C. Lenhardt as *Aesthetic Theory* (London, 1984).

    'Alienated Masterpiece: The *Missa Solemnis*', trans. Duncan Smith, *Telos* 28 (1976), pp. 113–24.

Agawu, V. Kofi, *Playing with Signs: A Semiotic Interpretation of Classic Music* (Princeton, 1991).

Althusser, Louis, 'Ideology and the Ideological State Apparatus', in *Essays on Ideology* (London, 1971), pp. 1–60.

Armbruster, Emil, *Erstdruckfassung oder 'Originalfassung'? Ein Beitrag zur Brucknerfrage am fünfzigsten Todestag des Meister* (Leipzig, 1946).

Arnold, Denis, 'Bruckner, Anton', in *The Oxford Companion to Music* (Oxford, 1983), p. 278.

Auer, Max, 'Anton Bruckner, die Orgel, und Richard Wagner', *Zeitschrift für Musik* 104 (1937), pp. 477–81.

Ayrey, Craig, 'Debussy's Significant Connections', in Anthony Pople, ed., *Theory, Analysis and Meaning in Music* (Cambridge, 1994), pp. 127–51.

Bailey, Robert, 'The Structure of *The Ring* and Its Evolution', *Nineteenth-Century Music* 1 (1977), pp. 48–61.

    'An Analysis of the Sketches and Drafts', in Robert Bailey, ed., *Tristan und Isolde: Prelude and Transfiguration* (New York, 1985), pp. 113–46.

Bakhtin, Mikhail, *Problems of Dostoevsky's Poetics*, ed. and trans. Caryl Emerson and Michael Holquist (Austin, 1984).

    *Speech Genres and Other Late Essays*, trans. Vern W. McGee, ed. Caryl Emerson and Michael Holquist (Austin, 1986).

Barry, Charles, 'Richter Concerts', *Musical Times* 28 (1 June 1887), p. 342.

Bärsch, Claus-Ekkerhard, *Die politische Religion des Nationalsozialismus* (Munich, 1998).

Beller, Steven, *Vienna and the Jews 1867–1938* (Cambridge, 1989).

*Francis Joseph* (London, 1996).

Benjamin, Walter, *Ursprung des deutschen Trauerspiels* (Frankfurt, 1955), trans. John Osbourne as *The Origins of German Tragic Drama* (London, 1977).

Benjamin, William, 'Tonal Dualism in Bruckner's Eighth Symphony', in William Kinderman and Harald Krebs, eds., *The Second Practice of Nineteenth-Century Tonality* (Lincoln, 1996), pp. 237–58.

Bent, Ian, ed., *Music Analysis in the Nineteenth Century*, 2 vols. (Cambridge, 1994).

Bloch, Ernst, *Vom Geist der Utopie* (Berlin, 1923).

Bloom, Harold, *The Anxiety of Influence* (Oxford, 1973).

Bonds, Mark Evan, *After Beethoven: Imperatives of Originality in the Symphony* (Cambridge, Mass., 1996).

Botstein, Leon, 'Music and Ideology: Thoughts on Bruckner', *Musical Quarterly* 80 (1996), pp. 1–11.

Bowie, Andrew, *Aesthetics and Subjectivity: From Kant to Nietzsche* (Manchester, 1990).

Boyer, John, *Political Radicalism in Late Imperial Vienna* (Chicago, 1981).

Brenner, Hildegard, *Die Kunstpolitik des Nationalsozialismus* (Hamburg, 1963).

Brett, Philip, 'Text, Context and the Early Music Editor', in Nicholas Kenyon, ed., *Authenticity and Early Music* (Oxford, 1988), pp. 83–114.

Bruckner, Anton, *Anton Bruckner: Gesammelte Briefe*, ed. Max Auer (Regensburg, 1924).

*Anton Bruckner: Sämtliche Werke, Band 24/ 1. Briefe, Band 1: 1852–1886*, eds. Andrea Harrandt and Otto Schneider (Vienna, 1998).

Brüstle, Christa, *Anton Bruckner und die Nachwelt: Zur Rezeptionsgeschichte der Komponisten in der ersten Hälfte des 20. Jahrhunderts* (Stuttgart, 1998).

Burleigh, Michael, *Death and Deliverance* (Cambridge, 1994).

*The Third Reich: A New History* (London, 2000).

Burnham, Scott, 'The Role of Sonata Form in A. B. Marx's Theory of Form', *Journal of Music Theory* 33 (1989), pp. 247–72.

Carragan, William, 'The Early Version of the Second Symphony', in Crawford Howie, Paul Hawkshaw and Timothy L. Jackson, eds., *Perspectives on Anton Bruckner* (Aldershot, 2001), pp. 69–92.

Chissel, Joan, concert review in *The Times* (22 March 1969), p. 19.

Cohn, Richard, 'Maximally Smooth Cycles, Hexatonic Systems and the Analysis of Late-Romantic Triadic Progressions', *Music Analysis* 15 (1996), pp. 9–40.

Cook, Nicholas and Everist, Mark, eds., *Rethinking Music* (Oxford, 1999).

Cooke, Deryck, 'The Bruckner Problem Simplified', *Musical Times* 110 (1969), pp. 20–2, 142–4, 362–5, 479–82, 828.

'Bruckner, Anton', in *The New Grove Dictionary of Music and Musicians*, ed. Stanley Sadie (London, 1980), vol. III, pp. 352–69.

*Vindications: Essays on Romantic Music* (Cambridge, 1982).

Letter to the Editor, *Musical Times* 98 (1957), p. 266.

Craig, Gordon, *Germany 1866–1945* (Oxford, 1978).

Dahlhaus, Carl, 'Bruckner und die Barock', in *Neue Zeitschrift für Musik* 124 (1963), pp. 335–6.

*Between Romanticism and Modernism: Four Studies in the Music of the Late Nineteenth Century*, trans. Mary Whittall (Berkeley, 1980).

'Anton Bruckner und die Programmusik: zum Finale der Achten Symphonie', in *Anton Bruckner: Studien zu Werk und Wirkung, Walter Wiora zum 30. Dezember 1986* (Tutzing, 1988).

*The Idea of Absolute Music*, trans. Roger Lustig (Chicago, 1989).

*Nineteenth-Century Music*, trans. J. Bradford Robinson (Berkeley, 1989).

Darcy, Warren, 'Bruckner's Sonata Deformations', in Paul Hawkshaw and Timothy L. Jackson, eds., *Bruckner Studies* (Cambridge, 1997), pp. 256–77.

Dawson-Bowling, Paul, 'Thematic and Tonal Unity in Bruckner's Eighth Symphony', *Music Review* 30 (1969), pp. 225–36.

Decsey, Ernst, *Bruckner: Versuch eines Lebens* (Berlin, 1919).

Derrida, Jacques, *Writing and Difference*, trans. Alan Bass (London, 1978).

*Margins of Philosophy*, trans. Alan Bass (Chicago, 1982).

Doernberg, Erwin, *The Life and Symphonies of Anton Bruckner* (London, 1960).

Eagleton, Terry, *Ideology: An Introduction* (London, 1991).

Eckstein, Friedrich, *Erinnerungen an Anton Bruckner* (Vienna, 1923).

Eisen, Cliff and Wintle, Christopher, 'Mozart's C minor Fantasy, K.475: An Editorial "Problem" and its Analytical and Critical Consequences', *Journal of the Royal Musical Association* 124 (1999), pp. 26–52.

Ehlers, Paul, 'Das Regensburger Bruckner Erlebnis', *Zeitschrift für Musik* 104 (1937), pp. 745–8.

Ellis, John, *Against Deconstruction* (Princeton, 1989).

Evans, Dylan, 'From Kantian Ethics to Libidinal Experience: An Exploration of Jouissance', in Dany Nobus, ed., *Key Concepts of Lacanian Psychoanalysis* (London, 1998), pp. 1–28.

Einstein, Alfred, 'Bruckner, Anton', in *The Grove Dictionary of Music and Musicians*, 3rd edn (London, 1927), vol. I, p. 482.

Fink, Robert, 'Going Flat: Post-Hierarchical Music Theory and the Musical Surface', in Nicholas Cook and Mark Everist, eds., *Rethinking Music* (Oxford, 1999), pp. 102–37.

Floros, Constantin, *Bruckner und Brahms: Studien zur musikalischen Exegetik* (Wiesbaden, 1980).

'Historische Phasen der Bruckner-Rezeption', in Othmar Wessely, ed., *Bruckner-Symposium Bericht. Bruckner Rezeption* (Linz, 1983), pp. 93–102.

'On Unity between Bruckner's Personality and Production', in Crawford Howie, Paul Hawkshaw and Timothy L. Jackson, eds., *Perspectives on Anton Bruckner* (Aldershot, 2002), pp. 285–98.

Forte, Allen, 'Liszt's Experimental Idiom and the Music of the Early Twentieth Century', *Nineteenth-Century Music* 10 (1987), pp. 209–88.

'New Approaches to the Linear Analysis of Music', *Journal of the American Musicological Society* 41 (1988), pp. 315–48.

'Debussy and the Octatonic', *Music Analysis* 10 (1991), pp. 125–70.

Foucault, Michel, *Madness and Civilization*, trans. Richard Howard (London, 1967).

*The Order of Things* (London, 1970).

*The Archaeology of Knowledge*, trans. A.M. Sheridan Smith (New York, 1972).

Freud, Sigmund, 'Obsessive Actions and Religious Practices', in *Standard Edition of the Complete Works of Sigmund Freud* (London, 1907), vol. IX, pp. 117–27.

'A Case of Obsessive-Compulsive Neurosis (the "Ratman")', in *The Wolfman and Other Cases*, trans. Louise Aday Huish (London, 2002), pp. 125–202.

Gault, Dermot, 'For Later Times', *Musical Times* 137 (1996), pp. 12–19.

Gilliam, Bryan, 'The Two Versions of Bruckner's Eighth Symphony', *Nineteenth-Century Music* 16 (1992), pp. 59–69.

'The Annexation of Anton Bruckner: Nazi Revisionism and the Politics of Appropriation', *Musical Quarterly* 78 (1994), pp. 605–9.

'The Annexation of Anton Bruckner: Nazi Revisionism and the Politics of Appropriation', in Paul Hawkshaw and Timothy L. Jackson, eds., *Bruckner Studies* (Cambridge, 1997), pp. 72–90.

Goebbels, Joseph, 'Reichsminister Dr Goebbels zur Kunstkritik', *Zeitschrift für Musik* 104 (1937), p. 259.

*Goebbels Reden*, ed. Helmut Heiber (Düsseldorf, 1971).

Göllerich, August, 'Anton Bruckner. Die beim Bruckner-Commers nicht gehaltene Festrede von August Göllerich', *Deutsches Volksblatt* 13 and 15 (1891).

Göllerich, August and Auer, Max, *Anton Bruckner. Ein Lebens- und Schaffensbild*, 4 vols. in 9 (Regensburg, 1922–37).

Gräflinger, Franz, *Anton Bruckner, Bausteine zu seine Lebensgeschichte* (Munich, 1911).

Grasberger, Franz, 'Das Bruckner-Bild der Zeitung "Das Vaterland" in den Jahren 1870–1900', in Rudolf Elvers and Ernst Vogel, eds., *Festschrift Hans Schneider zum 60. Geburtstag* (Munich, 1981).

Grasberger, Franz and Partsch, Erich, *Bruckner-skizziert. Ein Porträt in ausgewählten Erinnerungen und Anekdoten* (Vienna, 1991).

Grier, James, *The Critical Editing of Music: History, Method and Practice* (Cambridge, 1996).

'Editing', in *The New Grove Dictionary of Music and Musicians*, 2nd edn, ed. Stanley Sadie (London, 2001), vol. VII, pp. 885–95.

Grout, Donald J., *A History of Western Music*, 5th edn (New York, 1996).

Grunsky, Hans Alfred, 'Form und Erleben', in *Bayreuther Festspielführer* (1934).

*Seele und Staat. Die psychologischen Grundlagen des nationalsozialistischen Sieges über den bürgerlichen und bolschewistischen Menschen* (Berlin, 1935).

'Der erste Satz von Bruckners Neunter. Ein Bild höchster Formvollendung', *Die Musik* 18 (1925), pp. 21–34 and 104–12.

Grunsky, Karl, *Anton Bruckners Symphonien* (Berlin, 1908).

*Anton Bruckner* (Stuttgart, 1922).

'Bruckner als Künder einer neuen Zeit', *Die Musik* 24 (1932).

*Kampf um deutsche Musik!* (Stuttgart, 1933).

Haas, Robert, *Anton Bruckner* (Potsdam, 1934).

Habermas, Jürgen, *A Theory of Communicative Action* (Boston, 1984).

*The Philosophical Discourse of Modernity*, trans. Frederick Lawrence (Cambridge, Mass., 1987).

Halm, August, *Die Symphonie Anton Bruckners*, 2nd edn (Munich, 1923).

*Von zwei Kulturen der Musik*, 3rd edn (Stuttgart, 1947).

Hansen, Matthias, 'Die faschistische Bruckner-rezeption und ihre Quellen', *Beiträge zur Musikwissenschaft* 28 (1986), pp. 53–61.

*Anton Bruckner* (Leipzig, 1987).

'Persönlichkeit im Werk. Zum Bild Anton Bruckners in der Analyse seiner Musik', in *Bruckner-Symposion Linz 1992* (Linz, 1995), pp. 187–93.

Harrandt, Andrea, 'Students and Friends as "Prophets" and "Promoters": The Reception of Bruckner's Works in the *Wiener Akademische Wagner-Verein*', in Crawford Howie, Paul Hawkshaw and Timothy L. Jackson, eds., *Perspectives on Anton Bruckner* (Aldershot, 2001), pp. 317–27.

Harrison, Daniel, *Harmonic Function in Chromatic Music* (Chicago, 1994).

Harrison, Julius, 'The Orchestra and Orchestral Music', in D. L. Bacharach, ed., *The Musical Companion* (London, 1934), pp. 127–284.

Hatten, Robert, 'The Expressive Role of Disjunction: A Semiotic Approach to Form and Meaning in the Fourth and Fifth Symphonies', in Crawford Howie, Paul Hawkshaw and Timothy L. Jackson, eds., *Perspectives on Anton Bruckner* (Aldershot, 2001), pp. 145–84.

Hawkshaw, Paul, *The Manuscript Sources for Anton Bruckner's Linz Works: A Study of His Working Methods from 1856 to 1868* (Ph.D. dissertation, University of Columbia, 1984).

'The Bruckner Problem Revisited', *Nineteenth-Century Music* 21 (1997), pp. 96–107.

'A Composer Learns his Craft: Bruckner's Lessons in Form and Orchestration, 1861–3', in Crawford Howie, Paul Hawkshaw and Timothy L. Jackson, eds., *Perspectives on Anton Bruckner* (Aldershot, 2001), pp. 3–29.

Hawkshaw, Paul and Jackson, Timothy L., eds., *Bruckner Studies* (Cambridge, 1997).

'Bruckner, Anton', in *The New Grove Dictionary of Music and Musicians*, 2nd edn, ed. Stanley Sadie (London, 2001), vol. IV, pp. 458–87.

Hegel, Georg Friedrich, *Wissenschaft der Logik* (Nuremberg, 1812–16).

*Introductory Lectures on Aesthetics*, trans. Bernard Bosanquet (London, 1993).

Hepokoski, James, 'Fiery-Pulsed Libertine or Domestic Hero? Strauss' *Don Juan* Revisited', in Bryan Gilliam, ed., *Richard Strauss: New Perspectives on the Composer and His Work* (Durham, N.C., 1992), pp. 135–75.

*Sibelius: Symphony no. 5* (Cambridge, 1993).

Horton, Julian, *Towards a Theory of Nineteenth-Century Tonality* (Ph.D. dissertation, University of Cambridge, 1998).

Review of *Bruckner Studies*, *Music Analysis* 18 (1999), pp. 155–70.

'Bruckner and the Symphony Orchestra', in John Williamson, ed., *The Cambridge Companion to Bruckner* (Cambridge, in press).

'Recent Developments in Bruckner Scholarship', *Music and Letters* 85 (2004), pp. 83–94.

Howie, Crawford, *Anton Bruckner: A Documentary Biography*, 2 vols. (Lampeter, 2002).

Howie, Crawford, Hawkshaw, Paul and Jackson, Timothy L., *Perspectives on Anton Bruckner* (Aldershot, 2001).

Hruby, Carl, *Meine Erinnerungen an Anton Bruckner* (Vienna, 1901).

Hsu, Dolores, 'Ernst Kurth's Concept of Music as Motion', *Journal of Music Theory* 10 (1966), pp. 2–17.

Hussey, Dyneley, 'The Musician's Gramophone', *Musical Times* 98 (1957), p. 140.

Hyer, Brian, 'Reimag(in)ing Riemann', *Journal of Music Theory* 39 (1995), pp. 101–38.

Jackson, Timothy L., 'Bruckner's Metrical Numbers', *Nineteenth-Century Music* 14 (1990), pp. 101–31.

'The Finale of Bruckner's Seventh Symphony and the Tragic Reversed Sonata Form', in Paul Hawkshaw and Timothy L. Jackson, eds., *Bruckner Studies* (Cambridge, 1997), pp. 140–208.

'The Adagio of the Sixth Symphony and the Anticipatory Tonic Recapitulation in Bruckner, Brahms and Dvořák', in Crawford Howie, Paul Hawkshaw and Timothy L. Jackson, eds., *Perspectives on Anton Bruckner* (Aldershot, 2001), pp. 206–27.

Johnson, Stephen, ed., 'Bruckner: Guilty or Not Guilty?', *Independent* (10 January 1996), p. 7.

*Bruckner Remembered* (London, 1998).

Jonas, Oswald, 'Heinrich Schenker. Über Anton Bruckner', *Der Dreiklang* 7 (1937), pp. 167–77.

Kantner, Leopold M., 'Der Frömmigkeit Anton Bruckners', in *Anton Bruckner in Wien: Eine kritsiche Studie zu seiner Persönlichkeit* (Graz, 1980).

Kinderman, William and Krebs, Harald, eds., *The Second Practice of Nineteenth-Century Tonality* (Lincoln, 1996).

Klose, Friedrich, *Meine Lehrjahre bei Anton Bruckner* (Regensburg, 1927).

Kopp, David, *Chromatic Transformations in Nineteenth-Century Music* (Cambridge, 2002).

Korstvedt, Benjamin, 'The First Published Edition of Anton Bruckner's Fourth Symphony: Collaboration and Authenticity', *Nineteenth-Century Music* 20 (1996), pp. 3–26.

'Anton Bruckner in the Third Reich and After: An Essay on Ideology and Bruckner Reception', *Musical Quarterly* 80 (1996), pp. 132–60.

'The Bruckner Problem Revisited (A Reply)', *Nineteenth-Century Music* 21 (1997), pp. 108–9.

'"Return to the Pure Sources": The Ideology and Text-Critical Legacy of the First Bruckner *Gesamtausgabe*', in Paul Hawkshaw and Timothy L. Jackson, eds., *Bruckner Studies* (Cambridge, 1997), pp. 91–121.

*Bruckner: Symphony no. 8* (Cambridge, 2000).

'"Harmonic Daring" and Symphonic Design in the Sixth Symphony: An Essay in Historical Musical Analysis', in Crawford Howie, Paul Hawkshaw and Timothy L. Jackson, eds., *Perspectives on Anton Bruckner* (Aldershot, 2001), pp. 185–205.

Korsyn, Kevin, 'Towards a New Poetics of Musical Influence', *Music Analysis* 10 (1991), pp. 3–72.

'Brahms Research and Aesthetic Ideology', *Music Analysis* 12 (1993), pp. 89–103.

'Beyond Privileged Contexts: Intertextuality, Influence and Dialogue', in Nicholas Cook and Mark Everist, eds., *Rethinking Music* (Oxford, 1999), pp. 55–72.

Korte, Werner, *Bruckner und Brahms: Die spätromantische Lösung der autonomen Konzeption* (Tutzing, 1963).

Kramer, Lawrence, 'The Mirror of Tonality: Transitional Features of Nineteenth-Century Harmony', *Nineteenth-Century Music* 4 (1981), pp. 191–208.

Kreczi, Hanns, *Das Bruckner-Stift St. Florian und das Linzer Reichs-Bruckner-Orchester* (Graz, 1986).

Kristeva, Julia, 'Word, Dialogue and Novel', in *The Kristeva Reader*, ed. Toril Moi (Oxford, 1986), pp. 34–61.

Kulka, O. D. and Mendes-Flohr, P. R., eds., *Judaism and Christianity under the Impact of National Socialism 1919–1945* (Jerusalem, 1987).

Kurth, Ernst, *Bruckner*, 2 vols. (Berlin, 1925).

*Ernst Kurth: Selected Writings*, trans. and ed. Lee Rothfarb (Cambridge, 1991).

Lacan, Jacques, *Seminar VII: The Ethics of Psychoanalysis* (London, 1992).

'Subversion of the Subject and Dialectic of Desire in the Freudian Unconscious', in *Ecrits*, trans. Alan Sheridan (London, 2001), pp. 323–60.

Laufer, Edward, 'Some Aspects of Prolongational Procedures in the Ninth Symphony (Scherzo and Adagio)', in Paul Hawkshaw and Timothy L. Jackson, eds., *Bruckner Studies* (Cambridge, 1997), pp. 209–55.

'Continuity in the Fourth Symphony (First Movement)', in Crawford Howie, Paul Hawkshaw and Timothy Jackson, eds., *Perspectives on Anton Bruckner* (Aldershot, 2001), pp. 114–44.

Leibnitz, Thomas, *Die Brüder Schalk und Anton Bruckner dargestellt an den Nachlaßbeständern der Musiksammlung der Österreichischen Nationalbibliothek* (Tutzing, 1988).

Leichtentritt, Hugo, *Musikalische Formenlehre* (Leipzig, 1911), trans. as *Musical Form* (Cambridge, Mass., 1951).

Levi, Erik, *Music in the Third Reich* (London, 1994).

Lewin, David, 'Amfortas' Prayer to Titurel and the Role of D in Parsifal: The Tonal Spaces and the Drama of the Enharmonic Cflat/ B', *Nineteenth-Century Music* 7 (1984), pp. 336–49.

Lewis, Christopher, 'Mirrors and Metaphors: Reflections on Schoenberg and Nineteenth-Century Tonality', *Nineteenth-Century Music* 11 (1987), pp. 26–42.

Lewy, Günter, *The Catholic Church and Nazi Germany* (New York, 1964).

Lorenz, Alfred, 'Zur Instrumentation von Bruckners Symphonien', *Zeitschrift für Musik* 103 (1936), pp. 1318–25.

Macartney, C. A., *The Hapsburg Empire 1790–1918* (London, 1968).

Maier, Elisabeth, 'A Hidden Personality: Access to an "Inner Biography" of Anton Bruckner', in Paul Hawkshaw and Timothy L. Jackson, eds., *Bruckner Studies* (Cambridge, 1997), pp. 32–53.

Mann, William, 'Bruckner's Structures in Perspective', *The Times* (21 July 1967), p. 6.

Marx, Adolf Bernhard, B., *Die Lehre von der musikalischen Komposition*, 4 vols (Leipzig, 1837–47).

McClatchie, Stephen, 'Bruckner and the Bayreuthians: Or, *Das Geheimnis der Form bei Anton Bruckner*', in Paul Hawkshaw and Timothy L. Jackson, eds., *Bruckner Studies* (Cambridge, 1997), pp. 110–21.

McCreless, Patrick, 'Ernst Kurth and the Analysis of the Chromatic Music of the Late Nineteenth Century', *Music Theory Spectrum* 5 (1983), pp. 56–75.

McGann, Jerome, *A Critique of Modern Textual Criticism* (Chicago, 1983).

Mellers, Wilfred, *Man and His Music* (London, 1962).

Melman, Charles, 'On Obsessional Neurosis', in Slavoj Žižek, ed., *Jacques Lacan: Critical Evaluations in Cultural Theory* (London, 2003), pp. 117–24.

Mitchell, Donald, Review of Hans Redlich, *Bruckner and Mahler* (London, 1955), *Musical Times* 97 (1956), pp. 303–4.

Morgan, Robert, 'Dissonant Prolongation: Theoretical and Compositional Precedents', *Journal of Music Theory* 20 (1976), pp. 49–92.

Narmour, Eugene, *Beyond Schenkerism: The Need for Alternatives in Music Theory* (Chicago, 1977).

   *The Analysis and Cognition of Basic Melodic Structures: The Implication-Realization Model* (Chicago 1990).

Nattiez, Jean-Jacques, *Music and Discourse*, trans. Carolyn Abbate (Princeton, 1990).

Notley, Margaret, 'Brahms as Liberal: Genre, Style and Politics in Late Nineteenth-Century Vienna', *Nineteenth-Century Music* 17 (1993), pp. 107–23.

   'Bruckner and Viennese Wagnerism', in Paul Hawkshaw and Timothy L. Jackson, eds., *Bruckner Studies* (Cambridge, 1997), pp. 54–71.

Nowak, Leopold, Preface to *Anton Bruckner: Sämtliche Werke Band VII/2. VIII Symphonie C-moll, Fassung von 1890* (Vienna, 1955).

   *Anton Bruckner. Musik und Leben* (Linz, 1973).

   *Über Anton Bruckner* (Vienna, 1985).

   Foreword to *Anton Bruckner: Sämtliche Werke Band II. II Symphonie C-moll, Fassung von 1877* (Vienna, 1967, repr. 1997).

Oberleithner, Max von, *Meine Erinnerungen an Anton Bruckner* (Regensburg, 1933).

Oerley, Wilhelm, 'Von Bruckners eigener Hand. Revision der Revision', *Der Turm* 2 (1946), pp. 138–42.

Orel, Alfred, 'Original und Bearbeitung bei Anton Bruckner', *Deutsche Musikkultur* 1 (1936–7), pp. 222–5.

Paddison, Max, *Adorno's Aesthetics of Music* (Cambridge, 1993).

Parkany, Stephen, 'Kurth's *Bruckner* and the Adagio of the Seventh Symphony', *Nineteenth-Century Music* 11 (1988), pp. 262–81.

*Bruckner and the Vocabulary of Symphonic Formal Process* (Ph.D. dissertation, Berkeley, 1989).

Pascall, Robert, 'Major Instrumental Forms: 1850–1890', in *The New Oxford History of Music 1850–1890* (Oxford, 1990), vol. IX, pp. 534–658.

Philips, John A., review of Korstvedt, *Bruckner: Symphony no. 8* (Cambridge, 2000), *Music and Letters* 82 (2001), pp. 323–8.

Phipps, Graham H., 'Bruckner's Free Application of Strict Sechterian Theory with Stimulation from Wagnerian Sources: An Assessment of the First Movement of the Seventh Symphony', in Crawford Howie, Paul Hawkshaw and Timothy L. Jackson, eds., *Perspectives on Anton Bruckner* (Aldershot, 2001), pp. 228–58.

Pike, Lionel, *Beethoven, Sibelius and the Profound Logic* (London, 1978).

Pois, Robert, *National Socialism and the Religion of Nature* (Beckenham, 1986).

Potter, Pamela, 'The Politicization of Handel and his Oratorios in the Weimar Republic, the Third Reich and the Early Years of the German Democratic Republic', *Musical Quarterly* 85 (2001), pp. 311–41.

Proctor, Gregory, *The Technical Basis of Nineteenth-century Chromatic Tonality* (Ph.D. dissertation, Princeton, 1978).

Puffett, Derrick, 'Bruckner's Way: The Adagio of the Ninth Symphony', *Music Analysis* 18 (1999), pp. 5–100.

*Derrick Puffett on Music*, ed. Kathryn Bailey Puffett (Aldershot, 2001).

Rachman, Stanley and de Silva, Padmal, *Obsessive-Compulsive Disorder: The Facts* (Oxford, 1992).

Rado, S., 'Obsessive Behaviour: A. So-called Obsessive-Compulsive Neurosis', in S. Arieti, ed., *American Handbook of Psychiatry* (New York, 1974).

Ratner, Leonard, *Classic Music: Expression, Form and Style* (New York, 1980).

Redlich, Hans, 'Bruckner, Anton', in *The Grove Dictionary of Music and Musicians*, 5th edn (London, 1954), vol. II, p. 971.

*Bruckner and Mahler* (London, 1955).

Reed, Graham F., *Obsessional Experience and Compulsive Behaviour: A Cognitive–Structural Approach* (Orlando, 1985).

Richter, Ernst Friedrich, *Die Grundzüge der musikalischen Formen und ihre Analyse* (Leipzig, 1852).

Riethmüller, Albrecht, ed., *Bruckner-Probleme* (Stuttgart, 2000).

Ringel, Erwin, 'Psychogramm für Anton Bruckner', in Franz Grasberger, ed., *Bruckner Symposion Linz 1977* (Linz, 1978), pp. 19–26.

Röder, Thomas, *Auf dem Weg zur Bruckner Symphonie: Untersuchungen zu den ersten beiden Fassungen von Anton Bruckners Dritte Symphonie* (Stuttgart, 1987).

'Master and Disciple United: the 1889 Finale of the Third Symphony', in Crawford Howie, Paul Hawkshaw and Timothy L. Jackson, eds., *Perspectives on Anton Bruckner* (Aldershot, 2001), pp. 93–113.

Rosen, Charles, *Sonata Forms* (New York and London, 1980).

'Influence: Plagiarism and Inspiration', *Nineteenth-Century Music* 4 (1980–1), pp. 87–100.

*The Romantic Generation* (London, 1996).

Rothgeb, John, Review of Eytan Agmon, 'Functional Harmony Revisited', *Music Theory Online* 2 (2002).

Salzer, Felix, *Structural Hearing* (New York, 1952).

Salzman, Leon, *The Obsessive Personality* (New York, 1968).

Samson, Jim, *Music in Transition* (London, 1977).

Schmalfeldt, Janet, 'Beethoven's "Tempest" Sonata and the Hegelian Tradition', in Christopher Reynolds, ed., *The Beethoven Forum*, vol. IV (Lincoln, 1995), pp. 37–71.

Schoenberg, Arnold, *Fundamentals of Musical Composition* (London, 1967).

*Harmonielehre*, trans. Roy Carter as *Theory of Harmony* (London, 1978).

Schönzeler, Hans-Hubert, *Bruckner* (London, 1970).

Schorske, Carl, *Fin de Siècle Vienna* (New York, 1980).

Scott, Derek, 'Bruckner and the Dialectics of Darkness and Light', *Bruckner Journal* 2/1 (1998), pp. 12–14; 2/2 (1998), pp. 12–14; 3/1 (1998), pp. 13–15.

Sharp, Geoffrey, 'Bruckner: Simpleton or Mystic', *Music Review* 3 (1942).

Simpson, Robert, *The Essence of Bruckner* (London, 1967).

Sisman, Elaine, 'Haydn's Theatre Symphonies', *Journal of the American Musicological Society* 44 (1990), pp. 292–352.

Sked, Alan, *The Decline and Fall of the Hapsburg Empire 1815–1918* (London, 1989).

Skorzeny, Fritz, 'Anton Bruckner im Lichte deutscher Auferstehung', *Die Musik* 30 (1938), p. 311.

Solvik, Morten, 'The International Bruckner Society and the N.S.D.A.P.: A Case Study of Robert Haas and the Critical Edition', *Musical Quarterly* 83 (1998), pp. 362–82.

Straus, Joseph, *Remaking the Past: Musical Modernism and the Influence of the Tonal Tradition* (Cambridge, Mass., 1990).

'The Anxiety of Influence in Twentieth-Century Music', *Journal of Musicology* 9 (1991), pp. 430–47.

Street, Alan, 'The Obbligato Recitative: Narrative and Schoenberg's Five Orchestral Pieces, Op. 16', in Anthony Pople, ed., *Theory, Analysis and Meaning in Music* (Cambridge, 1994), pp. 164–83.

Subotnik, Rose Rosengard, *Developing Variations* (Minneapolis, 1991).

Swinden, Kevin J., 'Bruckner's *Perger* Prelude: A Dramatic *Revue* of Wagner?', *Music Analysis* 18 (1999), pp. 101–24.

Talmon, Jacob, *The Origins of Totalitarian Democracy* (London, 1952).

Taruskin, Richard, review of Korsyn, 'Towards a New Poetics of Musical Influence' and Straus, *Remaking the Past*, *Journal of the American Musicological Society* 46 (1993), pp. 114–38.

Todd, R. Larry, 'Joseph Haydn and the *Sturm und Drang*: A Revaluation', *Music Review* 40 (1980), pp. 172–96.

'Sturm und Drang', in *The New Grove Dictionary of Music and Musicians*, 2nd edn, ed. Stanley Sadie (London, 2001), vol. XXIV, pp. 631–3.

Tovey, Donald Francis, 'Sonata Form', in *Encyclopaedia Britannica*, 11th edn (London, 1911), p. 398.

*Essays in Musical Analysis*, vol. II: *Symphonies (II), Variations and Orchestral Polyphony* (London, 1935).

'Retrospective and Corrigenda', in *Essays in Musical Analysis*, vol. VI: *Miscellaneous Notes, Glossary and Index* (London, 1939), p. 144.

Tusa, Michael, 'Beethoven's C minor Mood: Some thoughts on the Structural Implications of Key Choice', in Christopher Reynolds, Lewis Lockwood and James Webster, eds., *The Beethoven Forum* (Lincoln, 1993), pp. 1–27.

Van den Toorn, Pieter, *Music, Politics and the Academy* (Berkeley, 1995).

Voegelin, Eric, *Die politischen Religionen* (Munich, 1996).

Wagner, Cosima, *Cosima Wagner's Diaries: An Abridgement*, ed. Geoffrey Skelton (London, 1994).

Wagner, Manfred, *Der Wandel des Konzepts: Zu den verschiedenen Fassungen von Bruckners Dritter, Vierter und Achter Sinfonie* (Vienna, 1980).

'Bruckner in Wien: Ein Beitrag zur Apperzeption und Rezeption des oberösterreichischen Komponist in der Hauptstadt der k.k. Monarchie' in *Anton Bruckner in Wien. Ein kritische Studie zu seiner Persönlichkeit* (Graz, 1980).

*Bruckner: ein Monographie* (Mainz, 1983).

'Response to Bryan Gilliam Regarding Bruckner and National Socialism', *Musical Quarterly* 80 (1996), pp. 118–31.

Wason, Robert, *Viennese Harmonic Theory from Albrechtsberger to Schenker and Schoenberg* (Ann Arbor, 1985).

Watson, Dereck, *Bruckner* (Oxford, 1975).

Webster, James, *Haydn's Farewell Symphony and the Idea of Classical Style* (Cambridge, 1991).

Wellesz, Egon, 'Anton Bruckner and the Process of Musical Creativity', *Musical Quarterly* 24 (1938), pp. 265–90.

Williams, Alastair, '"Répons": Phantasmagoria or the Articulation of Space?', in Anthony Pople, ed., *Theory, Analysis and Meaning in Music* (Cambridge, 1994), pp. 195–210.

Wingfield, Paul, *Janáček: Glagolitic Mass* (Cambridge, 1992).

Wintle, Christopher, 'Kontra Schenker: "Largo e Mesto" from Beethoven's Op. 10 no. 3', *Music Analysis* 4 (1985), pp. 145–82.

'The Sceptred Pall: Brahms' Progressive Harmony', in *Brahms 2: Biographical, Documentary and Analytical Studies* (Cambridge, 1987), pp. 197–222.

Zaslaw, Neil, 'Music and Society in the Classical Era', in Neil Zaslaw, ed., *Man and Music in Society: The Classical Era* (London, 1989).

Zimmermann, Reinhold, 'Anton Bruckner: der große Lehrermusiker', *Der Deutsche Erzieher* (12 June 1937), p. 370.

# Index